The Jewel and the Key

··

BY LOUISE SPIEGLER

Houghton Mifflin Harcourt
Boston • New York

www.hmhbooks.com

The text of this book is set in Abrams Venetian.

The Library of Congress has cataloged the hardcover edition as follows:
Spiegler, Louise.
The Jewel and the key / by Louise Spiegler.
p. cm.
Summary: After an earthquake, Seattle sixteen-year-old Addie McNeal
finds herself jolted back to 1917 just as the United States is entering
World War I, where she is drawn to the grand old Jewel Theater which
is threatened both then and in the present time, as the United States
again is about to enter a war.
[1. Time travel—Fiction. 2. World War, 1914–1918—Fiction. 3.
Theaters—Fiction. 4. Theater—Fiction. 5. Earthquakes—Fiction. 6.
Seattle (Wash.)—Fiction.] I. Title.
PZ7.S75434Je 2011
[Fic]—dc22
2011008149

ISBN: 978-0-547-14879-3 hardcover
ISBN: 978-0-547-72192-7 paperback

Manufactured in the United States of America
DOC 10 9 8 7 6 5 4 3 2 1

4500371206

For Richard, with love

CONTENTS

The world has been printing books for 450 years, and yet gunpowder still has a wider circulation. Never mind! Printer's ink is the greater explosive: it will win.

—Christopher Morley, *The Haunted Bookshop*

AUDITION

It wasn't a real theater and never would be.

Not like she'd dreamed about, with a wooden stage, and scenery, and lights, and an orchestra setting the mood.

It was the musty old auditorium of Lincoln High School, with Tom Stark running far too much of the auditions. The problem was that Mr. Crowley, the drama teacher, kept getting called out of the room—someone said his wife had gone into labor, but no one knew if that was true—and as soon as he was gone, everything fell apart. Music erupted from cell phones. People coughed and whispered. A group of boys kept sputtering with laughter and throwing wadded-up notes to the theater divas, Keira and her gang, who always got parts, no matter what. Addie looked over at the cluster of girls giggling and commenting acidly on whoever was onstage. *If this were an all-male production about sumo wrestlers,* she thought wryly, *they'd still get the leads.*

One of their pals finished, and, despite the rule about not clapping during tryouts, they broke into a storm of applause.

For the third time, Addie glanced over her shoulder toward the back of the auditorium. *None* of her good friends were here. Even Almaz and Whaley hadn't shown up. Almaz had a math competition and Whaley . . . he'd been so busy fuming about the hecklers at his all-ages show last night that he probably hadn't registered it when she'd reminded him about her audition this morning.

But even without her posse cheering her on, she was sure she could get a part this time. No one knew the play like she did.

She rolled her shoulders and smoothed the skirt of her dress. Most people hadn't worn costumes. But when she and Almaz had found this shimmery green gown at Deluxe Junk for just five bucks, she knew she had to have it. The only possible garment for a beautiful troll princess. She wished she'd painted her face with the glittery silver and green makeup she'd experimented with last night, but there hadn't been time.

"Addie? Addie McNeal? We're ready for you."

She jumped out of her seat and made her way past the divas. Keira said something and the other girls muffled their giggles.

Heat flooded into her face. She hated that she let them unnerve her.

Still blushing, she lifted her head and walked down the

aisle, climbed the steps, and crossed to the center of the stage. It was suffused with stale yellow light and smelled of old mops. To her dismay, Mr. Crowley's chair was empty. Tom was in charge again. He was a skinny, world-weary senior who was tapping his pen against his clipboard. Addie guessed he must be good to win the coveted student-director position for the spring *Short Takes*—the one-acts students could do instead of the musical. Mr. Crowley would be in charge, but Tom would have a lot of input. Somehow, he didn't fill her with confidence.

Now he was looking down at his notes. "*Peer Gynt?* Not *another* troll princess?"

Giggles rippled along the row where the divas sat.

"Act two. Scene five," Addie said.

"I know what scene it is."

"Can someone read Peer's lines for me?" Addie looked about for a likely candidate. She was pretty sure Sun was out there somewhere. Maybe Jake. Unfortunately, she didn't see either of them—she'd intentionally sat alone so she could concentrate, and now she didn't know where they were. But before she could suggest anyone, Tom spoke.

"Come on. We've seen this so much already. And we're almost out of time. *I'll* read them."

"But—"

Without preliminary, he tossed out the first line.

Addie froze. He couldn't expect her to play against him when he was sitting ten rows back in the audience, could he? Quickly she scanned the auditorium, as if Whaley and

Almaz might miraculously appear just when she needed them. Where the heck was Mr. Crowley? He'd never do an audition this way. He'd assign someone to read.

It didn't matter. He wasn't there.

Oh, well. Planting her feet firmly, she drew herself up to her full five foot nine. Height was good sometimes. When she stood up very straight, she could feel strength shooting up her spine. Tall and straight like a spruce, she told herself. With a deep breath, she stepped forward. If she concentrated, she could make the noise in the audience disappear. She could make Tom's bored voice not matter. It took a lot, but she could do it.

She conjured up Peer Gynt, onstage with her in the haunted grove, wearing his cap and peasant trousers. Yes, she could almost see him. He was a charmer—a rambler and a troublemaker. Kind of like Whaley. But she could outwit him. And with her trollish supernatural powers, he had no chance against her at all.

She pivoted on her heel, toward stage right, where Peer would be standing, and let a small, knowing smile touch her lips. Then she held out her arms, beckoning him.

I'm the Dovrë-King's daughter . . .
Deep in the Rondë has father his palace.

The rhythm of the words caught her. Now she was the beautiful, ill-meaning temptress, luring feckless males to her father's underground kingdom, and their doom. She could feel her own grace and malevolence. It coursed through her veins as she circled round Peer, cornering him like a cat.

She hardly noticed the boredom in Tom's voice as he bounced lines back to her like Ping-Pong balls. She was bringing the stage to life. The furled American flag in the corner had become a silvery weeping willow. The clock on the wall was the full midnight moon, pulling time and tide in its wake. Dark trees of the Norwegian forest loomed all around, hung with gold hoarded by the trolls. The clang of treasure in their branches chimed behind the lines she was half speaking, half chanting. In a small sliver of her consciousness, she thought, *It's working!* and a throb of delight passed through her.

"Zzzzzzzzz!"

She jumped.

It was the after-school buzzer. Chairs slammed, zippers zipped, shoes scuffed the floors. Conversations bubbled and popped as everyone got up to leave. The frozen forest of Addie's imaginings dissolved, and the auditorium shifted into sharp focus. She registered that Mr. Crowley was back in the seat next to Tom. He looked distracted, sticking his left arm into the right sleeve of his jacket and trying to shove a mess of papers into a folder at the same time.

"Oh, *Peer!*" Keira's voice rose above the confusion. "*Peer*, follow me to my forest realm for *I* am a princess!" The drama queens roared. Keira smiled at Addie as if Addie were supposed to find it funny, too.

"Thanks." Tom wrote something on his legal pad and put it away.

Addie turned to Mr. Crowley. "How did I do?" She knew he probably wouldn't say, but she wanted to find out if he had seen any of her audition.

But Mr. Crowley was jamming the folder into his briefcase, and it was Tom who answered. "You'll hear. We'll post the parts on the website."

He didn't sound very impressed.

But why not? Addie thought a bit indignantly. She'd thought the magic was working. When she'd played Titania in *A Midsummer Night's Dream* at camp last summer, people had actually used that word to describe her performance— *magical*. In neighborhood productions, she always got the accolades. What was it about acting at Lincoln that made her always miss the mark? She'd *felt* Peer's world alive—brought to life—around her. Hadn't anyone else been able to feel it?

"I didn't get it, did I?" The words just slipped out.

This time, Mr. Crowley looked up. "As Tom said, we'll post the parts on the website." For a moment, he actually seemed to focus on her. "Addie, right? Didn't you help Sun with makeup last time?"

Addie nodded numbly. She had. But she'd thought this year she'd get a part.

Then his focus was gone again. He was pulling out his cell phone. "I'm sorry. I've really . . . I've got to go. But you were good at that," he added vaguely.

"Good at—?"

"Yeah, that's right," Tom said. "If you don't get a part, you can help out with makeup and costumes again."

Addie stared at him. Had she sucked and just not realized it?

No. She was sure she could act. But it seemed strange not to be picked two years in a row. How could she get stuck with makeup again? She opened her mouth to say no. She wasn't going to settle for makeup! But something stopped her.

How was she ever going to prove herself if she gave up now? Lincoln had the best drama department in the city. They were famous for doing challenging plays, not the usual high school fare. If you had a lead, or even a supporting role, you could win competitions. Maybe get into a college with a good theater program.

If she kept doing makeup and props and soaking up all she could, eventually, it might all pay off. After all, she thought unhappily, there was always next year.

"Thanks, Mr. Crowley," she said.

He smiled and nodded absently. Then he bolted out of the auditorium.

Dispirited, she left the stage and trudged back to her seat. She gathered up her boiled wool coat, picked up her backpack, and made her way to the exit.

Outside, the trees were dark and slick with wet. It was a grizzly day. That was a word her brother, Zack, had made up. It meant so drizzly and cold and miserable, it just made you grit your teeth and say "grrr." At least it wasn't actually raining anymore.

She had to find Whaley. If anyone would understand, he would.

Hugging herself for warmth, Addie headed around the front of the school, scanning the sidewalk and the park diagonally across the street just in case he'd hung out and waited for her.

She heard yelling—a commotion back by the main entrance. When she turned to where the sound was coming from, she saw a crowd gathering into a tight circle in the small parking lot. People were yelling with excitement. An occasional groan went up from all of them at once.

A fight.

Addie's neck prickled.

She sprinted up the sidewalk and across the lot, elbowing her way into the crowd between two football players.

Oh, no. This was what she'd been afraid of.

Whaley was fighting the guy who had brought those knuckle-draggers to heckle his band last night. Kirk. That was his name. Big and dumb. The type who didn't know when to stop. Of course, Whaley had probably been all too willing. . . .

Her stomach clenched as Kirk grabbed Whaley's shoulders and bashed him into the side of a car. Under his shock of reddish hair, Whaley's narrow face was pale, but he was grinning like a madman. The second he hit the steel door, he twisted away and punched Kirk in the stomach, darting and dancing. But Kirk, slower moving but more powerful, turned like a Sherman tank and just came at Whaley again.

Addie spotted Whaley's bandmates, Cam and Enrique, in the crowd and rushed over to them. "Can't you guys break it up?"

"No way," Enrique said.

"This is Whaley's business," Cam told her. "It's his band."

"It's your band, too!" But she knew they were right. Whaley was the one who searched out the bookings, made the posters, wrote the songs. The way he saw it, if the band was disrespected, it was his job to defend its honor. And she knew that everyone would laugh if Whaley's friends dragged him out of this fight. She turned back to watch, every nerve in her body jumping.

Whaley was dodging Kirk's blows well, but his guard was slipping. He stumbled, and Kirk's fist smashed into his face. Blood sprayed from his nose.

Addie flinched and forced herself not to cry out.

Kirk flung himself at Whaley as hard as he could and slammed him onto the hood of a Subaru Outback. But then Kirk lost his balance and floundered onto the hood as well. Whaley leaped up, grabbed him by the waist, and smashed him into the windshield. The glass cracked. Kirk rolled over, flattening Whaley beneath him.

"Ooooh!" went the crowd.

Addie couldn't stifle herself any longer. "Stop it! Stop, now!"

Whaley twisted his head around from under Kirk's bulk and gave her a bloody-mouthed grin. "Hiya, Ads!" Distracted, Kirk turned too, and as he did, Whaley wriggled away from him and rolled to the ground. Before Kirk knew what was happening, Whaley yanked his legs out from under him.

"Whaley—"

Before she could finish, Cam and Enrique burst into cheers. Whaley had won. It happened so fast, Addie wasn't even sure how. But suddenly Kirk was down in a puddle, moaning, and Whaley had him pinned.

"Give up?" He was pressing Kirk's head to the ground.

"Unh." Glaring, Kirk gave a short nod.

Enrique and Cam helped Whaley to his feet. The three of them were crowing and high-fiving one another. People were slapping Whaley's back; some guy was pretending to be a fight announcer; and girls were snapping their fingers in the air.

Whaley was laughing, accepting their congratulations, already pulling out his tobacco tin and paper for a celebratory smoke. Addie just drew a shaky breath and turned away.

She crossed the street to the park and kept going until she reached the top of the hillock, where the benches hid among the cedars. It was later than she'd thought. In the west, a slab of sunlight poked through the mass of clouds hanging over the Olympics, painting the sides of the houses fiery colors. She took a deep gulp of air. Late crocuses poked through the mud. Purple irises were furled against the cold. Spring was here.

But the thought didn't cheer her. She drew her coat tighter over the gorgeous troll dress, thinking she'd left home this morning as shimmering silk but was coming back as nothing but boiled wool.

"Hey ya, McNeal!" Whaley had crested the hill behind her. His face glowed with triumph. He tossed aside his rollie and stamped it out.

Addie smiled, warmed that he'd left his cheering fans

to find her. But then she got a closer look at him. "Oh, wow. Look at you! Let me clean up that blood." She pulled a bandanna from her bag and went over to the water fountain to wet it. He followed and stood patiently, stooping a bit, as she dabbed at the caked streams of blood under his nose. "And you're getting a black eye."

Whaley touched his cheekbone gingerly. "Looks worse than it feels, I bet."

"Turn around. Let me see your back. Is there any glass in it?"

"I love it when you're Nurse Addie," Whaley grinned, looking more ragged and snaggletoothed than ever. "Naw. My back's okay." He winced a bit. "More than I can say for the Subaru."

"Did you leave a note or anything? So they can contact you?"

Whaley's eyes widened. He smacked his forehead. "Oh, crap."

"What?" Addie eyed him warily. "What is it?"

"It's just . . . I just realized." Whaley looked over her head, as if he were examining a peak of the Olympics in minute detail. "I think that was Mr. Nguyen's car."

"The principal's?" Mr. Nguyen was not a touchy-feely, let-bygones-be-bygones guy. He'd nail Whaley to the wall for this.

"Don't freak! I'll offer to fix it or something. I know how to replace a windshield."

"You do? But—" She remembered the last big fight Whaley was in. "What if Dad finds out?"

"Then I'll be in the doghouse," Whaley said mournfully. He caught Addie's eye, threw his head back, and howled.

Addie nearly laughed but managed to stifle it. Whaley had too many people charmed already and not enough people to tell him the hard truth. "You can't keep getting in fights, Whaley! Not after they suspended you the last time. Don't you care?"

"About school? What do you think?"

Addie didn't have to think. She knew. "Well, do you care about Dad?"

"Of course I do. If it wasn't for him, I'd still be sleeping on that bench right there." He looked down at his old Doc Martens and then back up at her. "And if it wasn't for you."

It was true. She'd been shocked to find him sleeping in this park last September after his stepmom had kicked him out, his head propped on his guitar case and his possessions stuffed into a bag at his feet. Since they'd been friends so long, it hadn't been hard to convince her father to let him move in with them. Dad was a sucker for strays.

"You can't let him see that big bruise," she said more gently. "You promised no more fights, remember?"

"It's a black eye, Addie. I don't think I can hide it." But he looked worried.

"Hmm. Actually . . ." She thought a minute. "Maybe I can." Here was one thing, at least, she could salvage from today's audition fiasco. "But you have to let me turn you into a troll."

"A troll?" He broke off, looking slightly abashed. "Oh,

man, I *am* a troll. I forgot your audition. Did you get the part?"

Addie ignored the question. "Wait here. I need to get something."

She sprinted down the hill and ran along the street until Victrola Books came into view. Upstairs, on the second and third floors, where her family lived, the lights were out. But in the warm glow of the lamps inside the secondhand bookstore on the ground floor, Zack was curled up in the window seat reading one of his Redwall books, with Magnesium asleep on his lap, a swirl of soft white fur. Dad's prized antique gramophone gleamed on the shelf above him. She caught a glimpse of Dad behind the counter, but thankfully he was reading the paper and didn't notice her.

She darted around the side of the building before either of them could spot her, went in the back door, ran up to her room, and dug out the tackle box. Dad had given it to her for a makeup kit, back when she'd staged *The Hobbit* with the neighborhood kids in the adjoining backyards. The face paint she'd been messing around with last night was in there, and pancake makeup with brushes and sponges for applying it.

She may have blown her audition, Addie thought as she left with the tackle box in her hands, but she could at least keep Whaley out of trouble by transforming him into the troll king.

MUSHROOM BOY

An hour later, they came home from the park, shivering. The bookstore was closed, so they had to walk around to the back door to get into the house. Shedding their muddy shoes in the hall behind the store, they climbed the stairs to the second floor.

Smells of tomato sauce and oregano floated out of the kitchen as they headed to the living room, the largest space in the house, where everyone ate and hung out and did homework. Looking nervously at the glittery silver and green designs she had painted over Whaley's battered features, Addie hesitated before going in. She wasn't sure how successfully she'd concealed his injuries, and she didn't feel ready for a confrontation if she'd failed. Whaley hung back, too. Gathering her nerve, Adie flashed him a quick smile and peeked around the door frame.

Someone had lit a fire in the fireplace. Its warm light

glowed against the dark paneling. Their neighbor Mrs. Turner was sitting in one of window seats that overlooked the street. Even from way back here, Addie could see her bright lipstick vying for attention with the latest dye job she'd inflicted on her gray hair. Mrs. T. was stout, well dressed (in a flowing-crepe-fabric kind of way), and dynamic, especially for her age, which Addie thought to be about sixty. Dad and Zack were at the big oak table; Zack had his colored pencils spilling everywhere, and Dad's round glasses were gleaming behind a newspaper with the headline CONGRESS VOTES FOR WAR FUNDING; FIRST OFFENSIVE EXPECTED SOON. He was reading the article out loud. Mrs. Turner was gripping an unlit cigarillo between her fingers, listening intently.

"'Despite war costs set to top one trillion dollars for ongoing operations, Congress has authorized war funding for the new theater of conflict, citing credible intelligence of imminent threats. This despite opposition from a vocal minority in Congress.'"

Addie glanced at Whaley. She knew he'd been following this a lot more closely than she had. He always got worked up over military stuff. It was hard to gauge his reaction under the heavy makeup, but his eyes glowed with interest.

"This can't be happening," Mrs. Turner burst out. "Not again! Are we sure the intelligence is accurate this time? Really sure?"

Dad lowered the paper. "I doubt it, don't you?"

"And is there a single reason to think it will do any good?

Any reason in hell . . ." Mrs. Turner pulled out her lighter, flicked it, and then remembered she couldn't smoke in the house. She dropped it back in her pocket with an impatient gesture. "It makes me mad! We've all been working so hard to stop this from happening—"

"Hey!" Zack spotted Addie and Whaley. "What are you guys hiding for? Is Whaley in trouble again?"

Whaley sliced a finger across his throat, but Zack only laughed and stuck out his tongue.

Addie gave Whaley a final once-over. Even the thick makeup couldn't completely hide the worsening swelling under his eye. Still, you had to be looking for it, she told herself, and Dad probably wouldn't be. Not with all the war news.

"Hi, Dad," she said, stepping into the room. Whaley followed. "Hi, Mrs. T. Isn't Almaz here yet?"

"Not yet." Dad glanced at the paper one last time and then shoved it aside. "What's with the face paint, Whaley? I thought Addie was the one auditioning."

Mrs. Turner put a hand on her chest and drew in a deep breath to compose herself. She crossed the room, gave Addie a quick hug, and looked Whaley up and down. "I know I should be the last to comment on anyone's makeup, but why, dear boy, is your skin the color of bread mold?"

"Just letting Addie practice on me. What do you think?"

There's blood on his shirt, Addie realized. And mud. It was a nondescript lumberjack shirt, a murky reddish-brown plaid, but you could see the stains if you looked closely.

The back door slammed and they heard feet thumping up the stairs. Almaz burst into the room, her hair in the elaborate shuruba braids she reserved for big occasions. She was wearing a purple skirt, a dark scoop-neck top, and a long white scarf.

"Hey, everyone!" She pulled off her scarf and twirled around happily, waving the scarf like a flag. "Guess what!"

"What is it, Supergirl?" Whaley was grinning at her. "Why are you dressed up?"

She waved two fingers in the air. "Respect and praise to the King County math silver medalist!"

"Almaz! That's great!" Addie exclaimed. Whaley grabbed the end of her scarf and tugged on it. Almaz laughed and yanked it out of his hands. "Whoa! What are *you* supposed to be, Whaley? The Tin Man?"

"If he only had a brain," Addie stage-whispered. Almaz giggled.

"Do I look like the Tin Man?" Whaley went over to the mirror that hung over the mantel.

"Nah." Zack stuck a crimson pencil in his mouth. "You look like a mushroom."

"Well, good," Addie said. "That's the effect I wanted."

"You wanted a mushroom? Why—"

"Speaking of mushrooms," Dad interrupted, "go throw the pasta in, Addie. The sauce is already made."

"I wanted a troll," Addie told Zack. "Same palette."

Whaley scrunched up his nose at his reflection and burst out laughing. "You're right, Zack. I *am* a mushroom." Abruptly, he crossed the room to pick up his acoustic guitar he'd left in the corner. He threw the strap across his shoulder and began banging out blues chords, singing in a scratchy tenor:

> *Well, I'm a mushroom, babeee,*
> *From Planet Zay-am!*
> *Not no shiitake mushroom, babeee,*
> *Like they got in Japan!*
> *Don't you know I'm a mushroom, baby?*

"You're a *troll*," Addie said.

Whaley dropped down into the rocking chair, picked up the tempo, and shook his head wildly.

> *Some girls love a fungus*
> *Some girls love a spud*
> *But I'm here to tell you*
> *That I ain't no dud—*

"A blues troll," Mrs. T. observed. "I wish I'd brought my camera."

"*Wait* a second." Almaz turned to Addie, narrowing her eyes. "What are you messing around with makeup for? I thought you were going to act." She was tall and beautiful, and really strong, and when Almaz asked questions in this way, Addie had no trouble imagining her in her position as the intimidating left forward on her soccer team, charging the goal. She often thought goalies must quake when they saw Almaz coming. Addie, however, was going to try to deflect her.

"Well, isn't it a good makeup job?"

"Sure." Dad looked up from the paper, which he'd started reading again. "But how'd the audition go?"

"I'll go cook the pasta," Addie said, heading quickly for the door.

"Hey, Ads—" Almaz followed, putting her hand on Addie's arm.

But Addie shook it off and hurried out into the hall. In the kitchen she found the Dutch oven full of hot water fizzing on the stove, about to boil over. She turned down the burner and dumped in two packages of spaghetti. The steam made her face hot. She didn't want to talk about the audition.

But really, there was no way to avoid it. She sighed and grabbed a stack of plates out of the cupboard, shoved the kitchen door open with her foot, and went back to the living room. Might as well get this over with.

"I'm probably doing makeup again," she announced as she plunked the plates onto the table.

Whaley put his guitar down. Zack looked up from his drawing.

"Oh, honey." Dad put an arm around her, but she wriggled away.

"Get the forks and knives," she ordered Zack. When he got up and did this without arguing, she knew she must really be pitiful.

Almaz put her hands on her hips. "That's ridiculous. I read through that part with you. It isn't like you weren't good. And don't tell me any of those drama queens were any better!"

Addie shook her head, but couldn't bring out any words in response. Instead she went to fetch the brass candlesticks off the mantel.

Whaley followed her, awkwardly patting her back. "They're morons, those theater people. Don't know a good thing when it smacks them on the head."

Addie glanced up at him and managed a smile. "I *wasn't* bad. But no matter what I do, they just never pick me." For some reason, she could take sympathy from Whaley when she couldn't from anyone else.

"Who's the student director?"

"Tom Stark."

"Case closed. Everyone knows he can't tell his butt from a hole in the wall."

"Thanks, Whaley—that's disgusting." Addie started pulling mismatched glasses from the cabinet behind the table.

"Didn't Mr. Crowley say anything?" Dad asked.

"He wasn't there most of the time. His wife is having a baby or something. And it wouldn't matter anyway. He didn't cast me last year—I only got that walk-on. . . ."

"So it was all Tom," Whaley said darkly, rubbing the knuckles on one hand. "Want me to pound his face in?"

"*No!*" Geez, you'd think he could keep away from the subject of fighting just for a second.

"My great-aunt was a director," Mrs. Turner interjected, settling herself at the table. She leaned back comfortably in her favorite chair. "Did I ever tell you that?"

Addie shook her head, grateful for the change of subject.

"She was. She lived in this house all her life, you know."

"This house?" Addie looked at her in surprise.

"Oh, that's right." Dad glanced up from the bottle of red wine he was uncorking. "I remember you said a relative of yours lived here before you sold us the place, Margie."

"That was Aunt Meg. I inherited it from her." Mrs. T. took the bottle from him and splashed red wine into her glass. "Directed until she was in her eighties, God love her! A real terror, too."

Dad looked at Addie thoughtfully. "What can I tell you, sweetheart? I've watched them pick other kids for the big parts as long as you've been at that school. We all know you're good." He shrugged. "Maybe they're just jealous."

Addie shook her head. Sorry for herself she might be, but she wasn't going to be that self-indulgent. "Or maybe I'm no good. You can't rule out that possibility."

"Nonsense!" Mrs. T. cried. "We've all seen you act. You're with people who don't appreciate you."

"True." Almaz stuck a candle in each candleholder and lit them. "Tom Stark's not a terror. He's a drippy dishcloth. And Mr. Crowley isn't much better. I don't care if his wife is having a dozen babies." The little flames danced as she blew out the match.

They were almost cheering her up. Then Dad said, "Poor Addie. I was sure you'd get the part."

"So was I." Addie was mortified to hear a catch in her voice.

"If it's any comfort, Whaley's makeup is brilliant," Mrs. Turner said. "Where'd you get the idea?"

"From a book downstairs. I'll get it and show you, if

someone else will drain the spaghetti." Suddenly, she was dying to be alone. Too much sympathy was as deadening as none at all. "Can I have the keys, Dad?"

"Just remember to lock up." He dug into his pocket and held them out.

She grabbed the key chain, darted out of the room, and headed down the steps to the back hallway.

"Whew," she said softly as she stepped inside the shop. She put the keys in her pocket, shut the door, and leaned against it. For a moment she just inhaled the comforting smells of coffee, yellowing pages, and furniture polish. A faint butterscotch light filtered through the big bay windows in the front, touching the book-lined walls. Shadows filled the store. Addie closed her eyes, savoring the moment of solitude.

But the humiliation still felt like a raw, ragged wound, and she couldn't get beyond it. Not yet. Because she hadn't told them everything. How Keira would skewer all the people who auditioned on her Facebook page. Sun was on her friends list (who knew why) and told Addie the sort of things she wrote there. God knew what Keira and her clique said about her behind her back. It was like getting bad reviews when you weren't even performing. Getting bad reviews just for existing.

She opened her eyes and went in search of the book, shoving the rolling ladder out of her way as she went.

The shiny oak floorboards creaked beneath her feet. How many afternoons had she spent here, dreaming, memorizing lines? Since she was eleven or twelve she'd been reading her way through the skinny Penguin editions of plays, eventually tackling the big, bound collections: Shakespeare, Shaw, Ibsen, Williams, Wilson. She loved them all. The words jumped off the pages. She could hear how the dialogue should sound, imagine how a scene should look onstage. She devoured actors' biographies and pillaged the DVDs and audio recordings. But her favorite book of all was definitely *A History of the Theater*.

She had shoved it into its place on the shelf spine-first to prevent anyone from buying it, and, as always, as she pulled it out she felt a twinge of guilt. It was a collector's edition, and Dad could have sold it for a lot of money. She *would* turn it back around someday. Just not yet.

But as she tipped it out of its place, a squeal of car tires outside startled her. She spun around to see headlights flaring crazily in the window, and the volume slipped from her hand, pages fluttering.

"Oh, no!" She dove and made a lucky catch. The book slammed shut as she caught it, but a stiff piece of paper about the size of her palm flitted out. Addie snatched at it, but it wafted over the row of books and stuck behind the shelf.

Ooh, Dad would kill her if she'd torn out a page! Carefully, she reached over the tops of the books to get at the paper. But it just slipped farther down and stuck in a jagged crack in the wall.

Darn it! Now the whole bookcase would have to be moved.

She put the book down on a stool. Then she leaned her

shoulder against the end of the shelf and rocked it gently back and forth. It groaned and scraped as she angled it away from the wall. When there was enough space, she slipped behind it and sneezed violently, trapped in a column of dust. Then she saw that the paper wasn't stuck in a jagged bit of plaster after all.

It was caught in a door.

Addie felt a tremor of excitement. She'd pulled books off this shelf a thousand times but had never imagined there'd be a hidden door behind it. It was as if it had just materialized. She had the most ridiculous feeling that if she came back later, she'd find nothing here at all.

Bending closer, she saw that the paper was an old black-and-white photograph, faded to a syrupy orange. Only the bottom of it was visible: the hems of long skirts, pleated trousers, feet in fancy shoes and boots. Intrigued, she took hold of the corner and gently tried to pull it out.

It tore.

She winced, let go, and tried instead to open the door to release it. But no matter how hard she twisted the knob, the door only gasped slightly, like a fat man trying to catch his breath.

Now she *had* to open it. Something good had to come out of this day. She dashed into the back hallway to the closet where Whaley stashed his tools and grabbed a crowbar. She slipped behind the bookshelf again and inserted its edge into the doorjamb. It was hard work. Dried paint had melded with the moisture in the walls and created a sort of seal. She had to pry the door loose from its frame bit by bit.

When she had maneuvered the crowbar halfway down the crack, she tried the handle again.

This time, the door breathed out a bit more. Addie dug in her heels, braced herself, and pulled with all her might. It flew open, and the photo fluttered to the floor.

For a moment, she could have sworn she heard a trill of laughter feather through the air behind her. Startled, she jerked around to see if anyone was there.

Of course not. It was just her overactive imagination. But her heart was beating fast, and it was a relief to hear faint laughter from upstairs, and footsteps creaking across the ceiling.

"Food's on the table!" Dad shouted down the back steps.

Quickly, she snatched the photo from the floor and held it to the light.

It was a scene from a play. Three women in long gowns, their hair piled on their heads, stood stage left, and three men in tails were stage right. They all wore hideous masks with enormous jutting noses, bristling eyebrows, and buckteeth. The men were bowing to a king on a throne, the women curtsying. The king's mask covered only the bottom part of his face, with a great frowning O for his mouth. His hand was stretched out in a gesture of command. Another man, wearing a loose peasant blouse, knelt before him.

Wait a second. A slight shiver played down her back. Wasn't this *Peer Gynt?*

But she'd looked in the section of the book about Ibsen's plays many times and never seen this photo. Where had it come from? Was it like the door behind the bookcase, something that had just this moment materialized for her eyes alone?

Oh, don't be a dork.

She picked up the book and flipped to the section on Ibsen, but there was no indication that anything had fallen out. She turned the rest of the pages, searching, but it wasn't until she reached the end that she figured it out. Someone had pasted one of those ex libris sheets inside the back cover without putting his or her name on it, and the sheet had come unglued at the bottom; maybe the photo had slipped out from behind it. Addie frowned. It certainly seemed odd.

She turned the picture over and found that there was writing on the back. It took a moment to make out the faded lettering: *R. before the mob—1917.*

Before the mob? What could that mean? The audience? Addie thought unhappily of the divas and their boyfriends at the audition and turned the photograph over, focusing on the actors once more. A yearning to be part of their world shot through her like an arrow.

"Addie!" Dad called again. "We're starting without you!"

She slipped the picture carefully into her pocket, then closed the book and slid it back into its space on the shelf.

But she couldn't leave without having a quick look behind the hidden door. She pulled it open wider and stuck her head in.

There was no light inside, but she could tell that it was a storage closet, six or seven feet deep, with a sort of bench built into the wall on one side. It smelled of camphor and cedar. And it was filled with dusty crates. Now that was intriguing. She stepped in and lifted the lid of the nearest one. It was hard to see much of anything, but the crate seemed to be filled with fabric.

Quickly, she dropped the lid and stepped out, then shut the door behind her. She'd move the bookcase back tomorrow.

Upstairs, everyone was already eating dinner. After the cold bookstore, the warmth and color of the living room made her head swim. The threadbare Persian carpet glowed with reds and blacks; the hanging lamp drenched the room in warm orange light. Addie shoved herself between Almaz and Zack at the table. No one seemed to remember what she'd gone down for; they were deep in a political conversation.

"We could have avoided it," Mrs. Turner was saying. "You'd think we'd learn. How many people have died so far in our other war? Thousands of our soldiers, thousands of theirs, and who knows how many civilians? Tens of thousands. And despite the fact that it solved *nothing*, we're going to war again." Mrs. Turner punctuated this with a gulp of red wine.

"And it's a good thing, too," Whaley said, twirling his spaghetti.

"Try not to sound so pleased about it," Dad grumbled. "That's the last thing we need, boys like you getting heroic ideas."

"That's me. Always the hero."

"Always *fighting*," Almaz corrected. "I don't know if that's the same thing."

"Hey, Dad!" Addie interrupted, not liking the direction the conversation was taking. "I found a closet behind one of the shelves downstairs. Did you know it was there? It's full of old crates."

"Behind what shelf?"

"Drama."

"The drama section?" Dad looked perplexed. Then light dawned. "Oh, wait. I do know. It's just been so long. You mean you got that door open? I remember it being jammed tight." He pointed a fork at Mrs. Turner. "It must be your stuff in there, Margie. We've never used it for storage."

"Not mine." Mrs. Turner looked at Addie with interest. "Did you open any of the crates?"

Addie swallowed a mouthful of pasta. "Just one. I couldn't really see in the dark but it felt like tablecloths or clothing or something."

Mrs. Turner thought a minute. Then her eyes lit up. "I'll tell you what. They probably belonged to old Meg—my great-aunt I was telling you about. How fun! I'll bet they're ancient."

Dad stood up and started stacking the empty serving dishes. "Well, if they belonged to your family, you're welcome to have them back, Margie."

"Thanks, Mike." Mrs. T. pushed back her chair. "If there's something obviously useful—or sentimental—I'll take it. Addie? Shall we look through them together?"

"Are you kidding? I'd love to." Addie put down her glass too quickly, splattering her water on the tablecloth. "Now?"

"Forget it," Mrs. T. said firmly. "I'm too old and gouty

for an unheated bookstore at night. How about Sunday morning? I'm on assignment tomorrow."

The phone by the window seat rang and Dad went to answer it.

"Sunday's good," Addie said, though it seemed a long time to wait.

Mrs. Turner took her last bite and pushed her empty plate aside. "Tell Mike thanks. He knows I have a meeting to get to." She left, and the door swung shut behind her.

"*What?*" Dad's voice boomed. Addie jumped.

She turned to see him clutching the receiver, a shocked look on his face.

Instantly, she knew who was calling and why.

"Are you sure it was him?"

Almaz glanced apprehensively at Addie. "Maybe I should go," she whispered.

Addie nodded and mouthed *I'll call you* as Almaz slipped out of the room after Mrs. Turner. She and Whaley exchanged a look. He knew as well as she did. She could tell because he had a look on his face like a condemned man. With a sort of resignation, he stood up and started stacking plates.

"What's going on?" Zack asked.

"Go to bed," Addie told him. He ignored her.

"All right," Dad was saying. "But I hope you're wrong. Either way, I'll make sure he calls you." He put the phone down and glared first at Addie and then at Whaley. "That was Mr. Nguyen," he said. "Anything you'd like to tell me? Either of you?"

Whaley looked down at the pile of plates in his hands. Behind the glittery makeup, Addie could see, there was a raw color in his face. He looked sick.

"I . . ." Addie started. "Um—like what?"

"For example, that Whaley is about to get expelled from school."

3

GREEN FLASHES

She was waltzing gracefully across the stage, her long white gown sweeping along the floor. *Turn two three, turn two three.* The lights were glaring, and it was so hot she could feel the perspiration running down her sides. Her partner's eyes crinkled into a smile behind the fleshy nose and bristling mustache of his troll mask.

"You can't be out of breath already! It's only the first dance." A warm voice, crackling with amusement.

Addie laughed, enjoying the easy way he glided her around the stage. "I'm hot, not out of breath. Don't worry, I could do this forever."

"Stop!" someone commanded.

They stumbled to a halt. The music from the orchestra pit died.

The troll king had risen from his throne. Above the

half-mask, his eyes blazed with indignation. He pointed at Addie. "What is *she* doing here?"

Before she could answer, another voice drifted in. The footlights were snuffed out; the troll king gone as suddenly as he had appeared.

Whaley was on the phone in the hallway outside her room.

Addie jammed the pillow over her head. Her feet had felt so right in those dancing shoes. The top of her head had glowed in the warmth of the spotlight. If only she'd had time to explain to the troll king that she belonged on that stage.

Then the previous night's arguments and endless discussions with Dad and Whaley flooded back into her brain. If that was Principal Nguyen on the phone, Whaley had better be making a good case for himself.

She tossed the pillow aside, got out of bed, grabbed her clothes, and went out into the hall. Whaley was sitting at the top of the stairs with the phone jammed between his ear and his shoulder, smelling faintly of the rollies he never smoked in the house. Addie walked past him to the bathroom, made a hangdog face at herself in the mirror, undressed, and got into the shower. Under the hot spray, she turned everything over in her head.

When Whaley moved in with them, they'd agreed he could stay until he graduated and could get his own place. But after last night . . . she had a terrible feeling Dad might not let him. He'd given Whaley second chances before. They were on to third and fourth chances now. And he'd been really, really mad.

Her throat tightened at the thought of Whaley leaving. She loved having him here. What would happen if Dad kicked him out? His stepmom would never take him back, that was for sure. Not with his dad gone, too. And no matter how tough Whaley tried to sound, he couldn't go back to sleeping on that bench in the park, lining up for meals in the Congregational church basement in the U. District like those kids they saw when they helped out at Teen Feed. Geez, they were nice enough, always grateful, but some of them were drugged out; some had babies they couldn't take care of. . . . And their lives were so hard. She couldn't stand to think of Whaley ending up like that.

She twisted the knob to turn off the water, stepped out, and dried herself off. Why did he need to get himself into trouble all the time? Almost angrily, she yanked on the beatnik-era turtleneck and miniskirt she'd gotten at the Ballard Goodwill and then pulled on a pair of black leggings.

When she emerged, Whaley was gone. She glanced up and down the hallway, feeling the peculiar emptiness he left behind. He wasn't a big guy, but he took up a lot of room — a lot of air and energy. It was funny, Addie thought. She imagined herself on the stage, but the person with real stage presence was Whaley.

The sunlight was beating through the thin curtains in the kitchen window as she entered, making her blink. Dad was leaning against the counter talking to Whaley's back as Whaley pulled an orange juice carton out of the refrigerator. Dad looked tired and rumpled; he was rubbing his forehead right above his nose, the way he did when he had a headache. His hair was shaggier than ever, and his beard needed a trim. "What did Mr. Nguyen say? Does he want us to meet with him like we did last time?"

Whaley shook his head. He didn't turn around. Just took a glass down from a cupboard and poured the juice into it. "He said I can still get my GED, but he can't let me back because they already suspended me twice this year."

"Jesus. Well, I'm not surprised. It's not like you're a child," Dad burst out. "You're eighteen. You're old enough to take responsibility. Why can't you stop picking fights?"

"I don't *pick* them." Whaley turned around, a dull crimson rising in his face. "They just happen."

"They don't just happen." The words slipped out before Addie could stop them. She didn't want to pile fuel on the fire, and she did sympathize with him, but it wasn't as if Whaley couldn't hold back sometimes. He just let himself explode.

He gave her a thin, hard look. "Thanks for the vote of confidence!"

"I've given you my vote of confidence! I mean, I understand why you were mad at Kirk, but it isn't worth getting thrown out of school for." She looked at Dad. "It was Kirk's fault. He and his friends were horrible at Whaley's show. Like baboons. The bouncer had to throw them out."

Dad poured himself some coffee that smelled like it had been boiling for hours. He tasted it, grimaced, and put it down. "Troll makeup, no less," he said sourly. "I'm *not* happy with you, Adeline, after that little deception."

She looked down at her feet. "I know."

The kitchen door slammed against the wall and Zack burst in. "Can I have a waffle?"

"In a second," Dad said.

Whaley slumped against the fridge. "All right. I know. I really know I screwed up. And I owe you an apology." He stood up straight and held out his hand. "Thanks for everything, Mike. I'll pack my bag."

Dad didn't shake his hand.

Addie looked at him in horror. "No, wait a minute!" She spun around. "Dad?"

"Don't be so dramatic," her father said impatiently. Addie wasn't sure if he was talking to her or Whaley.

Zack ran to Whaley and threw his arms around him; he was ten but was acting like a much younger kid. Surprised, Whaley rubbed Zack's head with the palm of his hand, and Zack hugged him harder.

"We can't just throw him out!" It was inconceivable. Dad would never do such a thing. Would he?

"Forget it, Ads." Whaley tried to pull away from Zack and leave. But Zack held on tight.

She had to think of something. Quick. Before Whaley walked out and never came back. "But what if he got a job, Dad? Then couldn't he stay until he gets his own place? He needs to live somewhere!"

"You've done me enough favors," Whaley protested. He looked almost angry.

Dad picked up his mug from the counter, sloshing his

coffee around inside it. "A job might be a good idea. If Whaley can take it seriously." He frowned. "You big enough for that, Whaley Price?"

Every nerve in Addie's body stretched taut. Whaley glanced over at her as if she had the answer. But how could she? It twisted her heart. She just shrugged and tried to look encouraging. Zack let go of Whaley and backed into the counter by the blender, watching closely.

Whaley took a gulping breath. "Do you really mean it?"

"I mean it." Dad looked more tired than ever. "You can stay with us if you can pay your own way. Then no one's doing you a favor."

Whaley looked uncertain. Addie held her breath. *Come on*, she thought. *Say yes. Don't be too proud.*

"All right, then," he muttered, looking at the floor. "I'll . . . um. I'll start looking for work. Today." Finally he looked up and met Dad's eye. "And I can keep the Saturday shift at the bookstore, right? Until I find something else?"

"Yes!" Addie crowed. She swooped over to Whaley and clapped her hands on his shoulders. He gave her a faint half smile and pushed her gently aside.

"Of course." Dad's stern expression relaxed. "In fact, for the next few months, you can have most of my shifts at the bookstore."

"Really?"

"Sure. I would have had to hire more temporary help anyway while I'm writing my thesis. And I need coverage for Sunday, since Zoe can't make it anymore." Zoe was the rather stern Greek woman who ran the store on Sundays, when Dad was out on buys at estate or library sales. She'd told Addie she was opening some sort of artsy preschool. Addie thought she would terrify preschool children, but so much the better for Whaley. "It would save me training someone new," Dad continued.

Whaley almost smiled. "For real? Are you sure?"

Dad nodded.

Whaley held out his hand again, and this time Dad clasped it and gave it a firm shake. Addie sprang across the kitchen and threw her arms around him. "You're awesome, Dad."

"Can I have that in writing?"

"Yay!" Zack cheered.

"Are you sure, Mike?" Whaley repeated. "I'll only stay if you really need me." The sunlight struck him full in the face, accentuating the purple bruise under his eye. He was too pale, Addie thought. And a little too thin, for all his strength. His face always made her think of a lonesome cowboy's, kind of gawky and weather-beaten. Or, too often, just beaten. "I mean, I'm not a charity case," he added.

"If you do a good job, I'll really need you," Dad replied. Addie squeezed him harder and let go. "And in case everyone's forgotten, it's Saturday. You open at ten, Whaley."

"Okay, Mike. But I'll . . . I'll look for my own place— when I can, I mean." He seemed overwhelmed by the thought.

And suddenly, all the emotion in the room was too

much for Addie. *And that,* she thought, *is saying something. For me, at least.* She swung around and opened the door. "C'mon, Whaley, I'm going to grab a coffee at the Brown Bear."

"What's this?" Dad complained, pointing at the full coffeepot on the counter.

"Black molasses and gasoline," Addie said. "Even you can't drink it!" She poked Whaley's arm. "Wanna come?"

"Sure. Now that I'm gainfully employed, I'll start an expensive coffee habit."

"You'll start a budget!" Dad yelled after him as he and Addie banged out of the kitchen.

They thumped down the stairs, and Addie raised her voice to be heard over the sound of Whaley's boots. "What's going to happen to you, Whaley? Why can't you stay out of trouble?"

"Dunno. Looks like I just dodge the bullets as they whiz past."

"You've got to learn to dodge faster!" She slipped her arm through his. "Right now, Dad and Zack and me are all the glue you've got to hold you together."

Whaley swung open the back door. The air goose-pimpled their skin.

"You think I don't know that?"

As always, the six-foot-tall bear, carved by a "chain-saw art-ist" ("A lumberjack on the Olympic Peninsula," Whaley had told her), loomed outside the coffee shop.

"This is on you, Whaley. You owe me for that makeup job, even if it backfired."

"Man! Your dad's right. I'm going to need a budget."

Addie laughed, turned the doorknob, and stepped inside. Immediately, she knew something was wrong.

The place looked as cheerful as ever, with its honey-colored wooden tables and posters of upcoming concerts and plays on the walls. But no one was sitting around lazily chatting over coffee or clicking away on a laptop writing the great American novel. They were all watching the TV in the corner, which Addie had never seen turned on before. Even Mrs. Jambloski, the owner, was leaning her fleshy arms on the display case, craning her neck to see. Distractedly, she turned to Addie and Whaley. "Know what you want?"

Whaley's gaze was drawn to the set. "What'll you have, Ads?"

"Americano," Addie said, finding her attention sucked over to the TV as well. Whaley ordered and paid, and they drifted closer to the screen.

It was CNN showing a nighttime view of a city from the air. The place looked eerie and desolate. It bobbed in and out of focus as they watched. Addie could see concrete buildings and telephone poles. TV towers. An ugly city. No trees, no flowers, no shrubs.

Then a flash streaked down from the sky, green and glowing. Dirt flew into the air. The side of a building caved in, crumbling soundlessly in a plume of smoke and debris.

Addie frowned. "Already? Are those our planes?" Of course she knew they were, but still, she felt startled, seeing these images on television like this. So soon.

Whaley folded his arms. "I didn't think it would be long."

Addie kept watching. The city looked real enough. But the green flashes looked like computer graphics.

"What *time* is it over there?" an old man asked. Addie recognized him from the bookstore. He had a white goatee, and a very old black miniature poodle sitting at his feet. "It's dark but what time is it? Night? Morning? What?"

"Does it matter?"

The old man jabbed his finger at Whaley, a look of fury on his wizened face. "What do you mean, does it matter? We're bombing a factory! It matters if there are people working in there."

"It's probably a weapons factory," Whaley retorted. "We've got no choice."

"No choice?" Addie said. "What do you mean?" Suddenly the whole thing filled her with revulsion. She hadn't been paying a lot of attention to the media coverage or going to the debates about the war at school, but now that it was happening, what Mrs. Turner had been saying for a long time made sense to her. "A war doesn't 'just happen,' like one of your fights, Whaley! I bet we had a choice."

"How would *you* know what's a choice and what's not?"

Addie stared, startled by the anger in his voice.

He put a hand on her arm. "Sorry, Ads. I didn't mean that." He gestured at the screen. "It's just—I get it. I get why we're bombing that city. Don't you? I mean, you don't want more terrorist attacks, do you?"

"Of course not! But remember what Mrs. T. said? We've gone down this road before."

"Well, we haven't gone far enough or we wouldn't have to keep fighting!" Whaley exclaimed. "I wish *I* was over there!"

Addie looked at him incredulously. "Aren't there enough people for you to fight right here, Whaley? Look where that's got you."

"It got *you* out of a load of trouble once," Whaley pointed out. "Remember that guy last year? What would have happened if I hadn't come looking for you? You didn't mind me bashing him."

"I know!" Why did Whaley have to mention that in such a loud voice? "But just because it was worthwhile once doesn't mean you always need to fight!" she spluttered. She looked at her watch. "It's nearly ten. Let's go."

Whaley dragged his eyes away from the screen. They picked up their coffees and headed out.

The wind had whipped up while they'd been inside. Leaves shivered in the high branches. Addie gazed up through the treetops at the blue-black clouds rolling in from the west like tanks.

Out of the corner of her eye, she caught a flash of green and started.

But it was only the cedar sprays, flicking to and fro in the quickening wind.

4

SHIFTS

Sunday morning, Mrs. Turner arrived out of breath, her face nearly as pink as her hair.

"Why is it that no matter where you walk in this city, it's always uphill?" she grumbled, fanning herself with her free hand. In the other she held a stack of flyers, which she plunked down on the table between the funny pages Zack was looking at and a review of a production of *Angels in America* that Addie was reading. "Good morning, all."

"Hi, Mrs. T." Addie looked up from the paper. "Ready to go through those boxes?"

Dad got up from the overstuffed chair where he'd been tying his shoes. "Are those the posters? Let's see."

Mrs. T. took a flier from the top of the pile and handed it to him. Addie went and looked over his shoulder. It showed a black cat hissing, back arched and fur on end, above the words *Rally Against the War*. Next Friday's date was below that. "I picked them up from the printer this morning. And I posted a bunch after I dropped the car off to be serviced up by the U. District. But then I walked all the way home, and now I'm pooped. Do any of you want to take over for me?"

"Looks like a Wobbly placard," Dad said.

"We stole the graphic from the IWW. And why not? This is a good old Wobbly town."

Addie leaned over to get a better look, intrigued by the stark image. "What's a Wobbly?"

"Who, not what," Mrs. Turner said. "It's a nickname for the Industrial Workers of the World. A bunch of union madmen who used to be thick on the ground around here. Not too in love with foreign wars, either. Their organization got crushed a long time ago, but they left behind a darned good songbook."

Dad pulled a few flyers off the top of the pile. "I'll put one in our window. And talk to the other business owners in the neighborhood."

"I'll post the rest for you, Mrs. T.," Addie offered, surprising herself. The argument with Whaley had stuck with her. Everywhere she went, the war was always on the news, in the papers. She couldn't stop seeing the TV images. People came into the shop and talked about it with Dad. And Whaley just couldn't let it go.

As if on cue, the door banged open and Whaley swept into the room, flannel shirt buttoned up wrong, toast and honey in one hand, the front page of the paper in the other. "'Marines have gained control of the capital and of key mountain passes,' " he read. " 'The fighting is expected to shift soon from urban areas into tribal zones outside of government control.' " His expression was wistful. "If it weren't going to be over in a few days, I'd get my butt over there."

"Good thing you have a store to run then." Addie wished Whaley would stop being so fixated on the war.

"And it won't be over in a few days," Mrs. Turner said grimly. "Believe me."

Dad pulled on his jacket. "Buying starts at eleven, Whaley. Don't be a pushover. I don't want junk I can't get rid of."

"Mike, can you spare some of your gunpowder coffee?" Mrs. Turner yawned. "These late-night meetings are killing me!"

"Help yourself. The cups are in the draining rack." Dad turned to Zack. "I've got to find the address for that estate sale. You be ready to go when I come back." Zack had his rocket science class every Sunday morning at the community center. Dad usually dropped him off and hit a book sale before picking him up again around noon.

He left the room, Mrs. T. in his wake, and Whaley folded up the front page, dropping it on the table. "Whatcha doing today, Ads?"

"Exploring that secret closet with Mrs. T. And I said I'd put up flyers."

"What flyers?" He picked up one and rolled his eyes. But to Addie's relief, he didn't try to argue about it. Instead, he asked, "You don't wanna help me with the store, do you? It's my first time with book buys. All those people dragging in cartons of old books. I might not say no as much as I should."

"Well . . ." Addie hesitated. She *had* helped Dad on buy days before. But she didn't want to be stuck working at the store all day.

Then again, if she had too much free time on her hands, she'd just keep checking the drama website to see who'd been cast for the *Peer Gynt* scene. Which was silly, since names probably wouldn't be up until Monday. Why bother anyway? There wouldn't be a part for her. She'd be better off keeping busy. And Whaley was looking at her with such a hopeful expression. She sighed. He *was* trying.

"Okay," she said. Then a thought struck her and she flashed Whaley a wicked grin. "Buuut . . . In exchange for my time, and expertise . . ."

"Here it comes," Whaley groaned.

"I get to emcee your next all-ages show."

"What? You mean do that Cruella de Vil act introducing the songs?"

Addie put on a stage-Russian accent. "But, of course, darlink. What, you think Cruella get old, get false teeth, go into retirement?" She lifted an imaginary cigarette holder to her lips and took a luxurious drag. Zack cracked up. They'd watched *One Hundred and One Dalmatians* again last week.

"Cruella doesn't talk like that," Zack said.

"So? I'm Cruella's cousin, Natasha. From Saint Petersburg." She pointed to Magnesium, who was yawning and stretching under Zack's feet. "Nice kitty for fur coat, yes?"

Zack snatched up the cat in pretended outrage. Magnesium yowled and leaped out of his arms, scurrying out of the room.

"Oh, all right, Natasha." Whaley grinned.

Dad came back into the room with a slip of paper in his hand. "Ready, Zack? Let's go."

"I'll catch you in a few," Whaley told Addie. "I gotta go to the People's and pick up some milk." Almaz's family owned the People's Grocery, down the block. "Need anything, Mike?"

"Bread. Canned tomatoes. Money's in the jar. See you later." Dad and Zack headed to the door, and Whaley followed them out.

Mrs. Turner bustled back into the room, a cup of coffee steaming in her hands. "Come on, Addie," she said. "We've got a mysterious cavern to explore."

Sunlight was streaming through the big plate-glass windows, warming the front of the store. In the back, it was still icy. Remembering how dark the closet was, Addie took a flashlight from the storage cupboard in the hallway and led the way to the drama shelves. Mrs. Turner put her coffee on a stool and helped Addie lever the bookcase away from the wall.

She'd expected the door to stick again, but when she gave it a good yank, it flew open. She fell backwards and landed on her butt.

"It'll heal! Strongest muscle in the body!" Mrs. T. held out her hand and pulled Addie to her feet.

"I thought that was the heart," Addie said, rubbing her tailbone ruefully.

The camphor and cedar smells enveloped her as she stepped inside. And no wonder: when she switched on the flashlight, she could see that the walls, the floor, and even the ceiling were paneled with golden-brown cedar. The crates were cedar as well. Only the narrow bench built into the wall looked like it was of some less sturdy wood, darkened and cracked.

"Can we both fit?" Mrs. T. was peering in.

"It's pretty cramped. But maybe you can slide in onto the bench. Just don't get a splinter in your strongest muscle."

Mrs. T. stepped in after her. "Well? What are we waiting for?"

For a moment they grinned at each other conspiratorially. Then Addie pulled up the lid of the nearest crate. The hinges creaked. Addie's eyes widened as she shined the flashlight in. "Wow!" She pulled out a glittering golden sheath and held it against her body. "Take a look at this! A flapper dress."

Mrs. T. stared, shaking her head in bemusement. "A flapper dress? Who knew?"

Addie shook her hips to swoosh the skirt and make the beads jangle while Mrs. Turner fished out a mangy fur stole and held it at arm's length, as if it might have fleas. "How bizarre that Aunt Meg kept all this stuff."

"Why wouldn't she? It's better than a vintage shop!"

"Yes, but Meg couldn't stand vintage clothes."

"You're kidding." Addie gave her an incredulous look. "Old clothes are fabulous."

Mrs. T. laughed and put the stole aside. "I can see *you* think so. But my aunt Meg wouldn't agree. Her fashion sense was up to the minute. I mean, look at this smoking jacket. Who would wear it? Not Uncle Stan, that's for sure."

"Why not?" Addie examined the stiff, shiny jacket with velvet lapels Mrs. T. was holding up.

"Because Meg had that man under her thumb. She wouldn't have seen him *buried* in anything this tacky!" She stopped and snapped her fingers. "Wait a second. I've just realized—you know what these are? They aren't my great-aunt's clothes. They're costumes. From the Jewel." At Addie's blank look, she added, "The theater downtown where Aunt Meg directed. My friend Becky owns it now."

"You're probably right." Addie folded the flapper dress and pulled out a lace mantilla. "I bet someone used this in a production." She arranged it on top of her head. "What do you think? *Carmen?*"

Mrs. Turner laughed. "You're in heaven, aren't you? Why don't you take something up to your room and try it on? I know you're dying to."

"Can I?" Addie dug through the crate, playing the flashlight along the rich fabrics and sparkling buttons. She hesitated. "Really? Aren't you worried about their getting damaged?"

"Not by you. You know how to take care of old clothes."

Addie smiled and went back to picking through the costumes. She felt like a spoiled kid on Christmas. There was just *too much*. Finally she pulled out a pale, goldish dress and stepped out of the closet, cradling it against her body.

"Oh, now, that's lovely with your chestnut hair," Mrs. T. said. She bent forward and looked more closely. "I'll bet it's nearly a hundred years old. Amazing it isn't in shreds." She pulled out some grainy, dark gold-colored material that had been folded beneath it and stepped out of the closet as well. "This shawl goes with it. It's heavy. Maybe there's a clasp or something inside." Addie held out a hand and gently touched the fine material. "Go on," Mrs. Turner urged. "Give it a try."

"All right." Addie took it from her. She was right; the shawl *was* heavy. "I'll be quick." She turned to go, but Mrs. T. stopped her. "We'd better put this all back first." She glanced at her watch. "I promised Becky I'd drop by. *And* I've got to stop by the hen house and feed the girls before I leave."

"You go, then. I'll take care of it. And I'll put the dress back when I'm done."

"All right. Bye, then." And Mrs. T. hurried off toward the back door.

Addie hung the dress carefully over the rolling ladder, laid the folded-up shawl down on a chair, and packed the costumes back into their crates. Then she ran up the two flights of stairs to her bedroom, the vintage clothes clutched in her arms.

She stripped off her T-shirt and jeans and pulled the dress over her head. The fabric rustled stiffly as she worked her arms into the sleeves and then smoothed down the skirt. It had a tight bodice and a sash. *This couldn't have been a costume*, she thought. It had the feel of a well-loved, much-worn dress. A springtime dress—not too heavy, but not light either. Addie examined herself in the mirror on her dresser and was surprised at the way the material hugged her body. Funny. It was so old-fashioned, but somehow it really suited her. She pulled on her ankle boots. Maybe wearing it would make the book buy more fun.

Then, just as she got up to head downstairs, she remembered the shawl. She sat down again and began unfolding the fabric in her lap. It was some sort of silk. Whatever was wrapped up inside it was round and smooth and felt like metal.

In a moment, the shawl was shimmering in folds on the ground, and she was holding a small silver mirror. The glass was clear in some places, dimmed with age in others, but before she could really look in it, she noticed there was something engraved on the other side. She turned it over and gasped.

Three dancers wearing long flowing dresses were etched in the tarnished silver. Their hair was bound and wreathed like Greek goddesses', and the silversmith had sketched a grove of laurel and olive trees behind them. It was one of the loveliest things she had ever seen.

Were the women the three Graces? Or the Muses? Or the Fates? They looked so graceful and fresh in the giddiness of their dance. *What a perfect image.* In her imagination, it burst into life. She saw the women onstage, dancing under greenish-silver branches. Now *that* would work in the scene in *Peer Gynt.*

Putting the mirror down, she lifted her arms above her

head and spun, letting the dress bell out around her calves. Oh, yes, that was perfect. . . .

Then she stopped. *I won't be in* Peer Gynt, she reminded herself.

She closed her eyes and saw herself twirling around the stage in this dress, turning and facing the troll king. His question from her dream echoed in her memory: "What is *she* doing here?"

But this time Addie was ready with an answer.

I belong here.

Opening her eyes, she picked up the mirror and slid it into the pocket of the dress. A wave of dizziness hit her.

That was odd. Why was she dizzy all of a sudden? She went to the back window and threw it open to get some fresh air. A breeze swept in, bearing a faint scent of wisteria. The day was clear and bright, and she could see for blocks from her third-floor perch. In the alley, Whaley was strolling home from the grocery, a bag in his hand.

"Whaley!" Addie leaned out and shouted. "What time is it?"

He squinted up at her and called back, "Almost time to open. What are you doing up there?"

"You'll never guess what we found!" But a mayhem of clucking swelled from Mrs. Turner's chicken coops and drowned her out.

"What?" Whaley shouted back.

Before she could get another word out, loud, high-pitched bird song burst from the cherry tree in Mrs. Turner's backyard. Addie looked around, bemused.

And suddenly it wasn't just birds. All over the neighborhood, dogs were howling; cats were crying. Frowning, Addie leaned out the window, half expecting to hear donkeys braying and elephants trumpeting.

Sparrows burst out of the baby green foliage, chirping like crazy. And then, just to add to the chaos, a truck drove by, rattling the window until it shook in its frame.

Uneasily, she spun around to see the walls of her bedroom rippling like a musical saw.

The door writhed in its frame, and the coffee cup she'd left on her dresser that morning crashed to the floor. Then the floor drew itself up like a cat arching its back. It stretched and sprang, once-solid floorboards flowing in waves under her feet. Framed photos on her desk followed the suicidal coffee cup. She looked out the window and saw Whaley sheltering his head under his arm as the gutters crashed around him.

The Douglas fir in their backyard thrashed in the bright windless sky, a giant trying to pull up its roots and run. Her books shuddered to the edges of the bookshelves and jumped.

Then something in Addie's brain clicked, and every earthquake drill she'd ever been in flashed into her head. She sprang away from the window into the shelter of her door frame.

Stay put, the earthquake-drill voice told her.

But the black power lines were thrumming across the blue sky, and someone was yelling her name, and she flew from the door frame out into the hall and down the stairs.

The steps to the second floor boinged beneath her feet like rubber. She darted through the hall and down the bottom flight of stairs as the walls cracked and sheets of plaster crashed to the ground.

A brick from the chimney careened past her head as she ran into the yard. She looked up to see masonry give way and bricks crumble down the slope of the roof.

Whaley sprinted into the yard, yelling, "Is anyone inside?" His hair was flecked with the cherry blossoms that had been shaken off the boughs.

"No," Addie croaked, realizing the shaking had stopped. Whaley ran his hand over her head and neck, feeling for broken bones.

"I'm fine!" Addie protested, examining him in turn. "Nothing hit you, did it?"

Whaley shook his head.

"Thank goodness. I'd better call Dad and see how he is." Her voice caught. "And if Zack's all right." She reached into her pocket for her phone and then realized that, of course, she'd left it upstairs in her jeans pocket. All her hand closed around was the handle of the small mirror. "Darn it! I don't have my cell."

"I'll call," Whaley said, and started dialing.

Addie waited nervously as he stood with the phone pressed to his ear. "Any luck?"

He frowned and shook his head. "Nope. No signal." He slipped the phone into his pocket. "Don't worry. I'm going to check around the front of the store anyway, see what the damage is. Maybe someone else's phone will be working."

"Oh . . . Okay. I'll go next door and see if Mrs. Turner's all right." She suddenly realized she was shaking.

Whaley headed off around the side of the building, and Addie crossed into Mrs. T.'s backyard, examining her house to make sure nothing had collapsed. It looked all right, but you never knew. . . .

Just then, a chicken burst out of the hen house and began running in circles, squawking. To Addie's relief, Mrs. Turner dashed out of the house after it. "Messalina!" she called. "Come back here, you addle-brained girl!" Addie felt her face relax into a weak smile.

The hen was big and speckled and completely out of her mind. She ran into Addie's yard and around the Douglas fir, white feathers flying, and then doubled back, *bauck-bauck*ing like a wind-up toy gone berserk. Mrs. Turner gave chase, swerving and feinting behind her, coaxing and scolding.

But then Mrs. T. ventured a full-out dive. Addie winced as Mrs. T.'s shoe caught on a tree root and her body hit the ground with a thud. Addie rushed over and squatted down next to her. "Are you all right?"

Mrs. Turner blew a strand of pink hair out of her eye. "Catch her for me, sweetie. I've corkscrewed my ankle."

Messalina wasn't hard to catch, but holding on to her was like hugging a windmill. Her legs churned and her wings flapped until every feather stuck out in distress. A sharp peck from her little beak broke the skin on the back of Addie's hand.

"Stop that!" She felt deeply moronic, yelling at a chicken.

The squawking bird tried to fly out of her arms, but Addie hung on. Pinned, Messalina stretched her neck and pecked frantically in the direction of Addie's face. "Here." Addie thrust the mass of bristling feathers at Mrs. Turner. "Here's your—chicken!"

Once in Mrs. Turner's arms, the hen folded herself up like a cat. The only remnant of her fit was a prolonged, muffled clucking.

"There, there. What an excitable girl! Watch out or you'll stop laying." Mrs. Turner looked up at Addie, shaking with laughter. "I'm sorry. She's high-strung, Messalina." She pushed herself up off the ground, but as she put pressure on her ankle, the color drained out of her face.

"You're really hurt!" Addie exclaimed, quickly offering her arm for support.

Mrs. Turner gritted her teeth, and with Addie's help, she lowered herself back down. Just then, Whaley came into the yard. "Sorry, Ads. I tried some other people's phones, but you can't get a signal anywhere. I think—"

"Mrs. T.'s hurt her ankle," Addie interrupted. "Can you take a look? I'll get the first-aid kit."

She ran to the back door, but Whaley sprinted after her. "Stay out here. There could be aftershocks. I'll get it."

"Do you even know where it is? And if I can't go in, why can you?" She dashed in after him. But when she caught a glimpse of the store through the half-opened back door, she froze. Then, fearfully, she entered.

Shelves were upended. Books were strewn all over the floor. Light fixtures had smashed, and tiny fragments of glass powdered the wreckage like confectioners' sugar. Dust and plaster granules floated in the air. The bay windows, where she'd seen Zacky curled up with Magnesium just two nights ago, were nothing but empty frames. Addie stared.

Then she heard Whaley coming down the stairs and went into the hall to meet him. The first-aid kit was in his hands. It was an old metal lunch box that Zack had painted white and put a red cross on for a play they'd done in the backyard. But it had real bandages and medicine in it.

"Whaley, did you look in the store?"

"I looked." He seemed almost angry. "So much for my job," he muttered.

"What?"

"Nothing. C'mon. I'm not kidding about the aftershocks. Let's go." They left the building and he handed her the first-aid kit. "You get Mrs. T.'s ankle fixed. I'll check on the neighbors."

"Tell Almaz I'll be over soon."

"Don't worry. I will."

Mrs. Turner was sitting on the tree root that had felled her, holding her twisted ankle. Messalina was calmly stalking around the yard, pecking at worms. Addie sat down beside Mrs. T. and took a roll of bandages and tape out of her kit. Gently, she propped Mrs. Turner's foot on her lap, located the end of the bandage, and pressed it against her ankle.

"Pretty silly to survive an earthquake and get injured by a chicken," Mrs. T. joked.

Suddenly, she jerked upright. "Becky! Oh, my God! I need to check on her!"

"Who's Becky?" Then Addie remembered. "Your friend

who owns the theater?" She got the tape into position and fastened the bandage. "Why do you need to check on her? Is she an old lady or something?"

Mrs. Turner gave her a look of mock irritation. "No, dear. *I'm* an old lady. Becky just isn't well. She had an operation and it left her partially blind. And when I think of furniture falling and windows breaking . . . and Dave's out of town." Mrs. Turner stood up again, but winced as her weight came down on the injured ankle. "I'm going to go see her." She stopped short. "Damn it! My car's in the shop. I guess I'll just have to hobble over on my own two hooves."

Addie shut the first-aid kit. "You can't walk anywhere!"

"Well, I'll have to. What if she's pinned under a big mantelpiece, or a bit of machinery in the shed? Your family hikes. Don't you have one of those hiking sticks? Loan me one of those."

"I'm serious! Sit down!" Addie looked at her sternly. "I'll go. Just tell me where she lives."

Whaley came back into the yard. Addie jumped to her feet and whipped around. "Is Almaz all right?"

"She's fine. Her dad's giving out bottled water to everyone in case the pipes are burst."

"Good. Listen, Mrs. Turner needs me to check on her friend. What's her name again?" she asked, turning to Mrs. T.

"Becky Powell."

"She's a blind lady or something. I think I should."

Whaley frowned. "I don't know. What if there's an aftershock? Why don't I go instead?"

"Whaley! I can manage. Besides, you should stay close

to the store until Dad and Zack get back. I mean, the windows are all broken, and—"

"Okay." He still sounded uneasy. "But if something looks unsafe—"

"I know, I know," Addie said. She grinned mischievously. "Hey, it suits you."

"What does?"

"Worrying." Then, more seriously, "Caring."

Whaley just made a face, turned, and headed toward the store.

"Try it more often!" Addie called after him. "Join the rest of the world!"

But he was gone. As her teasing words died away, Addie thought of the smashed-up bookshop and heard his muttered, "So much for my job," and felt that everything was broken.

REG

She made her way to the street through the narrow gap between their house and Mrs. Turner's, righting garbage cans as she went. *The buildings are all standing,* she thought, a bit dazed. Windows were smashed and chimneys had collapsed, but that was the worst of it. Roof tiles and bricks were scattered about. The sidewalk sparkled with shattered glass, and she had to pick her way carefully among the shards.

The girl with the fish tattooed on her biceps whom Addie often saw at the Brown Bear was wiping blood from the face of another girl. Addie went over to them and held up her first-aid kit. "Do you need bandages?"

"You got antibiotic ointment?"

She snapped open the lunch box and handed the girl a tube.

"Thanks." She squeezed some of the cream onto her fingertip. "They're not very deep cuts," she told her friend.

The other girl yelped as the cream touched the wound. "Doesn't mean they don't hurt!"

Addie cut off some gauze and tape for them, took back the tube, and snapped the kit shut. Lots of people were milling around in the street, but to her relief, no one else seemed to be injured.

People were clumped together in little groups everywhere, talking anxiously, examining their houses, fruitlessly trying to use their cell phones. Like Whaley, no one could get a signal. And Addie understood from a few overheard comments that the landlines were dead, too.

She headed to the bus stop, but after a few minutes, she couldn't stand waiting anymore. Would the buses even be running? It wasn't such a bad walk to upper Capitol Hill—kind of long, but under the circumstances, the wait for the bus might be longer. She made the decision and began walking east. After a block or two, she quickened her pace until she was almost running.

Beyond the houses and trees, she caught a glimpse of the ship canal; she saw, with relief, that the University Bridge was still standing. She got closer and then stopped and gazed along the canal. It sparkled, as blue as fresh paint; dotted along the shore were white trawlers and sailboats. To the east and west, she saw the ghostly white tops of the mountains; they looked peaceful, as if there had been no rending and grinding in their rocky hearts, no deep shift in their layers of time and sediment. As if nothing had been broken that couldn't be fixed.

Then she took off across the bridge and didn't stop all the way up Capitol Hill, turning off on Boston Street and rounding the bend in the road to Fifteenth. Almost panting, she continued past the cemetery until she reached Volunteer Park. Mrs. Turner had said that her friend lived on one of the streets bordering the south end of the park, so it made sense to cut through.

She walked along the road that wound toward the glass conservatory filled with tropical plants. But before she reached it, she turned and cut across the grass behind the Asian Art Museum, the imposing building disappearing from view behind the groves of giant oaks and maples and cedars as she pressed on, trying to keep up her pace as she headed toward the huge brick water tower at the south entrance. Tulips pushed up through the hard earth, petals still shut tight against the chill. By the time she reached the little yew hedge that surrounded the life-size statue of the angel, she was sweating and out of breath.

She dropped down on the marble bench at the angel's feet, gasping for air, and sat until her breathing slowed and her skin cooled down a bit.

She'd passed this statue so often, tucked away here among the trees, but she'd never really looked at it closely. Now, as Addie sat catching her breath, she noticed the tenderness in the angel's face as she gazed down at the dead soldier she was lifting in her arms. The sculptor had created the illusion that the angel was rising, her feet only barely touching the heavy base with its long list of names. They were carved under the words DEDICATED TO THE MEMORY OF THOSE SEATTLE NATIVES WHO GAVE THEIR LIVES IN THE GREAT WAR 1917–1918.

Addie thought of the bombs hitting the factory that she'd seen on TV. She looked again at the beautiful, sad angel and the names from those long-ago battles.

Long ago . . . She jumped off the bench and looked down at herself in dismay. The antique dress—she was still wearing it! And—oh, no. The hem was dirty from when she'd sat on the ground. The front was all right. But what about the back? She twisted around, trying to gauge the damage, but couldn't see.

Luckily, the little mirror was still in her pocket. She pulled it out and held it behind her to get a good look. There was some loose dirt along the skirt in back but no actual mud, thank goodness.

She brushed it off, then quickly examined her face to see if she looked as much of a mess as she felt. No, she was all right. But as she gazed into the glass, another wave of dizziness caught her. For a moment she was afraid it might be an aftershock. Hastily, she dropped the mirror back into her pocket and looked around, balancing carefully on her feet to measure the movement of the earth.

If there had been another shift, it was over. Now she was really nervous. She worked her wristwatch free from under the tight sleeves: 11:49. Getting late. She'd better hurry. The sooner she got there, the sooner she could go home. She wanted to be there when Dad got back with Zack. She pulled the sleeve down over her watch and set off again.

The day seemed suddenly warmer. The air was full of hyacinth as she left the park and turned onto Salmon Bay Drive.

Mansions lined the street, hidden behind chestnut trees in their first white bloom. Low stone walls guarded gleaming lawns. She looked around in surprise. The houses were decorated with red, white, and blue bunting, as if for a Fourth of July parade. Odd, since it was only April. But stranger still was the quiet. No neighbors gathered in anxious groups. No traffic. Not even a car parked on the street.

She found number 65 and walked up a sweeping drive to a Craftsman-style house of dark wood and cut stone with a big chimney and gables. Big, latticed windows looked out on a comfortable porch. Addie stared, thinking of the jagged shards of glass in front of their store. Mrs. Powell was lucky her windows were in one piece. She glanced up. The chimney seemed to have survived as well.

She glided her hand along the iron railing as she climbed the front steps. Then she crossed the porch and knocked at the door.

No one answered.

She waited and knocked again. When there was still no response, she walked over to a window and peered in through the pale muslin drapes. She saw a long mahogany dining table under a chandelier. A tall china cabinet with glass doors stood against the far wall. That hadn't broken either! She frowned. Almaz had once told her that the effects of an earthquake could be different from one part of the city to another. The house was pretty high up on the hill. Maybe that explained it.

She hesitated before knocking a third time. It didn't look as if there had been much damage, she reasoned, so Becky Powell was probably all right. If there was no answer, should she just leave?

But Mrs. Turner's worry pricked her conscience. She'd said her friend was sick. And partially—or was it completely—blind? Addie couldn't remember. In any case, it might take her a while to make her way through the house to answer the door.

"Say! Hello, there!" a voice called, and Addie jumped. "Are you looking for Mrs. Powell?"

She swung around to see a guy about Whaley's age wearing a suit with the jacket tied around his waist. He was walking slowly up the sidewalk, carrying what looked like a large sack of laundry.

"Yes, I am."

"My mother's not home, but I'm glad you're here. I can't put her down, you see, and I'll need you to unlock the door for me."

He was coming up the drive now, and as he got closer, Addie realized that what he carried was not a sack of laundry but a girl. And she was unconscious.

Startled, Addie hurried down the steps toward them. The girl looked about thirteen or fourteen. A purple bruise mottled her forehead around a deep cut, and sticky-looking blood seamed the wound. Freckles stood out against her waxy skin. Strings of reddish-blond hair straggled across her forehead.

"Poor thing!" Instinctively, Addie put her arm under the girl's back to help the guy support her weight. "She's been hit hard."

"As hard as she could be," the guy returned in a disgusted tone. He was tall, though not in the gangly way Whaley was, and good-looking. His face was flushed, and his dark hair was sticking up in places and plastered down in others.

"Where are you bringing her from?"

"Downtown, by the jail."

"Downtown!" Addie frowned. "Why didn't you take her to Swedish?"

"It didn't seem right to leave her at a hospital all by herself. I can telephone Dr. Wald. He'll come by." His blue eyes clouded with worry. "But you're right. I probably shouldn't have dragged her so far. It's just that it's crazy down there with the demonstration and everything."

"What demonstration?" But even as she asked, Addie remembered Mrs. Turner's posters. "I thought it was next week."

"It's today. The crowds turned out to support the Wobblies."

The Wobblies? Addie vaguely remembered Mrs. Turner talking about them. "What happened?" She looked more closely at the girl, alarmed by the shallow sound of her breathing.

"The bricks started flying and she got hit."

Addie thought of the bricks flying off the chimney at

home and winced as she imagined one of them smashing into someone's skull, the explosion of pain. She touched the girl's arm gently.

"Should I hold her while you open the door?"

"It's not worth the jostling. Any little jolt hurts like flaming devils. When she's awake, that is." The guy's face was open and good-natured. "Listen, I know it's not really the thing, but under the circumstances . . . could you reach into my jacket pocket and fish out the keys?" He jerked his head to indicate the jacket tied around his waist. The pockets dangled down near his knees.

"Sure." Addie bent down and reached into one. To her surprise, it was lined with silk. Below the cuff of his trousers, his shoes were polished leather. She wondered what he was so dressed up for.

The key was heavy, a long finger of iron with prongs. Addie held it up. "I don't think I've ever used one like this before." She studied the door. "Where's the keyhole?"

"Under the brass plate."

A moan escaped from the lips of the unconscious girl.

"She's coming around. Can you be quick about it?"

Addie flipped open the little oval of brass and slid the key into the lock. But she couldn't get it to catch. There seemed to be acres of space inside the keyhole. She fumbled around, turning the key this way and that, while the guy stood sweating with the dead weight of the girl in his arms.

Finally, she jammed it into the hole as hard as she could, muttering, "Go in, darn you."

It worked. The locking device clasped the key tight,

and Addie turned it until it clicked. "Aha!" she exclaimed. "Our heroine saves the day!" She turned the knob and opened the door. The guy raised an eyebrow and stepped past her. No one, Addie understood his look to say, had ever had so much difficulty with a key before.

She followed him into a grand entrance hall. A large gilt-framed mirror on the wall reflected them. Addie caught a glimpse of herself and was startled. Once again, she'd forgotten that she was wearing the antique dress. The guy must have thought she was a nut, dressed like this. Though his clothes were fairly out of the ordinary, too. It made her feel a little less out of place.

The injured girl murmured something unintelligible.

"Shh, now," the guy told her quietly. Addie followed him through the dining room she'd seen from the window. Then they were in a narrow corridor. Photos in silver frames lined the walls: black-and-white pictures of babies being christened, men and women in their wedding clothes.

"Papa?" the girl murmured.

The guy looked over his shoulder at Addie and said, "Could you open that door at the end of the hall?" He stepped aside to let her go ahead.

Addie opened it and they entered a bright, comfortable room. French doors in the back wall let in the brilliant sunlight. They were shut now, but Addie saw that they opened onto a stone porch with wrought-iron lawn furniture and, beyond that, a garden full of cherry trees in bloom. The room was cluttered and inelegant compared to the rest of the house, but that only made it more welcoming. There was an old writing desk against one wall, its cubbyholes overflowing with papers. A red couch was pushed against the other wall, with a low coffee table on which someone had left a cake with white icing and shavings of lemon peel, along with a few glasses and plates. A dressmaker's dummy with emerald fabric slung over its shoulder stood in one corner, and a wheeled croquet set in another.

"Rake Mother's trash off the sofa. I'll lay her down there."

But it wasn't trash on the sofa, Addie saw immediately. It was stacks of theater programs with some sort of bold black and white design on it—maybe a period drama. She studied the guy with greater interest. She'd forgotten. His mother owned a theater. Maybe that was why he was dressed like that. Getting ready for an opening night or something.

She cleared off the couch and helped him lower the girl down to it, easing her head onto a throw pillow. She sank into the cushions with a groan.

Addie knelt beside her. Lightly, she lifted the girl's hair away from her forehead to get a better look at the injury. The blood had already dried, but she still needed to clean it. "Do you have a damp cloth?" she asked, keeping her voice low.

"Sure." He left and returned a few minutes later with a warm, moist cloth. Addie took it and dabbed gently at the wound, careful not to open it again. Some blood had dripped onto the girl's blouse, which was frayed at the buttonholes and smelled oddly of fresh-cut wood.

"Who is she?" she asked.

Mrs. Powell's son was rolling up the sleeves of his shirt. "I don't know. I just saw her get hit, and no one was helping her. She might be one of the Wobs' kids. She keeps asking for her father."

"Wobs? You mean the Wobblies?"

"Who else? Their families were all there, singing their hearts out. Then vigilantes jumped in and trouble started. Whoever was with her must have got swept up in the panic." He looked at Addie and grinned. "I bet you're wondering what a gentleman like me was doing at such a sordid scene."

A gentleman? But she liked it. She liked people to dramatize themselves.

"And speaking of being a gentleman!" He put his hand over his heart and bowed. "Sincere thanks for your help, Miss—I haven't even asked your name."

"It's Addie. Addie McNeal."

"I'm Reg Powell."

"Reg?"

He made a face. "Don't rub it in. It's Reginald on the birth certificate. And I don't know what I ever did to deserve that."

Addie laughed. It *was* a pretty bad name.

"Some great-uncle of Dad's, I think. No one ever calls me by my full name, thank goodness. Here, I'll take the cloth if you're done."

"Oh. Thanks." Addie handed it to him and picked up the painted lunch box. She opened it and began rummaging for the antibiotic cream.

"Is that a first-aid kit? That's lucky. Are you taking one of those Red Cross classes?"

"I . . . No. I brought it just in case. Mrs. Turner asked me to come see if your mom was all right."

"Oh, Mrs. Turner sent you?" Reg smiled uncertainly. "But—why? Something to do with the theater?"

"She was afraid your mother might be injured. You know, like this girl. Knocked down by a piece of furniture or a brick or something."

"I appreciate your concern—or Meg Turner's," Reg said pleasantly. "But what has this girl getting hit with a brick got to do with my mother?"

Reg frowned. "What? Hold on. Let me get rid of this wet cloth." He stepped out of the room.

Addie found the antibiotic and applied it to Frida's wound. She put it away and snapped the kit shut. Reg came back, still frowning slightly.

"Well, if a brick could fly off a building downtown, why couldn't one fly off a building in Capitol Hill? Do you have some special kind of masonry or something?"

"What are you talking about? A vigilante threw that brick. Or did you think that those upstanding defenders of law and order wouldn't hit a kid?"

Addie frowned. "I don't understand."

A cry of pain interrupted them. The girl's eyes snapped open. She jerked straight up and clutched her head. "Oww! It huuuurts!"

Addie squeezed in next to her on the sofa and put her arm around her shoulder. "Shhh."

"I'll call the doctor." Reg headed for the door. "She probably needs laudanum."

"Laudanum?" Addie stared at him. "But—but that's morphine, isn't it?"

"I think so. Why?"

Was he serious? She examined him more closely, but he didn't seem to be joking. "What's wrong with a few aspirin? I've got some right here." There were a few loose ibuprofen rattling around inside the kit. She shook two out and held them in her palm. "If you get her some water, she can take it now."

"There's sherry on the mantel." He moved toward a crystal decanter half full of golden liquid.

"*Sherry?*" Now she was feeling alarmed.

"It's legal in your own home," he retorted.

"I *know* it's legal. That's not the point." For a moment she tried to step back and make sense of all this. Because something was really wrong here. She liked Reg, but—she shook her head and then started as the girl on the couch cried out.

"Owww!" She was lightly touching the wound and looking from one to the other of them in panic. "What happened?" She glanced down at her clothes. "*Blood!*"

"You got hit by a brick, and this"—Addie looked at Reg, who was mouthing *I'll get the water* as he left the room—"this very nice person is calling a doctor."

The girl stared at Addie as if she were the head of a human-trafficking ring. "Where am I?" Her voice had a lilting up-and-down accent, with heavy, round vowels. Scandinavian? Addie wondered. German? "Is this your house?"

"No. Reg lives here. My name's Addie. What's yours?"

"Frida Peterson." Gingerly, she settled back on the pillow. Addie patted her hands, remembering when she was ten and had her tonsils removed. When she'd woken from the surgery, her dad had been sitting like this on the side of her bed, and she'd felt warm and comforted.

In the dazzling sunlight, Frida's face was pale. Grubby, too. Addie noticed that there were grease stains on her dress.

"Too bright." She squeezed her eyes shut again. "The light's picking holes in my head."

Addie got up and pulled the drape across the windows just enough to shade the girl from the glare.

"That's better." She pressed her hand to her forehead, then suddenly jerked herself up. "Papa . . . I didn't see my father. I didn't give him the slippers. It's so cold in the jail. All that time waiting, and I didn't even give him the slippers."

"Your dad's in jail?" Despite herself, Addie felt shocked.

"Not that he oughtta be." Frida's weak voice mustered a defensive tone, but her eyes teared up. "He said a man got a right to shout about things that aren't right and not get arrested. But he was."

"People are getting arrested? At the demonstration?"

"Didn't you know?"

Addie swallowed and shook her head. How could Mrs. Turner be so excited about getting people to go to the march when here was this girl with her head cut and bleeding and her dad in jail?

Reg returned, carrying a china pitcher. He'd flung a towel over his arm like a waiter in a fancy restaurant. "What's this? Tears? Ah, no, no, no, mademoiselle! No tears in the Powell Luxury Sanatorium!" He put the pitcher on the table and filled one of the glasses with a flourish. "There you go, Miss . . ."

"She said her name's Frida."

"Miss Frida, get that down while the nurse gives you your horse pills." He turned to Addie, who pressed two tablets into the girl's hand. "Dr. Wald's coming. He says she probably has a concussion. If she falls asleep, we should wake her after a bit and ask her name, who's the president, questions like that."

Somewhere in the house a door slammed.

"Reg!" a musical voice called. "Are you home? More guests for dinner. And the cook's day off! Be a sport and help me rustle up provisions. Where are you?"

Reg opened the door to the hallway. "Back here," he called softly.

A click-clack of high heels approached. *This must be Becky Powell*, Addie thought. *The Becky Powell Mrs. T. was so concerned about.*

"You could run down to Paulson's. It's not too late to roast a chicken. Though what we'll do for dessert . . ." Her words trickled to a halt as she approached the doorway. "Reg? It's dark as the witch's glen in here! What's going on?"

A tall, slender woman with dark brown hair drawn back into an elaborate twist appeared in the doorway. Her face was delicate, and she wore a white blouse, a slim gray skirt that fell to midcalf, and a short, tailored black jacket. She glanced from the girl on the couch to Addie and finally to Reg, her light brown eyes curious and benevolent.

Addie stared at those eyes, and a chill feathered down her neck.

As Reg told his mother what had happened, her face

filled with concern. She opened a closet, pulled out a folded quilt, and tucked it around Frida, who was dozing off.

Addie watched as Mrs. Powell moved around the room with such grace and certainty. Feeling Addie's gaze, the woman turned and looked at her—*looked at her with both eyes clear and focused*—and smiled. She said something about how lucky Reg was to have her help, then shook her hand when Reg introduced her. Addie tried to smile back, but she couldn't.

Something was wrong. There was no way this woman was sick or blind.

"I'm sorry," she said awkwardly. "I think I've made a mistake. The person I'm supposed to be checking on is blind. Or partially blind, or something. Mrs. Turner wanted me to make sure she was all right." Addie shook her head in confusion. "She said her name was Mrs. Powell. But *you're* Mrs. Powell, aren't you?"

"Well, yes," the woman said guardedly. "In fact, I am. But I'm not blind."

Reg regarded Addie with a puzzled smile. "What an extraordinary thing to say! Meg Turner must be playing a joke on you. The only things my mother is blind to, Miss McNeal, are my faults."

ANGEL

Mrs. Powell regarded Addie quizzically for a moment then turned to open the French doors at the end of the room. "Let's go out on the back porch," she said quietly. "We can keep an eye on the girl until the doctor comes but not wake her up." She picked up three clean glasses from the coffee table and said to Addie, "Bring out that cake—and the knife, if you can manage. I think we all could do with a little sustenance."

Shaken, Addie got the cake and followed her out. Mrs. Powell put the glasses down on a wrought-iron table. Gently, she shut the glass doors and sat, gesturing for Addie to do the same.

Addie put down the cake and hesitated. Through the glass, she could see the girl turning restlessly on the couch. She felt torn: she wanted to go back home—surely Dad and

Zack would be there by now—but she couldn't leave quite yet. Not without figuring out what was going on.

"I just don't understand it," she said, pulling out a chair and sitting down.

"It's one of Meg's jokes. That's what I think," Mrs. Powell said.

Meg? Reg had called her that, too. But most people called Mrs. T. Margie.

"She plays them on everyone. Don't take it to heart."

"But she *looked* serious. And why joke about you being blind? It's not funny."

Reg opened the French doors and stepped out onto the porch carrying the pitcher of water. "Don't be confused. Meg's jokes aren't always meant to be funny. You know these artistic types. Meg Turner's one of the worst. A symbolist! A devotee of that crazy Isadora Duncan, no less."

"Who is a great artist," his mother contradicted. "And not crazy! Excuse Reg for being such a Philistine, Miss McNeal." She got up and closed the doors as Reg poured water into the glasses.

Addie frowned. Mrs. Turner was a photographer, if that's what Reg meant by artistic. But a symbolist? What was that? "Who is Isadora—" Then she recalled a photo she'd seen somewhere. "You mean that dancer?" Now she remembered. A dark-haired woman, twirling barefoot onstage, eyes closed as if in a trance. But there was something about her, Addie thought. Something sad. Oh! "She died when her scarf caught in the wheel of a car or something, didn't she?"

"God forbid!" Mrs. Powell's eyes widened. She balled her

hand into a fist and reached out to knock against the cherry tree behind them. "You must be thinking of someone else."

"Maybe," Addie said doubtfully. Uneasiness whispered through her again.

"What I'm saying, Mother, is that Meg probably meant you were blind as in *blind to the dreadful state of things*." Reg slipped into an impassioned falsetto. "There's a terrible state of things in the world, Miss McNeal. A conspiracy of the rich. Of big fat men with cigars! That's why we're at war."

Addie felt disloyal, laughing at Reg's impression of Mrs. T. "Maybe she does sound like that sometimes. But she's right. Not about the conspiracy, I mean. But everyone knows we wouldn't be fighting if it weren't for the oil companies."

Reg tipped his head, considering. "I guess they'll make a mint out of it, just like the banks and the munitions factories. But you can't really think that's why we're fighting." Addie frowned. She'd heard enough from Dad and Mrs. T. to disagree with him on this, but it wasn't polite to argue. Reg turned back to his mother. "Did you hear what Meg said about me joining the army?"

"Don't try to discuss the war with her, darling. She's convinced it's all a plot of the big bad capitalists." Mrs. Powell gave Addie a look of dry amusement. "I'd like to know where Meg thinks she gets her salary from. Perhaps she thinks I give away the box seats for free? And she's one to talk, the way she treats our poor electricians!"

"Wait a second." Addie turned to Reg. "You're joining the army?" The swaying branches of the cherry tree blocked the sunshine for a moment, and she felt a chill.

"Of course not. He's in college," Mrs. Powell said firmly. "And he's not serious."

"Why am I not serious?" Reg objected. Addie couldn't tell if he really meant what he said or was just teasing his mother. "Why wouldn't I go fight for freedom and democracy? Not to mention to stop people from murdering our citizens in cold blood? Someone has to do it, don't they?"

"But that's Mrs. Turner's point," Addie said. "It's *not* about freedom and democracy. The politicians just say that."

"So young and yet so cynical." Reg grinned at Addie. "In case you're confused on this point, it wasn't the oil companies that declared war. It was Congress."

"Congress didn't *declare* it," Addie protested. "They hardly ever do. Not since—"

"You think the president would commit troops without congressional approval? All for the benefit of Wall Street and a few bellicose millionaires? That's ridiculous. Didn't you read the speech he made when he introduced the war resolution?"

Mrs. Powell leaned in toward Reg. "Our president gives an impressive speech and you're off to solve the problems of the world with a machine gun? You're the mainstay of your widowed mother, remember? I expect help running the theater once you graduate."

"Why can't Charlie do that?" Reg groaned. "I keep telling you, I'm no good at business. I edit a student paper— and that's all. I couldn't keep the *Daily* going financially if someone threatened to draw and quarter me."

Addie hid a smile. It was clearly well-trodden ground. So much so that Mrs. Powell—just like Dad!—seemed not to hear Reg at all and simply continued with her thoughts. "Charlie can't, that's all. Your brother is quite happy in his law office. He'd be out of his depth dealing with late nights and temperamental actors and freethinkers!" Her expression softened, and she shaded her eyes from the bright sunlight to look in on Frida. "And I don't know how he'd cope with the waifs that pitch up on our doorstep. We'll have to find her parents, you know."

"Her father's in jail," Addie said, and immediately wished she hadn't.

"*Jail?*" Mrs. Powell turned to Reg in alarm. "Not one of that Everett mob, is he?"

Addie wanted to ask what the Everett mob was, but kept quiet.

Reg shrugged and looked away.

"Reg! I know it's out of the goodness of your heart, but why must you always get tangled up in lost causes? You only make life hard for yourself."

You're just making life hard for yourself. That was exactly what Addie's school adviser had said about her getting mixed up with Whaley.

Reg caught Addie's eye and winked. "My life is *so* difficult," he murmured, surveying the beautiful house and garden.

"All right," his mother said. "Point taken. But still!" She sighed. "Well, it's not the girl's fault. We'll just have to locate her mother. Out by the mills in Ballard, I suppose. She must be worried sick."

Guilt stabbed into Addie. Her *dad* would be worried

sick. How long had she been here? She pushed back her chair. "Thanks for the drink. But I've got to go. I shouldn't have stayed this long. And—" The unsettling feeling rippled through her again. "I'm sorry. That was just weird about your being blind."

"Don't apologize. We're in your debt. Honest." Reg grinned mischievously. "You've given us something to entertain our guests with tonight: What did Meg Turner mean by her fabulous fib?"

"That's not gentlemanly, Reg."

"Oh, come on, Ma. What good is being a gentleman around theater people?"

"I suppose you have a point." Mrs. Powell turned to Addie. "I own and manage the Jewel. Did Reg tell you that?"

Addie, about to stand up, found herself sinking back in her chair. "You're so lucky," she said, trying not to sound envious.

Mrs. Powell smiled and stretched her arms up to the sky. "I know! I'm the luckiest woman in this city, Miss McNeal. Not the richest. Not the prettiest. But the luckiest. Because I have work that I love."

"I wish I could work in the theater," Addie said, a bit wistfully.

"How old are you, dear?" Mrs. Powell asked.

"Seventeen—just."

"Well, seventeen's quite old enough. What kind of work are you interested in? Costuming?"

"No!" Addie replied so vehemently that Reg gave a surprised bark of laughter, and she looked down in embarrassment at the dirt-streaked dress. "I mean, wardrobe and makeup are fun, but they're not what I want. Though from the way I'm dressed, I can see why you would think that."

"You don't want to *act*, do you?" Reg inquired in mock horror, leaning back in his chair.

"Oh, shush, Reg. Don't tease."

"Well." Addie hesitated. "I thought that might be what I want."

"Find out if you're any good at it first," Mrs. Powell said, and Addie was struck by how her gentleness was instantly replaced by a brisk, no-nonsense tone. "Because most people aren't."

"I know that," Addie said, her face falling.

"Have some cake," Reg said solicitously, mimicking Addie's downcast expression so exactly that she had to smile. "It's perfectly safe. Mother had no hand in its making, in case you had any delusions to the contrary." He cut a slice and passed her the plate. Addie took it and had a bite. It tasted sharp and full of lemon, surprisingly less sweet than she'd expected.

Mrs. Powell was peering through the windows of the French doors into the study again. "Oh, dear. She's tossing and turning. Reg, did you say you gave her something for the pain?"

"Miss McNeal did."

That's right. Addie frowned to herself. Ibuprofen rather than morphine, fortunately! Reg couldn't possibly have a drug problem, could he? No. That was ridiculous. It was more as if—

Mrs. Powell stood up abruptly. "I'll feel a lot better once the doctor's had a look at her. How long has it been since you spoke to him?"

"Half an hour. He said he had to see another patient first."

Half an hour? Anxiously, Addie tugged back her tight sleeve to check her watch again. But it must have broken in the earthquake somehow, because its hands were still stubbornly stuck at 11:49. It had to be a lot later than that. Quickly, she pulled her sleeve down and sprang out of her chair. "I'd really better be going. I'll tell Mrs. Turner not to worry about you, Mrs. Powell."

"I can't imagine why she would." Mrs. Powell regarded Addie with gentle curiosity. "You know, I think I'll telephone Meg myself once I see how that girl is." She put her hand on the doorknob and then paused, as though debating something. "Would you like to come to a rehearsal sometime, Miss McNeal?"

"A rehearsal?" Addie had been pushing her chair in, but stopped short. "You mean at the Jewel?"

"Of course." Mrs. Powell gave her an appraising look. "If you're genuinely interested, perhaps I could find some work for you. And not in costumes or makeup, though those are very useful skills, if you ask me." She smiled. "We're doing the Scottish play, of all things. Lots of drama. Lots of scenery-chewing. You'll enjoy it."

"Work—in a professional theater? Really?" Mrs. Powell nodded. Addie had to restrain herself from jumping up and down. A rehearsal of *Macbeth*—and the possibility of being part of it! "Oh, thank you!"

"My pleasure." Mrs. Powell turned and went into the house, calling over her shoulder, "Charming to have met you, Miss McNeal."

Addie turned back to Reg. "Where is the Jewel, anyway?" She was so happy she thought she would float up through the blossoms and get caught in the branches of the cherry tree.

"Second and Pine." Despite all his teasing, he looked pleased for her. "You can't miss it. Don't you want to finish your cake?"

"No, I'd better run. I have to get home and make sure my dad and my brother are all right. When should I come by the theater?"

"Not tomorrow. The crew's working on the set. Tuesday? Rehearsals start midday and go until the wee hours."

"Will you be there?"

"Maybe." He grinned. "After all, I *am* the mainstay of my poor widowed mother."

Addie couldn't help grinning back. "Thanks for the cake. It was great to meet you and your mom. I'll see you soon."

She turned and walked off the porch onto the lawn, intending to go around the side of the house, but before she made it that far, Reg caught up to her.

"Sorry. I have to ask: Why are you worried about your father? He wasn't at the jail, was he?"

It was such an odd question that Addie gave a surprised laugh. "No, of course not! He was dropping my brother off at a class, and then the earthquake hit. I mean, I'm sure they're fine. Everyone in my neighborhood was. But I just want to make sure."

She turned to go again. But, to her astonishment, Reg grabbed her wrist.

"What earthquake?" He smiled at her politely.

"What do you mean?"

"I mean, what earthquake are you talking about?"

Uneasily, Addie slid her wrist out of his grasp. "The one this morning."

"This morning? I don't follow you."

"What's to follow? The earthquake this morning!" Addie exclaimed. "Why do you think I came here? I told you, Mrs. Turner was worried about your mother getting hurt."

He looked thoroughly puzzled. "Because she couldn't see well? And might be unable to find her way out of the wreckage?"

Addie opened her mouth and shut it again abruptly. For a fleeting moment, she felt as if she couldn't get quite enough air into her lungs. Was he teasing her? She wanted to tell him to stop playing games, but—she glanced at his house. She guessed he had some reason to doubt her. Nothing was damaged here. Not the delicate china teacups. Not the windows, not the chimney. Even the girl lying on his sofa had been hit by a brick someone threw, not by debris from a building cracking at its foundation.

"Miss McNeal, you must know there wasn't any earthquake." Now his voice had a humoring note in it, as if she were mildly insane and needed to be treated gently.

"Of course there was!" There had to be some logical explanation. "If you'd been in my neighborhood, you would have felt it for sure. Maybe it was just stronger in some parts of the city than others. Or—"

"Or there wasn't one," Reg said firmly.

"Don't be ridiculous!"

They stared at each other, and Addie could see her own distrust reflected in his eyes.

The sound of a doorbell startled her. "That's probably Dr. Wald," Reg said.

Addie stomped her foot, starting to feel angry again. "There *was* an earthquake!"

"A tremor, do you mean? I *could* imagine missing that—"

"No. Stronger. A lot stronger."

Reg shook his head. His white dress shirt was blinding in the sun, and his voice was suddenly formal. "I'm sorry. I'm not in the habit of getting into arguments with people I've just met."

"Neither am I. Why don't you just come by our house? Once you've seen the mess it's in—"

"Reg!" Mrs. Powell's voice rang out. "Come talk to Dr. Wald. He needs to know what happened!"

"All right!" Reg called back. He turned to Addie. "Look, I'm willing to be convinced. But not now. Give me your address. I'll drop by."

"Do you have something I can write it on?"

He patted his pockets, turned one inside out. "Darn it!

No. Just tell it to me. I've got a good memory." A grin flickered across his face and Addie relaxed a bit. There was something she really liked about this guy, even if he was strange.

Hurriedly, she told him the address.

"Near Meg Turner's?"

"That's right."

"Should be easy to find. I'll see you later, then." He turned and walked back across the garden.

As soon as he had disappeared, she took off running. She needed to see the wreckage from the earthquake. It wasn't as if she doubted it. Of course she didn't. But the sooner she got home, the better she would feel.

The antique dress whipped around her legs as she flew down the quiet, tree-lined street, past the mansions with the red, white, and blue bunting on their gates. It was only after she burst through the entrance to the park that she began to slow down.

Her boots hammered the asphalt drive and then crunched on twigs and stones as she darted across the grass and approached the yew hedges. She looked up to get her bearings.

And skidded to a halt.

The statue of the angel wasn't there anymore.

She stood stock-still, staring, as though if she looked hard enough, it would simply reappear.

But it didn't.

Slowly, Addie approached the fountain. She felt dizzy. Stunned. She couldn't tear her eyes away from the empty space where the statue should have been. And because she was staring so hard, she tripped over a tree root, pitched forward, and fell hard onto the ground. Something jolted out of her pocket and landed on the grass: the beautiful silver mirror she'd found that morning. Her hands were shaking as she reached for it.

This was insane. What was going on? Taking a deep breath, she pushed herself off the ground and continued right on through the gap in the hedge. There was the little fountain and the marble bench, right in front of her. But the statue was definitely gone.

She felt her forehead, hoping—actually hoping—that she was feverish.

But she wasn't.

What had happened then? Had she been hit by something in the earthquake? And if so, how could she have forgotten? She held up the mirror and examined herself. Same longish nose, same well-defined lips. No obvious injuries. Her eyes were green and clear, not dazed or unfocused. She pulled her coppery chestnut hair off her forehead to see if there were any bumps or bruises. But no. Nothing at all. She was fine.

Then, reflected in a corner of the glass, she caught sight of the cool white marble of the angel's wing.

She whirled around to look again.

The statue had been there all along.

A small sound, half sob, half laugh, burbled up from her throat. The bubble of unreality burst, and the sounds of the city came rushing back to her: the shrilling of an ambulance siren, the chatter of voices from the sidewalk just outside the park, the whoosh of a car speeding by. She was weak with relief as she set off once again, heading out the side entrance, back down the slope toward the ship canal and University Bridge.

A woman in a red scarf was puffing up the hill toward her, pulling a little boy by the hand.

"Let's just hope the chimney is still standing," she was saying to him.

"Why?" Addie called to her. "Why are you worried about your chimney?"

The woman looked startled. "Because of the earthquake, of course."

Addie's heart slowed, and she drew a deep breath. "Of course," she said. "Because of the earthquake."

DAMAGE

As she came over the hill, a block away from the house, she saw Dad standing in front of the bookstore examining a deadly-looking two-foot-long spike of glass that was all that remained of the pane in the door. He looked older all of a sudden; his shoulders were slumped, and his face was gray with worry. Addie's throat tightened.

"Dad!" She sprinted down the street toward him. "Is Zack okay?"

He turned and broke into a smile, the age dropping away. "Of course. What do you think? He enjoyed it. At least he says he did. You were quick."

Quick? She'd been gone for ages. Addie glanced at her watch: 12:30. That had to be wrong, but at least the watch was working again.

"Margie told me about your mission of mercy." Dad tousled her hair. "That was good of you, Addie."

Whaley came around the side of the building, carrying a dustpan and wheeling the garbage can behind him. He gave Addie a glum wave. "How's Mrs. T.'s friend?"

"Fine," Addie said, and frowned. "Better than fine."

Whaley looked at her curiously and began sweeping up the broken glass. The larger pieces had already been cleared away, and all that remained was this shimmering pile of broken shards.

"Owns a theater, doesn't she?" Dad asked. "I can imagine what the quake did to it." He shook his head. "We'll have to get that glass in the door safely removed. Until then, go in the back way, or do like so." He went over to the empty window frame, pulled some work gloves out of his big jacket pockets, and put them on. Then he braced himself against the sill, jumped up, and climbed into the bookstore.

Addie made as if to climb in after him.

"Don't touch the frame! Here." Dad stripped off the gloves, leaned out the window, and grabbed her hand. She braced a foot against the sill and let him pull her up and over. After a moment of scrambling, she found herself standing on the cushion of the window seat, which was white with plaster dust. Dad was already heading to the back of the store.

She stepped down. The front of the store looked even worse than the rear had. It had always been so inviting here, with the wool rug on the floor, the bright Ethiopian posters Almaz's family had given them, the tinted lamps, and the brass Victrola up on the shelf. Now the shelves were broken, and hundreds of papers and books were scattered all over. The imitation Tiffany lamp was upended, a pane of its ruby-colored shade cracked. The Victrola was nowhere to be seen.

She heard the crash of glass being dumped into the can outside. A few moments later, Whaley clambered into the store as well. Addie turned to him, indicating the chaos with a sweep of her hand. "It doesn't seem fair! Nothing was broken in the Powells' neighborhood. Mrs. Powell's son didn't even believe we'd had an earthquake."

Whaley snorted. "Theater people are so full of crap. He was just messing with you."

"No, they're not!" Addie hesitated. "And I don't think he was messing." She crouched down and began picking up books, testing their bindings. Even though she had denied it, maybe Whaley was right. Maybe Reg had been joking. But how could he have been? There'd been genuine concern in his eyes when he insisted there hadn't been any earthquake.

Maybe something *was* wrong with her. Considering that perfectly solid things were disappearing and reappearing ... The horrible moment when she found the angel gone flashed into her head, and a rush of dizziness overtook her.

She stuffed the memory away quickly into some hidden compartment in her mind.

"Hey!" Whaley tapped her shoulder. "Want to help out here?"

Addie shook herself and put her hands under a toppled bookcase. She raised it, and the rounded edge of a brass trumpet amplifier gleamed beneath the mess of books that had fallen from the shelves.

"Dad! I found your Victrola!" she called, righting the bookcase and bending down again to carefully uncover his treasured record player. "I think it's okay."

"It'll be a miracle if it is." Dad emerged from the chaos of fallen shelves, an anxious look on his face. His dark hair and beard were dusted in white plaster. "If you find the box of seventy-eights, would you check inside? I don't think I can stand to look."

Addie's heart went out to him, thinking of all the years he had spent searching for the records at antique stores and estate sales, cleaning them, cataloging them, and playing them on the Victrola at backyard parties in the summer. . . .

"They're all shellac, aren't they, Mike?" Whaley shoved a box he'd filled with books against the wall. "Man, I couldn't look either if I were you. Some of them must be one of a kind." He straightened up, and a look of panic washed over his face. "Oh, my God. Nothing better have crashed down onto my guitar. I left it out of the case."

Addie jumped to her feet. "I wonder if I put away the theater-makeup kit."

Dad looked from one of them to the other. Then he lifted his hand, curving his thumb and pointer finger together, like a statue of the Buddha. He lifted his head in a meditative pose. "Life is suffering," he declaimed. "Attachment to things causes suffering. To end suffering, detach yourself from antique record players and guitars."

"Speak for yourself, Buddha." And Whaley went running to the back of the shop. They heard him pounding up the stairs to his room.

"Release yourself from twenty-jar makeup kits and wardrobes full of vintage gowns and boots. . . ."

"Shut up, Dad." Addie giggled.

He closed his eyes and rubbed his forehead. "Ah, my head is clear. I feel free. . . ." He opened his eyes, winked at Addie. "Cheer up. We're out of business for a little while, that's all."

A moment later, Whaley thumped back down into the store. "I did put it in the case."

"That's good," Dad said. "Listen. I'll clear this stuff away. You guys go get some of that plywood out of the shed and hammer it across the window frames. We need something to keep the vultures out until we can get a glazier to fix us up. Oh, and Addie?"

"Yes?"

"Take off that marvelous costume of yours. It's your brawn I need, daughter dear, not your beauty."

"Oh, right." Addie glanced down at the antique dress. "I'll go change."

She began to pick her way through the ruins of the store, heading for the back stairs, but came to a sudden halt. The drama shelf had toppled over. Crouching down, she began picking up the books, carefully closing them, brushing off plaster dust. Her eyes darted anxiously until she found *A History of the Theater* splayed open on the floor. Thank goodness it wasn't squashed or ripped! Some pages were bent back, but the binding hadn't broken. She hugged it to herself. Where could she put it to keep it safe? She could take it to her room, but that would be plain stealing. Her eyes traveled across the wall to the hidden closet, exposed now. Perfect. She opened the door, placed the book on the little seat that protruded from the wall, and shut the door again. She'd put the book back once things settled down.

As she stepped into the back hall, she ran into Whaley coming out of the storage closet with his hammer and a jar of nails. His bleak expression startled her.

"Whaley? Something wrong?"

But he just ignored her and went out the door into the backyard.

Concerned, Addie followed him out, then stopped short.

Mrs. Turner was reclining on their flowered garden chair, her injured foot propped up on a stool. Zack was sitting on the old picnic table, reading one of his books to her.

"Addie!" Zack leaped up and charged toward her as if he'd been fired from a cannon, hair sticking up and smudges of dirt across his cheeks. "It was so cool! The teacher's helper hid in the broom cupboard. There were six of us under my table, and the table legs jumped like a frog, and one of the boys was hanging on to this girl's braids, and as soon as it stopped, she socked him—pow!"

"You're spitting on me!" Addie spluttered, holding him at arm's length, grinning.

"It was a six point eight, the radio said, but way deep down, not on the surface." It figured that Zack would know this, Addie thought. He loved earthquakes, volcanoes—any kind of natural disaster. He always wanted to go to Mount Saint Helens when they went hiking so he could look at the lava dome. "That's why there wasn't too much damage."

"This isn't much damage?"

"*And* we get to have a barbecue," Zack rushed on. "A barbecue in April! There's still no electricity, so Mrs. Turner said I could get those iron tong things, if it's okay with Dad, and she'll make toasted cheese over the fire pit."

Mrs. Turner was watching Addie with a sheepish look on her face. "It sounds as if I sent you on a fool's errand. I'm sorry, sweetie."

Gently, Addie pushed Zack away. "Go tell Dad about the barbecue." Zack ran into the house. She turned to Mrs. Turner. "What do you mean, a fool's errand?"

"I mean there was no need to send you after all. Becky Powell rang a little while ago to make sure I didn't come hitching across the city to check on her, since she was fine."

"The phones are working?"

"My cell is, now. Still no landlines."

"Well, she said she would call you." Addie leaned against the picnic table. "There's something funny there," she said slowly.

"Where?" Mrs. Turner looked around, as if expecting to see a rat by the chicken coops.

"At the Powells'." Addie hiked herself up onto the table and sat where Zack had been. The wood was slightly damp, and for the first time since she got home, she felt the chill in the air. "For one thing, there's nothing wrong with your friend's eyes, is there?"

"Of course there is! Didn't you notice? She's recovering from cancer."

"Cancer?" An image of a thin, withered-looking woman in a hospital bed flashed through Addie's mind. Her mom. So long ago. Addie could remember very little of her during that last illness, when she was in the hospital, but this image had always haunted her. She held it up to her image of Mrs. Powell from earlier in the day, and shook her head. "How could that be? She has so much energy."

Back by the alley, the shed door slammed loudly. She looked over at Whaley, struggling with a sheet of plywood. "Addie! You helping or what?"

"In a minute!"

Whaley heaved the wood up onto his back and stalked past her.

Mrs. T. eyed Addie quizzically. "Becky had brain surgery about six months ago. It nearly destroyed the vision in her right eye. She can see fine out of the other, but it affected her spatial sense—for example, she can't always judge distance. The other eye will eventually compensate, the doctor says. But it's good to hear that she was energetic."

The beautiful polished-agate color of Reg's mother's eyes rose in Addie's mind, and the whisper of unease she'd felt at the Powells' stirred again, stronger this time. It fit with that feeling she'd had from the moment she met Reg, that something was really off; things just weren't adding up.

She thrust the thought away. Looking around at the familiar yards, the houses, the big Douglas fir, the weathered picnic table, and the piled-up milk crates that Dad used and reused for transporting books, she found it all oddly comforting. She turned back to her neighbor. "I really liked her—Mrs. Powell. She invited me to the Jewel on Tuesday after school."

"Tuesday? *I'm* going there on Tuesday, to help her with the inspector."

"What inspector?"

"Building code. Becky wants to renovate the place." Mrs. T. shook her head. "It'll be a lot more than she was bargaining for now, with this earthquake."

Maybe Mrs. Powell had been lucky and her theater had suffered as little damage as her house, Addie thought. Though when she looked around at the roof shingles in the yard and Mrs. Turner's damaged chicken coop, it seemed unlikely. "What time are you going to be there?"

"Around two. Becky gave me a key. If you'd like, I could leave it in the mailbox for you—it's by the loading dock entrance in the alley around back—so you can just let yourself in when you get there." She paused, examining Addie. "She must have seen you were interested in theater. Did she think that old dress was a costume? Now that I look at it on you, I'm beginning to wonder."

Addie leaped off the picnic table. "Oh, gosh, I'm sorry! It's a mess. I'll get it dry-cleaned, I promise!"

"Stop apologizing! You ran halfway across the city just because I was worried about Becky. Besides, the dress isn't mine as far as I'm concerned. It's yours. I was thinking I'd offer most of the contents of the crates to Becky for the Jewel, since it seems they came from there in the first place. But of course you can keep anything you like."

"Really?" Delight flashed through her. This wonderful dress was hers! And maybe even—she reached into her pocket, pulled out the mirror, and handed it to Mrs. Turner. "I forgot I had this. Do you mind if I keep it, too?"

Mrs. Turner's eyes widened. "Where did this come from?"

"It was wrapped in the shawl that went with the dress. The shawl must still be up in my room. I forgot about it when I found the mirror."

"I don't blame you. This is gorgeous!" She held the silver closer to her face and squinted. "Do you see this here?" She pointed the manicured nail of her pinkie finger at some tiny letters along the edge of the metal. "The silversmith's mark. *T-a-g* . . . something."

Addie went and leaned over the edge of the lounge chair. "There's a date, too . . . 19—oh, I can't tell what the other numbers are. We need a magnifying glass." She looked up. "That's a great idea, giving the costumes to the theater. You'll need help getting them there, won't you?"

"I'm hoping your dad will offer to loan me the van." She looked down at her bandaged ankle ruefully. "And help me pack it too."

"Well, when I get to the theater, I'll help carry the crates inside. Actually, I'll get Whaley to help, too. How does that sound?"

"Perfect."

The sound of banging on the front door carried into the backyard, and Addie heard Whaley yell, "Don't come that way! Can't you see the broken glass? Climb through the window."

Addie straightened abruptly and bounded away. "Thanks, Mrs. T.!" she shouted over her shoulder and rushed around the side of the house, hoping she would find Reg there.

But it was Almaz who was standing on the sidewalk examining the empty window frames. She had a bandage on her hand, and her white T-shirt was stained with mustard. Addie guessed the jars in the store had shattered in the quake, and her friend had been helping clean up.

"Oh. Hey."

"Wow, I feel welcome already," Almaz said sarcastically. She slumped into a pantomime of disappointment. "Hey, back atcha."

Despite her teasing, there was a strained, upset look on her face. Addie caught up her nonbandaged hand and squeezed it. "Sorry. I just thought it might be someone else."

A faint smile flickered across her friend's face. "And I would be fascinated to hear who that might be, except right now I need to borrow Whaley. The banister on our stairs needs to be fixed before it falls down and kills someone."

As she spoke, Whaley emerged from the back of the store with more wood. "I'll come when we've finished boarding up here." He glared at Addie. "Which might take hours if I don't get some help. How 'bout you get out of that flouncy dress and lend a hand? Unless you're planning on declaiming Ophelia's death speech while we hammer— which, by the way, if you don't start helping, really will be a death speech."

"Ophelia doesn't have a death speech. She just floats and then sinks."

"Can you come soon, Whaley?" Almaz asked. "The food's going to spoil unless the electricity comes back, and we're so busy clearing up that I don't see how we're going to fix the banister before dark." To Addie's dismay, the unflappable Almaz looked close to tears.

"Sure I will," Whaley promised. "Go get changed, Addie!" He disappeared again into the backyard.

"We'll get right over as soon as we're done here," Addie told her.

Almaz gave her a quick hug and made an effort to look more cheerful. "Now you have to tell me. Who were you expecting?"

"A guy I met," Addie said, embarrassed. "Just some crazy guy."

Almaz looked Addie up and down. "Is that why you're so dressed up? You look *good*." She caught Addie's expression and laughed. "Don't worry. He'll come." With a wave, she turned around and headed back toward her house.

They worked all the rest of the day, helping at Almaz's and Mrs. Turner's places, clearing up debris, dragging stuff that was irretrievably broken out to the curb, and boarding the store up tight. And even though the lights and electricity came back on by evening, they still had the barbecue in the backyard, much to Zack's delight.

But Almaz was wrong. Reg never showed up.

AN ERRAND

On Tuesday, all the students were allowed back into the Lincoln building; they'd had a day off while the teachers put their classrooms back together. The whole school had a shaken, confused look, and boarded-up windows made it dark and gloomy. Addie couldn't even stare out of the math room to mentally flee the boredom of Algebra II. Almaz pointed out that Addie's math scores might actually improve because of this, but she wasn't convinced. Mr. Brent's droning didn't sink in any more than it usually did. And drama class was awful.

When she walked in, Keira was leaning back, and Taylor, a co-diva, was French-braiding her hair. Inevitably, a whole group of people were caught up in the hair drama. As Addie walked by, Keira murmured something that caused a ripple of giggles to run through the group. Pretending not to notice, Addie sat down on the opposite side of the classroom with Jake and Sun, and Brian, who had a wispy mustache and told geeky stories of weekends spent with the Society for Creative Anachronism.

"She's just jealous," Sun whispered. "I thought you were good."

Addie raised her eyebrows and shrugged.

When Mr. Crowley finally showed up, his shirt was untucked and he looked like he hadn't slept in days. Between the earthquake and Mrs. Crowley's blessed event, the parts for the *Short Takes* had never been posted on the website. So he just read out the names and promised to post a formal list when he had a chance.

Addie was paired up with Sun for makeup and costume design. It was no surprise. And she liked Sun a lot. But it still felt like she'd swallowed a rock when she heard that Taylor had gotten the part of the troll princess.

She'd seen Taylor's audition and it was blah. Just blah. Had Mr. Crowley even watched it? She glanced at Tom and saw him flash a thumbs-up at Taylor. Bile rose in Addie's throat. She wished Whaley were here and she could whisper something caustic in his ear like, "Who the heck do you have to bribe to get a part around here?" She almost laughed, imagining the changes he'd probably make to that question.

It doesn't matter, she told herself. After all, she was going to the rehearsal at the Jewel right after school. And that was going to be amazing. She just knew it.

When the final bell rang, she threw her books into her

backpack, squeezed through the crush of students, and ran out the door.

She scanned the park across the street to see if Whaley was there. Little kids on the playground leaped from the jungle gym to the climbing frame. Above their heads, the wind tore blossoms from the cherry trees and scattered them into the street in great sweeps of pink, like ripped crepe paper. It always made her a little sad, the first storms of spring and the way the wind plundered the flowers off the fruit trees.

No. She wouldn't think sad thoughts. And she wouldn't think about drama class. Only about the Jewel. Anticipation bubbled through her, and she almost danced with impatience. She still felt a little disturbed about that earthquake business with Reg, but the apprehension it caused her had faded. . . . Where was Whaley, anyway?

A finger poked her shoulder. She turned and grinned at Almaz, who had one ear bud in her ear and one hanging loose at her neck.

"Hey! Didn't see you at lunch." Almaz took in the green headband holding back Addie's hair and the 1920s vintage dress she was wearing. "Is this the big day? That why you're so decked out?"

Addie gathered her cropped wool jacket tighter over her dress. "Is it too much?"

"Not to those who know and love you. We're used to your wacky wardrobe."

"I'm serious, Almaz."

Almaz put her head to one side. "What? Were you supposed to bring your own costume? What if they're doing a modern play? Or Shakespeare or something?"

"They're *not* going to put me in a play. It's just—I guess I just want to make an impression."

"You always make an impression." Almaz started to bop her head to the music. "Hey, get this."

She put the other earbud in Addie's ear and Addie listened, her head bent close to Almaz's. She heard a distant sound, like a jet engine revving up or a bomb exploding. Then a voice from an old crackling recording began to speak. It was a speech—a famous speech. Someone explaining— or maybe excusing—something terrible. She thought she knew who it was, but the name eluded her. Chanting layered in beneath it, and as the speech finished, the explosion got louder, and dub bass and rapid-fire drums overwhelmed it all.

Addie pulled the earbud from her ear, fixing a quizzical look on her friend. "That speech . . . 'Now I am become Death, the destroyer of worlds.' . . . Who is that?"

"It's Robert Oppenheimer. The atom bomb guy. It's what he said when they first tested the bomb out in the desert." Almaz paused. "Oh, come on, why are you looking so worried? The band is the important thing. It's Tackhead. Whaley loves them. He loaded the song for me."

Addie shook her head. "It's creeping me out. All this stuff about war all the time. I wish Whaley would get over it."

"Don't be silly. You know he loves that kind of thing." Almaz pointed down the block to where Whaley was just rounding the corner, wearing a patched green sweatshirt and carrying his guitar. "There he is now. Gotta run. Call me later?" She squeezed Addie's hand. "Let me know how it goes."

She ran down the steps, slapping Whaley's hand as she passed him, and then, when he wasn't looking, she turned and gave him another glance. *Uh-huh*, Addie thought, and smiled to herself.

"Ready?" Whaley gave the school a glowering look. The streaks of purplish blue under his eye still stood out clearly. "I don't want to hang out here."

She hurried down to him. "Thanks for agreeing to help."

"No problem. I didn't think you and Mrs. T. could manage those crates alone. But I got to get to Rico's by five." He lifted up his guitar case, the one with the initials *W.P.P.* engraved on it under a sticker that said *This Machine Kills Fascists.* "Band practice. And I got some errands to do on Broadway."

Kirk brushed by, and Whaley flashed him a sardonic peace sign. Addie rolled her eyes. "Why is he still in school when you're not?"

"Come on," Whaley said. "Let's get out of here. Want to walk?"

She looked up at the low, mottled clouds overhead. "Okay. But we hop a bus if it starts to pour. I don't want to ruin this dress."

"Some Seattle girl you are. What's a little rain?" Whaley examined her with a faint, amused smile. "Why are you wearing that, anyway?"

"I just thought I should look nice. There's a rehearsal at the Jewel, and Mrs. Powell said maybe she could find work for me."

The smile disappeared. "Terrific. At least *someone* will be working."

"What do you mean?" She looked at him more closely, loping along, kind of hunched over and closed in. Despite what Almaz said, Addie thought he had been a little down the past couple days. She knew he was anxious because he didn't have any shifts to cover and he was supposed to be working. But he had to know that was out of his hands. Gently, she said, "It's only been two days since the earthquake. The store will reopen soon. You've got a lot of it cleaned up already."

He wasn't mollified. "It won't be that soon. There still aren't any windows. The walls need repair, and meanwhile, I'm not earning my keep. I feel like a leech."

"Can't you help fix the walls? You're good at that kind of thing. And no one thinks you're a leech!" She touched his shoulder. "Come on, Whaley. You're part of the family, all right?"

Whaley didn't respond. It was a familiar feeling, this ache she had in her heart for him. Like she would make his world better for him if he'd let her, but he never wanted her to.

Addie walked along beside him in silence, all the way down Fortieth and back up across University Bridge. The wind was cold here, whipping up whitecaps on the ship canal. *It's really too long a walk,* she thought. *We should jump on a bus.*

But already they were off the bridge, walking fast, climbing up Capitol Hill. She looked around and thought there was as much damage here as anywhere else in the city. Roof tiles littered people's yards. There were boarded-up windows in the florist's shop and the French bakery. Then again, this street wasn't as high up as Fifteenth Avenue was, and the Powells' house was much closer to Fifteenth, so perhaps it did make sense that there would be less damage up there. Still, a faint unrest crept into her mind once more.

They passed the big private school that was built like an Italian Renaissance villa, all brown stucco and tile roofs. The grass in the school's playing field glowed in the silver pre-storm glare. One of those rare spring thunderstorms was brewing. The wind spat Addie's hair into her eyes, and the electricity in the air made her skin crawl. Out of nowhere, the image of the angel's stone wings rising over the yew hedge troubled her memory. "Whaley?"

He turned sharply, as if she'd startled him back from some faraway place, and suddenly she wished she hadn't gotten his attention.

"What?"

The cold of the approaching downpour had gotten into her bones. It made her shiver. "You know the war memorial in Volunteer Park? The statue of the angel?"

He nodded.

"Last Sunday, when I was coming back from the Powells', it wasn't there anymore."

Whaley raised his eyebrows.

"I mean, I saw it when I went to their house. But when I came back, it was gone. The fountain was there, the marble bench, and the hedge. But no angel."

"So? Maybe a tree was in your way."

"Maybe," she said doubtfully. Now she felt foolish.

But Whaley wasn't making fun of her. "This happened on the way back from their house?" he asked. "After you met that guy who said there hadn't been an earthquake?"

"Yes," Addie said cautiously. Somehow she knew the two things were linked, but her mind shied away from examining it too closely.

Whaley frowned. "It's just strange, isn't it? He says something that happened didn't. You say something that's normally there wasn't."

They were passing St. Mark's Cathedral. The clouds overhead were blue-black. The whole thing with the angel was too spooky. Why had she mentioned it? She didn't want him to treat it as if it had really happened. What she wanted, she realized, was for him to convince her it *hadn't*. "It doesn't matter anyhow," she said hurriedly. "When I looked again, there it was."

"Maybe it was low blood sugar? From running all over town with nothing to eat?"

Yes! That could be it. But the bites of the lemon cake she'd had at the Powells' were still vivid in her memory.

Whaley swerved around a barrier that a road crew had put up on the sidewalk. He and Addie crossed the street. "You mean that memorial with the list of names on it, right? Guys who died in—what was it? World War Two?"

"One," Addie said. The park was only four blocks up along the next cross street. "Can I show you? You're not in a hurry, are you?"

"I thought you were."

"It'll just take a minute," she said, and they headed up the steep winding road that intersected Tenth, leading to the south entrance of the park. Near where the Powells lived.

She led him into the park and through the trees to the yew hedge and they came to a halt in front of the monument. Then Addie walked right up to the statue and touched the outstretched stone wing. The clouds had thrown a shadow over the angel's face. Her expression was unreadable.

She sat down on the bench and scanned the names on the statue's base. *Allen, Anderson, Bellows* . . . after every name was the same year: 1918. And next to the year, the names of battles: *Belleau Wood, Meuse-Argonne,* or, more infrequently, *St. Mihiel Salient.*

"Did you see the paper today?" Whaley said suddenly.

"No."

"Well, I've had lots of time on my hands," he said bitterly. "Just sitting around . . ."

"What about the paper?" Addie asked quickly.

"They published the names of soldiers who've died since the war started. Where they came from. How old they were." He pointed at the memorial. "Sort of like this."

"Oh, wait, I did see that." Addie looked up at Whaley in his patched sweatshirt, huddled against a cold gust of wind. She'd read that article while she was having breakfast. It had mentioned a few soldiers from Fort Lewis, the big army camp near the city. One guy had graduated from

Franklin two years ago. Another had been a lifeguard at Matthews Beach, where she and Almaz swam in the summer. Now he was dead.

She frowned. Mrs. Powell's son Reg was thinking about joining up, wasn't he?

"Doesn't it make you mad?" she burst out. "All those soldiers killed already? When there's no good reason."

Whaley looked at her as if she were insane. "Yeah, I'm mad. But I'm mad at the people who *killed* them. It sounds to me like you and Mrs. T. are mad at *our* folks for standing up and fighting back."

Addie opened her mouth to make a retort, but closed it again. She didn't want to get him angry. Besides, being here, in this quiet place with all the names of the dead, made arguing seem pointless. Whaley wasn't going to change her gut feelings about war, and she would never know enough about politics and strategy and boots on the ground and all that stuff that Whaley loved to convince him of anything. Instead, she just felt sad.

"There are so many names on this memorial," she said. "And now the names are just starting to come in from this new war. How spooky is that?"

Whaley just turned and walked back toward the park entrance. After a moment, Addie followed him.

In silence, they made their way back down to Tenth and headed to where the street merged into Broadway, and suddenly shops and restaurants and bars replaced the quiet houses.

"Spare some change?" A homeless girl sitting in a

doorway held out a cup. It was odd to see her here, Addie thought. Most homeless kids gravitated to the U. District. Maybe she was new in town. Her eyes were muddy, strung out. From Whaley she knew how easy it was to buy drugs just about anywhere in Seattle. He'd been mixed up in all of that before they became friends.

The girl's fingernails were black, and she was wearing two jackets, one on top of the other. Whaley rummaged in his pocket and gave her a five-dollar bill. The girl didn't thank him, just put her head on her knees and crooned a sad, wordless melody to herself.

Addie linked her arm through his. "You're so generous, Whaley."

"It all comes around. Who knows? I could end up like that again."

"No you couldn't!" Her vehemence surprised even her. "We're not going to toss you out on the street. And for the last time, it's not your fault there was an earthquake." She gave him a playful shove. "Or is it? I mean, did you *engineer* a quake just so you could spend the week jamming with Enrique instead of working in the bookstore?" He didn't laugh. "Oh, come on, Whaley. We *want* you to stay with us."

For a moment, his expression was naked and uncertain. Then he squeezed her arm. "Man," he said, "you are one of the five things that save me every day, Addie McNeal."

Addie glowed. "Am I? What are the other four?"

"Jimi Hendrix, Leadbelly, Muddy Waters, your dad, and my guitar."

"That's five."

He looked over his shoulder to where a bus had just rounded the corner. "Yeah? And guess what. There's the nine. Want to take it the rest of the way?"

"Sure." But the tone of his voice made warning bells go off inside her. There was something strange in it. Something *grim*. She wanted to find out what it was, but the first drops of rain were pelting their faces and they had to run to the Metro stop.

Addie jumped on the bus and began rooting through her purse. She needed to throw away some of the junk she lugged around! Finally she found a bill and some quarters, slipped them into the change machine, and turned to make a joke about it to Whaley.

But he was gone.

The doors closed and the bus swung away from the curb.

Where the heck was he? Addie grabbed a seat and looked out, only to see him striding away down the sidewalk. She pulled open the top window and yelled, "Hey! Where are you going?"

He waved. "I'll catch the next bus. Break an arm."

"Leg! And I'm not auditioning, anyway! Where are you *going?*"

But he either didn't hear or was pretending not to. "Whaley!"

The other passengers stared at her—middle school kids with instrument cases, old ladies with grocery bags, homeless guys with big beards and all their belongings in sacks.

Fuming, Addie slid back into her seat.

Half a block farther, the bus wheezed to a stop, stuck behind a SUV trying to edge its way into a tiny parking space. Addie turned again, craning her neck to see where Whaley had gone.

She spotted him standing in front of an ugly stone building near the community college. His hand was reaching for the doorknob, but then he dropped it and just stood there, hesitating.

Posters were plastered on the windows: action figures, guys in camouflage running with guns at the ready. A video store?

Then she made out the sign over the door: ARMY RECRUITMENT CENTER.

"Hey!" She gathered her purse and her backpack and pushed her way to the front of the bus. "Can you let me off?" she asked the driver. "You're stuck anyway."

But the SUV had angled into the last inch of the parking space, and the bus driver leaned on his horn. "That's it, buddy! Get outta my way!" He jolted past with less than an inch to spare. "Hate those goddamn monstermobiles."

"Good thing we're protecting the oil fields for people like him," a guy with a laptop observed.

"That's not why we're fighting," a woman snapped. She was carrying a toy terrier in a front pack. "I'm sick of hearing people like you—"

"Oh, shut the hell up," someone else said, and it was on.

"Can't you let me off? *Please?*" Addie repeated.

But the bus was already whizzing down Broadway. "No unposted stops," the driver said, accelerating so fast Addie pitched forward and nearly fell. "It's not safe."

She grabbed one of the poles and held on for dear life. "Where's the next stop?"

"Third and Broadway." They eased to a halt. "Sit down, miss. No passengers in front of the yellow line."

Addie threw herself into the closest seat and glared at him, imagining her eyes emitting cartoonish thunderbolts that would ignite the back of his head. Though even if he had let her off, it wouldn't have done any good. She knew Whaley. Rushing in after him, shouting, *No, don't do it!* wouldn't stop him.

Maybe he's just checking it out, she told herself.

"Third and Broadway," the driver announced.

Light burst in the sky as she got off the bus. Nervously, she jerked her head up, remembering the green bomb flashes on TV. The storm clouds had parted for a moment, and a sunbeam had glinted off the black edge of the Columbia Tower; that was all. In the clearing, she saw a thin vapor trail slice across the dome of the sky.

And then the light was gone, swallowed up in black thunderheads rumbling in from Puget Sound.

She hesitated. Should she go to the Jewel? Or should she jump on the next bus back to Capitol Hill, find Whaley, and bodily pull him out of the recruitment center?

She actually felt as if she might throw up. On one hand, what if Whaley really did sign up and went over to fight and for the rest of her life she regretted not stopping him? On the other hand, what if, because of Whaley, she insulted Mrs. Powell by not showing up at the Jewel? She couldn't mess up her chance to work in a real, professional theater, could she?

She closed her eyes, and took a deep breath.

No. She *couldn't* miss this chance.

She pulled her jacket tighter around her and headed to the Jewel.

THE JEWEL

Addie stared up at the theater's dirty gray façade in utter disappointment.

Rain was spattering the pavement as she stepped back to take it all in. The ticket booth windows were shrouded in dust. Boards blocked up the doorways. Lights were smashed, and the terra-cotta façade was filthy. But this wasn't just earthquake damage. There must have been decades of dirt embedded in the walls and coating the windows.

Maybe, Addie thought hopefully, maybe she had come to the wrong place?

But above the central doorway, in a big decorative arch, she spied a carving of a faceted diamond, and underneath, blackened by pollution, was the inscription THE JEWEL— EST. 1910.

It was a mess. Yet, Mrs. Powell had spoken of it with such pride, as if it were busy and successful. And maybe it was. After all, Mrs. T. had said they were renovating. Despite this, Addie felt that familiar disquiet.

It doesn't make any difference. No matter what the outside of the theater looked like, inside, the Powells were expecting her. Rehearsals were under way. That was the important thing.

The spark of excitement that had burned inside her all day rekindled. She'd better find that key and let herself in.

Leaving behind the dilapidated façade, she headed around the side of the building and followed the sidewalk toward the back of the theater. There was a loading dock with a ramp and a garage-size steel door. But she didn't see any regular door through which she could enter. Hadn't Mrs. T. said the loading dock entrance was in the back?

She continued on and turned right into the narrow alley behind the theater. The reek of garbage and decay nearly made her gag. A few motorcycles were parked here, but she didn't see Dad's book van. Maybe it was just too cramped. She saw a second loading dock halfway down the alley, and as she approached it, noticed a man with a tobacco-stained beard rummaging through a dumpster right next to it.

Hastily, she bounded up the steps of the loading dock, keeping her eye on the man, who didn't seem to notice her, and slipped her hand into the rusty mailbox. The key was there, as Mrs. Turner had promised. Addie jangled it in the keyhole, turned the knob, and heaved open the steel door.

"Mrs. Powell?" Propping the door open with one foot, she peered into the darkness. A dim passage stretched out before her.

"Mrs. T.?" Addie glanced over her shoulder. The man was pulling a pizza box out of the dumpster now, muttering to himself as newspapers and Styrofoam containers cascaded in its wake.

"Is anyone there?" she called more loudly.

The only answer was the wind rattling the papers as they spun down the alley behind her.

Her heart sank. Should she just leave?

But the thought of going home with nothing to show for the trip was way too depressing. And Mrs. T. had left the key, so she must be here somewhere. And Reg *had* said Tuesday, and here it was, Tuesday. They must be in the auditorium.

All right, then. Addie stepped inside and eased the steel door shut behind her.

Darkness enveloped her. A subterranean chill raised goose flesh on her arms. The place smelled ancient, like a crypt. She felt along the wall, found a light switch and flicked it, but nothing happened. Somewhere ahead of her in the darkness, a faint greenish light glowed. As her eyes adjusted, she could make out doorways with stippled-glass panes, recessed closets, crumbly walls. Carefully, she made her way down the gloomy corridor toward the light.

The corridor led to another hallway, perpendicular to it. The light was seeping out from under a closed door at one end. As she approached, something screeched behind it and Addie nearly jumped out of her skin.

"Mrs. Turner?" She gulped.

Oh, no, she thought. *This is the part of the horror film where the heroine is expecting to find her friend in the creepy old house, but the guy who's just escaped from the asylum jumps out instead. . . .*

She glanced over her shoulder. Shouldn't Whaley be getting here about now?

"Mrs. T.?" she called, louder.

"Addie?" a familiar husky voice called from within. "Is that you?"

"Yes! Yes, I'm here." Relieved, she flung the door open and found her neighbor leaning on one crutch trying to shove a threadbare pink love seat against the wall of a large, dusty office.

"Just making room," Mrs. Turner puffed.

"For what? Let me do that!" Addie grabbed the arm of the love seat and yanked it into the corner.

"Becky thought we could store the crates in here," Mrs. T. explained as she lowered herself into a wooden swivel chair behind an old rolltop desk.

"Oh, good. She's here after all. I was starting to wonder." Addie straightened up and brushed a cobweb off her jacket. Nervous excitement pumped through her once again. "Do you mind if I run out and tell her I made it?"

"Go on. The stairs to the stage are just down the hall. I think she's up there."

Addie left the room and dashed eagerly up the staircase, relieved that the lights were working in this part of the theater.

"Mrs. Powell! I'm here!" She burst out into the wings at the top of the stairs, her heart thumping. But instantly she stopped short. No one was here. Puzzled, she looked around.

The place was empty and silent. Lighting racks hung over-head in the gloom. The door leading backstage was open. She stepped through, but no one was there either. Old drops had been shoved against the cracked walls. Cans of dried-up paint had fallen off the shelves and been left on the floor. The air smelled like rotting wood.

Frowning, she turned around, catching a glimpse of the big loading-dock doors. Now she was beginning to feel a bit unnerved. It all felt so old and empty. And just as rundown inside as it was out front.

But there's supposed to be a rehearsal going on, she thought. Where were the actors? The crew?

Confused and disappointed, she went back into the wings and stepped through onto the stage. "Mrs. Powell?"

No. No one was here, either.

And yet . . .

As she gazed into the airy depths of the auditorium, she felt a lifting, an expansion—that feeling that she got when-ever she stepped into a theater, even if she was just in the audience, as if she were a bird about to take flight. A feeling of power, of potential, flooded through her.

Now *this* was a real theater.

But her elation was short-lived.

When she looked closer she saw that the stage floor was gashed and paint-spattered. Her gaze traveled to rows of seats in the orchestra that had been unscrewed and dragged out of place, and then up to the dress circle. There was a little bit of decorative plasterwork on the balconies, the box seats, the pillars supporting the roof, but she couldn't make out what most of it was, since what hadn't sheered off in the earthquake had cracked or crumbled. The proscenium rose above her, and as she stepped to the very edge of the stage, it was clear that something—sculptures or carvings—had been jimmied off the top of it. The ceiling was surprisingly low and tiles had fallen out, leaving black gaps. A huge burlap sack hung from the center of it, trailing great nets of cobwebs. There were even holes in the walls where light fixtures had been ripped out.

Addie sighed.

Still . . . you could tell the Jewel had been grand in its day.

She closed her eyes, and her imagination rolled crimson carpets along the aisles, applied shining paint to the walls, washed the grimy marble, and brightened the corners with huge vases of flowers. She could almost feel the warmth of the spots, could almost see women in sleek dresses and men in evening clothes shifting for a better view as the houselights dimmed.

She opened her eyes again. What had Mrs. Powell said they were rehearsing? Oh, yes. Well, she hadn't said it specifically because of that superstition. But there was only one play Addie knew of whose name must never be spoken for fear of catastrophe and bad luck.

Kicking imaginary robes away from her feet, she advanced to center stage holding an invisible piece of paper—Macbeth's letter to his wife, telling of his meeting with the witches and their incredible prediction of his rise to power.

Addie pretended to scan the letter, reading and projecting to the back rows.

> *They met me in the day of success; and I have learned by the perfect'st report, they have more in them than mortal knowledge. . . . Then came missives from the king, who all-hailed me—*

She lifted her head, as if taken with the wonder of it.

> *"Thane of Cawdor"; by which title, before, these Weird Sisters saluted me, and referred me to the coming on of time, with "Hail, king that shalt be!"*

She pressed the letter to her heart and turned suddenly, as if she'd been interrupted by Macbeth striding into the room. She ran toward him and threw her arms wide in greeting, letting her voice ring out across the auditorium.

> *Great Glamis, worthy Cawdor!*
> *Greater than both, by the all-hail hereafter!*
> *Thy letters have transported me beyond*
> *This ignorant present, and I feel now*
> *The future in the instant.*

A guitar chord rang out behind her. Addie leaped half a yard across the stage and spun around.

"Whaley! You frightened me!"

He was sitting on the floor with his guitar on his lap. "Sorry, Ads. Mrs. T. let me in." He bent his head and followed up the chord with a graceful but slightly eerie Elizabethan melody.

Addie listened, enchanted. In all the years they'd been friends, the music Whaley coaxed out of his guitar had never ceased to astound her. "What *was* that?" she asked softly as the notes died away.

"Don't know. Made it up. Lady Macbeth music. That was *Macbeth*, wasn't it?"

"Of course it's *Macbeth*," Addie said, and then, remembering Mrs. Powell's words, "or the Scottish play, if you're—"

A lone pair of hands clapping interrupted her.

"Bravo!" a soft voice called. "Lovely music! Nice job, Lady M."

Addie's face flamed as she peered into the gloom. Whaley put his guitar back in its case and came to stand next to her.

"Mrs. Powell?" she called. But it clearly wasn't her. Way in the back, near the exit, Addie made out a dim figure leaning on a cane.

"That's me."

The figure detached itself from the darkness, and Addie saw a small, wrenlike woman wearing a crisp white business blouse and a tweed jacket and skirt hobbling slowly toward them. Addie grabbed Whaley's arm.

"What's wrong?"

"That's *not* Mrs. Powell," she whispered.

"She says she is." Whaley shook her hand gently off his

sleeve, crossed the stage to the wing, walked down the steps, and made his way into the central aisle. The woman shook his hand and started chatting with him. Hesitantly, Addie followed.

When she reached them, the woman turned to her and held out her hand. "Becky Powell."

Addie shook her hand and introduced herself. But all the while her brain was reeling: Reg's mother was Becky Powell, wasn't she? She was tall and handsome and glowing with health. *This* Becky Powell was frail. She wore a silk scarf wrapped around her head with short wisps of hair peeking out from underneath. Her face was heart-shaped and drawn. Addie guessed her to be in her late forties or fifties. And though her left eye was perfectly normal, her right eye was dreamy and unfocused.

A smile brought a ghost of prettiness to her face. "Margie's told me about you, Addie. I'm glad she invited you to come by."

"But Addie said *you* invited her to a rehearsal," Whaley interjected.

"A rehearsal?" Surprise flashed across the woman's face. "Well, *I* certainly didn't. Who invited you to a rehearsal at the Jewel?"

Addie opened her mouth to respond, but something stopped her. "I think maybe I just misunderstood."

"Or someone was pulling your leg. There hasn't been a rehearsal here for years."

Addie's hands had gone ice cold. "For years?" she echoed faintly.

"Though, maybe Margie told you that I'm trying to change that? Now that I'm better . . ." She hesitated. "Now that I have the time, I'm going to try to restore the Jewel to its former glory. It was an important theater once."

The door to the lobby opened and a guy in a plaid shirt thumped down the aisle toward them. He had heavy jowls, like a bulldog.

"Hank! What news do you have for me?" Mrs. Powell called.

"Good news first or bad?"

"Bad. You know me."

He nodded at Whaley and Addie. "Beams and supports need replacing. And that plaster carving that survived the quake is in pretty bad shape. Original turn-of-the-century work, isn't it?"

Addie just listened to them. She felt stunned. This wasn't right. None of it was right.

Mrs. Powell nodded and sank into a seat. Dust poofed into the air around her. "I think there are more carvings. They've been plastered over or walled up or something." She pointed upward. "And that's definitely a false ceiling. The renters thought it would improve acoustics."

"Don't worry about that now. You've just got to get it up to code. First thing, the plumbing needs to be overhauled. No way the city will issue a permit in the state it's in now. Good thing the water's not hooked up—the pipes are definitely cracked."

So this theater isn't just a wreck; it's not even functioning, Addie thought unhappily. *And yet Mrs. Powell—the other*

Mrs. Powell—invited me here anyway! Why in the world did she do that?

"What's the good news?"

"Foundation didn't crack."

Mrs. Powell exhaled heavily. "Well, thank God for small favors."

"A sound foundation is not a *small* favor."

Mrs. Powell patted the seat in front of her. "Take a load off. Let's talk money." She glanced at Whaley and Addie. "This can't be interesting for you. Do you want to look around? I'll join you and Margie once we're done here."

"Sure," Addie said. Her stomach fluttered as she trudged ahead of Whaley up to the stage. She felt . . . confused. No. Worse than that. She realized that, for no good reason, she felt scared.

Whaley poked her shoulder. "Now, *that's* strange. How do you explain it?"

"I don't know!" She had to be rational. She couldn't let her imagination get carried away. "Do you think I got the name of the theater wrong or something?" Even to her, this sounded weak.

"You said you were going to the Jewel. Maybe the place is right, but those folks you met weren't really talking about rehearsing—"

"But that's exactly what they said: a rehearsal! I even know what play."

Whaley shrugged. "I don't know, Ads. It looks like they just stood you up."

Irritation washed over her. "Like you, you mean?"

"I didn't stand you up." Whaley gave her a prickly look and picked up his guitar.

"Sure you did. You ditched me and ran off to that army place. Couldn't you have told me where you were going?"

"Nah."

Addie glanced down into the auditorium to make sure Hank and Mrs. Powell weren't listening to their argument. To her relief, they seemed absorbed in their own discussion. "Why not? Don't you think it would have been good to talk about it first? To think about it?"

"I have thought about it!" Suddenly everything about him was tight and defensive, from the set of his shoulders to his grip on the handle of the case.

"You didn't promise them anything, did you? Didn't—whatchamacallit—enlist?"

Whaley narrowed his eyes, turned, and stomped off into the wing.

"Whaley! Wait!" She ran after him. Oh, she hadn't meant to start a fight.

Halfway down the stairs, he spun around. "It's my decision, Addie, not yours. And for God's sake, don't tell Mike."

"Fine," Addie spluttered.

As they reached the bottom of the steps, Mrs. Turner emerged from the office, awkwardly negotiating the door on her crutches. "Whaley! Just the person I was looking for."

"Sorry. I'm leaving." He pushed past her.

"But you said you'd help with the crates!" Addie called after him.

He stopped, but didn't turn around.

"If you could help, I'd appreciate it," Mrs. Turner said, pretending not to notice Whaley's mood. She handed a ring of keys to Addie. "Pull the van up to the loading dock, would you, sweetie? It's hard to drive with my wonky ankle."

Whaley came back and snatched the keys. "Addie failed her driving test. I'll do it." Mrs. Turner raised her eyebrows at Addie, but Addie just shook her head.

The rain was pelting by the time they brought the first crate into the theater. In a few minutes they were both soaked. They stumbled into the dark corridor, and again Addie was struck by its damp, earthy smell. She tried to catch Whaley's eye as they carried the heavy boxes between them, ready to make a goofy face, a silly remark, anything to break through the haze of ill will. But he wouldn't look at her.

As they lowered the last crate onto the floor of the office, Becky Powell and Mrs. Turner burst in. Mrs. T. was saying, "Now, just wait a minute before you call Dave—"

"No, I have to tell him. All that money! We'll never get a loan for that much!"

Addie looked from one to the other of the women in dismay. "What happened? Can't you renovate the Jewel after all?" Whaley leaned against the door frame, listening.

"I don't think I can." Mrs. Powell shook her head in disbelief. "An earthquake cracking the walls on top of everything! Who would believe it? It's like a sick joke. . . ."

Mrs. Turner maneuvered herself onto the love seat. "Can't you do some creative financing?"

"With what?" Mrs. Powell looked paler and more drawn than before. "My medical bills are eating up what's left of

Dave's money. I can get investors, but I'll have to sink a big chunk myself before they'll be willing to part with their capital."

The sadness in Mrs. Powell's voice went to Addie's heart. "Can I help somehow?" she asked. She knew it sounded silly, but she wanted to do something.

"That's kind. But I don't know how." Mrs. Powell slumped down on the arm of the love seat.

Addie glanced at Whaley. He usually had ideas. For the first time since they'd started bringing in the crates, he met her eyes. But he only shrugged.

"What about . . ." Addie paused, chasing a thought that had flickered through her mind. "Maybe this is nuts, but—remember, Mrs. Turner, you said your great-aunt worked at the Jewel a long time ago? Doesn't that mean this place is historic?"

"Of course it is."

"Well then, can't the city declare it a historic landmark?"

"I'm not sure how that would help," Mrs. Powell said.

But Mrs. T. gave Addie an encouraging look. "What are you thinking about?"

"Remember that church on Queen Anne? The one the congregation had to sell to a developer because they couldn't afford to fix it, but then they saved it? You took the pictures for the article, Mrs. T. The city helped fund the renovation because they proved it was a historic building."

"The city?" Mrs. Powell frowned. "I doubt it. They don't have any money. Maybe a foundation or something."

Mrs. T. snapped her fingers. "That's right! If the city decides it's a landmark, then it's eligible for foundation money. Addie's right. The deal is, you have to show you can restore the building to its original state. Do we know what that was?"

Mrs. Powell looked skeptical. "There's been a lot of remodeling. And a lot of damage. I'm not sure."

"I can find out for you!" Addie offered. "I could do a little research. I'm not bad at that."

"Well, there *are* some records somewhere, I'm sure. Some photos maybe. And"—she leaned over and touched the top of one of the crates—"was it only costumes you found in these?"

"No. There were papers, too. And books and boxes. We haven't really gone through them. But we could." Addie paused. "I could. If it would help."

Mrs. Powell gave Addie a faint smile. "You're starting to win me over."

Addie smiled back, thinking of the grand theater she'd imagined when she'd stepped onstage. "I could come back tomorrow after school." She looked at Whaley. "D'you want to meet me here?"

"Maybe. But there's some things I got to do. . . ."

"Pleeease, Whaley?" Addie slapped on a sappy, pleading expression.

Despite himself, he gave a small grunt of laughter. "Oh, all right."

A bit of animation had come back into Becky Powell's face. "If you're really serious, I can leave the key here for the two of you." She hesitated. "But you'd better let me show you around first. I don't want you to be under any illusions about the wreck I've got on my hands. Want to come along, Margie?"

"Nope. I'd better get moving." She patted Addie's shoulder. "Thanks, you two."

After Addie and Whaley said their goodbyes and Mrs. Turner had left, they followed Mrs. Powell back out into the hall. Though she still moved slowly, she seemed a bit more energetic now. "The dressing rooms were there," she told them, pointing at the first two rooms by the back door. "And the manager's apartment. The costume shop and the mechanical room were down at the other end of the hall." She thought for a moment. "But the auditorium and the lobby will be the most important for renovation. Come on. I'll take you out there."

She led them back up to the stage, pointing out the damage, speculating on how it might have looked in its heyday. "But it's just so hard to tell." As they walked, Whaley ran his hand along the walls, peering into corners, pressing on squeaky stairs. Addie smiled—he was such a fixer-upper.

Down in the orchestra pit, Mrs. Powell stopped suddenly. "Now, *that's* definitely original." She pointed. "Do you see that piano back there?"

Half hidden in the shadows behind a big trash can was a black upright. Its keys were yellow and cracked, and cobwebs drooped from it. A white marble bust rested on the top.

Whaley went over and blew the dust off the keys. "Do you mind?" he asked Mrs. Powell. She shook her head and he sat down and started to play, pulling faces at the sound of the out-of-tune keys. Addie came up behind him to get a closer look at the bust.

Then she froze.

It was, without question, Becky Powell.

Not the Becky Powell who stood leaning on her cane nearby, but the other Mrs. Powell. Reg's mother. The beautiful woman Addie had met the day of the earthquake, whom she had expected to see here today.

Her carved head was demurely bent to hide an irrepressible smile, and her hair was rolled into an elaborate up-do, the same way she'd had it arranged on Sunday. All her liveliness and grace shone through the curves of the marble. The only thing the sculptor couldn't do justice to were her eyes. They were cast down. When Addie bent to see their expression, they were as blank as the stone they were carved from.

Whaley was still hammering away on the keys, but Addie hardly heard.

She closed her eyes, as if doing so would shut out the fear that was washing over her like a cold tide.

"That's the stride piece Cam was showing me," Whaley said, lifting his fingers from the keys. Addie forced herself to open her eyes, to try to act normal. "Oh," she said faintly.

Whaley swung around on the piano bench to face her. "Hey, what's up?"

"Nothing. Just . . . that statue . . ."

"Emma Mae?" Becky Powell stretched out a hand to touch the marble. "Isn't she lovely?"

Addie said, "Who is Emma Mae?" Her voice was shaky.

"Emma Mae Powell. Her husband built the Jewel. But he died in a boating accident after the first season, so she took over and ran the theater. Really an amazing woman."

"But I thought you said the Jewel had been closed a long time."

Becky Powell leaned against the piano. "Of course. What's that got to do with it?"

"I'm confused. You just said that Emma Mae was the manager," Addie pressed.

"Owner and manager," Becky Powell said thoughtfully. "Now *she'd* be the ideal person to renovate this old wreck."

Addie hesitated, almost dreading to hear the answer to her next question. But she had to find out. "Why don't you just ask her, then?"

Mrs. Powell threw back her head and laughed. "What a terrific idea! I only wish I could, Addie. You don't know how much I'd love her help. There's just one problem."

"What?"

"Look at the base of the statue, the year it was carved."

Addie looked down where she pointed, to the numbers etched in the stone: 1919.

That couldn't be right. Her head swam. Her heart was racing. And yet somewhere deep inside, she realized she already knew.

"Too bad, eh?" said Mrs. Powell. "If we really wanted Emma Mae Powell to bring the Jewel back to life, I'm afraid we'd have to bring Emma Mae back to life as well."

A HISTORY OF THE THEATER

It was a blow straight to the chest.

Her head filled with echoing darkness, and for a moment she was the only passenger in an elevator that was plummeting down. 1919!

"That's impossible. . . ."

"Yes, unfortunately," Becky Powell agreed. She sat down on the piano bench next to Whaley. "Time has a way of depriving you of great companions. I would love to talk theater with Emma Mae Powell. But then, I'd love to have tea with Igor Stravinsky and catch a dance performance of Isadora Duncan's, too!"

Isadora Duncan. The floor seemed to pitch beneath Addie's feet.

"I'd—I'd better go," she choked out, and was happy that these were the words that actually came from her lips. Because the words in her brain were *I'm not crazy. I'm not.*

"Hey! What's up with you?"

But she hardly registered Whaley's question.

"Are you feeling all right?" Mrs. Powell asked. "You've gone pale."

"I'm fine." She mustered a faint smile. "I just . . . I think maybe I'd better get going."

"Wait a second. Don't you want to see the rest of the place?" Whaley asked.

"You can tell me about it later." She had to get out. Now. "I just remembered I—I told Almaz I'd get to her game. I'm late already."

Whaley looked at Mrs. Powell and shrugged.

"Nice to meet you, Mrs. Powell," she managed as she made her way to the stage. "I'll come back tomorrow." It was all she could do not to sprint into the wings cackling like a madwoman.

Once out in the rain again, she had to wrap her arms around herself to stop trembling. She *wouldn't* run. She would walk, slowly, in control, like any other sane person, to the bus stop. She would find an explanation for this.

That night, Addie huddled in her bed with the patchwork quilt pulled tight around her. She wanted to talk to Whaley, but he must have gone straight to Enrique's from the Jewel and he hadn't come home yet. A few times she picked up her phone to call Almaz, but each time she hadn't even pressed the button. It had been hard enough to talk about all this with Whaley. How could she bring it up with calm, logical Almaz?

Again and again she tried to close her mind to what had happened, to the marble bust of Emma Mae Powell gazing down serenely from the piano, where it had no doubt rested since it had been carved, nearly a hundred years ago. But she couldn't do it anymore. It was like the moment in *Peer Gynt* where he's wandering on the moor and he runs into the Boyg—the thing that is shapeless and inexplicable and can't be seen no matter how keen your eyesight. You can't go around it. You can't go through it. It won't budge; it demands you recognize its presence and resists any attempt to be reasoned away.

Well, if she couldn't bury the thought, at least she could take her mind off it. She picked up a collection of Shaw's plays and started reading an old, familiar one—*Saint Joan*. She loved Joan with her shining sword and her certainty and her good common sense. So reassuring.

But the image of the marble bust wouldn't leave her alone.

The idea that the people she had visited the day of the earthquake had been alive so long ago was impossible, she knew. But once she suspended her disbelief, it did make some of the pieces fit. For example, why Mrs. Powell and Reg hadn't met her at the Jewel. Why Reg hadn't believed her about the earthquake. The way they were dressed— strange how relatively normal it had seemed; she must have willfully ignored it. And what war was it, exactly, that Reg was so eager to go fight? If she had somehow stepped into the early twentieth century it must have been . . . the First World War? And—the red, white, and blue bunting—

America had just entered the war. So it must have been—oh, my God—1917.

She let *Saint Joan* slip from her hands. No. She didn't want it to make sense. Because if it did, then Emma Mae was dead. And then Reg was dead too, and Frida, and the doctor, and the people they were having over for dinner, and the guy who sold them the chicken they were going to roast, and . . . a shudder jerked down her spine: *And I just spent a whole afternoon visiting them.*

"No! No, no, no, no!" She jammed the pillow over her head, shaking from head to foot.

Then, with every ounce of control she could muster, she threw the pillow across the room and forced herself to sit up again. Furiously, she swept off her covers and jumped out of bed. She strode out of her room, went downstairs into the kitchen, and grabbed the keys to the bookstore from the table.

Whaley and Dad had been steadily cleaning, but the store was still a mess. Addie picked her way through the piles of books waiting to be reshelved and went to the drama section. The bookcase still hadn't been pushed back against the wall, so she had no trouble getting into the closet and picking up *A History of the Theater* from where she'd left it on the bench for safekeeping.

Back in her bedroom, she plopped down and opened the book. Her fingers were so cold she could hardly turn the pages.

But the reading lamp cast a circle of warm light onto her bed. The quilt was thick and comforting. She heard a little creak and saw the flick of a white tail through the crack of the door.

"Magnesium!" she called, making the tutting noises that the cat liked. Magnesium leaped onto the bed and turned three times before settling in a furry circle next to Addie's leg. He was always friendliest when you had a book on your lap. Especially if it was an old one with that musty used-book smell to it. Addie flipped through to the index, found the page number, and, with a quick intake of breath, turned to it.

The photograph of Isadora Duncan took up a third of the page. Addie examined the dark-haired dancer standing in an arbor wearing a diaphanous gown that hung in folds straight to her ankles. She looked like a Greek nymph or a goddess. A thin band circled her head, and laurel leaves were wreathed in her hair. Her hands were raised like a ballet dancer's. But the pose was more relaxed than a ballet pose, and she had a full, glowing smile on her face.

Slowly, Addie got up and lifted the silver mirror from her dresser. She brought it over to the bed and laid it down beside the photograph.

The dresses of the three dancers on its back matched the dress of the woman in the photograph, stitch for stitch.

Addie's skin crawled, but she just gathered the quilt more tightly around her shoulders.

So what? she told herself. *A Greek robe is a Greek robe is a Greek robe.* It didn't necessarily mean anything.

Except—except that Mrs. Powell had mentioned Isadora Duncan as if she was someone she knew. She shoved the mirror away and forced herself to look at the words on the page.

The heading read: *Isadora Duncan: 1878–1927.*

She exhaled slowly.

Both she and Emma Mae had been right.

Isadora Duncan had died when her scarf caught in the wheel of a car. But in 1917, she was still alive and dancing.

THE SCOTTISH PLAY

Addie was back on the loading dock behind the Jewel the next day after dropping off her backpack at home. She'd told Mrs. Powell she would help look through the theater's old records, and she felt guilty about leaving so abruptly yesterday. Plus, she hadn't been able to stop thinking about this place, about whether she'd find evidence of the Jewel as it had been in Emma Mae's time.

Whether the place was haunted.

And—really, the most key—whether she had gone completely and seriously insane.

She hesitated before opening the letterbox.

When exactly had it happened? It must have been when she stopped in the park on the way to the Powells'. She remembered the sudden warming of the air. The open flowers. It had somehow ceased to be this cold, rainy spring;

she had stepped into another spring, a warmer spring from long ago. That was why the statue of the angel was missing, of course. It hadn't existed.

But what had made it happen? She had racked her brain about this. Was it because she was wearing that antique dress from the crate? But she'd been wearing that dress before the earthquake hit. And how ridiculous, anyway—"magical thinking," Almaz would call it. She wore vintage clothes a lot; it didn't usually suspend the laws of time.

Still, she couldn't help glancing down nervously at the skirt she was wearing today, one of the pieces Mrs. T. had let her keep. It fell just to midcalf in a slim line. She wasn't sure what era it was from. She just knew that it looked good with the cropped velvet jacket she'd found at Value Village.

No. It wasn't the clothes. Was it something to do with the statue? Or the mirror? For the hundredth time, she wondered whether she'd bashed her head and it had all been a vivid hallucination. At least that was rational. Something she could say to Almaz without feeling like a lunatic. *If* she ever mustered the courage to tell her. She ran her hand over her scalp, feeling for bumps and bruises. But just like every other time, she found nothing.

Was it something to do with the earthquake itself? Of all the supernatural explanations, at least *that* felt believable. If the earth could shake a whole city and make it roll on its foundations, why couldn't it shake time out of joint?

The time is out of joint. Where had she heard that before?

It was a line from *Hamlet,* wasn't it? How did it go?

> *The time is out of joint—O cursed spite,*
> *That ever I was born to set it right!*

She wrinkled her brow. Was she supposed to set something right?

There was only one thing she could think of that she really needed to set right, and it didn't involve the past at all.

Guiltily, she reached into her pocket and curled her fingers around a folded sheaf of paper: Whaley's enlistment forms.

She *did* feel bad about stealing them from his desk before school this morning. So bad that she couldn't quite manage to throw them away. But she wasn't going to put them back, either. She had to do something to stop him from ending up in some strange country with a gun in his hand.

Stupid. Because of course he could always download the forms off the Internet again. But she had to try. And she'd have to get rid of the papers before he showed up here to help her.

Sighing, she pulled the key from the letterbox, fitted it in the lock, and opened the door.

The hall seemed even darker and danker than it had the day before.

Her eyes burned, and she rubbed them unhappily.

She'd gotten two hours of sleep last night, total. Then, when she'd finally fallen asleep, she'd dreamed. And that was worse. . . .

Okay. Come on, she thought. *Pull yourself together.* Whaley was going to show up at any moment. If he saw her looking so worn-out and nervous, he'd know something was going on.

Quickly, she reached into her jacket pocket and pulled out the silver mirror, hesitating before she raised it to her face. It didn't look very sinister. But it certainly looked magical. *Oh, stop being so ridiculous! Just get some makeup on.* With her free hand, she pulled out a tube of lipstick, applied it, and dropped it back in the bag. Then she took a look in the glass. For a moment, her eyes lost their focus and she felt dizzy. She blinked. Better. She ran her fingers through ringlets and knots in her hair. Now she looked okay. Good enough to be going to a rehearsal, actually. Despite the fear that hadn't quite departed since yesterday's shock, she felt a pinch of disappointment. If only she could have kept that appointment and seen the Powells again. She'd really been looking forward to that. After a final critical glance in the mirror, she shoved it back into her pocket and stepped over the threshold, letting the door close behind her.

She fumbled for the light switch and flicked it.

Lights blazed against honey-colored walls, little glittering bulbs in bright silver sconces.

Well, this was an improvement. Now, instead of the dank smell of the hallway, she breathed in the tang of fresh paint.

How was it possible? So fast! In amazement, she turned about, taking in the transformation.

A thumping piano rag, like the stride Whaley had been playing yesterday, pounded through the ceiling. The smell of furniture polish prickled her nose.

"Whaley?" Could he have fixed this up? It looked incredible! But he couldn't have done it all himself. Maybe he'd gotten some of his friends to help. She smiled to herself, thinking that maybe, with enough determination and enthusiasm, they could help Mrs. Powell bring the place to life.

But as she went along the hallway, passing doors with brass nameplates that read LADIES' DRESSING ROOM, POWDER ROOM, her smile faded.

No one could have done this all in one night. Not even Whaley with a bunch of his friends.

A heavy fire door swung open, and Addie nearly collided with a girl carrying an enormous tray.

"*Oj-då!*" the girl exclaimed and swung neatly away.

"Sorry—my fault," Addie said. And then she took in the girl's gray calf-length dress and white apron.

It was as if she'd been drenched in icy water.

The shock was so sudden that for a moment she thought she would faint.

"Some tea jumped out of the spout is all. No harm done," the girl said with a gap-toothed grin.

No, Addie thought. *It can't be. No.*

"Just push that door open for me, and I'll get a rag from the apartment," she continued.

"Apartment?" Addie said faintly, holding the door for the girl.

"Funny, in a theater, I know," the girl said. "But the

lady who owns the place likes to have somewhere to stay after a late night. And there's a kitchen, so I bake in there, or even cook a dinner sometimes."

Blinking, Addie did as the girl said. She followed her into a small, warm kitchen with walls that were papered a pale olive-leaf green. Muslin curtains on the window over the sink blocked out the ugliness of the alley. She could see a small bedroom through a half-opened door.

Stunned, Addie took in the room. The stove against the right wall was an enormous black iron monster with a heavy white door on the oven. The girl lowered the tray onto a table, and Addie saw it was heaped with jam-filled scones. She lifted the teapot and grabbed a towel to mop up the liquid. "Looks like a blizzard hit, don't it?"

The emptiness in Addie's stomach was turning queasy.

She drew in a deep breath. With deliberate calm, she walked over to the flour-covered table. Pastry had been rolled out and cut into tart crusts, and next to them was a bowl loaded with pitted cherries and scented with almond. She looked up at the girl, forcing herself to act normal. "Those smell good."

It was absurd—making small talk about baked goods when she had just slipped out of her own century. Again.

"Too early for Rainier cherries, but I couldn't wait." The girl gave Addie a confiding look. "I'm trying to measure up to the legendary Olga. Are you one of the people who tried to bribe her to stay even after her baby was born?"

"Bribe?" Addie felt like she was emerging out of some sort of deep sleep. A coma, maybe. "No," she murmured. "Who's Olga?"

"Aren't you one of the actresses? I'm sorry. Mrs. Powell only engaged me last week. I don't know everyone yet."

"*Engaged* you? What do you mean?"

"Hired me, of course." The girl laughed. "Isn't that right? We speak Swedish at home, and sometimes I confuse things."

"Are you . . . her cook?"

"Cook, maid of all work, wardrobe assistant—well, I iron a lot, anyway. Whatever she needs, I'll do." She hung the towel on the handle of the oven. "Hot work, though, when that thing's blazing. I wish she'd get one of those fireless stoves." She wiped her brow with her sleeve, revealing a puckered yellow-blue wound just below her hairline.

Addie clutched at the nearest hard surface—which proved to be the oven. "Ow!"

"You've burned yourself!"

"No, I'm okay." Addie stuck her hot fingers in her mouth. A wave of heat boiled the air around her, turning it viscous and slow and distorted. It was all she could do not to turn and run.

She took her fingers out of her mouth and drew in one shaky breath, then another, willing herself to calm down.

This girl, with the smudge of flour on the curve of her cheek, was the half-conscious girl she'd seen at the Powells' house the day of the earthquake. It was Frida. It really was.

"You're the girl that got hit with the brick," Addie said unsteadily. "One of the—what did he call it? One of the Wobs' kids."

Frida stiffened. "Who told you that?"

Addie shut her eyes as adrenaline surged through her. *The time is out of joint.* . . . She swallowed and opened her eyes, half expecting to find no one there. But Frida was standing not two feet away, looking at her with open suspicion.

Addie patted her pocket. She could feel the mirror. Irrationally, she was comforted to know it was there—the key, in some way she didn't understand, that unlocked the door between Frida's world and her own.

"I was at the Powells' house," Addie managed, feeling somewhat more confident, "the day you got hurt. Don't you remember?"

"No, I don't." Frida picked up the tray.

"You don't remember me?"

"Get hit with a brick and see what you remember," she said shortly and headed to the door.

"You've left the teapot!" There, Addie thought. She was acting nearly normal. She could feel herself shifting, fitting into this new reality, however insane it was.

"Pick it up, then." Frida kicked the door open.

Addie did and followed her into the hallway. "I'm glad you're better now." She could tell she'd offended her in some way, though she wasn't sure how.

Frida slowed her pace halfway up the corridor, allowing her to catch up. "Thanks," she said curtly. But then, seeming to sense that Addie meant well, she added, "I don't know what would have happened to me if it hadn't been for the Powells. Aren't they wonderful?"

Addie nodded, the sick feeling in her stomach starting to subside. A spark of anticipation lit inside her. After all, if Frida was here, might Reg be, too? And Emma Mae?

"What else can I do?"

"Help me get this food handed around to the cast. They'll be raising holy heck if they don't eat soon."

Addie followed Frida through the door and up a back staircase she hadn't noticed before. They reached the top, and suddenly she was backstage in the midst of a chaos of noise and people. Shock slapped into her again. One person she could handle, but here was a whole world—men in flat caps and suspenders were painting backdrops. Stage carpenters were sawing boards and hammering scenery together. Two boys about Zack's age were racing around, climbing over half-built sets. Addie's head spun. She stuck close to Frida, who swerved expertly around chairs and mirrors and painted panels as she made her way to a gap in a floor-length velvet curtain of deep, deep crimson.

Addie followed her out onto the stage and froze as she found herself gazing into the auditorium exactly as she had the day before. But this time her eyes traveled over a sea of green velvet seats rising in a gentle slope all the way to the exits. It was Becky Powell's theater, not dead anymore, not a ghost of what it had once been, but living and breathing and making a racket.

The stage swarmed with people, and Addie could see a long wooden table set up in the center. Six or seven chairs had been arranged around it, and two thrones were placed at one end. Actors perched on the arms of the chairs, laughing and chatting. The women were wearing dresses with fitted bodices and high-waisted skirts, hemmed just below midcalf, and the men wore white button-down shirts, pressed trousers, and suspenders. In the orchestra pit, a few musicians were putting away their instruments.

She made her way forward to the edge of the stage, craning her neck to see the proscenium rising above her. It was painted in glowing emerald green highlighted with gold and crowned with brightly painted sculptures. At the top of the arch stood an Egyptian Pharaoh, a brilliant ruby glowing in the head of the snake that rose from his crown. Attendants on either side of him carried food and drink and platters heaped with jewels.

Addie's gaze traveled up to where box seats protruded from walls gorgeous with carvings. Ibises, ankhs, and eyes were everywhere. Horus and Osiris and Isis and all the other Egyptian gods floated in barges down the Nile. Up above, rafts of electric lights were affixed to grids. A chandelier sparkled with cut crystal, like a cascade of diamonds. And to her amazement, it hung not from the ornate ceiling but from the center of a gorgeous dome, which was split into sections like an orange and painted with greens and reds and golds. Her eyes were drawn down again by regal crimson draperies that hid the entrances and exits.

"Wow," she murmured.

The rapid ragtime morphed into a waltz as she turned her attention back to the stage. Two couples who had been dancing frenetically drew closer and slowed their steps, and Addie was suddenly reminded of the dream she'd had the night she found that old photo. Down in the orchestra, she saw a man with his sleeves rolled up at the upright piano, fingers flying over the keys.

The same piano she had seen yesterday.

But the only thing on top of it now was a metronome.

"Come on," Frida beckoned her. "You can put the teapot on the table."

The waltz broke off, prompting a chorus of complaints, and the pianist called, "What have you brought for us, Frida, my love?" He twiddled the keys for punctuation and stood up, eyes sparkling. His mustache and pointy beard made him look like a merry devil.

A young woman with short, wavy dark hair clapped her hands above her head for attention and bellowed, "Provisions! Provisions for King Macbeth's court!"

"Don't say that!"

"You'll jinx us! We'll never sell any tickets."

"Someone will get sick. We'll have to cancel opening night."

But the woman just said, "Nonsense! Believe that and you'll believe what you read in the Hearst papers." Addie stared at the smoky gray scarf around the woman's neck, so much like the one in the photo of Isadora Duncan that it made her skin crawl. She turned away without looking and tripped over someone's foot.

"Watch out!" A hand grabbed her elbow. She'd let the teapot tip to a dangerous angle, and the person who was holding her arm—a tall, ruddy guy with a shock of blond hair—righted it just before it spilled. "Whew!" he said. "Disaster averted."

Addie smiled uncertainly at him, and put the pot down on the table.

"I'll run and get the cups and saucers," Frida told Addie. She set down the platter and announced to the others, "It's catch as catch can. No plates."

Within seconds, the table was mobbed by hungry actors and stagehands. Addie at first thought that she should be handing out the food, but abandoned the idea as one greedy hand after another whisked the pastries off the tray. Instead, she snatched up a warm scone before they were all gone and wriggled her way out of the press of bodies. She found a chair by the curtain dividing the stage from the wing and sank down onto it. The flaky pastry and oozing jam were reassuring. Something normal, to offset her prickles of fear and excitement.

But by now, excitement was starting to crowd out fear.

Could this Jewel of the past be the place she'd dreamed about? It seemed crazy. But then again . . .

"Which of you made these heavenly scones?" a voice thundered. It was the pianist, dragging a chair, which he positioned in the middle of the stage and sat down on backwards. Loud men always sat backwards on chairs, Addie thought, picturing her Algebra II teacher.

"I did." Frida had returned with a tray piled high with crockery. She put it down and began pouring tea into people's cups. "And there goes the last one."

"Go forth and fetch us more, Frida!" the pianist cried. "Banging these damned keys gives me an appetite."

"I'll do that for you," Addie offered, feeling sorry for Frida being ordered around so much.

"No. I'll bring another batch." Frida handed Addie the pot and rushed backstage again.

"My wife could use a girl like that," the pianist said to the blond guy who had caught Addie's elbow. "But would the Powells part with her, d'you think, Andrew?"

"Don't be silly, Peter," Andrew said mildly, holding out his cup to Addie. "Your wife wouldn't want a Wobbly brat in her kitchen, would she?"

Wobblies again? Addie's ears pricked up.

Peter fingered his mustache. "Maybe you're right."

Out of the corner of her eye, Addie saw Frida returning, a second plate of scones in her hand.

"And trust me," Peter added, "now that there's a war on, they won't even fight."

The war, Addie thought, and felt sick all over again. *World War One.*

"That's true," Andrew agreed. "Did you see the piece in the *Observer* last week? They're right, too. The Wobs are the best friends the Germans ever had."

Peter raised an eyebrow, but before he could reply, one of the actresses standing near the table spoke up. "What strong opinions you have, Mr. Lindstrom. When can we expect you to do your bit?" She batted her eyelashes and smiled coolly.

Color swept from Andrew's throat to his forehead, and

Addie felt glad someone had embarrassed him. She didn't like the way he talked about Frida. "As soon as this run is over."

The piano player threw back his head and guffawed. "Unless a really plum role comes up, you mean! You're as ambitious as our beloved thane, Andrew. Don't tell me you'd go jaunting off into all that muck and mud when you could see your name in lights."

Andrew flushed so deeply that Addie thought this must be true. She turned away for a moment and realized that a small line had formed, people waiting for tea.

"Maybe after the next run," she heard Andrew concede as she refocused her attention on filling teacups. "I can't throw it all away now, can I? Now that I've got a good part. I have to establish my career. No one else is going to help me." He turned to the lady who had teased him. "Some of us don't have family connections to get us work. But that doesn't mean I won't volunteer!"

"Of course you will," Peter said mockingly. "Just in time to miss the heavy fighting."

Andrew leaned angrily toward the piano player. "What do you mean?"

"Isn't it obvious?" he replied, unfazed. "The Hun will cave in once they've seen our boys on the battlefield! It'll be over a week after our ships touch the docks. Good timing, friend."

"That's not true," Addie interjected. The war didn't end until November of 1918. It was pretty much the only thing she remembered about this war from her American history class.

They all turned to stare at her, and instantly, she knew

she should have kept her mouth shut. "I mean," she amended, "it looks like it might drag on longer."

Peter gave her a patronizing look. "A bit defeatist, don't you think, Miss . . ."

"Addie."

He raised an eyebrow.

"McNeal," she added, remembering that Reg and his mother had always used her last name.

"That's not the word on the street, at any rate, Miss McNeal," Peter went on. "The enemy is demoralized. In retreat, in fact, on some parts of the line."

"True," the actress said. "It's go now or miss the chance of a lifetime, Mr. Lindstrom."

"Oh, I'll fight," Andrew retorted. "What about you, Peter? Can you miss the boat races this year?"

"Me? I'll get myself posted to Paris to play piano for the general staff. They say the girls are pretty, and the jazz clubs are open all hours for the boys on leave."

"Where's the tea girl?" the woman with the long scarf shouted from stage left, where she'd been talking to some of the actors. "I'm dry as a desert!" She was advancing on Addie, her cup and saucer extended imperiously.

But then a calm, lovely voice drifted across the stage. "That's not the tea girl. That's Miss Addie McNeal, and she's supposed to be my guest, not serving tea to you ravening monsters."

12

THE USURPER HIMSELF

Emma Mae Powell crossed the stage to Addie. "Welcome, Miss McNeal!" Her hair was pulled back into a businesslike bun, and she wore a short jacket and fitted skirt. "We wondered where you'd got to. Reg said you'd drop by on Tuesday."

"Oh—I—I'm sorry." Of course. They thought *she'd* been the one who hadn't kept her word.

Mrs. Powell clasped Addie's hands in her own, radiating warmth. "Don't worry. Today's actually a better day, since we've finally moved everything over from the rehearsal space. It's always such an upheaval. But so much more fun rehearsing in the theater."

A shudder rode down Addie's spine, and Becky Powell's words rang in her ears: *If we really wanted Emma Mae Powell to bring the Jewel back to life, I'm afraid we'd have to bring Emma Mae back to life as well.* For a moment, she held tight against panic. This couldn't be real. How could she get out of here? Was it even possible to get back to her own time?

Of course it was. As long as she had the mirror. "I—"

The woman with the scarf interrupted them. "Emma, did you see what Ben brought us for the cavern scene? Rhododendrons, for God's sake. In a big pot. Did Paul know about that?"

"Rhodis? Not *tremendously* Scottish. What was he thinking?"

It helped, Addie thought. Their normal banter helped the fear recede.

Besides, isn't this where you wanted to be? she reminded herself with a flash of irony. *At a real rehearsal?*

The scarf woman was rattling on. "Well, gorse wasn't native to the Northwest last time I checked. Or heather. Ben and I thought maybe rosemary. Emma, have a sit-down. You look tired."

"It was just the board meeting. I proposed the benefit, and they were fit to be tied." Emma Mae glanced at Addie. "Sorry, dear. It's a flying circus today." She turned back to the scarf lady. "I've missed the tea. Ask Frida to brew another pot, would you?"

"Sure." The woman headed into the wing, shouting "Frida!" at the top of her lungs. Did she ever use a normal tone of voice? Addie wondered.

"Sit down, Miss McNeal." Mrs. Powell sank into a chair and motioned to the empty seat next to her. "You take your breaks when they're offered here."

Addie pulled the chair out from the long table and settled into it.

"Freeeeeeda!" she heard the woman roar again from the stairs.

"Poor Frida," Addie said. "I wouldn't blame her if she's hiding in the pantry!"

"So you've seen our little invalid then? Up and fit as a corn-fed hen."

"Oh, fitter than that." Someone was leaning on the back of Addie's chair. She twisted her head and found herself looking up at Reg Powell. "Hello, Miss McNeal," he said, and sat down on one of the thrones at the end of the table. A tiny thrill shot through her, and the last remnant of her fear dropped away.

He's an actor, she thought in surprise. A metal circlet pressed his hair sleek to his head. He wore a tartan plaid across his shoulder, held in place with a pin, and a black shirt underneath.

"From what we've seen," he continued, "it would take a mountain of bricks to knock Frida out."

"Oh, don't tempt fate, Reg." Emma Mae rapped on the table smartly. "We're superstitious, we theater people." She smiled at Addie. "It's good to see you, Miss McNeal."

"Yes, welcome back." Reg hung his head in mock repentance. "I'm sorry I didn't come by your house. But it wasn't for want of trying. I must have mixed up the address because I just ended up at Meg's." He slid down off his chair and knelt ridiculously on one knee. "Say you forgive me!"

Addie tried and failed to stifle a smile. "So you're rehearsing *Macbeth?*"

"Can't you tell?" Reg leaped to his feet. "You're looking at the usurper himself! Thane of Glamis and Cawdor, unrightful regent of the fugitive Malcolm."

"*You're* Macbeth?"

"Miss McNeal, *must* you say the name quite so insistently?" Mrs. Powell exclaimed.

"Sorry," Addie said, embarrassed for forgetting.

Reg grinned and sat down again. "Well, today I am— the usurper, I mean. Harrison is home sick."

"So you're the usurper of the usurper?"

"That's right. Clever, aren't you? And not afeared to utter the name of the Scottish play aloud. The fellow who's the regular understudy enlisted, and he's already off for training." Across the stage, Peter started another rag, and Reg had to raise his voice. "Officer training, right, Ma?"

Emma Mae nodded. "We'll need to forward Saul's pay. Where's he gone again?"

"Montana," Reg said. "So here I am until they can find a real actor."

"Pooh! We don't need a 'real actor.' You're a wonderful understudy." Emma Mae turned to Addie. "It's not favoritism on my part. Just convenience. And he *assures* me he will pass his exams next month. If he'd just give up his idea of playing soldier, he might have a part in the next production."

"Stop worrying about that!" He pulled a face at Addie.

"Mother has started reading the news. *Always* a mistake. The yellow Hearst papers have filled her with dire forebodings."

"Says the editor of the university paper! For goodness' sake, Reg, I think there's *some* reason for concern. They never give us any real numbers, but Meg says the British have already lost more men at Arras than we have in our regular army."

Addie stared. "How is that possible? We have the biggest army in the world."

"Who told you that?"

Oh, no. It was Mrs. T. And there was a woman with the same name in their time, she reminded herself. She *really* had to be careful what she said. She hesitated. "Mrs. Turner," she said finally.

"Meg Turner says that?" Reg hooted. "When will that woman stop exaggerating? I'm sure she got that information from one of her women's peace organizations. Watch out, Ma, or she'll run for office and you'll be at loose ends."

Well, at least they both seemed to think it was something that their Mrs. Turner was likely to say.

"Where is she, anyhow?" Addie asked curiously, her eyes sweeping the crowd.

Mrs. Powell gave her a puzzled look. "But—"

"Far away, I hope," Reg said at the same moment.

"Reg!"

"Sorry." He took the metal circlet off his head and rubbed his temples. "I'm not trying to be unpleasant. But she's been bossing me all day!"

"That's her *job*."

"Yes, Mother," Reg said humbly. But his eyes were gleaming with mischief as he turned to Addie and stage-whispered, "There's the monster now!"

Addie followed his gaze and saw the woman with the short dark hair and the long scarf emerging through the curtain.

Oh. My. Goodness.

But the next second she thought: *Of course it's her.* The way the Powells described her, who else could it be?

"Five minutes!" the woman boomed to everyone in general. "Gulp your drinks! Put out your pipes! Al, get those rhodis out of here—no, wait. Get your fellas to drag the table away first."

A guy in overalls detached himself from the crowd and picked up one of the chairs from the banqueting table. "Okay, Ben. Jake. You too, Sven!"

Addie couldn't take her eyes off this new, younger Mrs. Turner—Meg Turner—who was plowing toward them, a steaming mug of tea in her hand. She handed it to Emma Mae. "Here you go, Emma. Get that dishwater down you." She shot a look at Reg. "Think you've got the lines, laddie-o?"

"Got 'em, Meggie-o."

The man named Al grabbed the top of his chair and gave it a shake. "Move the royal keister, Your Majesty. Gotta set up the next scene." Reg got up and calmly stepped out of their way.

"We've got defections in the ranks, Emma," Meg was saying. "I've just sent Janie Beckett home."

"Janie? Why?"

"She's come down with chickenpox. Or leprosy, or some other loathsome disease. I can't imagine how she has the nerve to come to work like that—pancake makeup a finger thick to cover it up! I told her not to come back. We can't have the whole cast infected." She lowered her voice. "She can stay home, if you ask me. She's useless as an assistant. Can't do the simplest thing. Even the prop table's in disarray! We're losing things right and left. I've been chasing after swords and shields and I don't know what else till I'm practically run off my feet."

"Well, I don't pay you to be a prop girl. I pay you to direct," Mrs. Powell said mildly. "If she's not doing a satisfactory job, you should hire someone else—I won't stop you."

Addie stared, remembering Mrs. T.'s words: *My great-aunt was a director. . . .* Why hadn't she put this together before? Meg Turner was Mrs. T.'s great-aunt. So that was why Reg had ended up at Meg's house when he went looking for her.

"Who else could handle props?" Emma Mae continued, getting up as another guy returned for her chair. "How about one of the boys? They don't have enough to do."

Meg gritted her teeth. "You're much mistaken if you think I would entrust props to any of *them*. You know I can't bear child actors."

"The play hardly works without child actors, dear. Lady Macduff's poor little chicks, you know."

"I feel like cheering when old Macbeth does them in," Meg muttered.

Addie thought of Mrs. T. and the hen Messalina and felt laughter bubbling up inside her. *So this Mrs. Turner can't bear little chicks.*

"What a bloodthirsty bat you are, Meg," Reg observed.

"Bloodthirsty! At least I'm not proposing to enlist in the army to kill and maim in some lunacy we have no business in. If I were your mother, Reg—"

"Ha! About as motherly as Lady M."

Meg Turner ignored this. "I suppose I'll just have to do without an assistant."

"Well," Addie began, and stopped. Was she crazy? She couldn't offer to work here! But Meg had already turned toward her. And somehow, she found herself saying, "I could help out, if you're in a tight spot."

A warm smile spread over the director's face. "Well, what a lovely young thing you are. *Would* you?" She threw the end of her scarf over her shoulder. "Emma, can we give her an hourly rate, just for today?"

"Of course."

"You don't have to pay me," Addie protested.

Meg looked at her incredulously. "You're turning down money?"

"That means you have to be nice, Meg," Reg pointed out.

The stagehands had just lifted the table by its corners when Meg whirled around and called, "Oh, my darlings, could you possibly put that down? And bring back those chairs? I didn't like the looks of that banquet scene, now that I think of it. I'd better run it again."

Al jerked his head, and the men put the table down

again. He was clearly trying to contain himself. "I'm sure there's something in our contract that says—"

"I'm sure there is," she said airily. "And if we rehearse well we'll have a nice long run, and your crew will have steady employment. So fetch the chairs back, dear lambs of my heart."

Reg broke up laughing at Meg's beatific expression.

"Yeah, yeah," Al grumbled.

"Are you sure you want to do this?" Emma Mae turned to Addie, putting her empty cup back on the table. "I promised to find you something besides costumes and makeup. But handling the props—for no wage!"

"I don't mind. If it needs to be done, I'll do it." This was nothing like being consigned to makeup by Mr. Crowley. She didn't care if they asked her to wash the floors. She was finally getting the chance to be a part of a professional production!

Meg nodded. "That's the spirit. We all need to shine. The prop girl is as important as the proudest lady of the stage. Unless it's that wretched Janie, of course." She grabbed Addie's hand and shook it. Her heavy perfume made Addie's nose prickle. "Much obleeged, as the Limeys say."

Addie grinned. "Obleeged myself."

"Watch out," Reg warned. He was twisting the golden circlet back onto his head. "Janie is Meg's personal slave. It's not just props. It's notes, and lines, and everything else—since for some reason there's no stage manager at the moment—"

"No stage manager?" Addie said incredulously.

"Meg fired her." Emma Mae sighed. "We'll need to hire someone new."

"And Janie's *supposed* to be assistant director—"

"Assistant *to* the director," Meg corrected. "Who ever said assistant director?"

Reg pretended not to hear. "But Meg is too much of a dictator."

"Yes, dear, I am." Meg spun about to face the chattering actors, clapped her hands over her head, and called out in a ringing voice, "One-minute warning! Miss McNeal will assist me the rest of the afternoon. Let her know who you are so she can help you."

Addie waved shyly at the crowd. A few of the men bowed and one or two of the actresses smiled, and then people were darting across the stage. Addie felt a surge of excitement as Meg Turner grabbed her wrist and led her behind the red velvet curtain to the prop table.

It was paint spattered and bore the marks of saw teeth and nails. Underneath and all along the walls were crates full of stuff. A woman in a black shawl was already waiting for her. "Hettie Longmere, First Witch." She handed Addie a battered copy of the script. "You'll need this for prompts."

Before she could ask a single question, actors swamped her. She was glad she knew the play fairly well and could figure out what item belonged to which character. The daggers belonged to the murderers. The candlestick was Lady Macbeth's. Still, it took a while to find what props were available and where. When she finally had a chance to pick up the script and go sit on a wooden stool in the wings, the banquet scene was over and a short scene between Lennox and some unnamed lord was already under way. Meg Turner was sitting on the edge of the stage, watching and writing notes to herself. Every now and then she'd leap to her feet and stop the action to say, "Put the emphasis on this word, not that one—see how that changes the meaning?" Or "Your light will be here, remember? Didn't we walk through this?" Addie watched, completely engrossed.

When the scene ended, she rushed backstage to the prop table again. Hettie Longmere and the other witches came to collect their cauldron and the toads and bats and other unpleasant things they had to throw into it, grumbling about some direction Meg had given them. Addie was mobbed with people needing crowns for the ghost kings' procession. Then she heard Meg roar, "Act four, scene one! Witches, find your places!" and they were all gone as quickly as they had appeared.

And then she was alone.

Her head was swimming. Sensory overload . . .

Carefully, she reached into her pocket and pulled out the mirror.

A step creaked behind her. Startled, she jerked around, hiding the mirror behind her back.

No. No one. She took the mirror out again. She'd been aware of it the whole time, her lifeline—her way back. But as she examined it, she began to feel anxious. What if it was damaged? Should she find something to protect it, to keep it from scratching or breaking—a handkerchief or something no one would miss from the prop box? She put it down, just for a moment, and went to look.

Just as she pulled a scrap of green silk from one of the boxes, Reg darted through the curtain.

She hardly had time to drop the silk over the mirror before he thumped his hands down on the table. "Hello."

"Hello, evil usurper."

"I need the looking glass for the procession of kings."

"But Macbeth doesn't carry the glass," Addie said, careful not to glance at the green silk lying on the prop table. "The last king does."

"Oh-ho! Our prop girl knows her Shakespeare." He smiled disarmingly. "All right. I'll admit it. I came to fetch it so I could see how you were doing."

"Oh." Addie blushed. She realized she was smiling like an idiot, and looked away. "I'm—I'm doing fine, thanks. Just a—just a second." Embarrassed, she crouched down to rummage in one of the boxes, hoping he hadn't noticed the color in her face. The prop must be here somewhere. The quicker she found it—

"Macbeth! Are you at your entrance?"

"Coming, Meg!" Reg shouted toward the stage.

Addie pulled out sashes, capes, and daggers, but no mirror. "Sorry. I don't see it. . . ."

"Well, I won't hold that against you. But I won't vouch for Meg." He leaned across the table, trying to peer into the boxes she was searching through. "Wait a second. What's this?"

With a sinking heart, Addie saw that he was holding her mirror. "Can't we use this?" he asked.

"No!" She scrambled to her feet. "I mean, that one's not a prop. Just wait. I'll find another."

He turned toward the curtain, frowning. "But it's here with the props."

"I know. But it's mine. It's—it's . . ." She floundered. "I'm sure I can find you something." She dived into another crate, practically throwing props around in her panic.

Nothing!

Then she felt his hand on her shoulder and glanced up to see him giving her a sympathetic look. "I know you want to impress Meg, but you don't have to try so hard," he said kindly. "I promise, I'll return it as soon as the scene's over."

"But—"

"Our thane! We await you!"

Reg flashed Addie a long-suffering look and rushed out to the wing, taking the mirror with him.

It was all she could do not to run after him and grab it out of his hand. What if someone looked in it? What would happen then?

But she couldn't barge in on the scene demanding it back. They'd just think she was crazy! Worried, she rushed out to the prompt stool to watch the rehearsal from the wing. All she could do was keep an eye on it.

But so far, there was no sign of it onstage. Reg was barging in on the witches' dance, looking every inch Macbeth even though he was way too young for the part. His black hair was crushed down under his crown, his face looked gaunt, and his every movement conveyed panic and distraction as he demanded the hags show him his future, demanded to know what threatened his hold on the throne.

The witches called up one apparition after another to bring cryptic messages of things to come—an armed soldier, a child in white robes splashed with blood, and, finally, the procession of the eight phantom kings. Addie remembered that the kings were accompanied by the ghost of Banquo, whom Macbeth had just murdered. They moved in a stately procession accompanied by a minor-key oboe melody.

Ah ha. She picked out the mirror in the hands of the last king and relaxed. He wasn't even looking into it.

But though she tried to keep her eye on him, her attention kept being drawn irresistibly back to Reg.

She was completely transfixed. Reg was the only person on the stage, as far as she was concerned. She watched him stare at the ghostly procession of kings in mounting horror as they wafted by him, evidence that all the crimes he had committed to win the throne were for naught He spoke the Elizabethan poetry with such familiarity that it sounded like natural speech, what anyone would say when confronted with a future he should never have learned about because all that was to be found there was woe. It sent chills down her spine, and she didn't know if it was because he was so good or if she was just totally falling for him. All she knew was she couldn't focus on anything else while he was onstage.

> . . . Filthy hags,
> Why do you show me this?—A fourth? Start, eyes!
> What, will the line stretch out to th' crack of doom?
> Another yet? A seventh? I'll see no more.
> And yet the eighth appears, who bears a glass
> Which shows me many more. . . .

She held her breath as the eighth king held up the silver looking glass to Reg to show an endless procession of Banquo's descendants, all kings of Scotland, all inheriting the throne that he had wanted for his own unborn children, wiping out his posterity.

And in that moment a truth hit her: Reg was an actor. A *real* actor.

And she . . . she was good. But she would never be *that* good.

Then Reg took the mirror. He held it at arm's length, as if it were a dangerous object, one that might burn or bite, and Addie was jolted out of her reverie. She jumped to her feet. She'd forgotten that Macbeth looks into it! Oh, why hadn't she stopped him? Now anything might happen. Why hadn't she been able to keep him from taking it? She braced herself, wanting to dash across the stage, but knowing she couldn't possibly do that.

Too late. He was already gazing into it.

And—thank goodness!—nothing seemed to happen. Addie let out the breath she was holding. It was fine. *Stop panicking.* In a few minutes the mirror would be back in her hands.

Reg was continuing on with the scene. As he stared into the glass, describing the horrors he saw there, he drew it closer, giving the impression that it was pulling him in, casting an evil spell upon him.

But then all the color drained from his face. He looked over his shoulder, and then back into the mirror again.

Silence filled the theater.

Addie froze. Ten seconds went by. Twenty. Reg stood there without saying a word. Addie saw one of the witches shoot a questioning glance at another.

She should do something, she thought. But what?

"Line!" a voice hissed. Andrew jostled her elbow. "You've got the script. Give him the line. He's dried up."

Flustered, Addie flipped through the pages until she found the procession of kings. More was wrong than that he'd just forgotten a line. She knew it. Reg was still frozen, holding the mirror close to his face.

" 'Horrible sight . . .' " Addie whispered.

Reg didn't seem to hear.

" 'Horrible sight!' " yelled Andrew. He winked at Addie. "Thank goodness we don't have to put up with the manager's son every day."

"What are you talking about? He's amazing!" Addie turned her attention back to Reg.

" 'Horrible sight!' " he cried in a strangled voice. " 'Now, I see, 'tis true; For the blood-bolter'd Banquo smiles upon me, and points to them for his. What, is this so?' "

Hettie Longmere stepped toward him, offering no comfort. " 'Aye, sir, all this is so . . .' "

He nodded slowly and slipped the mirror into a breast pocket. It was safe. But as Addie watched him pick up the threads of the scene, she was still filled with foreboding—of what, she didn't know. Lennox ran in at Macbeth's bidding, and the plot to attack Macduff's castle was hatched. But Reg's presence had changed utterly. He said his lines like a boy repeating the periodic table for a chemistry test.

"Oh, yes, he's quite amazing," Andrew murmured. "Speaking of which, I need Macduff's sword so I can get out there and start amazing all and sundry myself."

As she headed back to the prop table Addie could hear Meg Turner bawling Reg out. "What was that all about, King Macbeth? Has slaughter and pillage become dull all of a sudden? I know you're only filling in, but remember, understudies *do* perform on occasion!"

Addie handed Andrew his sword and glanced up to see Reg coming toward her. He looked furious. Andrew smirked at him and went off to his entrance.

"What *is* this?" Reg demanded, handing the mirror back to her.

Quickly, almost guiltily, she slipped it into her pocket. "What do you mean?"

"I think you know."

"It's—" She didn't know what to say. There was no way to explain. "It's just a mirror."

"No, it's not." Reg shot back. "I don't know what that thing is. But whatever gag you were trying to play, it wasn't funny. Who are you, Miss Addie McNeal? Where are you from, really?"

Addie's mouth went dry. "I told you. I live in Wallingford. Near Densmore Park."

"And you're a neighbor of Meg's. Isn't that what you said? I don't think you're telling the truth, quite honestly."

"Of course I am!" She managed to sound indignant, but she felt like a liar.

"Really? You'd obviously never met her before today. And she definitely didn't recognize you."

Addie caught her breath. If only she could explain. . . .

"You know what I think?" Reg went on. "I think you must be one of those girls they hire at the vaudeville houses, with a trick mirror like that. Are you trying to work your way into a legitimate operation? Is that why you're here?"

"What?" Addie blinked. "No!"

"That's why you've got props like that looking glass. Used it in a magician's act, did you? Though what you're trying to accomplish with a charlatan's trick like that—"

"What trick?" Addie stepped back as he leaned toward her across the prop table.

"The trick in the glass. The picture it shows."

"I don't know what you mean!" But her voice caught in her throat. She didn't know what the mirror was capable of. "What picture?"

"The kings? Carrying the coffin?"

"That doesn't make sense," she said faintly. "There's no coffin."

He gave her a withering look. "No, Miss McNeal. We *don't* have a coffin in the scene. Especially not with an American flag draped over it!"

Addie braced herself against the table. She glanced around quickly at the backdrops and furniture and machines all higgledy-piggledy backstage, half-hoping to see that he was wrong. But, no. He was right. No American flag.

"I have to tell you, Addie McNeal. You're uncanny."

"I'm *not!*" She insisted. "And it's not a trick mirror. I don't know what's with it. Maybe it's hexed or something." She gave him a pleading look. "I tried to keep you from taking it, didn't I?"

Reg considered this. "That's true," he admitted, sounding a fraction less angry. He pulled the crown off his head and unceremoniously dropped it into the open prop box.

"Maybe . . ." she offered hesitantly, "maybe, since you're thinking about joining the army, you just imagined it. You know, with all this talk of war . . ."

Reg had started unfastening the pin holding the plaid across his shoulder. He stopped, regarding her through narrowed eyes. "Imagined it? Are you saying I'm yellow?"

"Of course not!"

He went back to the pin. "Because if you feel that way, why don't you go on and find a white feather in those crates." When she looked at him blankly, he added, "Haven't you heard? The girls give them to fellows they think are shirking."

"A white feather?" Addie threw up her hands. "That's ridiculous."

Reg yanked the tartan off his shoulders and dumped it on the table.

She swallowed hard and said carefully, "I just . . . I don't want you to go fight. I'd like to—" A loud buzzer made her jump. "Oh! They're ready to start."

"That's not a stage call. It's the back doorbell." He turned and walked away.

"Wait a second!" Addie cried. She didn't want him to go. Not like that.

But he went. She watched his figure grow dim in the murky backstage light as he made his way to the stairs.

"Miss McNeal!" Meg Turner called from the stage. "Props for the mad scene! Are you ready?"

13

TWO GENTLEMEN

She crouched down and dug Lady Macbeth's props out of the crate. Her head was spinning. What did it mean, what Reg had seen in the glass? She shivered.

"That looks more like a dog dish than a washbasin, if you ask me." Addie looked up and saw Frida lifting the tea tray that she'd left on one of the chairs. "Just finished washing the tea dishes and already it's time to start tidying up the dressing rooms. It's as bad as when Ma and I slung hash at Dad's bunkhouse." She grinned. "More polite company, though."

Addie stood up slowly. Frida's grin faded as she examined her more closely. "Are you all right? You look like you've seen a ghost."

A ghost? She studied Frida's bright hair, the edges of the terrible bruise clear across her forehead. "Maybe I did," she said.

"It's a warning, then." Frida paused, looked around quickly, and added, "My dad seen a ghost once. Night before he went down to Everett, he saw his pal Abe, clear as day, lying in a pool of blood. And sure enough, next day Abe was one of them the deputies shot."

A stab of light dazzled Addie's eyes. Reg had swung open the door to the back staircase, and the brightness from the stairwell cut across the dim backstage area. She heard loud men's voices down below him, and then the door shut again and the voices were cut off.

He hurried over to Frida. "It's the police," he said quietly. "They want to talk to you."

Frida's freckles flamed against the sudden pallor of her skin. "Already?"

Startled, Addie looked from her to Reg, but neither of them seemed aware of her.

"It'll be all right," Reg told Frida. "I promise. I'll stick by you."

For a moment, the girl's lips trembled, but then she brought her features under control. "I ain't afraid," she said. There was a trace of pride in her voice.

"What's going on?" Addie asked.

But Reg just went and shouted down the stairs, "I found her. Come on up!"

Frida was searching frantically through the pockets of her apron. "Is this about the guy who threw the brick at you?" Addie asked.

"Hush! No. It's worse than that." The girl looked up. "Please don't ruin it for me!"

"Ruin what?"

Frida pulled something out of her pocket. "Don't ask, just—" She reached out and pressed an iron key into Addie's palm. "They can't find this on me." Her expression was fierce. "I'm trusting you."

Puzzled, Addie dropped the key into her skirt pocket. "I don't understand."

Footsteps were coming up the stairway. A moment later, two police officers came through the door behind Reg. Both of them were young and wearing blue serge jackets and trousers and hard helmets with chin straps. One was stocky, with a sullen expression and a close-clipped mustache that reminded Addie of photographs of Hitler (*who isn't even in power yet*, she thought). The other was tall and skinny, with a friendlier expression.

"Which of you is Frida Peterson?" the mustached cop asked.

"I am. What do you want?"

"Ah, don't be that way, gal." The skinny cop lifted his cap to reveal a shock of sandy brown hair. "We want to talk to you, not lock you up."

"'Less you got something to do with Gustaf's escape," the other added.

"My father?" Addie couldn't tell if Frida was delighted or frightened. "He ran away from jail?"

"And you didn't know?" The mustached cop jeered, examining Frida so intensely, it made Addie squirm.

For a second, she felt confused. Frida's dad was in trouble for who knew what—enough trouble to get locked up in jail—and Frida was definitely hiding something. And now her dad had escaped. She glanced at Frida, and drew in a sharp breath.

She knew already!

Was it as obvious to everyone else as it was to her? The pleading in Frida's voice came back to Addie: *Please don't ruin it for me!*

"I asked you if you knew anything about it."

"I don't," Frida said. *Oh, my gosh, she's unconvincing*, Addie thought.

"When did it happen?" Addie broke in, making her voice as nervously excited as she could. "Are you saying there's a criminal on the loose?"

It worked. Both policemen turned to her. The mustached one scowled. But the skinny officer said patiently, "Two nights ago, miss. But there's no reason to be concerned. We doubt he'd stay in the city once he broke outta jail downtown. But then we heard he had a daughter working here, so we thought we'd see what she knew."

Reg glanced over at Addie and raised an eyebrow when neither of the policemen was looking.

"I wouldn't go that far, Wallace," his partner snapped. "Peterson's wanted for murder." He turned back to Frida. "So what have you got to say for yourself?"

Addie's interruption had helped; Frida had collected herself. "I *didn't* know, but I'm glad he's out." She jutted out her chin. "My dad didn't murder anyone. It was the cops started shooting. They should be in prison, not my dad."

"Oh, we'll get him back in the clink, don't you worry."

"You couldn't even keep him there in the first place!" Frida said.

She's too reckless for her own good, Addie thought. What if they decided to drag her down to the police station? Could they arrest her for obstructing their investigation or something?

The skinny cop glanced at Reg, then looked back at Frida. "Your employer gave us his word you would cooperate with us."

"All right. I'll cooperate, if Mr. Powell says so. But I ain't doing anything to get my dad in trouble."

"He's *in* trouble already, you stupid—"

"Oh, lay off. She's just a kid," the skinny cop interrupted. He turned to Frida. "Just answer the questions the best you can."

"Don't you have to show me your badges first?" Frida asked. It was bravado, but she was scared. Her voice was small.

"I'll tell you what I've got to show you—" The other cop raised his fist. Instantly, Reg stepped between him and the girl. He was very still, very calm, but his eyes locked with the policeman's, and Addie felt the electricity of the moment before a fight.

But then the skinny cop put his hand on his partner's arm, and mustache man reluctantly backed off. "This is Detective Bryant," the skinny one said, digging a badge out of his breast pocket. "I'm Sergeant Price."

"All right, then." Frida pressed her lips together.

"Is there somewhere quiet we can conduct the interview?"

"You can talk to Miss Peterson in my mother's office," Reg said evenly, though Addie could see a spark of hatred in his eyes as he took the measure of Bryant. "You'll both interview her? Or would you like me to be present?"

"You?"

"No need for that," Price said. "We'll both talk to her."

That's a relief, Addie thought. *He won't let the other guy bully her.*

"You treat her well," Reg said to Bryant. Then, reluctantly, he added, "Go back down the stairs. It's at the end of the hall on the left." Addie bit her lip, trying not to think of the old musty office where she and Whaley had unloaded the crates only the day before.

"Much obliged, sir." Price put a hand under Frida's elbow and led her away. Bryant followed. When they reached the door, he nodded to Reg. "We'll let you know when we're finished."

"Thanks." Reg shut the door behind them, then turned to Addie. "Did she give you something?"

"A key."

"Good. I wouldn't put it past them to search her. I just hope Sergeant Price can keep the gorilla on a leash." He put a hand over his mouth, thinking. Addie watched him carefully and frowned. If Frida already knew her dad had escaped, then Reg probably did, too.

"Um, Reg?"

"What?"

"Are you going to tell me what's going on?"

"No. I can't. I—" He stopped, looking apologetic. "I feel

bad enough that you've gotten dragged into this. It would just be better if you didn't know."

A thump from the stairwell made them both turn sharply toward the door.

Reg grabbed Addie's arm. The touch raised the hairs on her arm. "I need you to help me. Without any questions."

"All right."

He glanced back and listened a minute. Then he said, "You know those stairs in the right wing? By the prompt stool?"

Addie nodded.

"Go down those and through the exit on your right. There's a hallway running to the back of the building. At the end of it, there's a closet marked *Custodian*. Just make sure it's locked—it should be. But if it's not, for some crazy reason, make sure you lock it. Then come right back. Can you do that?"

"Of course," she said, baffled, and a bit nervous. "You're not kidding about all this cloak-and-dagger stuff, are you?"

Reg half smiled. "No jest, lady," he said in his Macbeth voice. He let go of her arm and brushed his hand along her sleeve. "And I apologize for rumpling your clothes."

"Mr. Powell?" It was Bryant calling up the stairs. "Can you come down here a moment?"

"Go!" Reg gave Addie a gentle push. "I mean, please."

She nodded and quickly threaded her way through the clutter of chairs, candelabra, and thrones toward the wing, letting the curtain fall behind her. Fortunately, no one was there, though she could hear the cast milling around onstage.

"Is Reg hiding away somewhere?" Meg's voice floated above the rest. "Drag him out, will you?"

Addie found the little stairway beside a carving of a falcon-headed god, and she hurried down into the side of the auditorium and stepped out into a hallway. The walls were covered with emerald velvet. Far down at the end, she saw a broom and a dustpan leaning against a door. It had to be the janitor's closet.

She walked up to the door and stopped short. Now that she was alone again, a disturbing thought struck her: What if she wasn't back in time at all, and this was just a figment of her imagination? What if she had really been alone in the theater this whole time, psychotically talking to shadows, like old Macbeth and his crazy wife?

But then Meg Turner's voice thundered through the ceiling, berating some poor actor. "You're meant to be a villain! So be a villain! You're about as menacing as a stuffed bear!"

No. It was really happening. Someone that real couldn't be a figment of her imagination. Frida was in trouble, and Reg was tangled up in it, too. And she wanted to help. It was that simple. Whatever was happening to him and Frida involved her as well. She was tied to them and had been ever since the afternoon she first saw them, coming up Salmon Bay Drive.

She put her hand on the knob and tested it. It was locked.

She turned to go, but hesitated. What was so important it had to be kept locked up like this? How was she supposed to keep a secret if she didn't know what it was?

Frowning, she pulled out the key, turned it in the lock, and opened the door.

At first, she could make out nothing in the gloom. Then she jumped as a large shape detached itself from the darkness. A man in muddy overalls emerged, his eyes fixed on her face, the whites gleaming. Stubble bristled his cheeks, and a ragged mustache hid his mouth. As her eyes adjusted, she could see grime on his face and hands. Like the homeless man she'd seen in the alley.

With a muffled cry, Addie whirled around to make a run for the stairs.

But before she could, a heavy arm encircled her waist. The man dragged her into the closet and shut the door.

14

TIMBER WAR

Addie's heart pounded. She tried to yank herself away, but the man's arms were like iron. It was a nightmare she'd had many times, ever since the day John Dorsey had grabbed her after school and shoved her up against the lockers in the empty hallway. She remembered his tongue in her ear and the pressure of his body grinding against her. That time, Whaley had heard her scream. He'd found her and bashed John Dorsey's head into the wall. Now she thrashed about, trying to free herself, to no avail. And who would come for her this time?

"Wha—!"

The man shoved his hand over her mouth. She tried to jerk away, feet scuffing the floor.

"Calm down!" he growled.

She wrenched her head to the side, but his hand slammed over her mouth again as she started to scream.

"*Var tyst!*" His breath smelled of coffee and tobacco. "I won't hurt you." Addie's eyes darted around, looking for anything she could use to defend herself. She saw a lamp casting a dim light on a low table by a threadbare couch. Nothing there. The room was cluttered with buckets and mops. A mop wouldn't be very fearsome. . . . The only option was to be quicker than him if she could wrench free. But there was only one door, and the man had shut it tight.

She summoned all the power in her lungs and yelled straight into his hand.

"*Var tyst!*" he said again, and Addie realized he sounded frightened. "Please don't scream!"

She forced herself to look up at him. His face was twitchy. Bags hung under his bloodshot eyes.

"I didn't want to frighten you." His accent bloated his vowels. "But I can't have anyone coming here. No one. Do you hear?"

"Let me go!" Addie's words were muffled by the man's palm. She lifted one foot and smashed it down on his work boot.

"Ow. Look, I'll let you loose, I swear. I got a daughter your age. If I ever saw a fella holding on ta her the way I've got you, I'd rip out his teeth with pliers."

Addie's eyes darted back to his face. Of course. That's who he was.

"Wait. Why are you here?" Then, more forcefully, he added, "Did someone send you?"

Addie nodded.

"Who? Don't shout. If it's who I think, then we

can trust each other." Gingerly, he lifted his palm from her mouth.

"Reg," Addie croaked. "Reg Powell sent me. You're Frida's dad, aren't you?"

The man let her go. In an instant, she backed away from him, all the way to the wall. Every muscle hurt, as if she'd been in a fight.

In the silence, Lady Macduff's voice floated down from the stage, confronting Macbeth's hired assassins.

"'Where is your husband?'" the murderer demanded.

"'I hope, in no place so unsanctified where such as thou mayst find him.'"

Addie eyed the man guardedly. He had dropped down on the couch and clasped his hands between his knees. Frida's dad or not, he had just escaped from jail. And he was in for murder. Keeping her eyes fixed on his face, Addie inched toward the door.

"What'd he send you down here for?"

"To make sure the closet was locked." The door was within reach now. If he made a move, she could yank it open. "Frida gave me the key because the police came. She didn't want them to find it on her." It felt reassuring to tell him the police were here. If he tried anything, she could run out the door and get them. She'd been on Frida's side when that cop was bullying her, but now she wanted the police on hers. Peterson seemed less threatening, sitting on the couch like that, but . . . had he really killed someone?

"*Police?* When?"

"They're here now."

He smoothed his mustache nervously. "What are they doing?"

"Questioning Frida."

Peterson's head jerked at a clatter from the stage above. "My girl's a match for any of those timber lackeys. She'll shriek the place down if they try anything. Like a factory whistle, that girl's lungs." His eyes darted to the door. "They fixing to search the place?"

"I don't know. I didn't hear anything about a search warrant."

"Warrant! You think they bother with warrants? It's war, like Big Bill said. Full-out war between us and the timber barons. The cops just dance to their tune."

Addie edged closer to the door, frightened by the spike of anger in his voice.

Peterson's eyes followed her. "I know what you're thinking, miss. But you're wrong. I seen the papers, just like you, where they painted us dirty killers. But you know what we were fixing to do up there in Everett? Free speech campaign." At her blank look, he said, "Talk about the eight-hour day. And those sheriff's men were waiting for us on the dock. It was them fired the first shots. Got Abe Rabinowitz in the back of the neck—back of the neck!" His voice trembled. "That's the warrant they showed us."

"You didn't shoot them?"

"Some of the fellows *returned* fire. And two of them sheriff's men went down, to five of ours, and others missing, maybe drowned. So now the rest of my pals are waiting on trial while Tom Tracy's on the stand. You and I both know there's not much hope. That's why I ran." He jerked his thumb at the ceiling. "But that boy, he's a newspaper writer. He's gonna get the word out about what really happened, turn people's minds in our favor."

Addie blinked. "Did *you* shoot them?"

"I didn't have a gun then." Peterson glanced at the rucksack that lay on the floor at his feet, then back at Addie. "That's where maybe you can help me."

She reached for the doorknob. "I can't get a gun for you!"

"I ain't asking you to." Peterson looked straight at her. "I'm asking you to get rid of the one I got."

Addie stared at him incredulously. "Get rid of—"

"You've got to. The cops can't catch me with a piece!" He crouched down and picked up his rucksack, yanked the strap from its buckle, and emptied the whole thing onto the floor. Something heavy clunked onto the cement. A second later, Peterson picked up a pistol and pressed it into her hand. "Please." He touched her shoulder. "You've got to hide it. If they catch me, tell Frida where it is. She can get rid of it after they're gone."

Addie fought the urge to drop the gun like a hot potato. Peterson could be lying. He had a gun now. Maybe he'd had it on the Everett dock, too. Maybe he really was a murderer. What then?

"Hurry!" he urged. "If they come down the stairs, they'll see you!"

She looked at him uncertainly, teetering between trust and distrust.

"Please. If you don't hide it, I'm dead. Not just a fugitive, but a fugitive with a gun."

"Why do you have it, then?"

"Holy God! Why do you think? So what happened to Abe don't happen to me." There was a trace of pleading in his eyes. "I haven't been tried! No one's found me guilty, so how can you?"

That did it. She opened the door and slipped out quickly, turning the key in the lock as she left. The gun in her hands was as cold as the cement under the thin soles of her shoes. She tried to shove it in her pocket, but it was too big, so she held it down against her skirt, rolling the fabric over it.

Then she hurried back up the steps by the falcon-headed god. The rehearsal seemed be breaking up, and, thankfully, no one noticed as she slipped through the wing and backstage.

She found Reg, back in costume, searching for something in one of the boxes. He looked up with a harassed expression. "I thought you'd come right back. What did you do? Stop off at Western Union and send a telegram? You're still on props, you know."

Addie crouched down beside him. Keeping her hand low, she pulled out the gun.

Reg drew a sharp breath. "You *stupid* girl!"

Addie ignored him and slid the pistol carefully down into the jumble of swords and daggers.

"Why not a Lewis gun, while you're at it?" He reached out, but Addie grabbed his wrist. "Leave it!" she ordered. "We don't have time to find a better place."

Reg met her eyes and yanked his hand away, then slammed the prop box shut. The first of the actors were wandering backstage now, chatting and complaining about needing a smoke or a drink.

"Didn't you hear?" Andrew caught sight of Addie. "Break time while the coppers do their job." He pulled a pipe out of his pocket.

Meg Turner burst through the curtain. "First Janie, now *this!*"

"They're looking for an escaped criminal," said the actress who played Lady Macduff. "One of the Wobblies. How exciting."

"Good luck to him, I say," Meg Turner declared.

Reg had slid up to sit on top of the box. The whole thing had obviously thrown him off balance. Andrew seemed to notice, for he kept a considering eye on him as he lit his pipe.

"We'll start again in twenty!" Meg shouted after the departing actors. "Andrew, you're timekeeper."

"Right, Madam Director."

"Take the pipe outside, would you?" Reg told Andrew. "It smells like wood pulp."

Andrew gave him an unfriendly look and shrugged. "It's *your* theater." And he drifted out after the others.

As the last actor disappeared, Reg turned to Addie. "I'm sorry. I shouldn't have dragged you into this."

"That's all right." She sat down beside him, unsure of what else to say.

He gave her a rueful smile. His dark brows stood out against his skin, drawn together in worry. "It's not your fault Peterson's a fool. What's that crazy Swede doing with a weapon?"

"He was worried he'd be shot if the police caught him." Addie paused. "Are you really writing an article about the men in prison?"

He hesitated. "Well, yes," he said after a moment, and sat up straighter. "I know what you're going to say, but there's no way so many of them can be guilty, no matter what you think of their ideas. Someone shot and killed two deputies— no one's talking about who shot first, but the prosecutors and the press aren't too particular. They just want the whole pack of them convicted. It isn't right."

"You think Peterson's telling the truth?"

"Actually, I do. But I need to talk to some other witnesses. Some of the men in jail—I think I've got an in there." He grinned fleetingly. "For God's sake, don't mention that to my mother."

Addie met his eyes, smiled, and shook her head. For a strange, silent moment, they just sat there, side by side, as if waiting for something, until the creak of the floorboards broke the spell.

Detective Bryant stepped through the curtain.

"What's this?" he demanded, pointing at the crates. Addie's mouth went dry.

Reg looked puzzled and annoyed at the same time. "Prop boxes," he said.

"I'll have a look then, if you don't mind."

"Help yourself." Reg pushed himself off the box and stood aside. "But we don't usually keep fugitives in them."

"Reg!" Addie said. The cop shot a look at her, and she put on an ingratiating smile. "He's so silly sometimes."

"Stand up," Bryant said.

"What?"

"Stand up, miss."

Addie realized she was clutching the sides of Banquo's and Macbeth's box. Flustered, she let go and got to her feet.

Bryant tipped it open, and daggers, walking sticks, and swords cascaded to the floor. Addie couldn't help jerking her head as the pistol hit the ground, half expecting it to fire on impact.

Reg's gaze flickered across her face and away again.

"What the—" Detective Bryant exclaimed. He hadn't noticed the pistol yet, but that didn't make Addie's heart beat any slower. "What's this? City arsenal?"

A shaft of light fell across the confusion of props as someone opened the stage door.

To Addie's relief, it was Mrs. Powell, flanked by a flushed and indignant Meg Turner.

"What's all this hardware for?" Bryant demanded.

"It's for *Macbeth*, a tragedy by William Shakespeare. Perhaps you've heard of it?" Meg Turner snapped. "And what do you mean by upending our props? I thought you were looking for a fugitive! What do you think your commissioner will say about this if we make a complaint?"

Bryant was down on his hands and knees, searching among the clutter. Addie's heart thumped against her ribs as he spotted the pistol and lifted it up for all to see.

"Recommend me for a promotion, prob'ly," he said. He smiled sardonically at Meg Turner. "And I do, as it happens, know the story of *Macbeth*. For one thing, I know there's no call for any of the characters to be handling a 1911 Colt semiautomatic hot off the pawnbroker's shelf."

Emma Mae stared at the pistol. "But—I've never seen that before in my life."

Meg bristled at the detective. "You put it there yourself!"

"Hush, Meg! What a ridiculous thing to say!"

"Well, Emma, what am I supposed to think? Are they so desperate to convict that—what a surprise!—a pistol conveniently turns up at my theater?" She looked about to explode.

"*My* theater, Meg," Mrs. Powell corrected.

Reg looked studiously innocent. Emma Mae's gaze lit on him and sharpened with suspicion. *Oh*, Addie thought. He hadn't told his mother about Peterson.

"Whose is this?" the detective demanded.

"Well, *I* don't know," Meg said. Emma Mae shook her head in bewilderment. Reg just shrugged.

"So none of you have the faintest idea how a loaded gun got into this theater?" Bryant looked incredulously from one of them to the other. "What if I go downstairs and get that little cook of yours? Peterson's daughter?" A sadistic gleam lit up his eyes. "I have a feeling that, with a little persuasion, she might decide to help us after all."

Addie regarded him with loathing. He really was a bully. "I know how the pistol got here," she said with sudden decision.

Everyone turned to stare at her.

"It's my friend Whaley's."

"Who?" Reg asked.

"Whaley. I told you about him." She hadn't, but it didn't matter. Reg wasn't going to contradict her. "He lives with my family. I stole it from him this morning," she continued with all the conviction she could muster. "He's always liked shooting and now he's all raring to get out and fight in the war and I can't stand it, so I just took his gun." An image of Whaley standing on the curb outside the recruitment center flashed in her head. If only it were that easy! She talked faster. "And when you asked me to do props, Mrs. Turner, I thought what a great place to dump the stupid thing—in the prop box."

"You ought to be ashamed of yourself," Bryant said, "interfering with our men-at-arms." But he looked disappointed. Addie hung her head to conceal her flash of triumph.

"Good job, Miss McNeal." Meg Turner chuckled. "I'll sign you up for the anti-militarism union."

But Mrs. Powell was livid. "Don't you realize how dangerous this is? I can't have firearms lying about! What if one of the actors picked it up and it went off?"

"I know. I'm sorry." She was right, Addie thought unhappily. It was pretty irresponsible.

"They're not *stupid*, Mother," Reg said.

"I beg to differ." Meg sniffed.

"Don't know how to shoot, more likely." Detective Bryant sneered, and his mustache nearly disappeared up his nose. "All right, miss, tell your friend he can collect this at the Twelfth Street Precinct, if he can confirm your story. And no more nonsense. You should be proud of him." He looked at Meg and said dryly, "Parting is such sweet sorrow. I'm done here, if my colleague is."

"I'm done." Sergeant Price emerged from the wing with Frida in tow. She looked all right, so Addie guessed that the interrogation hadn't been too awful. "Miss Peterson has been very forthcoming," Price added firmly. "I think we can leave her alone for a while."

Bryant considered this. "Maybe. But don't be going anywhere, will you, Miss Peterson?"

Frida opened her mouth, and then, with a glance at Price, shut it again. "No. No, I won't."

The police officers left, and when their steps grew fainter on the stairs, Addie dug the key to the janitor's closet out of her pocket and handed it to Frida. The girl slipped it back into her apron with a guilty look at Emma Mae. "Mrs. Powell," she said, "I swear, I didn't mean to—"

Emma Mae stared at her. "Mean to do what?" she cried. "I don't understand anything!"

Reg put his hand on his mother's shoulder. "It's not her fault, Ma. It's mine."

"What now, Reg?" his mother said in despair. "You've mixed yourself up in something, haven't you? Again?"

Reg looked slightly abashed. "He's here, Ma. Frida's dad. We can explain, but I guess you'd better come and meet him for yourself. You want to make the introductions, Frida?"

The girl nodded and rushed off toward her father's hiding place. Emma Mae put a hand on her chest, as if to slow her heart, and followed her without a word.

Reg caught Addie's eye, and she could tell he was ashamed of not telling Emma Mae but also sort of proud of what he'd done. It was just a quick look, but she felt as if she'd had a whole conversation with him. It was the way she felt with Whaley a lot of the time. But different, too.

Meg Turner watched them all go. "So *that's* what's been going on," she said thoughtfully. Then she turned to Addie. "And you, Miss McNeal, are a fast thinker. You're welcome to work with me anytime. But right now, you look as peaked as that poor idiot Janie. Go splash your face and comb your hair. Emma's apartment is open. Make us a pot of tea and come running back. I'll gather the troops. We've got a long night ahead of us."

"All right." She *did* want to splash her face and collect her thoughts.

"And—Addie, is it? May I call you that?" Addie nodded. Meg Turner's voice was unexpectedly kind. "I was serious when I said I could use a new assistant. If you're at liberty to work, that is."

"Oh," Addie said, surprised. No—stunned. If she'd been in her own time, it would have been a dream come true, but now . . . "Thanks," she mumbled, and turned away.

By the time she pushed open the door to the apartment, she felt cold to the bone, despite the heat still radiating from the big iron stove.

"I know when this is," she said to herself. "And I know how I got here." She went to the large sink and turned the spigot. Cold water gushed out, spattering as it hit the ceramic. "I just don't know why."

She scooped the water into her hands and drenched her face.

Suddenly she was shaking. Shaking, with the water dripping off her nose—the water that wasn't hooked up yet to run through those pipes, that hadn't been hooked up for years.

Two sheets of reality crashed together, like tectonic plates. Fear rippled through her the way the seismic wave had rippled the floorboards in her room.

Hurriedly, she pulled the silver mirror out of her pocket and focused her gaze in the glass. She had to get home.

She stared and stared. But nothing felt different. Her face in the glass was pale and splotchy. She could feel this other time, the time that wasn't her own, all around her still. It wasn't working.

Perhaps she was too drawn to it. Too pulled toward all of them. Too in love with the Jewel as it was long ago. Perhaps she had to try harder to break away.

She kept looking, focusing until her own face nearly disappeared. . . . Hoping, wishing . . .

Then, in the corner of the glass, she saw the door creak open behind her.

"Hey, girl!" It was Whaley.

Addie nearly jumped out of her skin.

It was all she could do not to drop the mirror. She slid

it back into her pocket and swung around, steadying herself with a hand on the lip of the sink.

He was carrying a jug of bleach in one hand and a sponge in the other, wrinkling his nose. "I think something may have died in that refrigerator."

"Is that what the bleach is for?" she asked faintly.

Whaley shrugged. "You asked me to come. You were going to look for photos and stuff, right? I thought I'd get rid of some of the mold while you're busy with that. Now that I think of it, maybe I'd better run around the corner and buy one of those five-gallon jugs of water." He frowned. "What are you doing in this old apartment anyway?"

"Making tea," Addie said, and then wondered why she had told him that. Because of course, there were no packets of tea to be seen. No sacks of flour on the shelves, no bowls of cherries on the counter. The window that had been covered with pale muslin was boarded up, and only thin rays of grayish light filtered through the chinks.

"How are you going to make tea without water? Didn't that guy Hank say the pipes were cracked?"

"Yeah," Addie said faintly. "I guess so."

But her face was still damp.

RAGS OF TIME

Mrs. Powell's office was piled high with the clothes and books and photos Addie had pulled out of the crates, and she sat on the floor, sifting through them bit by bit. She was trying to be organized and systematic, as if throwing herself into the work would force time to become logical and unified on one plane again, not layered and permeable.

It was a vain hope. Sorting through those old objects, stored away so long, only led her back and forth between the two different planes on which she was living. Again and again she would pause, putting down this pair of shoes, that old magazine, to gaze off into space, and the wonder and terror of what had happened would flood through her. Then she'd try to shake it off and force herself to return to her task.

Whaley had brought a radio and was listening to a news program out in the corridor as he scrubbed down the walls. She was glad for the noise. It helped distract her from what had just happened.

Words drifted in: "An American bomb has leveled a hospital and surrounding buildings in a remote village. . . ."

Addie put down a pair of cracked leather boots and listened more closely.

"Fifty-eight are confirmed dead. More than one hundred injured. An air force spokeswoman stated that the intended target was an insurgent training camp. . . ."

A small rural hospital? Addie could almost see the wards full of patients, some getting better, preparing to go home, mothers having babies. . . . All that hope and struggle, only for a misfired explosive to rip away their lives.

She'd ignored a lot of news about the old war—the one the country had been fighting for so long that she couldn't even remember when it started—and even about the buildup to this new one. But now that Whaley might enlist, that world across the ocean was suddenly real. Though it was still foggier to her than the world of the Jewel, nearly a hundred years ago.

Out in the hallway, the radio continued to report the story, and a horrible thought struck her. If a trained pilot could mistake a hospital for a military target, what about Whaley? Would he be able to tell civilians from enemy combatants? The soldiers they were fighting didn't wear uniforms, she knew that. She'd been worried about Whaley getting hurt. But what if *he* hurt an innocent person? What if he killed a civilian? It wasn't like he was known for being careful or anything.

She was glad she'd stolen his enlistment papers.

They were still in her pocket. She had to get rid of them.

Suddenly she didn't hear the radio anymore. Whaley had switched it off. She could hear his footsteps approaching.

Hurriedly piling up the photos she had assembled for Mrs. Powell, Addie carried them to the desk by the back wall. She shoved aside the old swivel chair and slid back the roll top. An old green blotting pad still covered the writing surface. She laid down the photos and pulled open the top drawer. She'd just managed to take the crumpled enlistment papers out of her pocket, stick them into the drawer, and jam it shut when Whaley came into the room.

Bleach fumes streamed in behind him. "Mrs. Powell's here."

Innocently, Addie stepped away from the desk. "Was she surprised you were cleaning the walls for her?"

"Surprised?" Becky Powell's voice drifted in from the hallway. "Delighted! Though I hate for you to work so hard when it might be love's labor lost." She stepped into the room, leaning on her cane. "Don't mind me," she added. "I'm a pessimist. It works out better that way. Hello, Addie."

"Hi, Mrs. Powell." Addie cleared a path to let her cross the room. She noticed the cherry red silk scarf Becky Powell had wrapped artfully around her partly grown-back hair, and she felt a swell of admiration. Mrs. Powell was obviously weak, and yet she had taken on this huge project. How could someone who had battled through so much be a pessimist? Addie just didn't believe it.

"Did Mrs. Turner find out anything about the historical preservation people?" Addie asked, settling down again to her spot on the floor.

"She did." A smile lit Becky Powell's drawn face as she lowered herself into the swivel chair. "And they *do* provide grants. I'm so glad you thought of that!"

Addie smiled back at her.

"You mean, like, million-dollar grants?" Whaley pulled off the rubber gloves he'd been wearing and cracked his knuckles.

"Don't do that," Addie ordered.

"Keeps my fingers supple." He sat down on the floor beside her, cracking his knuckles one by one right under her nose. She shoved him away. "Whaley! It's like nails on a chalkboard!"

Mrs. Powell laughed. "Are you sure you two aren't brother and sister?"

"Definitely not! I'm sorry he's so immature, Mrs. Powell. We've tried to train him. . . ."

Whaley put out his tongue and panted like a dog. Addie sputtered with laughter. "*Do* they give grants for millions of dollars, Mrs. Powell?"

"Sometimes." Becky Powell reached out and pulled the chain of an old glass-shaded lamp that sat on the desk. Nothing happened. "You have to present an investment plan, but I'm not worried about that."

"But that's fabulous! Isn't that what you'd hoped?"

"Sure. But they only consider buildings for which the city's granted landmark status. And to get that, we'll need good documentation of the theater's original state. Have you found anything, Addie?"

"Yes!" Addie bounced up from the floor. "See that pile on your right? It's all photos." She went over to watch as Mrs. Powell shuffled through the pictures. Whaley got up and leaned over her shoulder. "Most of them are from the seventies and eighties. But this one—" Addie pointed at a black-and-white photo that showed the façade of the Jewel lit up with glaring electric bulbs against a night sky. A throng of people streamed in past the ticket booth and through the front doors. "I think it's from the twenties—see all the dropped waists on the women's dresses? They're like the flapper dress we found."

Mrs. Powell squinted. "Drat it, I wish there was a light bulb in this lamp. My vision isn't what it used to be." She picked up the picture and held it so that its edge nearly touched her nose. "I think you're right! Are there more like this?"

"A few."

"Any interior shots?"

"Only pictures of performances, so mainly the actors. Not the architecture so much. And that's what you need, isn't it? The carvings and the proscenium and the dome and the rest of it?"

Mrs. Powell lowered the photo from in front of her eyes and examined Addie curiously. "What dome?"

Addie started. "I—uh, I just thought there might be one," she said uncomfortably. "You never know what a false ceiling conceals. Sorry. Maybe I'm confusing it with another theater. Doesn't the Neptune have one?"

"Don't think so," Whaley said.

"Well, it's an interesting thought, Addie. Very interesting. If only we could rip out that horrible ceiling! Wasn't there anything else?"

"Nothing useful." The whole time Addie had been searching through the crates, she'd hoped to find some evidence of the Jewel back in Reg and Emma Mae's time. But she hadn't found anything. "Mostly costumes. Do they count?"

Mrs. Powell shrugged. "Probably not. But you never know."

"Well, I've tried to separate them by decade, anyhow. There's some great stuff." A sudden inspiration hit her. "Hey! I know what you should do, Mrs. Powell. When the place reopens—"

"*If* it reopens."

"*When*," Addie insisted, laughing. "You should get some mannequins and display the costumes from Mrs. Turner's crates."

Whaley squatted down by a pile and pulled out a purple paisley shirt with ruffled cuffs. "What do you think, Ads? British psychedelic band?" He held it against his chest.

Addie wrinkled her nose. "You look like Syd Barrett. Don't go there, Whaley."

"Hey, you know what else, Mrs. Powell? You should have benefit concerts here. It would be a quick way to raise funds."

"You and your band would play for free, wouldn't you, Whaley?"

"Sure thing. If Rico and Cam are up for it. But I know some of the Sub Pop bands, too. Maybe I could talk a few of them into it."

Addie gazed up at the green glass over the light fixture hanging from the ceiling, envisioning the musicians on the stage, and crowds dancing in the aisles. "That's a great idea. We could have concerts leading up to the grand reopening. Tie them in to whatever the first play is going to be." The living bustle of the Jewel came rushing back to her. What would Emma Mae and Meg do if they were about to launch a new theater? She thought a minute. "Something really exciting that everyone's going to want to come and see. And there should be some big bash to celebrate."

Mrs. Powell pretended to be alarmed. "I'd *better* get that renovation grant. I don't think I dare disappoint the two of you." She turned to Addie. "Where else can we look for documentation? I've poked around at home, thinking Dave might have some family albums or scrapbooks, but no luck."

Addie frowned. She'd been through everything in the crates and in the desk already. Her gaze drifted over to the panelled walls. "I tried opening those cabinets there, but—"

"Stuck. I know." Mrs. Powell's brow furrowed. "I don't want to do more damage, but . . . maybe we should just force them open. Would you like to try, Whaley? I don't care if you bang things up a bit. The preservation people aren't going to care about the offices."

Whaley went over and yanked on the black knob on the cabinet door. It didn't budge. "You got a crowbar?" He punctuated the question with a sneeze.

"Bless you. And yes, there's one in a janitor's closet in that little hallway down the stairs on the right side of the stage. There's a door that opens to it. Do you know what I'm talking about?"

Addie's eyes widened. Peterson's hiding place.

"Sure. I found a lot of the cleaning stuff back there."

As Whaley left, the "Ride of the Valkyries" burst from the tiny leather purse Mrs. Powell had thrown onto the desk. She grinned at Addie. "Must be Margie calling." She retrieved her cell phone. "Yes? No, of course not, Margie. How can I? . . . All right, I'll spread the word." Then she glanced at Addie. "Yes, she's here. Of course I'll tell her."

She hung up. "She wanted to remind me about the demonstration against the war this Friday. As if I'm going to march across the city!" She shook her head. "I've known Marge for twenty years, and I can't believe she's never landed herself in jail. Oh, and she said to ask your dad if she can get a ride to the protest. She can't reach him. Is he likely to go?"

"Definitely," Addie said, glancing at the drawer where she had hidden the enlistment papers. "He feels pretty strongly about it. He already asked Whaley and me to cover the store and watch Zack for him."

"What, no school?"

Addie shook her head. "Nope. Professional development day for the teachers."

She went over to the cabinet and ran her hand along it. "Are you sure you want Whaley ripping this open? It's going to look pretty trashed. I can give it another try, if you like."

Mrs. Powell shrugged. "That's thoughtful of you, but I think it's been stuck for a long time. Be my guest, though."

Addie crouched down and braced herself, taking hold

of the knob and pulling. It didn't budge. She tried twisting and shaking it. Nothing. She stood up to give herself more leverage, bent over, grabbed the knob and strained back, until she felt like she was going to end up on the floor. "Geez!" She shook out her hand, which now had red streaks across the palm. "I give up."

Whaley reappeared with a crowbar in his hands. "Are you sure you want me to use this?"

Addie and Mrs. Powell looked at each other. Mrs. Powell chuckled. "Definitely. Go right ahead."

With a splintering sound, a rich stream of expletives, and a halfhearted apology to Mrs. Powell, he soon had one door ajar.

Addie went over to peer into the dusty-smelling cabinet. Piles of programs, scrapbooks, ledgers, and scripts in varying stages of decrepitude were piled on the shelves.

"Pay dirt." Whaley grinned.

"Let me see." Mrs. Powell got up from the swivel chair and hobbled over.

Addie picked up a playbill. "*The Children's Hour* by Lillian Hellman—1936!"

"We'll need something older than that. But it's a start."

They sorted through the papers excitedly. There were stacks of material from the 1980s and 1970s. But it thinned out in the 1950s, and there was even less from the '40s. "Oh, look!" Addie cried. "*Henry V* . . . Whaley, it's from 1944. Isn't that the same year Laurence Olivier made the movie we saw at the Neptune? Remember, you said it was made during the Battle of Britain or something? To boost morale?"

"Closer to D-day," Whaley said, and put on an unconvincing English accent. "'We shall fight on the beaches, we shall fight on the landing grounds, we shall fight in the fields and in the streets . . . we shall never surrender!'"

Addie rolled her eyes. "That's not Shakespeare."

"It's Winston Churchill, when his country looked like it was going to be invaded. Sometimes people actually need to fight, Addie."

We haven't been invaded, Addie wanted to tell him, and you're not Winston Churchill. But she kept her mouth shut. An argument would just get his back up. Instead, she returned to the cabinet and thumbed through every program, newspaper notice, and review while Whaley and Mrs. Powell sorted through the rest. Finally, she reached the bottom.

"Is this everything?" she demanded in frustration. "What about the other cabinet? Whaley, can you open it?"

"If Mrs. Powell says it's okay." Becky Powell nodded, hardly looking up from the old account ledger she'd found. Whaley pried open the other cabinet doors and they dove in.

The papers on this side *were* older, mainly from the 1920s. Still, it wasn't until she'd dug through a mountain of them that Addie found a leather-bound scrapbook, its corners black and soft with mold. She lifted it out and opened it gently, since the binding seemed fragile. Embossed on the outside of the book's cover in gold ink were the initials *E.M.P.*

"It's Emma Mae's."

She'd spoken softly, almost to herself, but Becky Powell looked up sharply. "Emma Mae Powell's?"

"Yes!" The wonder was quickly overtaken by excitement.

"Oh, wow, look at this. Did she run the theater all the way up until 1942?"

"Yep. Even kept it afloat throughout the Depression." Becky Powell looked off into space for a moment. "And if she could do that . . ." She shook her head wonderingly. "Let me see that when you're done, okay, Addie?"

Addie nodded, already turning the pages carefully, feeling their stiff, easily crumbled paper, brown and stained with age.

And a quarter of the way through, there it was: the program from *Macbeth*.

The small hairs rose on the back of her neck. She opened it and read: *Directed by Mrs. Margaret Turner. Starring Mr. Frederick Harrison.* Her eyes flew to the cast list to check the understudies. Reg's name wasn't there. But then she remembered that Frederick Harrison had had a professional understudy, and Reg had only taken over temporarily.

She flipped the pages. There were a few photos. Not from *Macbeth*, but from other productions. And none of them showed much of the theater's interior. She had to remind herself to keep focused on that. But she couldn't help searching for actors she would recognize, for a glimpse of Meg Turner or Emma Mae Powell, of Hettie or Andrew. Or Reg.

And as she did, that other world shifted forward in her mind. She saw Meg assembling the actors back onstage once the police had left, calling for Addie to assist her—she'd be responsible for more than props, wouldn't she? Wasn't that what Meg had implied? What would Meg think when she found Addie had simply disappeared? And Frida and Reg—

would it look as if she had abandoned them after learning their dangerous secret?

Becky Powell clicked her tongue loudly. "Oh, dear. Nothing!"

"Don't give up yet," Addie said. She forced herself back to her task. It felt so frustrating not to find even one black-and-white photo when she could still see the rich red curtains and the shining brass of the real thing. The survival of the Jewel now depended on finding evidence of the Jewel then. How ridiculous that a thin veil of time was all that separated them.

She turned another page of Emma Mae's book and stopped short. "Hey! Mrs. Powell! I think I found something."

"What is it?" Becky and Whaley crowded around to look.

It was a photo of one wing of the foyer. They could see a molded ceiling with diamonds carved into it. A mirror covered the wall behind an elegant-looking bar strangely lacking in bottles. A woman—not beautiful, but compelling, with her strong, squarish face, high cheekbones, and short, wavy hair—leaned back against it, surrounded by a lively crowd who seemed to be toasting her with cups of coffee. She was clearly the leading lady who had just made her entrance into the bar following the performance. On the bottom of the photo, someone had written *Katharine Cornell and road company at the Jewel in* The Barretts of Wimpole Street, *1933*.

Mrs. Powell whooped. "Fab-u-lous! That's exactly what we need. Katharine Cornell, no less." Addie promised herself that the first thing she'd do when she got home was look up Katharine Cornell in *A History of the Theater*. "Let me see." Mrs. Powell took the scrapbook out of Addie's hands and thumbed through it.

"Anything else?"

Mrs. Powell turned the last page. "Bah, humbug. Nothing."

"What about in one of these drawers?" Whaley asked. "I mean, I can't believe there isn't *anything.*"

He went over to the desk.

Addie leaped up off the floor and rushed over to him as he pulled open the top drawer. "Wait a second! Whaley!"

Too late. He had the enlistment papers in his hand. For a second he just stared at them in confusion. Then he straightened, folded them up, and slapped them hard against the desk. "Well, well. Looky here."

"Whaley! Listen! I don't think you know what you're getting yourself into."

He glared at her, shoving the papers into the inside pocket of his jacket. She had never seen him this angry. "And *you* know better?"

She swallowed. "No . . ." But she didn't mean it.

Whaley could hear it in her voice. The moment prickled between them.

Then he turned and stormed out.

Addie stared out the doorway at the cobwebs swaying in the wake of his departure, and her self-control crumbled. She blinked her eyes, trying to stop the tears, but they dribbled out anyway, and she swiped them away furiously.

Mrs. Powell looked at her in dismay. "What was *that* about?"

So Addie told her.

IN THE CITY

The street was lined with mud-brick houses that had been there for centuries. Their doors were closed, their windows shuttered. Vines spilled from hidden roof gardens, and the scent of flowers hung heavy in the air. Addie followed the road as it twisted this way and that. More like a labyrinth than a city. She couldn't see beyond the next turn.

Was it an address she was seeking, that she had lost? Or a person?

The sky overhead was pitiless, the heat of the sun drilling into her skin. She clung to the shadows. Now the ground was rising steeply below her feet, and ahead, she finally saw a shop with open doors. She stopped in front of it. Dusty wooden bins, which must normally have been full of food, lined the walls. Only a few papery onions and some withered peppers were left. The cash register sat open and empty.

Above the shop, on the second-floor balcony, two men in strange uniforms sat at a table. Behind them, a door stood ajar, and a light from within silhouetted their bodies. Rolls of fabric hung off the backs of their helmets to protect their necks from the sun. Their fingers traced lines on a map, and Addie knew they were officers in a long-ago war. Their words were secret. They would give her no information. As she turned away and walked past the shop, she heard a voice.

"Miss!"

She spun around, but no one was there.

"Miss!"

She looked down and saw a cellar window, its shutter broken and hanging, and behind it, in the shadows, a girl in a headscarf, beckoning frantically. "You can't stay in the street!"

From inside the building, Addie heard the crackle of a television and words she didn't understand.

"Come inside with us," the girl said. Somewhere in the cellar a child began to cry.

"Just a second!" Addie ran back to the empty store. Jagged green light cut across the sky and was gone. She looked up again at the balcony, searching for the officers. Maybe they could help. Or at least tell her what was happening. But the light was off. The men had disappeared. And she heard a sound she didn't recognize—the sound of some mechanical beast coming from the labyrinth of twisting streets.

Bullets sprayed against a wall.

She dashed inside the empty store and snatched some onions and peppers, then rushed back into the street.

"Down here!" the girl called. Addie found the door leading to her cellar and tumbled into the dark, clutching the vegetables in her hands.

Children cowered along the walls. The grownups were crowded around a television, and Addie saw the same images on the screen that she and Whaley had seen a few days ago at the Brown Bear. The girl took the vegetables from her. "A guest gift," the girl said, and Addie felt ashamed.

The sounds of the mechanical monster drew closer, so close the children all rushed to the window to stare. It seemed to Addie that their noses nearly touched the caterpillar treads of the tank. Walkie-talkies crackled. Behind the tank, soldiers advanced—modern soldiers, in camouflage, guns at the ready. The smell of unwashed bodies made her choke.

Suddenly one of the children grabbed a sad, wrinkled pepper and flung it into their midst, screaming with rage. Shrieks broke out as the soldiers spun about, raising their guns and pointing them straight into the cellar. The roar of machine gun fire filled her ears.

Addie jerked awake. She was curled into a tight ball at the bottom of her bed, her hands pressing against the side of her head, adrenaline pumping through her body.

Even when her heart stopped thumping, there was no way she could get back to sleep.

She threw on her fleece and clogs, went downstairs, and opened the back door. The cold air shocked her, but she made herself go out and circle around to the front of the bookshop to pick up the newspaper. Down the street she saw a light on at the back of the People's Grocery—Almaz's parents were stocking for the day. Then she turned to examine the progress Dad and Whaley had made on Victrola Books. The glazier had replaced the glass in one window, and they had cleared away the wood Whaley had hammered on to cover it. But the other window was still boarded up—something had been wrong with the frame. Whaley was going to fix it—what a relief it was that Dad had found repairs for him to do.

She breathed in shakily. A few repairs . . . how long would that take? A day or two? So what? It wouldn't keep him here. He had his enlistment papers back now. He could fill them out any time.

They'd been half filled out already.

More than anything, she wanted to stop him. She didn't need horrific dreams to tell her what she already knew— that war was hideous, not glorious. That Whaley might come back broken, missing an arm or a leg. With PTSD. Or not at all.

But she'd thought about it a lot. She'd been wrong to steal his papers. What if he had torn up her script for *Peer Gynt* because he knew she wouldn't get a part? He might have been right, but she wouldn't have thanked him for it. If he was determined to go, she probably couldn't—and maybe shouldn't—stop him.

She just wished there was *something* she could do. Some way to make things better.

She took the rubber band off and unrolled the newspaper. A small item caught her eye: *Traffic delays are expected on major downtown arterials due to anti-war march. Use alternate routes.*

That's right, she thought.

Dad told her there would be demonstrations all across the country. San Francisco, Chicago, Detroit, Atlanta, New York—the protests would spread from the East Coast to out here on the west. How could the government ignore that? Wasn't that what had stopped the Vietnam War? Mrs. T. had been part of that. She had always told Addie that it was the people out in the streets who had forced the war to end. *What if protesters could force the government to pull the troops out?* After all, like Dad and Mrs. T. said, people knew that the last war had been a mistake. It might not be as hard to persuade the government that this one was as well. Then it wouldn't matter if Whaley joined up or not.

She hurried around to the back of the house, went in, and ran up to the living room, flicking on the lights and cranking the thermostat. The furnace in the back of the bookstore growled, and a breath of warm air wafted from the vent by her feet.

All week, she'd heard people arguing over the war, defending the war, shrugging their shoulders and saying, *What can we do? It's started.*

Well, she wasn't going to shrug her shoulders.

She picked up the phone and called Almaz.

SOAPBOX

The old VW van was crammed with people and loaded with boxes of books from an estate sale. Dad was in front with Whaley; Zack was on Addie's lap engrossed in a graphic novel; Almaz was trying to keep Whaley's djembe drum from falling off her own lap; and Mrs. T. was squeezed in by the window with her crutches. Whaley was going to drop all of them off at Volunteer Park, where the rally was already under way.

Now and then Addie exchanged a look with Almaz and they both smiled nervously. For the first time, she was going to a demonstration, and even though she was excited, she couldn't help remembering the huge gash on Frida's head. That had happened at some sort of rally, hadn't it? At least Almaz was going with her. Of course, Dad was going too, and Mrs. Turner. But that didn't ease her feelings as much as having Almaz there. It had been such a relief to go to her house this morning and tell her about Whaley trying to join the army and what she'd decided to do about it. She wished she could have spilled everything—all the strangeness and terror of what had happened to her in the Jewel.

But of course she couldn't.

"I can't push on him anymore," she'd told Almaz. "He's really mad at me, and I guess he has a right to be."

Almaz had laughed incredulously. "Of course he has! What were you thinking, stealing his papers? But going to the demo is good. After all, Whaley isn't the only guy—or girl—who's going to get swept up in this. If you think the war is worth stopping, then it's worth showing up to say so." She'd thought for a moment then said, "I'll go, too."

The fact that Almaz wanted to come along made it easier to convince Dad to let her go. He'd wanted her to stay home with Zack but finally agreed he would take all of them as long as they kept track of Zack at all times.

"Drop us by the south entrance, near the water tower," Mrs. Turner directed as the van rattled over potholes. They were fairly near the Powells' house now, Addie thought. Just over a few blocks. . . . She forced herself to put it out of her mind and peered over Zack's shoulder as they approached the park, taking in the crumbling stone walls and tall trees and hints of movement behind the dense foliage. *The angel is just over there.* . . . "We'll join up with the march as soon as people start coming out of the gates," Mrs. T. was saying.

Whaley grunted—he hadn't been very happy with the role of driver, though Addie wasn't sure if it was because he disagreed with the protest or because he was so annoyed with her that he didn't even want to be in the same vehicle. He drove on until they could see the top of the water tower through the trees, and then he squeaked the van into an illegal parking space. Dad jumped out and slid the door open.

Zack just continued reading his book. "Zack!" Addie shoved him. "Get off me! I'm squashed!"

He stuck out his tongue and bounced fiercely. Addie shoved again, not hard enough to spill him onto the sidewalk, but strongly enough.

"Get a move on, Zack!" Almaz urged. "I can't get out of here until Addie moves her regal behind!"

"Regal behind!" Zack cackled. But he put the book down and hopped out.

"How'd it get promoted to royalty?" Addie jumped out after him.

The sunlight was golden, and the air throbbed with voices; someone was talking over a loudspeaker. Through the trees, Addie caught glimpses of the crowd inside the park, and banners rippling in the wind. Magnolia blossoms shivered on their branches, and the sweet scent of wisteria washed over her. The breeze was cool, snapping with energy, and Addie suddenly felt like she was snapping with energy, too.

Whaley jumped down from the driver's seat and came over to the sidewalk. He'd been icy all morning, but as he watched Almaz struggling to strap on the drum, he thawed. "Hey, Almaz," he stage-whispered. "How about you ditch these clowns and come jam with me and Rico? I know you can wallop that thing."

Almaz tilted her head as if considering the invitation. "You'll have to do better than that to woo me away from here. Candlelit dinner, roses . . ." But she couldn't help a pleased smile.

Zack pretended to barf.

"You don't want Whaley cooking you any candlelit dinner," Addie pointed out, "unless you want to eat the candles."

Whaley pointedly ignored her, and she looked away to hide her quick hurt. *I know I was wrong,* she felt like blurting out. *Please stop being so angry!*

"No dinners of candles or otherwise," her dad cut in. "Whaley's minding the shop."

The noise of the crowd swelled, and Addie distinctly heard a clatter of feet. The march was beginning.

"Are you going to be okay, Mrs. T.?" Whaley asked.

Mrs. Turner waved a crutch gamely. "Don't think a little sprain is going to stop me."

"All right. But call me if your ankle hurts too much. I'll come pick you up."

Addie bit her lip as she watched him slam the van door and start the engine. The first marchers burst out of Volunteer Park and began to pour onto the sidewalk and into the street. Whaley lurched the van out of the parking spot. Angry guitar riffs blasted from his radio.

Almaz followed Addie's gaze and gave her drum a bash. "Testosterone," she pronounced. "That's why men fight. They're slaves to their hormones. Women are the voices of reason."

"Tell Whaley that!"

"Don't you worry. I will."

They joined the demonstrators heading east toward Broadway under the swaying spring-green leaves, and Addie's heart lifted. There was such an energy running through the crowd. People laughing, greeting friends, chanting slogans, beating drums. What had she been worried about? It felt like a carnival. They moved past the stone mansions by the park, down onto Tenth and onward to the gaudy storefronts of Broadway. People came out of their houses to watch. A few shouted at them, but most people just gaped. Some clapped or waved.

The crowd grew thicker as people joined in. Ahead of her, Zack was holding up a sign one of the organizers had given him, and Almaz banged as loudly as she could on the djembe. Mrs. Turner limped along determinedly.

Soon they were heading into Pioneer Square. Addie glanced at the tall old buildings and felt a squeeze of longing. This whole part of town reminded her of the Jewel—not today's decrepit old theater, but the sparkling new one where the 1917 production of *Macbeth* was being mounted. These buildings had been here in Reg's time, too, she was sure of it. They were old and grime-encrusted now—taverns and bookshops across from the triangular park littered with bottles and whiskery men sleeping off their liquor. A restored streetcar trundled up the hill. She wondered if Reg had brought Frida up to Capitol Hill on it. But no. It only ran on a short track, for the tourists. . . .

She caught herself. Again, for the hundredth time, she was thinking of Reg and Frida as if she could turn the corner and run into them, as if Frida might at any minute dart out of the butcher's shop on the corner with a big roast wrapped in paper. But of course, that was ridiculous.

Then, all of a sudden, onlookers were pressing in on all sides. Shouting matches were breaking out. Shoulders crushed against hers, elbows jostled. Addie stumbled forward into Almaz.

Her friend turned and put out a hand to steady her. "You okay?"

"Yeah. But it's getting—"

"Hairy. I know."

"Have you been at a protest march before?"

"The one for immigrant rights. Remember? But I was with a big group from the East Africa Center. I didn't feel scared." Almaz paused and admitted, "I do a little, now."

Addie examined the thickening crowd ahead. Angry people on the sidewalks were shouting and shaking signs— it looked like a counterprotest.

Almaz nudged her. "See that lady over there?" Addie looked where she pointed, and her eyes met those of a slight old woman leaning on a young guy's arm—her grandson, maybe. The old lady held a picture of Martin Luther King Jr. and flashed her a peace sign. Addie sent her a grateful smile, pulled herself up tall, and pushed on. Almaz started beating the djembe again. The sounds of the crowd roared in her ears: showers of clapping and whoops from some, shouts and angry voices from others.

A guy their age was standing just a few feet away, shaking a hand-printed sign above his head that read LEAVE OUR

COUNTRY! "Traitors! You like those folks so much, you go live over there! This country is for pro-America Americans."

"Don't be stupid!" Almaz snapped. She broke away from the march and went to give him a piece of her mind. "First of all—" Addie heard her say. Of course Almaz would explain her reasoning, even to some jerk! But the guy just started yelling at her. Addie tried to reach Almaz and extricate her from the argument, but she found herself swept irresistibly forward by the current of the march.

Suddenly, a man in a baseball cap sprang into the thick of the demonstrators. He grabbed hold of a bearded guy right next to her, and hauled off and punched him.

"Hey!" Addie shouted. The bearded guy doubled over, holding his belly, and the other guy twisted his shirt around his neck, choking him. Then he slammed his fist into his face.

Furious, Addie grabbed the attacker by his shirt, trying to yank him away. He shook her roughly aside. She stumbled but managed to keep her balance.

Almaz was pushing through the crowd toward her. "Come away from here," she called. "You can't stop them."

Addie hesitated. She could see Dad far ahead, Zack clinging to his arm in a way he normally wouldn't be caught dead doing. The man in the baseball cap was still beating up the guy with the beard. Other people were trying to drag them apart, without success.

High above the heads of the crowd, she saw a mounted policeman. *Thank goodness!*

"Over here!" she cried, waving her arm above her head.

The horse plowed straight toward her. She dodged out of its way. The policeman's face was hidden behind the visor of his riot helmet, and once in range, he struck out indiscriminately with his billy club, hitting both of the men. Addie could see blood oozing from the bearded guy's head. His attacker let go of him and bent over, sucking in his breath in great gasps.

"Not the guy with the beard!" she shouted. "He didn't do anything!"

But the policeman kept striking out. The bearded man had fallen to the ground. Stunned, Addie kept yelling until she was forced to scramble out of the cop's way as he backed his horse into the crowd. The surging crush of bodies had separated her from Almaz again.

Out of the corner of her eye, she saw Dad dragging Zack away. Mrs. Turner was struggling to keep up but clearly was having trouble maneuvering.

"Mrs. T.'s in bad shape," Almaz called. "I'd better go help her."

"I'll be there in a second. I've got to tell the policeman what really happened—"

"Be quick," Almaz shouted over her shoulder. She pushed her drum to one side of her body and disappeared into the chaos.

Then someone shoved Addie so hard she flew forward and crashed to the ground. Everything spilled out of her bag. To her horror, the silver mirror skidded along the pavement and stopped just out of reach.

"Oh, no!" She lurched forward, crawling between

people's feet. After a second, she managed to grab hold of the strap of her bag. Her wallet was close by, her brush, her cell phone. Quickly she swept them back in. But where was the mirror? In a panic, she twisted her head this way and that, searching. Finally she caught sight of silver flashing here, then there, as the mirror was kicked farther and farther away. The horse's hooves clopped down close to it as the policeman tried to break out of the crowd. Lunging forward, Addie closed her fingers around the handle, pulled it close as she scrambled to her feet, and flipped it over to make sure it hadn't shattered.

Behind her in the glass she could see a tall, heavy woman standing on a wooden crate, haranguing the crowd. Her brown hair was gathered in an untidy knot, and her voice thundered like a church organ.

"Don't believe the lies they tell you," she roared. "This isn't a war for democracy! English workers and French workers are fighting German workers to fill the coffers of the banks and the war industry! American workers, will you throw away your lives to join them? We say no!"

Somewhere in the background she could hear a brass band blaring a military march.

Panicking, Addie tore her eyes away from the mirror and spun around. "Dad? Where are you?"

The street was filled with marching men in uniform. Sailors in dress whites. Soldiers in khakis and round helmets and boots. Women in white aprons with red crosses sewn on the fronts. A familiar image on a poster on a nearby street lamp sprang out at her: the yowling cat of the Wobblies,

behind bars and paired with the words CLASS-WAR PRIS-
ONERS: WE ARE IN HERE FOR YOU. YOU ARE OUT THERE
FOR US!

Suddenly, a sailor ripped the poster from the lamppost
and tore it up. A man who'd been listening to the speaker
took off after him, yelling and shaking his fist.

That other time shimmered around her, and Addie
fought against it with all her might.

She squeezed her eyes shut, closing it out.

Then, gathering her courage, she opened them again,
stared fixedly into the mirror, and saw . . . not the woman
on the soapbox, but Whaley, of all people, shoving protesters out of his path. He was only a few feet away, but the
crowd crushed in around them crazily.

"Addie! Where are you?"

She slipped the mirror into her bag and waved her arms
above her head. "I'm here!"

He turned toward her voice, and relief flooded into his
face. He reached over and grasped her hand so hard she
could feel the bones in his fingers crushing hers.

"Oh, my God, Whaley, I'm so glad to see you. I thought
you were back at the bookshop."

Whaley looked over her head, surveying the scene.
Addie's gaze followed his. The mounted policeman was gone,
but other police officers in riot gear were heading their way.
Fights were breaking out. For once, Addie was glad for
Whaley's crazy haircut and the look he got, when he was
angry, of being ready for a brawl.

"The radio said it was getting rough." His hands

clenched fiercely down on her shoulders, and he steered her ahead of him through the chaotic mass of people. "The cops are wearing riot gear, for chrissake. I'd better get you home. I'm sure that's where your dad's heading."

But the march bottled up and she and Whaley were squashed between the protestors who had stopped in front and marchers coming up from behind.

"They're blocking the road!" a girl yelled. Addie peered ahead to the intersection and into a police barricade of glittering plexiglass shields.

One officer stepped out in front of the line of riot police and spoke, his voice crackling through the megaphone: "You have exceeded the limits of the protest zone. Disperse now."

"What protest zone?" an old woman shouted. "There's no protest zone!"

"Go home now, or we will disperse you!"

"What the *hell* were you thinking, Addie McNeal, coming out into this mess?" Whaley released her shoulder and gripped her hand again, yanking her toward the sidewalk.

"I'm trying to stop the war, Whaley! *That's* what I was thinking!"

Whaley made an exasperated noise in his throat and pulled harder. But before they could break free, a wave of panic swept through the crowd.

"Someone threw a rock!"

A man tripped over Addie's foot. A woman with two children clinging to her elbowed people aside. One of the kids was wailing, and the sound was the wail of the child in

Addie's dream. Protesters surged forward, shouting, and suddenly it was like swimming against a deep current.

"You can't stop a legal demonstration!"

A resounding slap, and then a thud.

"Disperse now! This is your last warning!"

Suddenly, there was a loud report, like a gun going off. Black smoke billowed up and wafted through the crowd. Addie's eyelids burned. Her throat stung as if she'd swallowed something caustic.

"*Tear gas!*" Whaley yelled through the commotion. "Cover your eyes!"

The skin on her cheeks was blistering. Tears flowed from her stinging eyes. She pulled open her bag and jumbled through bus transfers, keys, lipstick. Finally, her fingers closed around a bandanna.

"Here!" She thrust it at Whaley through the rising fumes, but he pushed it away.

"You put it on! I'm okay!"

Addie tied it over her eyes in a single layer, so she could just manage to see through the thin fabric. Choking, they clawed their way to the sidewalk. Her heart thumped in her ears; her feet itched to sprint, but too many people blocked their way. The voice was still crackling through the megaphone. "Your time is up!"

They were caught in a tidal wave of people running, darting down the side streets, dodging into bars, barbershops, anywhere a doorway beckoned or an escape route opened up.

She spied a narrow alley between two buildings. "Whaley! This way! Over here!"

But he was gone.

She searched up and down the street as well as she could through her own tears and the red fabric of the bandanna. And then suddenly she heard Whaley's voice behind her.

"I'm not demonstrating!" She whirled around to see him spluttering with fury as a police officer pinned his arms behind his back. "I'm *enlisting*, for chrissake."

The cop was clicking handcuffs around Whaley's wrists. With the riot helmet on his head and gas mask on his face, he looked like an insect. But he was even taller than Whaley and had a huge club and a gun hanging from his belt.

"I'm not protesting!" Whaley repeated.

"He's not!" Addie shouted.

The faceless officer ignored them. To Addie's horror, he simply swung Whaley around and frog-marched him up the block.

Then another cloud of tear gas exploded and she could see nothing at all.

LOCKUP

"Sorry, I didn't see you there." The woman at the sink in the bathroom of the doughnut shop looked up at Addie. She had short black hair in a jagged cut and was wearing a plaid flannel shirt. Her eyes were bloodshot, the skin puffy and damaged around the lids. "Here. I'm almost done."

Addie nodded numbly. The woman moved aside, and Addie took her place, turning the spigot and splashing cold water into her stinging eyes. It was hard not to blink, but she knew she had to wash out the chemicals.

She'd kept running once she'd broken free of the crowd and finally ended up in this skeevy doughnut shop where a bunch of people from the demonstration had taken shelter. There'd been no sign of Dad or the others. More than anything, she wanted to go home. But she couldn't. She was the only one who knew what happened to Whaley, and she had to help him. After all, if it hadn't been for her, he'd be free right now.

The woman who had spoken to her was wiping her face with a paper towel. "Are you okay?"

Addie nodded. "But my friend was arrested, so I probably need to get over to the jail."

"Unless he's in juvie. How old is he? Your age?"

"He just turned eighteen."

"He'll be at the jail, then. Do you know where it is?"

"On Third, right?"

A woman with long gray hair and lots of beads around her neck emerged from a stall. "No, darlin'. Fifth and Jefferson. Near the courthouse. Your friend'll be in the lockup."

Addie tried to marshal her thoughts. "So I go there first? Or do I—"

"You go to the courthouse first." The older woman examined Addie sympathetically. "Is this your first time, sweetheart?"

"Yes." To her embarrassment, she found herself tearing up. "My eyes still hurt," she muttered.

"It's okay." The old lady patted her shoulder.

Somehow, the touch put heart into her. Addie pulled herself together and said, "Thanks. I'll—I'll get down to the courthouse." She left the bathroom and crossed the shop, ignoring the unfriendly gaze of the guy wearing the little paper hat behind the counter.

Outside, the sky had gone overcast, the air damp and chill; all the promise of the glorious morning was gone. In the distance she could hear sirens and people still shouting slogans. She pulled out her phone and called Dad. It rang a few times and then went to his voice mail. Addie opened her mouth to explain everything, and then thought better of it. "It's Addie," she said. "I'm all right. Just call me, okay?"

Now she was passing the jail. For a second, she stopped and gazed up at the ugly building with its long black windows like suspicious eyes. In the small courtyard out front, weird sculptures of blocks and cones were strewn about like dismal children's toys. Reg's voice echoed in her memory: *I bet you're wondering what a gentleman like me was doing at such a sordid scene.* How could he joke about it? It wasn't sordid; it was terrifying. Whaley was locked up in one of those cells. And who knew who was in there with him. Robbers? Sex offenders? Murderers?

She sprinted across the street to the courthouse. A line of anxious people snaked out the door and down the steps. It took ages before she was finally inside.

"Whatcha want?" The woman behind the security desk looked at Addie as if she were some kind of rodent. Addie took in her dyed orange hair and the wad of pink gum she was chewing. Her desk was next to one of those metal-detector machines like they had at the airport, and two security guards stood waiting on the other side of it.

"I . . . I think my friend is in jail. But it's all a mistake. He wasn't even demonstrating. He—"

"Wha's his name?" The woman snapped her gum.

"Whaley Price."

The woman tapped at her computer. "I got a Price here," she said. "They booked him at four thirty."

"How . . . what do I do? To get him out?"

The woman gave her a bored look. "Unless you're gonna smuggle in a file in a cake, you better find out what bail they posted."

"Where do I go?" She pulled her cell phone out of her bag. She'd better try Dad again now that she knew something.

"Upstairs. Just follow the crowd. But you're not going anywhere unless you turn that thing off," the woman said severely. "Can't you read?" She pointed to a sign that said NO CELL PHONE USE IN COURTHOUSE.

"Can I—just make a call first?"

"If you wanna hold up the whole line." Flustered, Addie looked back over her shoulder. There were a lot of people behind her. She turned her phone off, shoved it back in her bag, and put the bag on the machine's conveyor belt before walking through the metal detector.

The elevator was jammed with people. A woman with patchouli wafting out of her hair was yakking away. "I told him to make them read him his Miranda rights. Why'd he go along? How many times did I tell him, George?"

Addie stepped out into the hallway and went from there into a huge waiting room overflowing with people from the demonstration. "How do I find out about my friend's bail?" Addie asked the nearest person, an old man in a knit vest.

"You have to talk to the gentleman at the desk," he told her. "We're all waiting our turns."

She sighed and went to the back of the line.

"Price?" the guy at the desk repeated forty minutes later

when Addie finally reached him. He didn't even look up from his computer screen. Addie had the feeling he'd gotten fed up with the entire human race ages ago. "What did you say his first name was?"

"Whaley."

"I got a W. P. Price. That him?"

Addie thought of the initials on Whaley's guitar case: W.P.P. "Yeah."

"Two thousand dollars."

Addie's mouth fell open.

"They take cards, cash, or a check."

It wasn't even worth looking in her wallet. *Two thousand dollars?* If she had twenty, that would be a lot.

"What if I don't have enough money?"

"There's a bail bond agency around the corner. You pay ten percent, they put up the rest. Next!"

Addie stared. *Bail bond agency?* Images of muscled bounty hunters sprang into her mind. Didn't they come and beat you up if you couldn't pay? No. She wasn't going there. She needed Dad, that was all there was to it.

Nervously, she glanced at the clock on the wall. Geez, look how long it had been already. She needed to let Whaley know she was here.

She hurried back downstairs, left the building, and turned her phone on. There was a message. Thank goodness! But when she listened, it turned out to be from Almaz, just saying she was home and was Addie okay? It was tempting to call her right back, but Dad was the one she had to get ahold of. She punched in the speed dial number. But once more, his phone was off. "Dad, it's me again. Call as soon as you can." She tried home, but no one was there, either.

The clock on the building across the street read 6:49. What if there was a cutoff time? Maybe they didn't let people out of jail after seven or something. She thought for a minute. She could head to the nearest Wells Fargo. She had a bank account but there wasn't anything remotely like two thousand bucks in it. Not since she'd paid for drama camp. Forget it. She just had to find Dad. He was probably on his way home. It would take half an hour by bus if she caught one right away.

All right, she thought. *But I have to get word to Whaley before I go.*

With a sudden decisiveness, she turned and headed back toward the jail.

As she reached the steps, her phone rang. "Addie! Thank goodness." Mrs. T. was on the other end. "Your phone was off."

"Mrs. T.! Why didn't you leave a message? I can't get ahold of anyone!"

There was a pause. "Now Addie, just promise me you won't panic."

"Why? Don't panic about what?"

"We're at Swedish. We can't have cell phones on. A doctor just finally looked at me, so I wheeled myself outside to call you."

"Wheeled yourself! You're in a wheelchair?"

"Don't worry. I just put too much strain on my ankle. It's not life-threatening."

"So Dad and Zack are there because they took you to the hospital?"

There was another pause. "No. They came because of Zack."

"Zack?" Her breathing tightened. "Is he okay?" Frida's unconscious face with the huge gash across her forehead flashed into her mind.

"He had a reaction to the tear gas. They're still in with the ER doctors."

"But is he okay?"

"The nurse said he'll be fine once they've treated him, but that's all I know. Listen, Addie, where are you?"

It was all she could do not to start laughing hysterically; everything was such an incredible mess. "I'm at the King County jail, Mrs. T. I need to bail Whaley out. He came to rescue me, and now I need to bail him out and I don't have any money. I mean, I have thirteen dollars. Could you tell my dad to come?"

"He can't leave Zack right now, Addie."

"Can you come? Dad could give you the money and—"

"Oh, sweetheart! I can't drive! But, listen—I'll think of something, I promise. Where are you?"

"Outside the jail. I'm going in to see about Whaley. I'll be in the waiting room, if they have one."

"Okay. Just sit tight. I promise, one way or another, someone will come."

Drawing in a deep breath, Addie ran up the stairs and pushed her way through the doors. It was crowded here, too, and there was another wait to go through security. She recognized some of the people from the courthouse. One or two of them nodded at her or shook their heads sympathetically.

Once through the metal detectors, she entered a large room. Reflections of the buzzing ceiling lights skidded greasily on the yellow linoleum floors. People paced nervously, and cops kept bringing in handcuffed prisoners. To the left was a crowded waiting area with rows of plastic seats. Cashier's desks were spaced along the far wall, with more lines of people stretching up to them.

How could she contact Whaley? Addie drifted over toward the cashiers, but something in her balked at standing for ages in another line, especially when it was just to pay—which she couldn't do—and they probably wouldn't help her get a message to Whaley anyhow. There had to be a quicker way. She looked around for someone to ask, but everyone, from the security guards to the people selling snacks at a kiosk, looked incredibly busy. Down the hall, she saw ranks of elevators, and just past them, another corridor. She wandered over in that direction.

A cop was leading a handcuffed prisoner down the hallway. A young guy, eyes puffy from tear gas. Addie overheard him ask, "Are these the holding cells?" The cop nodded before opening the heavy door at the end of the corridor. Raucous voices spilled out and were swallowed up again as the door shut behind them.

Holding cells. That must be the lockup, Addie thought. *That's where Whaley is.*

An idea began to form in her head. Probably no one would notice if she slipped down there, just for a moment.

As long as she was quick. Addie shrugged aside her uneasiness. Checking to see if any of the guards were watching, she darted swiftly down the hall.

She pressed her ear to the door, straining to listen as hard as she could. There was no way to tell for sure, because the door distorted the sound, and so many people were talking. . . .

But then she heard a muffled yet unmistakable scratchy tenor singing something. Singing! She almost laughed. That maniac. Singing in a jail cell.

"Whaley!" She thumped her palms against the door.

The singing stopped. Could he hear her?

"Whaley! It's Addie! I'm going to get you out!"

"Hey! What do you think you're doing?" Someone yanked her arm and twisted it behind her back. She jerked her head around and saw an enormous police officer with a gun strapped to his belt. He swung her around and marched her back up the corridor. "You think just anyone can go up there and interfere with the prisoners?"

At first she was so shocked she just let herself be pulled along, but once she got control of her feet, she tried to set her own pace. It didn't work. The guy was so humongous, it was like fighting gravity.

"I . . . was trying to let my friend know I was here—"

"Oh, yeah?" He dumped her into one of the plastic chairs that lined the wall. "I can just throw you outta here, you know that, don't you?"

Every muscle in her body clenched. She tried to speak, but no words came out.

"No more trouble from you or you're out on the street, you understand?"

Addie just stared up at the mountain of blue uniform.

"Do . . . you . . . understand?" he bent down, emphasizing each word.

She nodded, her head bouncing on her neck like a bobble-head toy's. "I understand," she whispered.

"Good." He turned away, and her heart thumped. She watched his broad back and the fold of flab on his neck as he receded toward the holding cells.

For a long time, she hardly dared move. She just sat in the chair where he'd left her, seething with anger at the cop. But also at herself. He was right. Of course it had been a stupid thing to do. This was a jail, for Pete's sake. You didn't run up and pound on locked doors. What had she been thinking?

The clock on the wall ticked loudly, and she could have sworn that there was progressively more time between each tick, until the minute hand was practically not moving at all.

Seven thirty. Seven forty-five.

The wait stretched on like saltwater taffy. Her anger seeped away and became a dull shame and then an even duller resignation. Finally, her head started to droop. She rested it awkwardly on her shoulder and closed her eyes.

Then she heard a door creak on its hinges—it sounded like it was near the elevators. Vaguely, in the velvety blackness into which she'd sunk, this disturbed her.

A voice said, "You sure you want to see these fellas? Rough bunch, I gotta warn you. No manners."

Addie forced herself to lift her heavy eyelids. It was darker now. Much darker. They'd turned off those ugly fluorescent lights, she thought.

But then she saw Reg emerging from an alcove at the end of the hall, a police officer at his side, and she knew there were no fluorescent lights to turn off. *Reg,* she thought drowsily, and felt a stab of happiness. What's he doing here?

"That's all right," he was saying to the cop. "I suppose a lot of other fellows have interviewed them already?"

"Not many," the policeman answered. He had light brown hair and a droopy mustache.

Addie jerked herself upright. "Reg!"

But he didn't react to her voice. She saw him pull a notepad from the breast pocket of his jacket and then look around, frowning, as if he could feel someone watching. Addie knew he must be going to interview Peterson's friends in jail. Her heart expanded in her chest as she watched him wait for the warden to turn an enormous iron key in the lock of the door. If only he could see or hear her.

But he stepped through the door and was gone.

"Addie?" A hand was shaking her gently by the shoulder.

"Ow!" Addie opened her eyes and saw Becky Powell's concerned face hovering over her. The scarf around her head was black today, and she was wearing very thick but still fashionable glasses.

"Are you hurt?"

"Just a bruise," Addie mumbled. And then, shaking off the last shreds of the dream, she sat upright. "What are you doing here, Mrs. Powell?"

"Margie asked me to come."

"But—you're not well. Couldn't she—"

"No. She couldn't," Mrs. Powell said dryly. "We took a quick pulse check and decided that, for once, mine was stronger. So I've paid Whaley's bail. They'll bring him out soon." Mrs. Powell lowered herself into the chair next to Addie, leaning her walking stick against the wall.

"*You* paid it!" Addie burst out. "But—but—I didn't mean for you to pay it! Oh, Mrs. Powell, I'm sorry. I thought Mrs. T. would come. Or Dad." She looked into Becky Powell's drawn face. The shadows under her eyes were dark enough to be visible even through the distorting lenses. "You don't feel well, do you?"

"My doctor says it's good for me to walk. And I need to adjust to driving again. Even at night." She laid a hand on Addie's wrist. "You didn't think I was going to leave you and Whaley here, did you?"

Down at the end of the hall, a policeman opened the door leading to the cells, and a swell of singing surged out, many voices together. It was "The Battle of New Orleans," a song Whaley had taught Zack. The two of them had driven her crazy with it.

Someone whooped and Addie could hear Whaley's voice leading the chorus: "Down the Mississippi to the Gulf of Mexico!"

Mrs. Powell arched an eyebrow. "Not really appropriate for that bunch of peaceniks, is it?"

Addie broke up laughing as they heard Whaley's voice

lurch into the second stanza. "What'd you expect? 'Kumbaya'? This is Whaley we're talking about."

"Pipe down in there!" the policeman at the door shouted. "Who's Whaley Price?"

"That's me, Mein Führer!" A ripple of laughter ran around the cell.

"Don't push it, boy."

"Did I get a candygram?" Whaley asked.

"You got out of my hair, that's what you got." The door swung closed as the policeman entered the cells. A minute later, a muffled cheer went up from inside as it opened again.

And then Whaley was coming down the hall behind the officer. He grinned when he saw Addie and Mrs. Powell waiting for him.

Addie sprang forward and threw her arms around him. "Whaley, I'm so, so sorry."

"Sorry? What are you sorry for?" Whaley hugged her back and then pulled away, rubbing his wrists. There were marks on them where the handcuffs had been.

"It's my fault. You wouldn't be here if it weren't for me."

"Don't be silly. It's not you that put me in here. It's those *fascist cops!*" Addie flinched, half expecting someone to come and drag Whaley back to the cell. "No way is it you, Addie." He turned to Mrs. Powell, and his cocky expression disappeared. "You bailed me out, didn't you, Mrs. Powell?"

"It's all right, Whaley."

Whaley grasped her small hands and held them between his red, calloused ones. "Thank you. I never expected—"

"It's all right," she said again.

"No. No, it's not," he insisted. "I'm going to pay you back, Mrs. Powell. I swear."

Mrs. Powell's mouth quirked into a half smile. "It's just a loan, Whaley. Besides, I'll get it back when you show up for trial. You don't owe me anything."

Whaley straightened his back. "Yes, I do," he said. "I'm going to help rebuild that place for you." He held up his hand to ward off her protests. "No, I am. Anything you need, that's what I'm going to do."

For the first time since the tear gas, Addie felt a small glimmer of hope.

ENTRANCES AND EXITS

Hope is a weird thing. It's a thin melody that flickers through you, disappearing and reappearing like a moth at twilight. Addie felt it when she got up Saturday morning and Dad told her Whaley had gone to the hardware store to pick up some wood finish Mrs. Powell had ordered for the Jewel.

She was superstitious, though. If she even *thought* about what she hoped for, she was convinced it wouldn't happen. So every time the moth fluttered its wings, she looked away, telling herself that nothing was there.

But then Almaz called and she found herself blurting out everything anyway.

"I'm with you," Almaz said. "If you think he might give up on the army to stick around and renovate that theater, fine. But if you need me to saw off his legs to get him to stay, I'm up for that, too."

"He'd go over on his stumps. I think he needs something to stay *for.*"

They said goodbye, and Addie went to the kitchen to make pancakes for Zacky. His eyes still looked terrible from the tear gas. He leaned against her side, watching the golden circles of batter bubble on the griddle. She drew him to her and squeezed. They could hear Dad on the phone with Mrs. Turner, arranging to pick up groceries for her so she could stay at home and rest her ankle.

After breakfast, Addie went to her room and took out the old photo she'd found the night she discovered the hidden closet.

She'd looked at it over and over again since that day in the Jewel, comparing it with what she'd seen in Reg and Meg's time. Was it really the Jewel? It was hard to tell. She couldn't catch a glimpse of any specific thing to confirm it, couldn't see the brass heating grate above the orchestra pit or the Egyptian carvings on the walls. She couldn't see the actors' faces clearly behind the masks. But it *felt* right.

She closed her eyes, and immediately the Jewel came to life around her. She smelled the sweet curranty smell of Frida's scones, heard Meg clapping her hands imperiously to summon the cast. What had they all thought when she'd disappeared? Was Meg angry? What did Reg do? Surely they would wonder why she had been gone so long. And Reg—she saw him again as she had in the jail and remembered the dismay she felt when she wasn't able to speak to him. But that had been a dream. She was sure of it. As real and immediate and uncanny as the other dreams that had started to trouble her sleep.

"Addie!" Dad called from downstairs. "Whaley's on the phone. He says can you get his camera and bring it to the theater."

Carefully, she slid the photo back into the book. "Tell him I'll be there in twenty minutes."

Whaley trusted her again, she thought. He must. Asking her to search for his camera in his bedroom was as good as saying he forgave her for stealing the enlistment papers. Happiness swelled inside her and she bounced up the steps to his attic room two at a time.

When she got to the theater, she found him in the lobby rubbing foul-smelling wood filler into the scratches on the surface of the grand mahogany bar, gently scraping off the excess.

"Brought the camera," Addie said, waving it in the air.

In his ripped Muddy Waters T-shirt, he looked somehow wirier and more like he was running on fumes than he usually did. But she could tell he was genuinely glad to see her.

Addie flopped down onto the single barstool in front of the bar.

"Hey there, Natasha de Vil. I was thinking you could take pictures of the inside of the theater. We can match them up with any other old photos we find, you know? Like the 'Now and Then' section in the Sunday paper," he said.

"That's a good idea." Addie hesitated. She was so excited

by the thought that maybe Whaley would stay here and help rebuild the Jewel for Mrs. Powell instead of joining the army that she was tempted to push him on it. But she didn't. There was no point trying to force Whaley into anything. She realized that now. She also realized that he had a debt to Mrs. Powell. A pretty serious one. Addie suspected that Mrs. Powell had covered the whole of his bail, not just the 10 percent. And Whaley took debts seriously. Still, she wasn't going to say anything.

So she just told him, "I'll get started," and headed into the auditorium. She began in the back and worked her way around, taking pictures of the arcades, the false ceiling, and the walls where the murals from Reg's time were all white-washed over. Somewhere, buried under layers of paint and dust, warm colors must still pulse like living things. Just as somewhere underneath all the decay, the Jewel of the past was still alive. For a moment, she stood still, listening intently, drawing in the smell of the place, as if an echo or a scent might waft to her out of that distant past.

A creak came from the foyer. That was all.

And yet, she thought, *I could shift away all these layers of time. I could see them all again.* Longing flared in her, and she had a sudden giddy thought: *Why not?* Take the camera and snap the pictures for Whaley—but in the past! The whole problem would be solved, and she'd see Reg and the others again. . . .

It took only a second for her to see why this would never work. For one thing, how could she possibly explain photos from 1917 in bright color, stored on a memory chip? She nearly laughed at herself. She'd just stick to what Whaley had asked her to do.

From the stage she snapped shots of the orchestra and balcony. Then she headed down to the lower level where the offices and dressing rooms were. The wardrobe shop still had clothes racks in it and an ancient sewing machine tucked away in the corner. She found the room where the sets were constructed and snapped a few more pictures. The place was huge, much bigger than she'd realized. Fixing it up was going to take a lot of effort.

Finally, she ended up back in the lobby.

Whaley was rubbing wax into the front of the bar now. Behind him, a huge mirror speckled with gray age spots took up most of the wall. Three shelves where bottles of wine and bright-colored liqueurs once must have stood rested against it. Addie imagined how the bartender's back and the theatergoers in their evening dress must have been reflected there. She walked behind the bar, licked her finger, and rubbed at the silvery discolorations in the glass.

"I wonder if there's any way to clean this off."

But Whaley was lost in thought and didn't answer

She examined herself in the big mirror, imagining how she would look decked out in a sleek evening gown surrounded by admiring fans, like Katharine Cornell on her West Coast tour. She could almost hear the tinkle of glasses, the light ripples of laughter, the appreciative applause; could imagine the fun of staying up to get the early editions of the papers to read the glowing reviews.

But then the image melted away.

And all of a sudden, she wasn't sure that was what she wanted after all. It was just a fantasy, wasn't it, all that glamour and adulation? And this place was so real.

Somehow, the Jewel had transformed that dream of stardom into something that rang a little hollow. That moment at the *Macbeth* rehearsal, when Reg was performing, flickered into her mind. She felt a pang, remembering the sudden knowledge of what her talent was compared to his. But it didn't upset her so much. It was more as if she had simply come to see something more clearly . . . that perhaps her dream was the wrong dream in the first place.

But then, what was the right one?

"Whaley?"

"Mmm."

She slid onto the barstool. "What would you do if you owned a place like this?"

Whaley's hand slowed a moment. "Fix it up, just like Mrs. Powell is." He stopped and gently ran his fingers along the bar. "It's one of the only things I'm good at."

"You're good at a lot of things!"

He gave a mirthless laugh. "Good at getting in trouble—"

Addie ignored this. "Music, for a start."

He just shrugged.

"*Whaley!* Can't you imagine yourself performing in a theater like this? Can't you picture it? People dancing in the aisles?" As she spoke, she could almost see the future rising into view, just on the rim of vision. She saw the place rebuilt. Whaley, Cam, and Rico up on stage. Lights. Music . . .

For a moment his eyes lit up. Then a closed-down expression came over his face. "Naw. I imagine myself playing in the bus tunnel with a hat to throw quarters in." He hunched back over his work. Addie could see the knobs of his spine through his T-shirt.

"Come on, Whaley," she said gently. "You're the best guitarist I've ever heard. Don't you think you'll be more successful than that? *I* think you will!" He just shrugged again. "Besides, aren't you going to do a benefit here once it's fixed up?"

Now he did turn and meet her eyes. "After what Mrs. Powell did for me? Of course I will."

"So, there. Already you'd be doing better than busking."

"What's so bad about busking? You can play good music anywhere. Same with theater, right? You don't need a fancy venue like this. Remember those plays we saw in the parks?"

"Sure, but . . . you *can* do plays outside a theater, obviously, but—" She paused to put her thoughts in order. "But a place like this . . ." She found herself suddenly totally inarticulate as she struggled to express what moved her about the Jewel. It was so important to make him understand. "I mean, yes, you can do it in a park, like that production of *Cymbeline* we saw. Or in your backyard."

She cast her eyes around the room, as if the words she needed would suddenly spring out from behind the bar.

She had to convey this to him! This feeling she had that every inch of this place teemed with life, the lives of so many people in so many layers of time, their struggles and their failures and their triumphs. You couldn't find that just anywhere. "But drama is a living thing. It's the performers and the directors and the magic they make working together—and the audience, too. It needs a place to grow." She stopped, shaking her hands in the air in frustration. Then it came to her. "It needs a home."

"Don't we all," Whaley said softly, and turned back to the mahogany.

Addie watched his arm moving round in patient circles, restoring the wood, and felt suddenly timid, not wanting to push, not wanting to kill the little moth of hope that was once again flittering within sight. "Whaley?" She was almost holding her breath. "How long do you think you'll help out with the renovation here?"

He shrugged. "Until I've worked enough to pay Mrs. Powell back." Suddenly his voice warmed. "I'd like to, too. No offense to your dad, but working in a bookstore is kinda dull compared to bringing a wreck like this back to life. But"—he twisted around to her again—"I guess how long I work depends on whether we find any old pictures to match up with those shots you're taking. Otherwise, Mrs. Powell won't be able to renovate anyway. But if she does, sure, I'll stick around for a while."

"What if we don't find anything?" It slipped out before she could stop herself. She grimaced, feeling as if she had struck a match and invited the moth to immolate itself.

"The army, for sure." He narrowed his eyes at her. "Now that I've got my papers back."

Zap! The moth flew straight into the hot center of the flame.

Addie turned quickly and hopped off the barstool. "Well, I'd better finish up these shots." She hurried back into the auditorium.

She *had* to make sure Mrs. Powell got the information she needed to get the place declared a landmark. She had to. But as far as she could see, there was nothing here to help them.

Unless . . .

She hesitated only a second. Then she marched back down the aisles and up onto the stage. She crossed it, plunged backstage, ran down the stairs and into the back hallway.

Her heart was racing as she entered the office and scanned the mess she and Whaley and Mrs. Powell had left there just a few days ago. Costumes were heaped everywhere. She knew there was a pile here of the oldest clothes she'd sorted out—where was it?

Ah, there. She went and knelt by a mound of clothes on the love seat. But as she reached out to pick up the top garment, she stopped. These weren't the clothes that Mrs. Turner had given her. They belonged to the Jewel. Should she really be wearing them? What if she ripped something?

Well, a dress can be sewn back together, she thought. But if she didn't do something right now, the Jewel might never be restored. And then Whaley would leave, and then who knew what would happen.

Hurriedly, she began searching through the jackets and trousers and vests, picking up, inspecting, and rejecting, until finally she found herself a dress. She peeled off her sweatshirt and her T-shirt. Then she wriggled out of her jeans and tossed them into the corner.

The dress crinkled and breathed as she shook it out and pulled it over her head: a pale, tea-colored dress of soft linen, with a square neck. Seed pearls were sewn into the yoke, and the sleeves ended halfway down her forearms. The skirt was straight, but then fanned out and swished at midcalf.

Once she had it on, she picked up her sweatshirt and took the mirror out of its zippered pocket. Holding it carefully at arm's length, she set it on Emma Mae's desk, face-down.

And now she started to feel nervous. Despite the damp spring chill seeping through the walls, sweat was trickling down her sides.

The dust in the air seemed to shimmer. She sat heavily in the chair, trying to psych herself up, like a diver standing at the edge of a cold, cold lake. Once you plunged into that water, what if you never came up again?

Fear rippled through her for a moment. But then, slowly, she reached for the mirror.

Trembling slightly, she held it up, hesitating to turn it over, like a solider about to throw a grenade for the first time. Then, deliberately, she brought it closer to her face and looked in. And for a flickering moment, she thought of Reg and realized there was something that scared her even more than diving back into his time.

It was looking into the mirror and seeing that nothing had changed at all. Because then she would never see him again.

The moment stretched, suspended like a bridge over a raging river. She could feel herself set foot on that bridge and step out into cold fog, icy uncertainty. It was as if she could hear the rush of passing decades clashing against one another and breaking on the rocks below. Her throat closed up.

And then she became aware of a whiff of heavy fragrance. Not the choking patchouli she'd smelled in the elevator at the courthouse. Something more complex, and elegant.

Behind her, in the glass, she caught a glimpse of a gray smoky scarf and the edge of a jade green blouse.

Nerving herself, she turned around.

Across the room, a woman stood in the doorway, her hand on the doorknob.

"My God, you frightened me!" Meg Turner said.

REAL TROLL LAND

"**W**hat are you doing here?" The director was gaping at her as she crossed the room. For a moment, Addie was afraid she had simply materialized in front of Meg Turner, like someone in a cheesy sci-fi show.

"I . . . uh . . ." Quickly, she palmed the mirror and slipped it into her pocket. Then she jumped out of the chair. "I was looking for you." It was the best she could come up with.

"Here? But this is Emma Mae's office." Meg's green eyes narrowed suspiciously. "Mine is down the hall. Why were you looking for me here?"

"I didn't know whose office it was," Addie began, but then remembered that the names were on the doors. Hurriedly she amended, "I was just looking for you. You said to drop by sometime—that you might need an assistant?"

Meg put her hands on her hips. "As I recall, I said that,

and then—hey, presto!—you were gone like the magician's assistant."

Oh, dear. What excuse could she give? She thought quickly. The gun. The police. "My friend came looking for me. About the gun. And then there was an uproar at home. I'm so sorry. I didn't mean to just leave like that—"

To her relief, the director's face cleared. "That's right. Has your friend enlisted after all?"

"Not yet." It felt odd to have this conversation—talking about Whaley with Meg Turner! "But he still wants to. And I keep having these bad dreams about it."

"Dreams?" Meg looked as if she was about to say something but then thought better of it. "Well, if you think he might be open to persuasion, there's a woman I know who speaks around town against enlistment. Louise Olivereau. She and Kate Sadler. You've probably heard of them. If you can get him to listen to one of their speeches, it might convince him." She began rummaging through the pile of papers on the desk—the very same desk that sat in the middle of the office of the present-day Jewel. "There should be a score here. . . . Not that I know if we'll even use it, but I wish I'd asked Emma Mae where she put it. Ah, here it is!" The director lifted a crisp white sheaf of papers lined with bars and musical notes. She began flipping through it. "Now," she said, "about your question, Miss McNeal."

Addie blinked. "My question?"

"About working as my assistant? Real assistant this time,

not prop girl. Do you want to show me what you can do?" Meg glanced at her watch. "This is your chance. I've got time to observe you a bit."

"I . . . uh . . ." Now? Was there any way she could be less ready for this?

Meg leaned back against the desk, examining her appraisingly. "You seem hesitant."

Addie took a breath and, with conscious decision, threw herself into this new reality. "Of—of course," she stammered. "I'd love to. Is it still *Ma*—the Scottish play?"

"*Macbeth*, you mean? Don't even mention that cursed thing! Everything is going wrong, and opening night less than a week away! We've had pretty sparse audiences for previews. Not to mention advance sales are sluggish. We need publicity." She threw up her hands. "Sorry. The short answer is *no*. Mercifully, the cast of *Macbeth* won't be coming in until early evening. With our new stage manager, thank goodness! Right now, I'm fooling around with a new project, with some of the actors helping me. In exchange for food, of course. Lesson one: Actors will do anything for a good meal." She laughed. "Oh, don't look like that! You make me feel like a wicked witch trying to lure you into my gingerbread house. This is extremely informal. Do you want to give it a try or not?"

"Sure." Addie gulped. "I mean, yes. I'll . . . I'll try to help you."

"Come on, then. Into the dragon's lair."

Carrying the score, Meg led her out of the office

and up the stairs. Addie dragged behind a bit, feeling apprehensive.

What if I'm nothing special, even as Meg's assistant? The memory of the *Short Takes* audition still stung. These were professional actors. Addie glanced at the slender but sturdy figure ahead of her. What would Meg's scorn be like if she said or did something naïve? She was so inexperienced.

The voices of the actors rang out as she and Meg emerged into the wings. Addie peeked through the curtains. A few actors in their street clothes were reading through lines, scripts in hand. The stage was warm and buzzing with a relaxed energy, nothing like the tension of the *Macbeth* rehearsal.

"Come on. This way," Meg said. Addie followed her down the steps and into the orchestra.

Instantly, her heart beat faster. It was like a jolt of caffeine: the stage lights, the smell of sawdust, the voices projecting against the back walls. The gorgeous colors in the auditorium, Isis and Osiris welcoming her back as if she were an old friend, the boats carved onto the balconies, gliding along the Nile, dodging hippos and ibises. Even with no sets, no costumes, no backdrops, it still ignited her imagination.

Meg had said *actors* but—would it be only the professional troupe here? Would Reg be helping out as well? She didn't see him.

No one paid any attention as they slid into seats in the third row. Purposefully, she scanned the group onstage until—yes—there he was, lounging on a wooden foldup chair in the center of the stage. His hand was on his chin, and there was a tremendous frown on his face. Andrew stood before him, clutching a cap in his hands, with Hettie Longmere by his side. Peter, of the devilish mustache and pointed beard, was sitting at the piano, hands poised on the keys, and Addie recognized a few other members of the cast of *Macbeth* gathered in a semicircle around the three main actors. They seemed to be blocking the scene, not just reading it.

Her eyes wandered back to Reg, as they would have even if he had not suddenly roared, "It's my daughter, then, you demand of me?"

Andrew preened like a fighting rooster. "Your daughter and the realm to her dowry, yes."

Addie jerked upright in her seat.

Meg Turner noticed her reaction. "Do you know the play?" she whispered.

Addie barely managed a nod.

She watched Reg rise from his chair and stroll across the stage with the rolling gait of a much heavier man, full of middle-aged self-importance, like a college professor. But he wasn't playing a professor.

He was playing the old man of the Dovrë.

The troll king.

Her breath caught tight in her chest. It *was* the Jewel in that photo she'd found. And Reg—she thought of the masked figure in the photograph. Was he the troll king? How long would it take—a month, two, three?—to get to a full-fledged production in costume? Would he be acting in it? Her thoughts galloped. She couldn't wait to look at the picture again.

Ay, but stop, my lad;

Reg fixed Andrew with a baleful stare, then glanced at the script in his hand.

You also have some undertakings to give,
If you break even one, the whole pact's at an end,
And you'll never get away from here living.
First of all, you must swear that you'll never give heed—

In her mind, Addie joyfully joined in:

To aught that lies outside Rondë-hills' bounds;
day you must shun, and deeds, and each sunlit spot.

She turned to Meg Turner. "It's *Peer Gynt!*"

Meg laughed, taken aback. "I'm surprised you know it—at your age! Ibsen's quite shocking."

"Really?" Addie's eyes fastened again on Reg, who was swaggering about the stage, having a fine time. Upstaging Andrew even in a read-through.

Meg Turner leaned back and put one foot up on the arm of the chair in front of her. It was a startlingly modern pose. *Ooh,* Addie thought, *won't she be happy when trousers become fashionable for women. When will that be? The thirties? But . . .* An odd dismay filled her. *She'll be middle-aged by then! They'll all be . . .*

"So," Meg whispered as the banter continued onstage, "what do you suggest? How can we bring this scene to life?"

Startled, Addie stammered, "B-Bring it to life? Um . . ." The performances already looked pretty good to her. Was that because she didn't know any better? What more could she do to stage this scene? Her thoughts spun. She'd directed all those backyard productions, hadn't she? Read director's notes? Yet it seemed pathetic. No preparation for the real thing.

"Let me . . . um . . . let me watch a bit more."

Meg nodded, but her mouth betrayed impatience.

Addie bit her lip. She watched intently as Peer and the troll king bargained. Sometimes the actors stopped and suggested things to each other, but mainly they kept the scene rolling. The king's courtiers set about transforming Peer into a subhuman troll like themselves. He drank the trolls' sour wine, and they fastened a tail on him. Addie couldn't help noticing that Reg was hugely enjoying making Andrew look ridiculous. He was overflowing with geniality and good cheer as he joined Andrew's and Hettie's hands and commanded:

Music-maid, forth! Set the Dovrë-harp sounding!
Dancing-maid, forth! Tread the Dovrë-hall's floor!

Down in the orchestra pit, Peter began to play. A waltz rolled off the keys, and Andrew and Hettie turned smoothly across the stage while Reg tapped his foot and beamed like a proud papa.

Okay. Something's wrong here, Addie thought. What was it? She watched the two dancers flow effortlessly around the stage. They danced so perfectly, and yet somehow it wasn't right. They looked like a couple waltzing at a ball, not trolls in the realm of the Dovrë king. She'd thought a lot about this scene when she was preparing to audition for *Short Takes,* and the picture of it in her head was very clear.

"It's not right," she murmured.

"I agree," Meg said, as if she'd been waiting for Addie to notice. "But tell me why."

Addie pointed at the dancing couple. "Because they're too . . ." She hesitated, but Meg was listening attentively. With more conviction, Addie went on, "They're too elegant. I mean, it's not a royal palace. It's the hall of the troll king— more like the monkey house at the zoo. So that music's too pretty. Hettie and Andrew are dancing too well." *And Reg should definitely not be so good-looking,* she added to herself. *They really need to do something about that.*

Meg Turner's bright red lips crooked up on one side, and for a horrible moment, Addie felt like the director had read her mind. "Good. So tell *them.*"

"What? Now? You mean, interrupt them? *On the stage?*"

"That's a director's job description," Meg said. Her smile became positively impish, and Addie thought, *She's not the wicked witch; she's the big bad wolf!* "What? You can't be scared of a pack of actors, can you?"

"No-o," Addie said, as bravely as she could. She licked

her lips and half rose from her seat. "Excuse me," she squeaked, trying to get their attention.

But Peter just went on with his sweeps and flourishes. Hettie and Andrew continued waltzing. And Reg stared pointedly at Andrew's tail and inquired, "How like you it?" with infinite courtesy.

Okay, Addie thought. *Actors project. So if you're going to interrupt them, you have to project, too.*

"Excuse me!" Still no one heard. Her legs felt weak. Soon the scene would be over and she would have lost her chance.

Quickly, she slid out of her seat, went along the side aisle and up the little staircase into the wing.

The piano player had just lifted his fingers from the keys when she stepped out onstage and waved her arms for attention.

"Excuse me!"

This time, they heard. Andrew let go of Hettie. Reg, who had been thumping him heartily on the shoulder, dropped his arm as he caught sight of Addie, his stage smile fading.

She stood there, stupid with nerves. Her hands clenched in front of her chest as if ready to catch her heart if it leaped out of her rib cage.

"Hello, Miss McNeal," Hettie Longmere said warmly, a smile creasing her round face.

"Welcome back," Andrew chimed in.

Reg didn't say anything.

Addie's insides contracted. She'd really thought he'd be happy to see her. Why wasn't he? For a moment, she couldn't remember anything she'd been about to say.

Thankfully, Meg Turner interjected, "I've asked Miss McNeal to make some suggestions for the scene. If you don't mind?"

Andrew shrugged. "Fire away. Anything goes at this point."

Addie's gaze jumped to Reg and away again. His face was emotionless. What was that about? Did he still think she was someone from a vaudeville house trying to worm her way into his mother's theater? *Ignore him*, she told herself. *Concentrate.* She stood up straighter, gathering her nerve. "All right." Her voice sounded strange to her. "I think . . . that is, you need—you need to think more about where Peer has just found himself. He's in the underworld, the kingdom of the trolls, where nothing is what it seems."

They listened politely, but they already knew all this. Of course they did, she thought. They were professionals. Professionals would know the script.

She forced herself to continue. "So when you're in this scene, it's like . . . everyone is living sort of this delusion." *God, I barely sound literate!* She made herself slow down and speak in full sentences. "Every troll has a mote in his eye that lets him taste the sour wine as sweet, see the troll hags as gorgeous maidens, and the trolls' disgusting behavior as . . . I don't know . . . court etiquette." She could feel herself gaining momentum. "But Peer's human. He's able to be fooled, but he's also got the ability to question. So he should be half hoodwinked and half aware." She dared to look around at the actors, fearing their boredom. But then she caught a glimmer of interest in Reg's eye, and she said, more decisively, "I think the trolls really have to be trolls. You look too nice, all of you. Too smooth and polite. Trolls need to be much more . . ."

She was going to say *gross*, but she knew it wasn't a word they'd understand.

"Offensive?" Reg suggested.

Addie looked away quickly. "Maybe. Disgusting? Abrasive? I mean, Reg should laugh at his own jokes, slap his thigh and guffaw like a buffoon. But a threatening one." She turned to Andrew. "And Peer should join in. He can mug to the audience to show he knows how obscene it all is, but then be sort of seduced by it, too."

She turned to the piano player. "And you need to make that waltz wilder."

"Wilder?" Peter plunked out a faster version of the same music. "Like that?"

"Maybe. . . . Try it and see, but the dance has to change. Andrew and Miss Longmere are dancing too well. Do you know what I mean? You should . . . you should sweep along gracefully—that's when Peer's hoodwinked by the enchantment of the trolls, and sees you as a beauty—but then, Andrew, you can blink and see her as she really is. Then, Miss Longmere, you need to slow down and plod awkwardly, right? He's just discovered you're not a princess, you're a troll!"

"Men always discover that about me," the actress joked, and Addie instantly loved her for it. "So I dance like a princess, and then a troll, and then back again? Can you show me?"

"Well . . . I'm not very good." But when she glanced over at Meg Turner, she knew she had to.

Andrew held out his arm. Gritting her teeth, Addie stepped into position. "All right!" she cued Peter, who turned back to the keys and swooped into a waltz.

Andrew spun her around and she did her best to float along with him. She'd never waltzed, but it took surprisingly little effort. "Okay," she called over her shoulder to Hettie. "So, three turns like this, and then"—she hunched her shoulders and slouched against Andrew—"look disconcerted," she stage-whispered, and Andrew pulled a terrific face that made Addie laugh. "Now hustle me back up into princess form."

"You mean, pull you up . . ."

"Jerk me to my feet. You can make it funnier as you practice it."

Andrew yanked her up by the waist. Addie flopped over his arm like a rag doll.

"That's it!" she cried, pleased.

Hettie Longmere clapped her hands.

They stopped. "What do you think?" Addie called out to Meg in the audience.

"Brava!" Meg called. "Now what?"

"Well—" Addie looked up and saw Reg watching her. His expression seemed a fraction warmer. Maybe because he could see she was serious about this, not a fake or whatever he had been thinking. She returned his look and found herself smiling, just because it was so good to see him.

Slowly, he smiled back. Addie looked away to hide the color that shot into her cheeks. Then she turned to the rest of the actors with a sudden burst of confidence. "The music should get wilder, and the whole cast should join in. Doesn't Peer have a line soon about a cow strumming a lyre, and a cat, or a—"

"A sow," Reg broke in. Even he was starting to sound enthusiastic.

"That's right. A sow dancing! So the whole scene should get out of control, and Peer should get scared. It's real troll land now." She frowned. "I'm not sure the waltz is right for that. Any other ideas?"

"A mazurka?" Peter suggested.

"What about the Grieg I've got?" Meg called from the audience, waving the score. "It was written for *Peer Gynt*, after all."

Peter frowned. "No. Something Scandinavian."

"Grieg *is* Scandinavian!"

"But his music is so ominous! I mean more like a folk dance. Something from a peasant wedding." He plunked out a chord or two. "Needs a fiddle," he complained. He attacked the keys again, stopped, thought a moment, and then snapped his fingers. "All right. Try this. Ready?"

"Sure," Addie said. Peter swung into a wild polka, and she and Andrew launched themselves back into the dance. But it still didn't work. They were lagging, and the music was accelerating.

"It's better, but still not right."

"We can go faster," Andrew suggested.

They tried to speed up, but Addie stumbled, and not to bring out the troll nature of the princess. It was a real stumble.

"Too many beats?" she asked in frustration.

"Possibly," Peter said.

"I think I know," Reg broke in suddenly. "Let me show you. Do you mind, Andrew?"

Reg was smiling at her, really smiling now, as he took her hand out of Andrew's and pulled her other arm around his waist. Then the music began again and he spun her across the stage, half jumping, half twirling in time with the wild melody. Addie raced to follow. At first she felt hopeless, like a klutz, but then she caught the rhythm of it and she was able to match his steps, heart thumping, feet flailing.

Both of them were laughing simply for the joy of it. Under the bright worklights, Addie noticed how blue his eyes were, as blue as the lake on a day of sun and wind. It felt as though the only thing anchoring her to the stage was his hand firm on her waist, pressing the thin fabric of the dress. It was the most wonderful feeling—the breathlessness, the warmth where their hands met, the slap as their feet touched down on the beat and flew up again.

Out of the corner of her eye, Addie saw Andrew grab Hettie and swing her into the dance. The others joined in. The whole stage came alive with the thumping of their feet. And the harder they thumped, the better it sounded. In her mind's eye, Addie could see the set swirling with dancers, could hear the stage ringing with stamping feet, and she knew this would be the scene everyone remembered.

The dance crashed to a conclusion. She and Reg whirled one last time and came to a halt, his hand still on her waist, their raised hands still clasped.

And then there was a burst of out-of-breath laughter and clapping, and Peter spun around on his bench shaking his long hands and crying, "Ow! That's stretched my poor fingers more than a week of ragtime!"

Meg Turner had climbed up onto the stage with the rest of them. Addie dropped Reg's hand and met the director's long, considering gaze.

"Not bad." Meg Turner nodded.

"Thanks," Addie managed to say, catching her breath.

Meg cocked her head. "You've got a job, if you want it. And if you work hard, Miss McNeal, someday you'll be sitting in my spot." She grinned as wickedly as ever. "But remember: I don't intend to give up my place at the Jewel until they put me in the ground!"

TIN LIZZIE

They fiddled around with *Peer Gynt* for another hour, and then Meg declared that she needed to rest before tonight's rehearsal. As soon as everyone started to disperse, Reg grabbed Addie's arm. "Come on, let's get out of here. You need to breathe something that isn't actors' hot air. That can be lethal." He put a hand to her forehead in mock concern. "It's affecting you already. You look dazed."

"I'm not dazed!" Drunk with excitement, maybe. Dizzy with delight. She was so happy she hardly knew what to do with herself, and yet she suddenly felt she could do anything. Without a second thought, she followed him down the stairs and along the corridor to the back door.

Reg opened it and let her through first. "Wait here. I'll be back."

Her head felt light. She paced back and forth on the loading dock, peering up at the nearly century-younger sky. It must have rained earlier. The air seemed washed and dazzling, and there were just a few tattered clouds lingering in the east. Even the alley smelled different, no longer reeking of pee and stale beer. The bins were piled high with garbage. She could detect rotting cabbage, coffee grounds, and a faint, delectable smell of baking wafting from the kitchen in the apartment. And beneath it all, the pungent smell of horse manure.

Reg emerged from the theater and handed her a green-tinted glass. "Early-crop cider. You'd better drink it before you get brain fever from all that dancing and pontificating."

Addie sank down onto the top step and gulped the cider, surprised at how thirsty she was. "I *wasn't* pontificating!"

"Isn't that what directors do?" Reg asked innocently.

She ignored his teasing. "Listen, I've just realized something." And it came to her that of all the people in the world, Reg was the one she had to tell this to.

"So have I." He lowered himself onto the step below hers. "But tell yours first."

She put her glass down. "I've realized—" She stopped and gave him a quizzical look, suddenly struck by the oddness of his appearance. He'd thrown on a jacket and buttoned one side of a collar onto his shirt and then forgotten about it. The other side was springing out at a right angle to his neck. "Do you know your collar's sticking up?" She made as if to button it for him. He slid closer to her, and she dropped her hands, suddenly shy.

He met her eyes in amusement and buttoned the collar himself. "What have you realized, Addie?"

It was the first time he'd called her by her given name,

she realized, astonished by the rush of pleasure she felt at such a small thing. "I auditioned for a part in *Peer Gynt* with . . . another troupe. And I didn't get it. Did I tell you that?"

"What part?"

"The troll king's daughter."

"Ha! You're joking. The Green-Clad One? Wraithlike creature of the shadows . . . Why in the world didn't you get it? You'd be perfect."

"Yes, but the director didn't think so." She turned it over in her head for a moment. "And it really gnawed at me. I felt like I'd been cheated out of something. But, now I think . . . I wasn't. Not really." She hesitated, not wanting to remind him of the mirror. But it couldn't be helped. She wanted to explain. "Do you remember the first time I saw you acting? In *Macbeth*? I knew then. I just knew I would never be as good as you were."

"What are you talking about?" He sat up straighter and somehow it was as if he'd moved away from her.

"Come on, Reg!" she exclaimed. "You're a real actor. You *must* know that. Everyone else does." Her voice softened. "*I do.*"

"Maybe," he said uncomfortably. He picked up her empty glass and rolled it between his hands so it caught the light. "Though it's too . . . easy. And even if I am," he gave his head a dismissive shake, "why would it mean you're not?"

"Don't you see? I *thought* I was. But I don't anymore. Because when Meg put me in charge just now"—a rush of excitement caught her. "I belonged there!" The echo of the words from her dream of the troll king made her laugh in sudden delight. "I'm a . . . director." She said the word softly, tasting it in her mouth. Then, more firmly, added, "That's what I am."

"A director?" He craned his neck and pretended to scrutinize her from different angles. "Ah yes, I *can* see it, now that you mention it. Commanding. Dictatorial . . ."

"Oh, thanks!"

"You're welcome." He bowed slightly and put the glass down on the concrete. "So, now that you're Meg's disciple, what's next? Long scarves? Painting your face?"

"She's just dramatizing herself. Maybe I'll do the same when I'm in her position."

"Don't bother with the face paint." He put his head to one side. "Why try to improve what nature did right the first time?"

That shut her up.

After a moment, she reached out and lightly touched the lapel of his jacket. Her fingertips brushed the rough interlocking tweed. She wanted to touch his smooth black hair, his earlobe, the warmth of his neck, but the moment was too delicate. She held back, savoring it, wanting only to be anchored in the here and now, not aware of any other time.

He reached out and took her hand, curling his fingers around hers. She looked away, and the desire to tell him absolutely everything was suddenly overwhelming.

But then he let go of her hand and the moment was gone. "Can I ask you something?"

"Maybe."

"Why do you disappear and reappear all the time, like Hamlet's father's ghost?"

"I—" What had she told Meg? Oh, she didn't know. Somehow she felt he wouldn't buy some made-up excuse.

He frowned. "It shouldn't be *that* hard to answer. You were here when the police came, and then suddenly you were gone. No one knew where. And I still have no idea where you live."

"I told you where," she protested, but she knew she was being disingenuous. He deserved some sort of explanation.

"Do you live with anyone? Other than that fellow you mentioned?"

"What fellow? Whaley? I'm not *living* with him like"— she groped for a phrase he'd understand—"like living in sin or something. He's more of a . . . foster brother." *All right*, she thought. If she was careful, she could tell him at least some of the truth. "I have a real brother, too. A lot younger. He's ten. And a father. He runs a bookstore," she added, as if this would make him more real to Reg.

"What about your mother?"

"She died a long time ago." Oh, it felt strange to tell him this. It flashed into her head that her mother hadn't even been born yet. From this point in time, she still had her whole life to live. . . . Oh, my God. She caught herself, too scared to continue that train of thought.

"Me, too. My dad died when I was twelve." Reg looked away, his dark eyes focused on something at the other end of the alley. "But he's still here, all the time. Still real to me."

For a few seconds neither of them spoke. But it was a good silence. Not awkward.

Then, after a moment, Reg said, "Last question. What about that mirror of yours?"

Addie pressed her hands against her temples. "No. I *can't* answer that. I barely know myself. But I'm not . . . I'm not a charlatan or whatever you thought I was. You can see that, can't you?"

"I shouldn't have said that. I'm sorry. That was pretty caddish. I'm just not used to occult visitations." He grinned. "Unless that's what you are. Then maybe I could get used to it."

She smiled back, then the memory jolted her. "Occult visitations! I . . . I think I had one. At the jail."

"The *jail?* What were you doing there?"

"Trying to get Whaley out of the lockup. There was a demonstration against the war—"*Oops.*

But Reg only looked amused. "Why is everyone I meet nowadays some sort of mad radical?"

"I'm not! I just don't believe in this war." She paused. "You're not still going to go fight, are you?"

Reg shrugged. "It's out of my hands, isn't it? The conscription bill's already in the House. I expect I'll be hearing from Uncle Sam soon enough."

Addie stared at him. Conscription? A *draft?* That hadn't occurred to her. No one got drafted anymore, she thought. No one even talked about it.

"Though I still might enlist under my own steam," he added. "But that's neither here nor there. Tell me what happened at the jail."

A black crow swooped down into the alley, cawing, and perched on the edge of an open garbage can. Addie watched it, uneasily. "I was there for ages, waiting to bail Whaley out. And I had this . . . dream. About you."

"You *dreamed* about me?" He took a lock of her hair and rolled it between his fingers. Addie pretended not to notice, though for a moment it felt as if her whole being was concentrated on the slow twisting of his thumb and forefinger on that one coil of hair.

"It's my turn to ask the questions." She pressed on, trying to keep her focus. "Did you interview those men in jail?"

"Yes." He glanced over his shoulder. "It was true what Gustaf said. The sheriff's men fired first. The fellows in prison confirmed that. The dockworkers in Everett did, too."

Now Addie looked over her shoulder as well. Behind them, the kitchen window in the apartment was cracked open. The yeasty smell of baking was even stronger than before. She dropped her voice. "What will happen to Frida's dad?"

"We're going to have to move him. It's not safe here." He looked thoughtful. "Actually, I think Peterson might have made a mistake, running. His buddy's trial is going to end soon—Tom Tracy's. If he's convicted, the other fellows are likely to be as well. But the IWW lawyer is pretty good. People are talking acquittal. Even if the other fellows get off, though Gustaf can't come out of hiding and get acquitted with them. I think he's shot himself in the foot, really." He shook his head. "All we can do is make sure he gets safely out of town."

Addie thought this over. Reg was right. She did understand why Gustaf had run away. She actually admired him for it. But now it was a gamble that might not pay off. "Have you published your article about it yet?"

Reg grinned. "It'll be in tomorrow's issue of the *Daily*. That reminds me—" He let go of the strand of Addie's hair and got to his feet. "The fellow who usually delivers the papers to the newsstands is sick. I told Tom I'd help him do it."

"Who's Tom?"

"Tom Buchanan. Our printer. He takes the pictures, too." He held out his hand to Addie. "Want to come with me?"

She let him pull her to her feet. "Come with you where?"

"To the *Daily* office. You could help me deliver the papers." He looked awkward suddenly. "I mean, if you like. I could buy you dinner. If you don't mind the kind of hash houses that are near campus."

Addie hesitated. She was here at the Jewel in 1917; she could cope with that. But somehow, the thought of venturing out into the broader world, even with Reg, was frightening.

Then a thought struck her. "Would your friend Tom have a camera at the newspaper office?"

"I doubt it. But he'll be there, and his lodgings are pretty close by if you need a camera." He looked at her quizzically. "Do you?"

She nodded, hope flaring in her again. Maybe she *could*

get the pictures she'd come for after all. But what could she tell him they were for? What made sense?

She had it. "For publicity shots for *Macbeth*. What if we got your friend to come back to the Jewel with us? He could take some pictures and Meg could use them to promote the show." Yes! Perfect!

Reg whistled. "And I thought *Andrew* was burning with ambition. You're set on impressing Meg, aren't you?"

She didn't know if this was a compliment or a criticism. "I just thought it would be helpful."

"All right. Though it will mean coming back here before rehearsal." He looked a little disappointed, and Addie felt a throb of dismay as well. She would have loved to have dinner with him. Even at a hash house, whatever that was. "Oh, well," he said. "Follow me. The motor's around the corner."

The "motor" proved to be an ancient contraption of a car, the kind she saw in the Greenwood vintage car parade every summer. It was parked with one skinny wheel up on the sidewalk, and its windows were wide open to the world. Or—no, it wasn't that the windows were open; there were no windows. The only glass was the windshield.

Addie examined it doubtfully. "Is it yours?"

"Mother and I share it. She wanted a Pierce-Arrow, but I thought we'd get more use out of a flivver."

"Flivver?"

Reg laughed. "Tin Lizzie. Ford Model T. What world do you come from, Addie McNeal?" He opened the passenger door and helped her in. Addie slid onto the leather upholstery and searched in vain for a seat belt.

He closed the door for her, went around in front of the car, and started fiddling with something attached to the grille.

"Why don't you get in?"

"I'm cranking the engine! Don't tell me you've never been in a motorcar before."

Not like this, she thought.

The engine caught, and Reg jumped into the driver's seat and pulled away from the curb. Addie felt as if she might fly through the roof if she bounced any higher; the thin tires did nothing to insulate them from bumps. She could feel every pebble in the road.

It was hard to talk except in yells. There were no traffic signals. Oncoming traffic swerved toward them and away again. Addie focused on the city flowing by, which looked, at first, so much the same as in her own time it was un-canny: brick buildings with arched windows and fire escapes running down their sides. The white marble walrus heads stuck out from between the windows on the Arctic Build-ing, just as they always did. But no hundred years of smog and soot gummed up the terra cotta. The marble gleamed white, and the iron rails were black and shiny.

"Are we going the wrong way?" she shouted.

Reg shook his head and yelled, "Detour! We'll turn around up ahead!"

Every few blocks, she saw men swinging hand bells and holding out buckets for donations next to placards that read BUY WAR BONDS! EVERY PENNY COUNTS! Passersby threw money in. Women in long dresses and hats held the hands of children coming home from school. Girls her own age, with pencils tucked behind their ears, emerged from office buildings. They were hanging on each other's arms and giggling. People who had lived out their days and come to the end of them long ago . . . She glanced at Reg and quickly away, shoving the thought aside.

By habit, she turned and looked south of the city, and there was the mountain. Fourteen thousand feet above them, the snows of Rainier gleamed white and ghostly and dearly familiar. Now *there* was a place where a hundred years, give or take, made no difference at all. She wished they could turn the car around and head out. If they were hiking there, on her favorite trail to the Alpine Lakes, it would be as if there really were no difference between them, nothing separating her world from his.

But then Addie's eyes were drawn to a poster plastered to a brick wall across the street.

The face on it was Gustaf Peterson's.

The drawing was rough, but accurate. And underneath Peterson's face was the word WANTED.

She turned to see if Reg had noticed, but, of course, his eyes were fixed on the road.

How many of those posters were there around town? Did anyone look closely and think, *I'll be the one to turn him in?* Suddenly, she couldn't believe the risk Reg had taken by hiding him at the theater.

But then she thought of the demonstration she'd gone to—only yesterday!—and felt glad that he had. Peterson's arrest was as unfair as Whaley's had been. She was sure

Frida's dad hadn't shot anyone. Thank goodness that, in their different times, Becky Powell and Reg had both been willing to help. What would have happened to Gustaf and Whaley otherwise?

They were approaching the ship canal and getting closer to her own neighborhood. And now the strangeness hit her hard. It was so bare! So few houses, so few trees, and where was the bridge? The towering span of I-5 was gone. Well, of course. She knew it would be. But so was the University Bridge. That was what threw her. Suddenly she was lost and began looking around in panic for familiar landmarks. The canal seemed so freshly dug, the houses so rough-hewn. And then, farther east, they approached another bridge, one she had never seen before. It was low and flat, with a trolley car trundling along one side. The noise was unbelievable as the Model T clattered across. Addie looked down over the side. The water seemed so close. . . . And then they were off the bridge, on the north shore of the canal, and Addie's heart skipped a beat as they crossed Fortieth—*her street*. She twisted her head to look west, where she knew her house was already standing. But somehow, it was a relief when they turned east instead and began climbing a steep hill.

Those wide lawns and scattered buildings she saw rising ahead of them must be the University of Washington—what else could it be? But where were the trees? The towering cedars and hemlocks? All she saw were little saplings. The university neighborhood looked as if it had been clear-cut. The houses were so new that some of the lots were just dirt. As they swung onto the campus and followed the twists and turns of Stevens Way, she searched for the huge fountain in the rose garden that sent cascades of water into the air in front of the ghostly silhouette of Rainier. It wasn't there, either. Just a sort of pool.

"Here's the office." Reg parked the car next to a building that Addie thought she remembered from her own time. The windows were opaque green glass, with moss already clinging to the moldings.

In a daze, she got out and followed him up the steps.

"Tom!" Reg knocked on the big double doors. "You still here?"

No one answered. "Probably ran out for a pint at that speakeasy in Lake City," Reg grumbled.

"A *speakeasy?*"

"Sorry. Didn't mean to shock you." He actually looked shamefaced. "I shouldn't have mentioned that."

"I'm not shocked!" Addie snorted. "You can tell me about a speakeasy. I won't faint or anything."

"Oh, all right." He laughed. "If you're so worldly, I'm amenable to corrupting youth." He knocked again. "The speakeasy used to be a medium's house. We've laid bets on who makes more appearances there, Tom or the medium's ghost." He knocked yet again. "Tom was winning until the Theosophical Society had a meeting in town. Then you couldn't walk down the street without tripping over someone who'd had a spiritual sighting over a few highballs." He began fishing around in his jacket pockets. "I *think* I've got the keys somewhere."

A moment later he produced a key ring and unlocked the door.

The office was one big open room with a door in the back wall marked DARKROOM. There was a smell of something like new paint—printer's ink, probably. Piles of freshly printed newspapers tied with heavy string cluttered the floor, while others hung on lines across the room, the ink drying. Hulking typewriters sat atop heavy wooden desks. Addie shuddered, thinking of the time it would take to type an essay on one of those things. Wooden cubbyholes for mail lined one wall, and what she guessed was a printing press loomed against the other.

"Now let's see," Reg began, and broke off suddenly, a startled look on his face. Addie spun around to see what had surprised him.

Someone was in the office after all.

Leaning back in an imposing wooden chair, his perfectly shined shoes resting on top of a desk, was an old man in a herringbone suit. The man's silver-rimmed glasses rested far down on his nose, and strings of fine white hair straggled over his high, bony scalp. His eyes, as he fixed Reg with an unfriendly stare, reminded Addie of the eyes of the fish on ice at Pike Place Market.

No way is this Tom, she thought.

"Greetings, Mr. Powell." The man's voice hit each syllable like a bullet hitting a clay pigeon.

"Hello, sir," Reg said, suddenly very formal. From his tone Addie couldn't tell if this man belonged in the newspaper office or not. "May I introduce Miss Addie McNeal?" He pushed Addie slightly forward.

"Delighted." The man swung his feet off the desk and rose, offering Addie his hand. "I have the honor of being the provost of this great university. You may call me Professor Hanson—no need for the full title."

"Pleased to meet you," Addie said.

Reg began, "We were looking for Tom—"

"Thomas Buchanan is gone," the old man interrupted. "How fortuitous you arrived, Mr. Powell! I had just been considering the very tedious prospect of returning to my office to put a telephone call through to your house."

Reg blinked. "You wanted to speak to me, sir?"

"Yes. About your lead article." The provost held the newspaper he'd been reading aloft for a moment before slapping it back on the desk. "You see, I'm afraid you can't publish it."

"Can't—?" Reg looked completely dumfounded. "I'm sorry. I don't follow you."

Professor Hanson shuffled around to the front of the desk and seated himself upon it. "This is the trouble with student publications. So much enthusiasm! So little experience. And young people have such a deplorable tendency to simplify."

Addie remembered Almaz describing one of her teachers as a person who needed binoculars to look down his nose at her. Suddenly, she knew exactly what she'd meant.

Reg still looked puzzled. "If you mean my article, it's as

accurate as I could make it. I double-checked everyone's statements, and the sources—"

"This isn't about accuracy." The provost's fish eyes fixed on him. "Mr. Powell, since you are clearly a well-informed young man, would you mind giving me the details of the act that the Congress is debating to address the current emergency?"

Reg wrinkled his brow. "You mean the Espionage Act? Why?"

"Because of what you've written here, dear boy. You know that already."

"No, I don't. I don't know what you're talking—" His eyes widened suddenly. "Wait a minute. The article isn't disloyal. Or useful to spies or enemies of the state or whoever—" He stopped, as if realizing something. "You know that already."

"Perhaps," Professor Hanson said evenly. "But in this climate, my opinion doesn't matter. If I can keep the university from becoming a lightning rod, I am going to do it. So, unless you can find another story to take its place, I think it would be better if the *Daily* wasn't published on Monday."

"But—the bill hasn't even passed the House yet!"

"Do you think there's any chance it won't?"

"You want to *censor* the paper?" Reg had given up trying to sound calm. His voice echoed off the back wall.

The professor's lips went very thin. "No. I simply said that in this climate it would be best—"

Reg raised his hands in an elaborate, sarcastic gesture.

"Best to do what? Keep quiet and let other people do our thinking for us?"

"I hardly think that tone is necessary."

"But he's right," Addie interjected, trying to sound calm and reasonable. She had a feeling that Reg was about to get into a shouting match with the professor. "Isn't speech supposed to be free here, at a university, of all places? You can't ask him to throw out an article just because some people might not like it."

"Excuse me?" The professor looked at Addie as if she were a dog that had stood on its hind legs and begun to speak. "I find it so distasteful when young women trumpet their opinions."

Addie's jaw dropped. *"What?"*

"Now who's being offensive?" Reg said angrily. "She can say what she likes! Can't she? Or is that another new rule?"

The old man ignored this. "If I tell you the article shouldn't be published—"

"But why shouldn't it? It's just a story about those fellows in jail. Giving their point of view. That's been difficult in this . . . this *climate!* Miss McNeal is right— shouldn't we at the university try to change that? As far as I can see, this *climate* is all about not letting people say what they think! Isn't that the newspapers' job? To give people a voice?"

"A journalist's job is to *inform*," Hanson corrected. "Not to incite."

"I'm not inciting anyone to do anything! I've written about this before. About the vigilantes attacking the Wobbly supporters at the jail. If it's such a dangerous topic, why didn't you stop me from publishing that story?"

"We had only just entered the war. Things have changed."

A loud knock made Addie jump. "That'll be Tom," Reg said.

"Allow me." The professor opened the door and admitted a man in denim overalls and a flat cap. He was middle-aged and had a sort of mournful basset-hound face.

"You got some trash you want hauled?" he asked the provost.

"Yes. Right here. Thank you, Ulleman." The provost pointed to the bundles of newspapers on the floor. "You can take them to the incinerator."

Reg spluttered, "Wait a second! You're—you're not going to burn it?"

Addie watched in horror as Ulleman whistled and a younger man appeared. The two of them began hauling the tied-up piles of the *Daily* out the door.

The provost didn't answer. Instead he turned to Reg and said conversationally, "Have you registered for military service by any chance, Mr. Powell?"

"What's that got to do with it?" Reg's eyes followed Ulleman as he carried off another batch of papers and shut the door behind him.

"Imagine those revolutionists out of jail and undermining the war effort while you're in France. One strike in the lumberyards, and there's no spruce to build the airplanes that provide cover for ground troops. You might not feel so tolerant then." Hanson smacked his hands together and headed to the door. As he turned the knob, he added, "I'm sorry to have to take such drastic steps. Truly. If I'd known earlier, I could have just asked you to pull the story. It's a shame to do away with the entire edition." A slab of sunlight hit the floor behind him as he opened the door.

Reg leaned against a desk, lost in thought. After a moment, he said, "So you won't object to a reprint of the edition? If my story is gone?"

The provost gave him a distrustful look. "Well . . . do you have the budget for that?"

"I—uh—yes. Yes, we have the budget."

"You're the editor. It's your responsibility." And the old man turned his back on them and left.

The minute the door closed, Reg burst out with a loud "Aargh!" He ran a hand fiercely through his hair until it was standing on end. "We speak no treason here," he said bitterly and sank down on top of the desk.

Addie lowered herself next to him and tentatively patted his back. She'd recognized the line from one of Shakespeare's plays. "No, I know you don't, King Richard. Now you're supposed to run out on the quad yelling, 'A horse! A horse! My kingdom for a horse!'" she joked, and then she added, "I can't believe that old buzzard had your paper burned!"

"Oh, you don't think I'm letting him get away with that, do you?" Reg got up and went to the desk the provost had been sitting at and picked up the edition the old man had left behind. A determined look crossed his face. "Besides, we don't need a horse. We've got the flivver."

289

THE IMAGE IN THE GLASS

Tom Buchanan was exactly where Reg said he would be: in a seedy speakeasy hidden behind a hardware store up in Lake City. Reg refused to let Addie come in with him, so she waited impatiently amid the shovels and rakes while Reg went and dragged Tom out.

He was a short, whiskery young man with a book called *Thus Spake Zarathustra* sticking out of his coat pocket.

"Did he tell you his plan?" Tom asked Addie once they'd been introduced.

"You mean *my* plan?" she corrected sweetly.

"Ah," Tom said airily. "I must listen more closely to Mr. Shaw on the cunning of the female sex. But—" He hiccupped, releasing a sour aroma of hops in Addie's direction. "But how exactly will it help to replace our piece of truth-telling journalism with a mildly inspiring jaunt into Mrs. Powell's undertaking to buy socks and bandages for the troops with proceeds from a benefit performance?"

"You'll see," Reg told him as they reached the car.

"When's opening night, anyway?"

"Friday." Addie glanced at Reg to double-check. He looked up over the hood and nodded as the engine started to splutter.

They stopped at a three-story apartment building long enough for Tom to run in and return with a canvas bag slung over his shoulder and a rectangular leather-covered camera in his hands. Then they roared across town at twenty miles an hour, maximum. It was crazy, the amount of roaring you could do at that speed with no muffler and no windows.

"As I see it," Tom continued when they climbed out of the flivver near the Jewel, "there are two possibilities. Either Reg is selling out—"

"Or I need a new cover story to fool the provost and we put the Wobbly story on page two."

"You'll get in trouble," Tom said mournfully. "Booted out of school, I bet."

"Don't be ridiculous. The worst that can happen is I get fired as editor. It's nearly the end of the quarter in any case, and who knows where we'll all be next year?"

They walked around to the front of the theater. It was the first time Addie had seen the outside of the Jewel in Reg's time. She fell back, staring. The ticket window was ready for business, the brass on the doors was shining, the doorways were swept, and the early dahlias were blooming in pots by the entrance. The place was positively majestic against the clear blue sky. If only Becky Powell could restore her sad wreck to this! Addie's gaze traveled up to the marquee and she read MR. FREDERICK HARRISON IN *MACBETH*—RED CROSS BENEFIT OPENING NIGHT.

"Take a shot of the front," Reg told Tom. He stepped back on the sidewalk. "This is a good angle, over here."

"You'll need interior shots as well," Addie put in quickly. She felt a little guilty, using their difficulty with the provost to further her own ends. But how did it hurt anyone if she helped get Reg's article published while Tom shot the pictures Becky Powell needed at the same time?

"Interior shots?" Reg said impatiently. "What's the point of that?"

What is the point, as far as they're concerned? Addie wondered. "Well, you're not going to have a lot of text, are you? Why not fill up space on the front page with photos?"

"But Tom will be taking pictures of the rehearsal, right? Isn't that what you wanted?"

"Right, but . . ." Addie scrambled to think of something convincing. "The promotion shots for *Macbeth* are one thing, and the photos for your decoy story are another. Besides, if you get interior shots of the Jewel, they can be standbys, you know, any time a freelancer wants to write an article about the theater."

Tom, who was surveying the façade with a critical eye, said, "It's probably worth taking extra shots of the theater anyway. Candids are tricky. If they turn out, we'll use them. But if not—we just need *something* to paste into that story tonight." He gestured at the big camera bag at his feet. "Good thing I've got flash equipment."

"As long as you don't set the place on fire." Reg sounded as if he thought this marginally possible.

"Take a lot of pictures," Addie told Tom, trying not to look too delighted. "The stage and the box seats, and the pharaoh above the proscenium, and the dome. All of that. We'll also need a photo of the auditorium," she rushed on. "And, Tom . . . can you develop an extra set for me?"

"An extra set for Miss McNeal," Tom said pleasantly and, looking through the viewfinder, stepped back as far as he could on the sidewalk. "No, this is no good," he complained. "I'll have to stand in the middle of the road. Be a good fellow, Reg, and hold the traffic at bay while I get this shot."

Reg looked dubiously at the carts and automobiles careening along the street behind them. He pulled the rolled-up copy of the *Daily* out of his jacket pocket and handed it to Addie. In a low voice, he said, "Give this to our friend, will you? I mean, in case I perish in the attempt to get this shot."

Addie nodded and went inside. She headed to the stage and then went through the door leading to the small side hallway.

Outside the janitor's closet, she saw a girl placing a tray carefully on the floor.

"Frida," she said quietly.

The girl whirled around, her hand on her chest. "Sweet Saint Lucy!"

"I'm sorry I scared you."

"It's all right." Frida flung her flour-covered arms around her. "I never got to say thank you for what you did!"

"What did I do?" Addie asked, hugging her back.

"When the coppers were here. You were so smart and quick!"

Addie smiled and pulled the *Daily* from her bag. "Reg wanted your father to see the article he wrote."

"He'll like that." Frida gave a soft knock and hoisted the tray from the ground. Addie could see that it was heaped with cold chicken and cooked carrots and bread and a hunk of cheese. Frida must have been cooking for her dad in Mrs. Powell's apartment.

Peterson opened the door and they stepped in. Frida put the tray on the low table and hugged him with her usual rough enthusiasm. "Hello, darlin'," her father said.

Addie closed the door behind them. As her eyes adjusted to the dim light, she regarded Frida's dad with concern. He didn't look ill exactly, but he didn't look well either. His face was pale, his brow furrowed with worry. His hands, creased and scarred with the marks of old injuries, clasped each other nervously. When he released Frida, he turned to Addie and said, "Welcome, miss."

"Hello, Mr. Peterson. Are you—are you all right?"

"Stir-crazy." Lightly, he slapped his hand against the door. "I ain't free yet, I guess that's all it comes down to."

"I brought you something." Addie handed him the paper.

Peterson managed a weary smile. "Now that brings some light into the day. Stay a minute. I'll read while I eat."

Poor man, Addie thought. The Wanted poster with

Peterson's picture flashed into her mind. How much were they offering for a reward? And what would happen to the Powells if he was caught? Considering how much trouble the provost thought Reg would get into for just *writing* about the men in prison, the punishment for hiding one of them must be pretty severe.

"I got to get to work, Dad." Frida smoothed her apron. "I'll come back and get the plate later."

Addie said goodbye and followed her back out into the hall and then started violently as a voice called, "Miss McNeal! Is that you?"

She swung around and saw Andrew Lindstrom heading down the corridor toward them.

"Oh—hello," she managed to say. *Don't look guilty*, she told herself. After all, there was nothing wrong with being back here, was there? Nothing at all.

Except that Peterson picked that moment to stick his head out of the closet and put the newspaper in Addie's hand. "I'd better not keep this—"

"Who the devil are you?" Andrew demanded.

Oh, no. This is it. Addie's mind whirred. What should they do?

Frida grabbed her hand. To Addie's dismay, a spark of defiance had flared in Peterson's face. She and Frida exchanged a frightened glance. But then—thank goodness— Peterson slumped his shoulders and looked deferentially at the ground. "I'm the new janitor," he said, "sir."

"Let me see what you gave Miss McNeal." Andrew grabbed the newspaper out of Addie's hand. " 'Wobbly

Prisoners Held Under False Charges.'" His eyebrows shot up. "What's this?"

"It's the *Daily*, that's all," Addie said quickly. "I must have dropped it."

"Dropped it where?" Andrew asked, but he wasn't paying attention. His eyes swept across the page and stopped as they came to the byline. "'Reg Powell,'" he read and looked up at Addie triumphantly. "Well, well. The things you learn about people."

Addie had to fight down the desire to smack him. "Can I have it back now?" she asked, but Andrew was reading and didn't seem to hear her. *Pretended* not to hear.

Frida glanced at her dad and jerked her head toward the auditorium. He gave a faint nod and went off in that direction, careful to pull a mop out of the closet as he went. Andrew raised his eyes from the page and watched him. Could he have recognized him from the Wanted poster? Addie wondered nervously. Even though the picture on it was only a sketch, it was a fairly good likeness.

"Come on, Miss McNeal," Frida said, as if resuming a conversation. "You too, Mr. Lindstrom. I've got a roast chicken upstairs for all of you, nearly ready for carving. Aren't you lucky I work Saturdays?"

Andrew stuck the paper in his jacket pocket, still gazing suspiciously at Peterson's retreating back. Addie's ribs ached with tension. He wasn't going to follow him, was he?

"Mrs. Powell was setting up the table," Frida continued, with a worried look. "I know she's waiting for you."

She took a step in the direction of the auditorium entrance and glanced back to see what he would do.

Addie put a hand on Andrew's elbow for a second. "We'd better hurry," she said. To her relief, the light touch caught his attention and he turned and accompanied her as she set off toward the entrance to the auditorium.

"Meg's looking for you," he said. "Where did you and the heir apparent disappear to?"

"Out for a drive."

"Oh, that's what they call it these days?"

Addie shot him a look as they mounted the stairs to the stage. She hadn't disliked Andrew before, but suddenly she was beginning to.

A table had been set up backstage and Meg, Emma Mae, Hettie, and Peter were settling down around it. Emma Mae had an earthenware jug in her hand and was pouring cider into everyone's glasses.

Meg scowled at Addie. "Well, well. If it isn't my assistant. If you're going to be slipping out with Emma Mae's wicked son at every opportunity, I don't know how we can work together. I don't need a helper who's asleep at the switch."

Addie froze, stricken with remorse. It was true. She'd just run off without a word. *Again.* And Meg had told her there was an evening rehearsal. "I'm so sorry! Please, Mrs. Turner, I didn't mean—"

The director's stern look dissolved. "Ooo, I love a little kowtowing from my troupe," she teased. "It's all right. *This* time. I've already told Emma you'll be working on *Peer Gynt.*

Just keep your eye on the track. And come have some supper, unless that boy fed you in some unsavory den of vice somewhere."

"No, no, he didn't." She turned to Emma Mae, who had finished filling the glasses. "And I'd love to work on *Peer Gynt.* If that's all right, Mrs. Powell." She knew she was ignoring all the problems with this scenario. But it was just too tempting. The thought of working with Meg, becoming part of the life of this theater—it all made her feel so happy, she couldn't let herself come to her senses about it. Not quite yet.

"Of course it's all right," Mrs. Powell said, picking up the jug again and pouring her a glass. "Though I'm not sure about disappearing with Reg. We may need to have a talk about that." Addie's eyes widened in alarm, but Emma Mae went on, "Not now. Please, do sit down and have some food."

"I'd love to . . ." *Remember what you're here for,* she reminded herself. "But I'm supposed to be helping Reg and Tom. With publicity shots for *Mac*—the Scottish play. Have you seen them?"

"Oh, yes. Pointing that silly Brownie camera at everything. Apparently we rate a headline in the college news. A tiny conflict of interest, I thought, but Reg didn't seem bothered. They've gone back to the newspaper office to develop the film. He said to tell you he'd be back soon."

"I thought they were staying for the rehearsal." Addie clicked her tongue in annoyance.

"It seems not. Something about meeting a deadline. I couldn't understand what they were going on about." Emma

Mae turned back to Meg and the others. "So tell me what you think about the new play—"

Addie stifled a groan. She'd meant to go with them. How else would she get the photos? *Besides*, she thought with a pang, *I can't stay here forever, can I?*

"How long till dinner?" Meg called after Frida, who was on her way to the stairs.

"Ten minutes," Frida called back.

"Good. We have time." She sprang out of her chair. "Come with me, Addie. I have something to show you. Excuse us, all of you."

The theater was strangely quiet as Addie followed Meg down the stairs and into Mrs. Powell's office. Inside, Meg swept aside the papers on the desk (as if it were hers, Addie thought) and stooped down to pull some things out of a box on the floor.

"Come take a look," she said. "I'm so proud of my acquisition!"

Addie watched curiously as Meg placed four or five carved wooden objects on Emma Mae's desk. It was a set of brightly lacquered masks painted red, yellow, and green with bold black lines around the eyes and lips, and golden designs on the cheeks. The noses jutted like huge curved beaks. The one on the far left was a half-mask. Under the nose, a black mustache bristled in every direction. The mouth was a large empty O.

It was the mask in the photo from the bookstore.

Wonderingly, Addie picked it up and held it to her face. "Reg will wear this one," she said quietly, almost to herself.

Meg's lips crooked in a quizzical smile. "That's right.

How did you know? The next time we do the troll-king scene, I'll have him try it out. What do you think?"

Addie's throat was dry. "I think they're wonderful. Are . . . are you going to cast Reg for sure?"

"If he'll take it." Meg's elfin features pinched in exasperation. "Stupid boy. Everyone seems to know how good he is except him. I actually wanted him for Peer—*don't* tell Andrew—and the only reason I didn't broach it, other than the small matter of college, is that he's so unreliable. It seemed safer to offer him a smaller part."

Addie walked over to a mirror on the wall and held the mask to her face. She knit her brows into a terrific scowl, the way Reg had during the read-through. It made her laugh. "This will look fantastic."

"*I* thought so." Meg beamed. "And I've got another idea. Remember what you said about the motes in the trolls' eyes?"

"Yes."

"We can get that across using pocket mirrors."

Addie turned around to face her and lowered the mask. "How?"

"By catching the light on—oh, never mind. Here, I'll show you. Where's my mirror?" Meg thrust her hand into the pocket of her jacket, and drew it out again. "Drat! I don't know where it's gone. You don't have one, do you?"

Addie put the mask back on the desk. "I do," she said slowly. "But it's kind of special."

"Oh, I won't hurt it." Meg held out her hand and snapped her fingers impatiently.

Addie hesitated, wishing she hadn't said anything. But what did it matter? Meg wouldn't run off with it. She'd just have to get it back quickly. Carefully, she pulled out the mirror and passed it face-down to Meg Turner.

Meg's face froze. "Where did you get this?" she demanded.

"I found it."

"You *found* it?" Meg gave her a look of incredulous fury. "But this is *my* mirror!"

Addie actually took a step back, as if dodging a slap. "What? How—how could that be?"

But even as the words were leaving her lips, she knew Meg was right. She should have realized! Those were all Meg's things in the crates, weren't they? The costumes. The props. The papers. Even—she glanced down at herself in dismay—even the dress she was wearing.

A dull heat spread across her face. Meg must think she was a thief! "I had no idea it was yours! I found it in an old crate in my dad's bookstore—"

"Well, I don't know how it turned up there . . . *if* it did."

"I didn't *steal* it, if that's what you're saying." Addie's head was pounding. She pressed her fingers to her forehead, wishing just once she could blurt out the truth. "I think . . ." she began unhappily. Oh, how to explain it? "I think it's both of ours. I think it's a very weird, creepy mirror, and it belongs to both of us at the same time."

Meg threw herself into Emma Mae's leather chair and put the mirror down on the desk. "I don't know what you mean," she said shortly. "But it's certainly ridiculous to say you discovered it in some bookstore when I'm the one who had it made in the first place! How is that even possible?"

Addie stared. "You . . . had it made?"

"Of course I did. Which is why I have trouble believing—"

"Oh, please don't be so angry!" Addie burst out. She felt near tears. "Please, please believe me. I would never steal anything from you. I don't understand at all," she went on softly, "but—please just tell me about it. About how you had the mirror made. Maybe I can figure it out then."

Meg examined her warily. "All right," she said. "But only because up to this point, I've had a good impression of you, Miss McNeal." Addie's heart sank. *Up to this point . . .* But to her relief, Meg went on. "I designed the mirror specially. And I paid a silversmith to make it."

"Why?"

Meg smiled a thin, sardonic smile. "Because I had no luck," she said flatly.

"What do you mean?"

"Have you never been down on your luck? Have you never thought other people lived charmed lives and why didn't you? That it's all so hopeless that you need *something*, some kind of lucky amulet or wishing ring to help you change your life?" She raised her eyebrows in self-mockery. "Sad, yes? But that was how I felt once, long ago. And since no fairy godmother seemed likely to swoop down and give me anything like that, I custom-ordered it."

Addie dropped onto the love seat like a marionette whose strings had been cut. Meg had "custom-ordered" the mirror, the way Dad had custom-ordered the windows for the bookshop? How was that possible? To custom order something so magical? "Do you . . ." she began.

"Do I what?" Meg's voice was still unfriendly.

"Do you know what the mirror . . . how it works?"

"What do you mean?" Meg clicked her nails against the desk. "It works like any other mirror."

"But is that *all?*" Addie was starting to feel desperate. "Because—" She stopped herself. "Because I think—it *does* things."

Meg leaned forward, focusing intently on Addie, scanning her face for signs of something. Insanity? Disingenuousness? Addie forced herself to meet her eyes directly. Finally, Meg's gaze dropped to the mirror on the desk, and she ran a finger over the embossed dancers, the laurel and olive trees. "All right. I suppose there is something to this mirror. I'll tell you honestly, I've always had a superstition about it." She paused. "Tell me what it does, Miss McNeal."

"When I look in it, things . . . change." Addie tried not to let Meg's tone intimidate her. "I don't think I can explain it more than that. It brought me here, that's the only thing I know for sure, and—"

"It led me here, too," Meg said unexpectedly.

The two of them looked at each other in surprise.

"How?"

"Through a dream." Addie watched with sharpened interest as the director picked up the mirror and turned it slowly in her hands so that it caught the light from the hallway. "When I was your age, Addie, I was a lot like you. I was bright, though with little experience. I had energy and talent—oh, yes, you do too, you know—but in one way, I was very different. I worked in a factory. Every day but Sunday. Rolling cigars, as I'd been doing since I was ten years old."

"Ten!"

Meg made a sour face. "Which is why I don't smoke. I had to run to my shift at the factory after school every day. And then I'd force myself to stay awake past midnight to finish my schoolwork. And in the morning, it would all start again." For a moment, she looked out into space, remembering. Then her gaze snapped back to Addie. "Can you see why it seemed only some sort of magic could transport me from that life to this?"

Addie nodded. She thought of hanging out with Almaz after school, going to secondhand stores, listening to Whaley practice his guitar. Sure, she helped out in the bookstore, but not if she had homework or some after-school activity. "Go on," she said.

"My parents had been on the stage, back in Prague, and they told me stories of the theaters where they'd performed, the great actors they had worked with. I vowed I would follow in their footsteps, no matter what. But the years passed, and I started to feel it was an impossible dream."

Addie looked more closely at Meg. She really was young, but there were tight lines at the corners of her eyes. It must have been a struggle to get where she was now. "But you made it come true, didn't you?"

"Yes. I worked double shifts in the factory and then at different little theaters around town. Vaudeville, too. If you had told me I would one day be the director at a place like the Jewel, though, I would have laughed in your face."

"But what did the mirror have to do with it?"

"Nothing!" Meg Turner laughed, and then looked serious. "Or rather, nothing I can prove. When the Powells advertised for a director, I *knew* it was too much to wish for. But . . ." She paused. "But then, I had a dream. I dreamed I was leading a production here, that I was a grand lady in charge of creating . . . enchantment. There's nothing strange in that, is there? I'll bet you've had dreams like that." She looked straight into Addie's eyes, and Addie felt as if she were staring right into her soul. "Except that when I came to the Jewel for my interview, it was the exact same theater as the theater in my dream." She settled back in Emma Mae's chair. "And no, I'd never been here before. But when I walked in, I knew instantly that I *belonged* here. That this was my future. Does that sound crazy?"

"No," Addie said, and then added softly, "And you're right. I have had a dream like that."

"In my dream, I was holding a mirror, a silver mirror with gorgeous embossing on its back." She shook her head. "I try not to be superstitious. I'll shout the name *Macbeth* from the rafters if I feel like it. But this dream was something I couldn't ignore. So while I waited to hear whether Emma Mae and her husband would allow me to have the future I was burning to have, I took all my savings—and the little twisted handkerchief of money my grandmother left me when she died—and I went to the best silversmith in town, Sven Taggerud. I ordered this mirror from him. I told him I was going to work at the Jewel, and I would pay the balance with my salary, though for all I knew, it was money I might never have." She picked up the mirror by its handle and held it out to Addie. "He did a beautiful job, don't you think?"

"Yes," Addie said softly, taking it and glancing from the lithe flowing forms of the dancers to Meg Turner, all of them draped in scarves and sparking with life. She smiled. "It's like you."

"I'm no lovely dancer." Meg snorted. "I'm a raging Medusa. Ask any actor. But it's like my imagination, you can say that. It's like what I bring to life here at the Jewel." She smiled. "They gave me the job. And I never put on a production without that mirror. Do you understand?"

"Yes," Addie said slowly. "I've thought about the mirror a lot, and what it has to do with the Jewel. But all I can think of is"—she looked up at Meg, a bit uncertain—"that the theater's sort of a mirror itself, isn't it?"

"Some people think so. A mirror in which the world is made magically clearer, brighter, less confusing. Complete, in a way our jagged, messy world can never be." Meg stood up. "Now, maybe I'm a fool, but suddenly I don't think you stole this at all. Though I still don't understand how we've come to have the same mirror." She wrinkled her brow. "How do you explain *that*, my apprentice?"

Addie drew in her breath and looked steadily at Meg Turner. *I'll tell her*, she decided. *I never thought it would be her, of all people, but now I see it has to be.*

But suddenly the door to the office opened, and Emma

Mae Powell stuck in her head. "Meg," she said, "I've just got a letter. For Reg. Can you come out here a moment?"

"Yes, of course, Emma," Meg said, quick worry in her voice. She went over to her friend and put a hand on her arm. Emma Mae squeezed it.

"Are you all right, Mrs. Powell?" Addie asked.

Emma Mae looked stricken. "I'm fine," she said. "Excuse us a moment, Miss McNeal. We'll join you at supper." She linked her arm through Meg's and the door closed after them.

Addie went over to the desk and sank down shakily into the wooden chair. What did it mean that the mirror had once been Meg's?

She turned it over and caught her reflection in the glass. And though she knew what the consequences would be, she couldn't tear her eyes away. It was as if some force were pulling her out of the past, out of Reg's world and Meg's, and back to her own, whether she wanted to go or not.

When she finally tore her gaze away, there were no troll masks, no inkwells and pens on the desk in front of her. The walls of the cabinet were still scraped where Whaley had used the crowbar to force them open. The costumes that had accumulated over the many years since she had sat here with Meg Turner were piled up around the room.

Slowly, Addie raised herself out of Emma Mae's chair and stood perfectly still, catching her breath as the new century settled around her like dust particles drifting in the beam of a spotlight.

NO JEST

The battlefield was silent. Not because everyone was dead, but because everyone was waiting. She was waiting, too. She felt the same watery sickness in her stomach that she'd felt when she'd tried out for *Peer Gynt*, but none of the elation. She was in the dark, in a trench, walls shored up with sandbags. Ladders climbed to the lip of the ground above. Wreaths of mist curled around her. When she tipped up her head, she saw washes of gray clouds across the sky, heard the lonely caw of a crow. Slick brown mud squelched under her feet, and the smell in her nostrils was clay and worms and something like wet dog.

There were many others with her, pressed against the ladders and sandbags. An occasional cough broke the stillness. The soldier beside her was so close that her sleeve brushed his. She had one foot on a ladder—she knew already they were heading to the surface. Her weight made it tip to one side and sink deeper in the mud. She climbed to the top and lifted her head over the edge of the earthworks.

Trenches zigzagged to the horizon, guarded by forests of barbed wire. Beyond the wire stretched an endless field of churned mud and torn-up grass. Huge craters dotted the landscape. What trees remained were leafless, bullet-ridden.

Forms thrust up through the mud. Arms, feet. Even faces. All caked in mud and the same color as the earth into which they had been driven, as if pounded in by hammer blows.

A soldier grabbed her arm and jerked her down. "What are you doing? They haven't signaled, you idiot." It was Whaley.

"But we need to look!" She inched back up the ladder. "Don't you want to know what we're getting ourselves into?"

"You wait for your orders. That's what the officers are for."

"But then how can we protect ourselves?"

He pulled her down again and she saw that she'd been mistaken. The soldier wasn't Whaley.

"We're not here to protect ourselves," he said. "Why can't you understand that?"

A high-pitched whistle shrilled, and the darkness of the trench suddenly swarmed with life. Uniforms brushed against one another, boots squelched, bayonets were fastened with a clink. Sharp, pungent sweat broke out on unwashed bodies.

The soldier leaned in toward Addie, and his eyes were blue-black, like clouds blowing in on an ocean front, bringing a storm. His hair was black and straight. And on his head, instead of a helmet, he wore a battered tin circlet: Macbeth's crown.

"No jest, lady," he said.

A second whistle blew. "Go! Go! Go!" The ladders swarmed with bodies. Addie managed to get her hand on a rung and climbed up while others jostled and pushed.

They breached the top and started running.

A whining shriek arced across the sky toward them, like a mosquito coming closer and closer and getting louder and louder, until above their heads the air split apart. A body flew back, knocking Addie to the ground—

She jerked up, gasping.

The hands on the clock beside her bed pointed to four thirty. She was in the civilian world of quilts and alarm clocks and pillows. But the chill of the underworld was damp on her arms. And her body ached, as if she really had slammed against the hard, frozen ground. She had a feeling that the dream had opened a door, and if she wasn't careful, she could slip back through it into that unprotected place where you had no choice but to rise and face the enemy.

And then she was fully awake.

What had brought *that* on?

She thought a moment. She'd still been angry with herself for losing track of Tom and Reg. She'd left—again!—without determining if the photos had been developed, without making sure she had them. But how could that have caused such a vivid and terrifying nightmare? Well, dreams didn't have to mean anything, did they? But even as she thought it, she didn't believe it. She'd believed Meg's story about her dream. A dream had introduced both of them to the Jewel before they'd even set foot there. . . . No. The dream was telling her something.

She shuddered and threw back the quilt. The cold seeped through the wood floor into the soles of her feet. Quickly, she pulled on a shirt, a sweater, and a pair of jeans, went to her chest of drawers, and picked up her brush. Mechanically she yanked through the tangles in her hair. Why was it *Reg's* war, not the one Whaley was so eager to join, that she was dreaming about?

Suddenly she remembered something Reg had said to Tom, something she'd barely even noticed at the time: *Who knows where we'll all be next year?*

She frowned. What did he mean? She was pretty sure he wasn't graduating. He was too young to be finished with college.

Then something else clicked. The letter that had arrived for him. That had upset Emma Mae . . .

A draft notice?

She flew down the hall, past the closed doors of the bedrooms where Dad and Zack were still asleep. She took the steps two and three at a time, stopping just long enough by the coat stand to dip her hand into Dad's jacket pocket and pull out the bookstore keys. This time, she ignored the drama section and headed right toward the military history shelves.

No jest, lady . . .

She gathered every book on World War I that she could carry and headed back up to the living room. Then she went back down for more.

Two hours later, she was still sitting at the big oak table, hunched over an open book, when Whaley wandered in, his hair standing up like a rooster's comb. He ran his hand through it and yawned loudly to get her attention.

"That's a good chunk of Mike's inventory you've got there. Grand reopening's tomorrow, you know. Better put it back before then."

Addie's eyes didn't leave the page in front of her. "There's coffee in the pot."

"Ow!" Whaley banged his leg on the table as he went back to the kitchen, then returned a few minutes later holding a steaming mug. "Want an omelet?"

"As long as it isn't tomato and sauerkraut."

"Which was delicious, by the way. You need to expand your horizons." He put down his mug and leaned over her shoulder. "What battle is that?" Of course he was interested. He loved military history. Addie was past feeling interested; she just felt sick. Whaley pointed at the photo. "There's an arm sticking out of the mud there." He brought up his own arm, pretending to snap his fingers like a crab's claw at her. "Rising out of the trenches, the ghosts of the fallen battalion, coming to take their revenge."

"Shut up, Whaley."

"What is it, then?"

Addie read part of the caption out loud. "'Hand-to-

hand fighting. American troops at the Meuse-Argonne.'"
She saw his blank look and explained, "World War One.
Remember that war memorial in the park when we were
walking to the Jewel?"

Whaley nodded.

"A lot of those guys died in that battle."

Whaley examined her face with puzzled concern. "Why
is *that* bothering you?" He looked at the caption under the
photo. "It says here it was a victory. One of the final offen-
sives of the war."

"It also says a quarter of the American force was wiped
out. Twenty-six thousand men were killed." The sick feeling
churned inside her again. She turned the page to a photo of
a line of soldiers in greatcoats, their eyes wrapped in dirty
linen, each with his hand on the shoulder of the man in
front of him, the blind men following their injured leader
to a casualty clearing station. "They used chemical weapons.
The gas burned their eyes. A hundred times worse than
what happened to Zack. And these guys were the lucky
ones. It says here that mustard gas ate through lung tissue.
Men would suffocate. And —"

Whaley shrugged. "Yeah, I know. We lost lots of people
back then." He looked at her more closely. "You're kidding,
Addie. You're not about to cry, are you?"

"No." She blinked hard.

"Come on, it's different now. We've got air superiority.
Our weapons are more accurate. And if you're on the ground,
you've got body armor." He paused. "You're thinking about
our war, aren't you? Not World War One."

"I'm thinking about *both*."

"What's World War One got to do with anything?"

She wished she could tell Whaley. Maybe then he'd understand how she felt about his joining up. She wanted to tell him about Reg, about how he could be sent to a battle where one out of four American boys ended up dead. But what was so real to her would just be craziness to him. So what if a huge number of guys died so long ago?

"Whaley? Have you ever had a dream that was so real it was like it actually happened?"

"Hasn't everyone?"

"But I mean dreams that really *did* happen. Last night I dreamed *this*." She pointed at the photo. "The men were jammed down in these trenches—the Germans on one side of the field, and the Allies on the other. They'd lob grenades or poisoned gas or there'd be huge artillery bombardments. And the officers would blow whistles and everyone would climb out and attack the trench on the other side while people fired machine guns at them."

Whaley stretched and picked up his mug. "You had a dream like that?"

"Sort of. I was in a trench. . . . They were ordering us to attack."

"C'mon, though. You studied it in American history, didn't you? The *Lusitania* and whatever."

"Mrs. Reich skipped it. She liked the twenties better." She gave him a wan smile. "Flappers, you know? Cute dresses?"

"Mrs. Reich!" Whaley pretended to stick his finger

down his throat. "C'mon. If you want that omelet, I'd better get cooking."

Addie closed and stacked the books, then followed Whaley to the kitchen. A weak morning light was coming in through the window over the sink.

Whaley opened the refrigerator and after a contemplative moment pulled out a jar of capers, wilted collard greens, and a sad-looking onion in a sandwich bag. He got a knife and started chopping with neat, decisive movements. "Maybe you saw a movie about it."

"I've never seen those images before! How could my mind just dredge them up out of nowhere?" She glanced at the clock over the sink. "Oh, geez, it's almost six thirty. We'd better hurry." She slid a knife out of the wooden block on the counter and began slicing the fibrous greens.

Whaley took out a frying pan, threw it on a burner, and dropped in a knob of butter. "Your mind can do amazing things. Like when I'm writing a song. My brain sucks up images. Like a taproot sucking nutrients up from the ground. Memories that don't even belong to me. And it all comes out as I play it." He scraped the onions into the pan. They sizzled, filling the kitchen with their sweaty tang.

"It *was* like that. Like someone else's memories." Addie pushed the sliced greens into the pan with the onions. "They were fixing bayonets on their guns. I didn't even know they fought with bayonets! It was so clear, I could do it right now if you handed me a rifle." She put down her knife and reached for an invisible gun, making the twisting motion the soldiers had used to attach the sharp blades. "How do you explain that?"

Just for a moment, she was sure Whaley could see it as clearly as she did. But then his lip twisted. "That's pretty cool, Ads. If you have a dream that tells you how to fire an A Four, let me know so I can impress the sarg when I get to basic."

"*When* you get to basic?"

"*If*," Whaley said. "Don't freak on me." He picked up the spatula and shoved the collards around the pan.

"Whaley, don't get mad. I just want to know. Why do you want to fight so much?" Her brain was tired, and she struggled to frame her thought in a way that wouldn't make him explode. "Is it because you don't feel like you're doing anything important in the real world?"

"The *real world?* What's not real about a war?"

"You know what I mean!" But the irony smacked her. Who was she to talk about the real world? She pulled out the egg carton and began cracking eggs into a bowl.

"It's a stupid question, Addie. You've watched me crash and burn all year."

"You haven't! Everything was fine until you got expelled." But she knew he was right.

Whaley took the bowl of eggs and started beating them with a fork, as if he were holding them personally responsible for his shortcomings. "Come on. We both know I wasn't going to graduate."

"It's not like you couldn't! You're smart. You just don't care."

"Got that in one, Sherlock." He poured the eggs over the vegetables in the pan. "It just doesn't seem worthwhile."

"Well, what *does*, for goodness' sake?"

Whaley leaned against the counter. "You know that bar I was working on yesterday?"

Addie nodded.

"Some parts of it were so beat up, they looked like drift-wood. But when I filled it in, sanded it down, and put the wax on, it came to life. I swear, it was like I could hear people sitting at the barstools and having drinks."

"You could?"

"Not really." He grinned at her. "I'm not as spooky as you. What I mean was, I felt like John Hammond must've with Robert Johnson."

"Like *who?*"

"That blues guitarist from the twenties. The guy who supposedly went to the crossroads and sold his soul to the devil to play guitar better than anyone in the world?" His voice warmed as it always did when he talked about his old bluesmen. Delicately, Addie nudged the edge of the omelet with the spatula, almost holding her breath. "Remember, his recordings were so damaged that his music almost disap-peared? But then John Hammond remastered them. It's like that. If someone really cares and tries to preserve something, they can stop it from disappearing for good. That's worth doing. Besides," he added, "I really owe Mrs. Powell."

Addie sighed. "Then *why* would you join the army? When you have so much worthwhile stuff to do right here?"

"Because . . . come on, Addie. I told you. I doubt Mrs.

Powell is ever going to get the money she needs. And besides, this war . . . it isn't like that mess you were reading about. World War One. This war really *will* make the world safe for democracy. Isn't that what they said back in the day? Believe it or not, that's another thing I care about." He looked at her. "One day, even Mike will thank me for it. And you will, too. I'll set the table. You've got to wolf that down if you want to get to school on time."

"There's enough for three people here. You want some?"

He grinned. "Does the bear—"

"Yes, it does. Shut up."

Zack rushed in, still in his pajamas, and nearly collided with Whaley, who was on his way out with the plates and forks. He took one look at the omelet and said, "I want a waffle."

"Philistine," Whaley grumbled, and disappeared into the hallway.

Where'd he get that word? Addie wondered. He sounded like Emma Mae.

Dad came into the kitchen close on Zack's heels. "Hup, two, three. I want everyone out of this house in twenty minutes."

"Not me!" Zack protested. "School starts at nine thirty."

"He means me," Addie said, carrying the omelet out to the table. School *did* seem irrelevant this morning. It was the closest she'd ever come to Whaley's point of view. "Bring the cups, Zack."

She moved the books off the table and perched them on the mantel. Then she put the pan down on a red place mat.

Whaley returned and dished out their breakfast. "Did you know Mrs. Powell's got a meeting at the Preservation Commission office tomorrow morning?" he said.

"*Tomorrow?* But she hasn't got the interior photos yet! She needs them."

"We couldn't find anything, remember? There probably aren't any."

Addie groaned. *But I bet there were,* she thought. *I just don't have them now!* "Are you going to see her today?"

"Yeah." He looked a little embarrassed. "I said I'd go over and sort of estimate how much of the place I could fix myself, so she won't need to pay a contractor for that bit. If it's a go-ahead for remodeling, I mean. Like a work plan."

"Good." Addie plopped down in a chair and took a bite of the omelet, hardly noticing the rubbery texture of the undercooked collards. "Listen. When you see Mrs. Powell, tell her to let them know we're still looking for evidence of the theater's previous state." He opened his mouth to object, but she rushed on. "I *am*, Whaley. I'm still looking. Maybe I should come with you today."

"Maybe you should go to school," Dad said, carrying in a waffle for Zack, who had put his head down on the table. "Though I tremble to ask, Adeline: Would I be correct in assuming you'll pass your Algebra II test tomorrow?"

"I'll call Almaz. She's good at research," Addie continued, talking to Whaley. "Tell Mrs. Powell."

"Did you hear me?" Dad's voice heated up. He leaned over the table toward her.

"Algebra II, yes." Addie smiled brightly at her father,

who scowled at her. "Almaz's helping me study tonight. She promised."

She took another bite and looked up at the clock. Seven. She turned back to Whaley. "Tell Mrs. Powell I'll definitely find something before her meeting tomorrow. I'll bring it over tonight."

"What's with you, McNeal? You sound very sure of yourself. Another revealing dream?" Whaley teased. "Did it point you in the direction of the photographs we need?"

"You could say that." She looked up at her father. "All right, all right. I'm going."

MELTED INTO AIR, INTO
THIN AIR

Addie sat in the back row in every one of her morning classes, reading the local history and theater books she'd brought from home under her desk. Except in AP Biology. Ms. Rosenthal caught her immediately and told her to put the books away. No one messed with Ms. Rosenthal.

When the bell rang, she made a beeline to the chem lab. The door was open, and Addie could see Almaz hanging up her lab coat and grabbing her bag off the floor.

"Almaz! Come with me. I need to get my Algebra II book." She grabbed her friend's elbow and linked her arm through hers. "I got your text. Sure you have time tonight?"

"I'm sure. You know how I love a treasure hunt. Where do we look?"

"The U. We've got to check the *Daily*. Dad said we'd have to go to their morgue."

"Their *morgue?* Have you been reading too much of that vampire crap?"

Addie laughed, pulling her along past the crowd by the open door of the cafeteria. The smell of greasy pizza and burned hamburger meat followed them down the hallway. "It's where newspapers go to die. Where they store back issues if they're not online."

Almaz looked at her curiously, pulling a container of blueberry yogurt out of her bag and ripping the aluminum top off. "Last I heard, you'd looked everywhere. What makes you so certain there's something out there waiting for you to find it?"

"Just trust me on this!"

Almaz offered her the plastic spoon she'd rummaged out of her bag, and Addie scooped up some yogurt. "Mm. Thanks. I hardly got any of Whaley's omelet."

"That's probably lucky." Almaz grinned. "So I'll meet you—"

Her words were drowned out by raucous voices. A bunch of students from the drama club were pushing past them, yelling lines at one another, falling over with laughter. The divas and their entourage—no one Addie was friends with, like Sun or Jake. Addie had to fold her biology textbook against her chest and flatten herself against the wall. Almaz stepped into the alcove between the rows of lockers. The drama crew was so full of their own noise and hilarity that they didn't even notice her. Only Taylor, who'd gotten the part of the troll princess, saw Addie. She whispered something to Keira. Keira smirked.

When they'd passed, Almaz stepped out from between the lockers and made a show of dusting herself off, as if they'd clattered by her on a dirt road. "Oh, my God, Addie, how can you stand them? They're so *annoying!*" She scowled. "That was so unfair you didn't get that part."

"You know what?" Addie straightened her back and snapped her fingers, just like Meg had the last time she saw her. "I—don't—care." She gave Almaz a radiant smile. "I don't care about their little world."

Almaz did a double take. "You—really?"

"Really." And it was true. The horror of the audition seemed much farther in the past than the *Peer Gynt* read-through at the Jewel. She'd forget the humiliation of that audition someday, she knew, but she'd always remember dancing with Reg in the hall of the Dovrë king.

They reached Addie's locker, at the end of the hall near the band room. "You want to know why?"

"Why?"

Addie stretched, smiling and reaching for the ceiling. She inclined her head from one side to another, cracking her neck luxuriously. It was her favorite warm-up exercise. "Because I'm going to work at the Jewel when Mrs. Powell gets it fixed up."

"Really?" Almaz looked delighted, though doubtful. "What are they going to pay you to do?"

"I don't need to be paid. I'll do anything." As she turned the dial on her locker, she saw the Jewel rebuilt, buzzing with energy just like Emma Mae's theater had been. Maybe someday she could assist the director Becky Powell would hire. Though she wouldn't say this to Almaz—she knew how outrageous it would sound. "Maybe they'll start a youth program. I'd definitely try out for that. Or I could even help set it up." Excitement bubbled inside her. Props. Makeup. Publicity—suddenly the desire was pounding inside her for the theater to come to life again. Not for Whaley or Mrs. Powell this time. For herself. "I mean, you never know what'll happen in the future."

"If the Jewel has a future," Almaz said.

"Sometimes you really are a poop." Addie poked her in the ribs and dialed in the last number of her combination. The lock clicked, and she opened her locker and pulled out her math book.

"That's why I'll make the big bucks. Someone will hire me to be head poop at their big research lab someday, you just wait."

Addie laughed, feeling lighter and more full of purpose than she had all day. She shut the locker and headed off to class.

"See you after practice!" Almaz called after her.

In sixth period, they were supposed to be working on an essay, so it was easy to keep reading her book with the computer screen blocking her from the teacher's view. By then, she'd skimmed through all but one of the books she'd brought. And it was there that she found the only reference to the Jewel. It was in an interview with Katharine Cornell, the actress who'd been photographed in the theater bar in 1933. Floods had delayed her train in eastern Washington, and the whole troupe had to transfer to some trunk line that ran into Tacoma and then catch a train up the Sound. "I've never been so happy to see any place as I was to see that grand playhouse," Cornell told the interviewer, "with the lights shining through the windows, and the radiators—thank goodness!—hissing away merrily. Emma Mae Powell, the manager, bustled us into dressing rooms without once letting us feel our delay had inconvenienced her. It was already midnight, but the audience had waited, and we drew the curtains and let them watch us set up the scenery. The play started at one in the morning!"

A great story, Addie thought. But no photos, and no reference to where photos might be found.

And no mention of Reg.

She knew better than to expect it, but she was disappointed nonetheless. She'd hoped to find that he'd finally accepted his talent and become part of the troupe.

The hands on the wall clock seemed to have come to a standstill. She groaned. Why couldn't she have been like Whaley for once and skipped school?

She logged on and did a quick search for the *Daily* but found that the paper was only archived back fifteen years. She'd Googled the Jewel many times over the past few days and didn't find anything new as she repeated the search. The Powells, she knew, had never posted their family or professional history on a genealogy page. Nor had Meg Turner. She cast another agonized glance at the clock and wondered once again why she hadn't walked over to the U. first thing that morning instead of torturing herself all day.

When the last bell rang, she tore out of the classroom,

dumped everything but her math text in her locker, and rushed to the bus stop. If the 44 hadn't come immediately, she would have run all the way. As it was, she leaped off the bus at the north end of the campus and sprinted to the building she'd visited with Reg. The tinted green windows had been replaced with clear ones, but otherwise it looked exactly the same.

Except that the *Daily* office wasn't there anymore.

After a long, frustrating search, she finally found it in another building. Inside, students were working on computers, surrounded by a mess of coffee cups and Styrofoam boxes exuding teriyaki smells. They were friendly, and Addie felt hopeful as they led her to the archives. The room that housed them was dank, cold, and dark—*morgue* was definitely the right word for it! Nonetheless, she dove into the work with alacrity. But she was disappointed when she found hard copies of the newspaper went back only twenty years.

"It'll be on microfiche, bet you anything," the editor, a girl with a blond buzzcut, told her. "At Suzzallo. You know where that is?"

Addie nodded. It was the huge Gothic library in Red Square with buttresses and gargoyles and stained-glass windows. She and Zack often had to dig Dad out of his grad-student cubicle there on weekends so they could go eat pho in one of the cheap Vietnamese restaurants on the Ave.

A librarian in a brilliant gold and red sari showed her how to set up the microfiche. "A database would be easier, of course," she told her, "but there are so many of these small papers that haven't been digitalized yet. You'll just have to suffer with our Stone Age technology."

Images of cavemen bashing clubs into microfiche machines flashed in Addie's mind as she settled herself in front of the ungainly contraption.

It took a few moments to get the hang of it, cranking the knob to straighten the picture, pressing the button forward and back to move the film. But once she did, the years spun by in a blur of black typescript, which she stopped now and then to hunt out the dates in the thick-crammed pages.

Finally, she reached the spring of 1917 and began turning the knob more slowly. What day had it been when she went to the campus with Reg? A Saturday. And the following Friday would have been May 4, the opening night for *Macbeth*.

She found Friday, April 27, and inched the next newssheet up onto the screen. This had to be Monday's paper, since the *Daily* wasn't published on weekends. It was hard to read the old type. Addie leaned in so close that she actually squashed her nose against the screen and jogged the machine. The image went fuzzy.

But once she managed to get it in focus again, she felt triumphant. Under the masthead, the page was thin on text and heavy on photos, just as she'd suggested to Reg, centered around a large picture of an imposing building. Ha! Who would have thought it would be so easy?

Reg's article about the Wobblies must be tucked away on the second page. She smiled to herself, thinking of him pulling that trick on the provost. It would be fun to see what he had written.

She put her hand on the knob and was about to roll the film forward when she realized she'd made a mistake.

The building in the photo under the masthead wasn't the Jewel at all.

It was Denny Hall, one of the buildings on campus. Dad had told her the name a million times when they walked by it. How could she have confused it with the Powells' theater?

She looked more closely at the rest of the pictures. They weren't the ones Tom had taken, either. There was the big open quad with spindly cherry trees in bloom, crowded with girls in white dresses wearing caps on their heads and bending over people stretched out on the pavement. The caption read: *Red Cross training.* Another shot showed an ambulance drill down by the canoe dock.

So where were the pictures of the Jewel? What had Reg and Tom done with them?

She made an exasperated noise. Boys! They were useless! Why had they left the theater without letting her know they hadn't taken the shots?

To be fair, though, it wouldn't have mattered to them what was on the front page. As long as the article about the Wobbly trial made it into readers' hands. But to her, it was a disaster.

Addie groaned. "What am I going to do now?" she muttered.

An old man with a bluish five o'clock shadow who was

being helped by the librarian glared at her from a neighboring microfiche machine.

Think. Don't panic. Maybe they had run the pictures and the article on another day?

Addie spun the film forward into the week, to check.

Nothing . . . nothing . . . wait a second.

She stopped turning the knob, puzzled. Was it a four-day week?

There wasn't a holiday she'd forgotten about, was there? Memorial Day? No, that was the end of May, not the beginning. And was it even a holiday back then? May Day? No. Well, it didn't matter. Maybe they'd held off until the day *Macbeth* opened. Friday, right? Where was it? Oh, yes, she saw it. But even on *Macbeth's* opening night, there was nothing about the Jewel at all. What had happened to the photos, then? And why was this week so short?

She counted back. Friday was here. Thursday, Wednesday.

Addie looked more closely at the edition with the pictures of the Red Cross nurses in the quad. The lights above her head buzzed like irritated bees.

The date on the masthead was Tuesday, May 1, 1917.

She flopped back into the grainy plastic curve of her chair, folded her arms, and took a deep breath. There was no Monday edition.

She needed help. Thankfully, the creepy old man seemed to have released the librarian. "Um, excuse me?"

"Yes." The librarian turned and walked over to Addie. The silk of her sari fluttered.

"Why would an edition of the *Daily* be missing from the microfiche? Could it be lost?"

"I hope not!" The librarian bent down to look at the screen. "What are you looking at, 1917? Wow. That long ago, anything is possible. Isn't there a note? We usually flag it when a day is missing."

Addie scanned through. "No note," she said.

"Let me check." Frowning, the librarian pulled up a chair and settled her glasses on her nose. "Mmm." The frown deepened. "I transferred these images myself, a few months ago. You know—this is May, right?" She paused and tapped her pencil in a light rhythm. "I had a few copies of the *Daily* from that week, but none of them had the date you're looking for. I remember thinking it was strange. There wasn't any notice explaining why in the paper." She shook her head. "No, I don't think the issue was lost. I think it just wasn't published in the first place. It *would* be the one you're looking for, wouldn't it?"

Numbly, Addie thanked her. She removed the microfiche, handed it back, and stumbled out of Suzzallo in a daze. Only vaguely aware of the crowds of students, the skateboarders, and the last lonely blossoms on the cherry trees, she slowly circled the library, trying to figure out what to do.

The pictures weren't there.

Not only that, an entire edition of the paper was missing. Had the provost discovered the deception? Had he destroyed yet another pile of the papers? Had Tom's film been ruined? Or maybe never developed?

And then, finally, she thought, *Did Reg chicken out?* Maybe he'd decided it was too risky, that he really would get kicked out of school. Addie shook her head. She couldn't believe it. He wasn't the type to chicken out.

Once again, she was thinking of him as though he were as real, as present in her own time, as Whaley.

Whaley, who was going to be at the meeting tomorrow when Mrs. Powell showed up empty-handed.

That couldn't happen!

She turned abruptly and pulled out her cell to call Almaz.

Then she sat, deep in thought, on the library steps for half an hour until her friend finally appeared, wearing shin guards and her soccer uniform. She ran up the steps two at a time and grabbed Addie's hands. "Don't look like that!" She pulled Addie to her feet. "And don't give up. You're good at research, but I'm better when it comes to finding a needle in a haystack. I've got to get home by six, but I can help until then."

"My brain's dead-ending, Almaz."

"Yeah, and when I called Whaley he said you forgot to tell your dad where you were. They're going nuts over there, getting the store ready for tomorrow. He told me to remind you about your Algebra II exam."

"Who *cares* about Algebra II?" Addie yanked the library door open. "I need to find these pictures. And there's nothing in the microfiche of the *Daily*."

They stopped for a moment in the foyer, where the two great marble staircases coiled up to the second floor on each side.

"Why don't you ask that Reg guy to help? I thought he was connected to the Jewel. Maybe he knows where some photos are."

"He's helped a lot already," Addie said quickly. It was all she could come up with.

"Really? When do you ever see him?" Almaz asked curiously. "I'm beginning to wonder if he even exists." Addie looked up at the huge chandelier hanging over her head, wishing she had never mentioned Reg in the first place. It wasn't as if he would ever meet Almaz, or anyone she knew. Her stomach twisted. She had never kept secrets from Almaz before.

"And why were you only looking through the *Daily*?" Almaz continued. "I don't get that. Why wouldn't you look in regular newspapers, or arts publications or something?" Addie opened her mouth to respond, and then closed it again. After all, she might have a point. Who knows? Maybe Reg and Tom had given the photos to Meg and they'd been published somewhere else. "Dawit's girlfriend is in the drama department here, and she says the *Daily* only reviews student productions," Almaz went on. Dawit was her older brother. "What years are you guys looking for, anyway?"

"From the year the theater opened—1910, I think—until maybe the forties? But I read there was a good series taken in 1917, so I've been trying to track that down."

"Okay," Almaz said briskly. "Tell you what. We'll ask the reference librarian what the biggest arts publications were in the city. I'll go through microfiche, or databases if anything's online."

"Good idea." Addie was starting to feel her optimism return.

"Did you think of special collections? That's all local history." Almaz pointed to a library guide posted on a pillar beside them.

"It *is*? I wish I'd known."

Once they'd gotten the list of probable publications from the reference desk, they split up. In the special collections room, where she had to take all pens out of her pockets before she was allowed to enter, Addie checked for primary sources from the Jewel: diaries, letters, published programs. But there weren't any. She tried records from other theaters. There were a few mentions of the Jewel, but none with photos.

At five thirty, Almaz came down to find her. She had a list of productions that had been advertised in local papers. "It's spotty, but I copied some ads for performances at the Jewel." She laid three dark Xeroxes in front of Addie, one for *Antigone*, one for *The Corn Is Green*, and one for *The Tempest*. None had an actual photo of a performance. Meg, Addie noticed with a pang, had directed *Antigone* in 1932.

"There were reviews, too. But none of them have photos that are going to help us." She put her hand on Addie's shoulder. "I wish I could tell you some good news, but that's the best I could do."

"Don't worry. You were a big help," Addie assured her, trying to look cheerful. "You'd better get home."

"All right. And I'll drop by your house at eight. You're going to pass that test whether you want to or not."

Addie managed a faint smile. "All right."

After Almaz left, she ran to a nearby cafeteria, grabbed a slice of pizza, and ate it while walking back to the library. She phoned Dad and felt relieved when the answering machine picked up and she didn't have to face his wrath about shirking the cleanup for the grand reopening.

Then she went back to the special collections room and continued her search.

A picture of children gathered around a flower-strewn coffin made her catch her breath. Their mothers and fathers stood behind them in patched coats and black hats. Some of the men were holding up books with the title *IWW Songs* on the covers. It was the funeral of someone named Felix Baran, an IWW member. The writing on the back of the photo said that he had died in the Everett massacre in 1916.

One of Gustaf's pals.

She knew Gustaf and Frida were real, but to see the photo here, in a history archive . . . how could any of this be? Should she call Dad and ask him to check her into an asylum?

No. She was too busy.

She glanced at the clock. Six thirty already. She should be home.

But she plowed through photo after photo. There were pictures of soldiers leaving for France. Pictures of the university. Of other theaters. But none of the interior of the Jewel.

Finally, a bell rang to tell her the special collections room was closing.

And she gave up.

CENOTAPH

The next morning, she knew she should tell Whaley she hadn't found anything. He was going to see Mrs. Powell today, after all, and he should know all the details. But she only managed to mumble "No, not yet," when he asked, and pretended to be very busy getting ready for school. *Not yet,* she told herself fiercely. Because she *would* find something. She didn't know where. And maybe not in time for that meeting he was going to today. But soon, one way or another.

She jammed her shoes onto her feet. Why was it so hard to find evidence of people and places from the early twentieth century? It wasn't like she was digging up relics of the Stone Age!

There was only one solution: she'd need to go back. If only she could just whip out the mirror and do it now! *Theoretically,* she thought, *yes, I could. But practically, no.* She couldn't end up on this end of town in 1917, with no money and no transportation, and expect to make her way to the theater to find Reg. Nor did it make sense to go over to the Powells' house and start there. How could she explain simply turning up on his—their!—doorstep? The only place people were expecting to see her was at the Jewel. She needed to start there.

Then that's what I'll do, right after school, she decided. *If I can get hold of the key* . . . Oh, it was more complicated than she'd thought. She'd have to stop by the Powells' after all, just to pick it up.

All right, then. And she flew down the back steps.

But when she opened the door, she ran straight into Dad, carrying grocery bags. Three whole salmon wrapped in paper were sticking out of one of them. "You see this?" Dad said, lifting up the bag.

"That's a lot of fish."

"Darn tootin'. We've got a lot of people to feed tonight. And I can't run the store and fire up the barbecues at the same time. So you need to come straight home after school. Do you hear me? No drifting off to the theater or wherever you get to."

The grand reopening. "Oh, *God.*" Why today of all days?

"What was that?"

"Nothing," Addie grumbled. But when she looked up at Dad in his rumpled corduroys and sand-colored sweater, she remembered that he had been working long into the nights, thumping around the bookstore, making calls, designing flyers. . . .

"I mean it, Addie. I need you here. It's important for all of us." He glanced up the stairs and added, "For Whaley, too."

"I *know*. I hear you, Dad." She looked at his tired eyes and forced herself to sound less annoyed. "I mean, of course I'll be here." Her heart sank. "You can count on me."

But it was exasperating to have to come home and work at the store. And even worse to waste her time at school taking a test she didn't care about. How could Algebra II possibly be important? Who *cared*? But she owed it to Almaz to try to pass, since she'd come over last night to help her study.

A twinge of guilt hit her as she wrote her name on the test and settled into her seat. She hadn't been such a great friend to Almaz lately, hadn't gone to any of her games or dropped in on her shift at the grocery. Too busy obsessing about the Jewel and its inhabitants, living and—

"You have the whole period," Mr. Brent told the class. The prospect of handing out bad math grades made him happy and at peace with the world. You could almost see him rubbing his hands with glee. Addie forced herself to stop wondering what was happening at the meeting with the preservation society long enough to write equations that—she hoped—made sense. But as soon as she finished, the thoughts came rushing back.

When she got home, she found the grand reopening in full swing. Through the brand-new plate-glass windows, she could see Dad behind the counter chatting with customers. Almaz's dad was serving up Ethiopian dips and injera from a hot plate on the sidewalk in the shade of the red cedar. People were gobbling up the free food and basking in the bright, cool sunshine at the card tables and chairs they'd placed on the sidewalk in front of the store. Mrs. T. had stuck new anti-war posters in the windows.

Despite itching to get away, she was glad to see the bookstore hopping with life again. Dad's Victrola was back from the repair shop and in its place of honor on the shelf by the cash register. From the open doorway, Addie could hear an old Django Reinhardt recording spinning on the turntable. Gypsy jazz. It was one of Dad's oldest and most treasured 78s. From 1929, she remembered him saying.

She smiled to herself. Wouldn't it be fun to swipe the album and play it for Reg? He wouldn't even have heard of Django. Suddenly, she saw herself dancing with him to this music. Outside, on some green lawn. A late-night party . . .

Don't be an idiot.

She crossed the street, pushed her way through the small crowd of people. The bell on the door jingled as she entered, and Dad looked up.

"There she is now," he remarked to Enrique's mom, Mrs. Paseo. Whaley and Rico were playing tonight, and Mrs. Paseo loyally turned up for most of their performances. She'd been to more shows than even Addie had.

"Have you seen Whaley?" Addie asked.

Dad shook his head. "He left for that meeting at the Jewel and I haven't seen him since. Not that I haven't needed him."

"Was he at your place, Mrs. Paseo?"

"No. But Enrique was expecting him any minute." She

wagged her finger at Addie and said to Dad, "Like twins, those two, aren't they? If they're not together, they're looking for each other."

Dad raised an eyebrow. "Well, since her twin has gone AWOL, Addie's in charge." He jerked his thumb at the banner plastered on the wall behind the counter: GRAND RE-OPENING—BARBECUE AND DANCING TO FOLLOW. "Go, mistress of the festivities! Make our backyard festive." He winked at Addie. "You know what to do." He turned away to ring up a pile of books for an old man with a nervous black poodle on a leash. "Nice to see you again, Morris."

"Take more than an earthquake to keep me and Buñuel away," Morris wheezed. Addie realized he was the man Whaley had argued with at the Brown Bear the other day. She bent down and patted the poodle, who snarled at her. She snatched her hand away and headed toward the backyard. Zack was loafing in the stacks and she dragged him outside with her.

Nothing was ready. Oh, well. It didn't matter. After years of backyard productions, she was pretty adept at pulling together cast parties. This would be the same sort of thing, but bigger. She rolled a large aluminum garbage can into the yard from the alley and dragged the recycling bins over. With Zack's grudging help, she set up two big folding tables and wheeled out their barbecue grills. Then she pulled the fire pit out of the garage. Whaley had insisted that they needed a bonfire.

Zack found the strings of chili lights she had used for A

Midsummer Night's Dream, and they wrapped them around the trunk of the Douglas fir before plugging them into the outlet in the shed.

Up in the kitchen, she discovered that someone—hopefully not Whaley—had marinated chicken kebabs and wrapped the salmon in foil. By the time she brought the food down, the neighbors had started to arrive with curries and bowls of potato salad and chips and coleslaw.

Enrique's van suddenly squealed to a halt in the alley behind the house. Abandoning the cooler she was filling with drinks, Addie ran over to him. "Hey, Rico! Where's Whaley?"

"I thought he was with you." Rico climbed out. "Me and Cam had to load all the equipment ourselves."

"So where's Cam?" Addie pressed her face against the window of the van, looking for the pimply drummer.

"Pulled a muscle loading." A grin split Rico's broad face and he punched Addie's arm. "That leaves you and me to set up, Addiebelle!"

"I'm in charge of everything already! Besides, I twisted my ankle the last time I tried to carry that hardware duffel, remember? Can't you wait for Whaley?"

"No way, friend. It's late already. And it's *your* party. You're lucky you're getting quality entertainment for free."

He was right. It would be ungrateful not to help. Addie sighed. "What's the band name this time?"

"Groovy Like a Pig," Rico said proudly, opening the back door of the van. "Whaley wanted Whaley and the Chain Gang, but we said no."

They started unloading. Whaley still didn't show up.

By the time Addie had carried a few drums and helped Enrique lift the old Fender amp out of the car, she wasn't just worried about Whaley—she was ready to kill him. He must know she was dying to hear how the meeting with the preservation commission had gone. Where was he?

"I think you should leave that for Whaley," she said, gazing unhappily at the duffel full of drum hardware in the back of the van.

"Leave what?"

She whirled around to find Whaley right behind her, standing by the shed. "Where have you been?"

"I'll get the rest of this," he said, without meeting her eyes. "Come on, Rico."

"Yeah, thanks, big help," Rico said sarcastically. "Poor Addie had to do the heavy lifting. She—"

"Tell me what happened at the meeting, Whaley," Addie interrupted. But Whaley just picked up the duffel and walked off to set up the PA.

Just then Zack crashed into her, waving a box of camping matches over his head, a delirious grin on his face. He slid it open and pulled out a match, lit it, and threw it into the air. "Can I start the fire?"

"No way, you little pyro! That's all I need." She snatched the box from his hand, took them over to the grill, and set about lighting the coals.

A few minutes later, Almaz showed up, holding an enormous bowl of spicy lentils and grinning from ear to ear. "Dawit took over the cash register for me. Mom sent this."

Addie maneuvered the other dishes around to squeeze the bowl onto the table.

"Thanks, Almaz. That looks great."

Almaz looked out toward the corner of the yard where Whaley was sliding a cymbal onto its pole. "Excellent! I forgot the band was playing!" She tossed the hem of her embroidered skirt. "Does this mean you're doing the Cruella act—emceeing?"

Addie slapped her forehead. "Oh, darn, I forgot. Whaley promised me I could, didn't he?" She shook her head. "I guess it slipped my mind."

"Everything's slipping your mind lately. Maybe you've run out of room in your in box," Almaz teased. "What happened at that meeting you were so worried about?"

"No idea! Mr. Rock Star over there can't spare a minute to tell me anything." Addie gave the half-empty bag of briquettes a vicious shake.

"It's tough being so cool." Almaz smoothed her skirt with her hands and called across the yard, "Hey, Whaley! Addie wants to talk to you!"

But he only waved in her direction and began fiddling with the amp.

"See what I mean?"

"Come on, I'll help you with the rest of the food. And cheer up. Maybe that guy Reg will show."

Oh, if only, Addie thought. It was easy to picture Reg here. He'd be nowhere near as freaked out as she'd been in his time, she bet. Probably get along with everyone, too. Except Whaley, maybe.

"Hey, your fire's going out." Almaz grabbed the newspaper that Addie had been absent-mindedly feeding in between the charcoal and stuffed in a long strip. "I'll handle this."

"Thanks. I'll get the tongs."

The yard was filling up. Addie threw the salmon and chicken on once the coals were just right, and Almaz helped her man the grills. People loaded their plates. Enrique, Whaley, and Cam started their first set. Mrs. T. emerged from her house and lit the bonfire, using wood and kindling that Zack had carried for her. Its flames licked out against the suspended twilight.

Addie didn't get a break until the moon rose. Then she darted over to Mrs. T.'s side.

"Did you get to the meeting today?"

Mrs. T. shook her head. "No, darling. I'm really supposed to rest my foot if I want to start walking again in a day or two. After the march, I'm not taking any chances. I invited Becky to this shindig, but I haven't seen her yet. Can't Whaley tell you what happened?"

Addie shrugged. "He's kind of busy right now," she said, and jerked her thumb toward where Whaley and Enrique were banging out a punk love song.

Mrs. Turner chuckled. "He loves that, doesn't he?"

Smoke wafted from the barbecue, carried on the faint chilly breeze. Dad closed the till and locked up the store, and Zack and his friends put grapes in their mouths and spit them at each other. Addie got up and began wandering around among all the friends and well-wishers, searching for Becky Powell. If Whaley wouldn't talk to her and

Mrs. T. didn't know anything, Mrs. Powell was the only person to ask.

But she didn't seem to be there yet. Giving up, Addie just plunked down on a bench next to Almaz, who had been dancing and was fanning herself despite the evening chill.

"This is our last song, and it goes out to our very own Whaley Price," Enrique was saying in that corny master-of-ceremonies voice he used onstage.

"Someone should tell him how cheesy he is," Addie said to Almaz. "It would help the band."

"True." Almaz took a cherry tomato off a dish and delicately bit into it. "But I *like* Rico. I don't want to hurt his feelings."

"Constructive criticism shouldn't hurt his feelings," Addie said, grabbing a slice of corn bread. "There are people who can do that." *People like Meg Turner,* she thought.

Meg. Wait a second.

She sat bolt upright. *This is Emma Mae's office. Mine is down the hall.*

That was it. She'd told Reg and Tom that the photos were for Meg to use for publicity. What was wrong with her? Why hadn't she searched Meg's office at the Jewel? She'd been through half the stacks at the university and every website in the virtual universe, but she hadn't even thought to look there. Oh, she had to tell Whaley. She leaped to her feet and waved to get his attention.

"What's up?" Almaz was staring at her. "You look like you're trying to summon a lifeboat."

Self-consciously, Addie dropped her hand. "I just

realized—the photos—there's another place at the theater where we might find them. The director had an office, too. Not just the manager. It's a long shot, but if there's still a desk or cabinets or something . . ."

Almaz got up and put a hand on her arm. "I guess that's an idea. But don't get your hopes up. I mean, if all that searching last night didn't turn up anything . . ."

"I know! But our chances are slipping away and I have to keep trying."

At that moment, Whaley glanced in their direction. She waved again, but he didn't register it. Then she realized it was Almaz he was looking at, an expression of surmise on his face and something else—a sort of hopefulness. Almaz was picking up paper plates. She looked beautiful, Addie thought. Tall and strong, with thin gold earrings setting off the lovely lines of her features. But she hadn't seen the look Whaley sent her way.

"Almaz . . ." Addie ventured, forgetting her own urgency for a second. But Almaz had already set off toward the side of the house to throw the plates in the compost bin. Oh, well. If Whaley had something to say to Almaz, she was sure he could say it himself. All she wanted was to catch him as soon as he got off the stage. But the band was attacking their instruments again, launching into "I Fought the Law."

During the chorus, Mrs. T. called out, "No jail time for Whaley!" The backyard resounded with cheers and whistles.

Whaley bashed the song to an end, and Addie bounded

across the yard to where he and Rico were leaning their instruments against the amps.

"Sorry for not showing up this afternoon," Whaley was saying. "I had to sign up for that test to join the army."

Addie froze.

"I didn't think you'd go through with that, man." Rico's voice was always slow, as if he were pondering what he said while he said it. "Don't you have some project at that theater? I thought we were going to get a gig there."

"It doesn't look like that'll pan out."

Stunned, Addie slipped back into the darkness by the shed. So that was why he was avoiding her.

"Besides, what if the war is over before I can get there? If there's nothing going for me here, I don't want to miss my chance."

"Gotta respect that." Enrique clapped his big hand against Whaley's shoulder. "But what about your trial? You can't leave the state, right? And can you join the military if you've got a conviction?"

"I won't get convicted! And anyway, you can get a waiver—"

Addie couldn't listen to any more. It was all crumbling around her, the carefully constructed future she'd imagined. Whaley, the Jewel, a youth program . . . and just because she hadn't tracked down a few old photos.

Disappointment bit into her. No. She couldn't let this happen.

Without a second thought, she dodged around the side

of the shed and took off running. She ran out of the alley and onto the street and headed east, block after block, up and down hills. A bus was approaching. With a burst of speed she made it to the nearest stop and jumped on.

As the bus crossed the University Bridge, she watched the ship canal gleaming like obsidian far below, remembering how it had looked from Reg's flivver, crossing the bridge that no longer existed. She got off at the stop by the park but didn't take the shortcut through it. Not on her own at night. Instead, she walked all the way around to Salmon Bay Drive. There were no tulips blooming in front of the Powells' house anymore, only straggly, unkempt rhododendrons.

Taking a deep breath, she marched up the steps, trying not to feel shy as she rang the bell.

The door was answered so immediately she startled. A man she had never seen before was standing there, wearing a dark gray pullover and jeans.

"Hello," she said uncertainly.

"Hello."

"Um, I'm Addie McNeal. I'm sorry to bother you so late. I just wondered if I could have a word with Mrs. Powell."

"Oh, *you're* the famous Addie." The man gave her a tired smile, looking anxious, and sort of overworked, but friendly.

Looking—Addie realized as he stepped into the pool of light from the porch lamp—a lot like Reg.

For a second she had a sensation of free fall, like someone on the downhill drop of a roller coaster.

"I'm Dave, Becky's husband." He shook her hand. "I've heard so much about you."

He was maybe fifty, with crow's feet at the corners of his eyes, wire-rimmed glasses, and a bit of a paunch. But there was something about the deep-set eyes and the very thick, dark hair. She'd known Becky Powell was married. Why had it never occurred to her that she was married to someone related to Reg? Her heartbeats seemed to speed up, and to her chagrin, she found herself blushing.

She remembered the black-and-white photographs on the walls when she'd followed Reg into this house: babies in baptismal gowns, young men in graduation robes or soldiers' uniforms, young women posing in their wedding dresses. She peered around the man in front of her, thinking, *What would I see if he asked me in now?*

But he wasn't asking her in; he was apologizing for keeping her out. "It's been a long road for Becky. I'm afraid she's already asleep. That meeting today took it out of her."

"I—I understand," Addie faltered, guilty at forgetting that Becky Powell was still recovering from a grave illness. "I hope I didn't wake her."

"No chance. Doorbell hardly rang. I haven't dashed so fast to answer it since Julie was a baby." Dave Powell looked at her very seriously. "There's *nothing* worse than waking a sleeping baby."

He even sounded like Reg.

Over his shoulder, Addie could see a girl's graduation photo on the china cupboard in the foyer.

"I'll tell Becky you came by. Is there a message you want me to give her?"

"I just wanted to ask how it went with the preservation people." She dared to look him in the face again, and, now that the shock was over, she saw that he had kind eyes. Suddenly, she blurted out, "My friend Whaley was hoping to work for her. If it doesn't work out here, he's going to go off to fight in the war. I thought, if Mrs. Powell can save the Jewel . . ."

"I know. Becky's told me. But the preservation people weren't too encouraging. They need clearer evidence of the original state, and we haven't got that." He looked at her sympathetically. "Still, she convinced them to come and look at the place on Saturday. So it's not all over."

"Saturday?" It was like a reprieve. "We could find something before that! Would you mind if I went to the Jewel tomorrow, Mr. Powell? I thought of a place we haven't looked yet."

"I'd be delighted for you to search around the Jewel. But not tomorrow. Or the next day either." He laughed. "Becky's having it fumigated! Did you know there's a mouse problem?"

"When's the earliest I can go?"

"Friday, I'm pretty sure."

"All right." Addie tried to hide her disappointment.

"I'll tell Becky to leave the key for you when she goes to air it out."

"That's great. Thank you. And please tell Mrs. Powell I hope she feels better."

"I will. Goodbye, Addie."

She walked down the steps and along the moon-dappled sidewalk, almost trembling with frustration. Three whole days before she could search the Jewel! Four before the inspectors came. And if she couldn't search it, she couldn't get over there to use the mirror. . . . Either way, she just had to *wait*. It was intolerable.

The memory of *Peer Gynt* on Meg Turner's stage came back to her, almost unbearably. She felt Reg's hand on her waist, heard her own voice telling the actors how to dance, how to play the scene. *Someday*, Meg Turner had said, *you'll be sitting in my spot*.

Addie closed her eyes and wished hard that someday she really would be in Meg's place. At the Jewel. And she wanted Whaley there, too. Playing his guitar here in Seattle, with her and Dad and Zack and Almaz and all the people they both loved, not across the world in the middle of a war. She tilted her head back, looked up into the sky with its skeins of gray clouds, speckled with stars like sequins in a thin black scarf. And in the blackness, time seemed to melt away, the different layers to merge into one.

Her feet had automatically taken the familiar route back across the park. She was walking like someone in a dream, her steps muffled by the grass. It could be any time at all in here. The twenty-first century. The twentieth. Even earlier.

As if following some long set-out path, she turned toward the yew hedge.

The angel and the soldier were waiting for her, strangely unfamiliar in the patches of shadow and light, where the street lamps speckled them through the tree branches. The moon was reflected in the waters of the fountain at their feet, like a silver fish in a black, black sea.

Addie crouched down in front of them, balancing herself with a hand on the pedestal, and read the words: DEDICATED TO THE MEMORY OF THOSE SEATTLE NATIVES WHO GAVE THEIR LIVES IN THE GREAT WAR. She leaned back thoughtfully, keeping a hand on the base, near the angel's foot.

It was cold all of a sudden. She huddled into the light sweater she had thrown on earlier in the evening and let her eyes rest on the list of names on the base, wandering from A down the alphabet, as if reading a poem.

And then her blood went cold and sluggish in her veins.

There, carved in the marble, was the name R. Powell.

26

FOUR-MINUTE MAN

Addie didn't know how long she stayed in the garden. She lay on the frigid white marble bench and cried until the stinging in her eyelids was as bad as the tear gas.

Time had been her friend. She'd crossed its borders and found the Jewel, the living, breathing home of her heart. She'd found Reg and Meg. She'd found her calling.

But now she'd found out too much.

So time was her enemy, and it was an enemy no one could fight. Not with a Lewis gun or an A4 or a hundred yards of microfiche.

When she got back home, Dad was furious at her for disappearing without a word. Whaley was worried, but she didn't even want to talk to him. She raced upstairs, locked her door, and pulled the photo of the *Peer Gynt* performance out of the frame of her dresser mirror where she'd stuck it. Once again, she read the faint, pointy script: *R. before the mob.*

And the realization hit her: R. was certainly Reg. But *the mob* didn't mean the audience.

It meant "the mobilization."

Someone had written that after he'd left for the war.

She got into bed, but the clock dragged its hands around like a ball and chain. Sleep fled from her as thoughts looped through her brain. *He died in 1918. . . . But maybe it isn't him. . . . His name is right there on the monument. . . . But R could be Robert. Or Ron. Or Ross. . . . How did he die? Artillery fire? Or gas? Or . . . no, he couldn't have . . . he couldn't have. . . . But it's right there. On the monument. . . .*

The words dissolved and she was sitting on the marble bench beside the cenotaph. The stone angel looked down at her. The feathers on her wings stirred.

The earth was hurtling around on its axis under an electric blue sky. She could actually feel it spinning. Mountains, plains, and oceans flashed by like time-lapse photography, a film speeding over time zones, flashing over longitudes. The air sizzled above a desert landscape. Far away, the sound of women wailing. A fighter jet swooped in at unbelievable speed. Monuments to ancient kings exploded and were gone.

Then the world was spinning faster, and a vast snowy steppe spread out before her, tanks and trucks bogged down in the drifts. Horses hitched to big guns frozen where they'd fallen. Across a frigid river stood a city of factories and brick apartment buildings. Frightened eyes were peering out, watching, as the army slowly advanced, leaving behind their dead animals, their frozen jeeps, pushing on toward the river.

The snow melted into a lush field of poppies, flaming orange in tall grass, farmhouses in the distance. The poppies dissolved into churned mud, and Addie saw gashes in the earth where men writhed like worms, packs on their backs and guns useless in their hands. Gas hung in the thick, choking air.

She couldn't look. She jerked her head up to see a sky lashed with white tongues of cloud. The sun burned through them, showering the muddy fields with gold. A biplane dived like a hawk, wings rattling with speed. A second plane rose to meet it. Sprays of bullets flew from beneath the wings, and the first plane spiraled down in a swirl of black smoke and the reek of gasoline.

The angel's wings beat, powerful eagle wings churning the air. But she couldn't rise. She strained and sweated, holding the soldier's motionless form, and Addie understood that he was as heavy as wet earth and clay, while the angel was frail flesh and bone. She hovered over the pedestal, struggling, wings thrashing. The tip of her foot barely left the ground.

Addie grabbed the angel's foot, tried to fling her up into the heavens. The winged girl tripped into the sky, but still hovered low. Addie climbed up onto the empty pedestal, banging her knees and scraping her hands. She grabbed the heel of the soldier's boot, to push him up, too. Cold bit her hand like a serpent.

The angel shook her head. "I can only raise them one at a time," she whispered, "while they cut down thousands."

Addie jerked out of bed, ran to the bathroom, and threw up.

Her next days were leaden. She could barely push herself through the hours. Almaz kept asking what was wrong, what had happened the night of the party. Nothing, Addie said. Nothing. What could she say? She couldn't confide in her or Whaley, and that hurt, but it wasn't anything compared to what she was feeling about Reg.

She passed her Algebra II test. She helped Dad and Whaley in the bookstore. She found herself crying at odd moments. Was there any way to stop it from happening? How could she? It seemed impossible. His name was already listed among the dead. She'd searched and searched for evidence of the past, evidence of its breathing life, and instead this was all she'd found: blunt proof of a life cut short. And yet she couldn't help wishing, hoping . . .

But all I can do, she thought, *is try to change what happens now.*

No matter what, she would find those photos. And wait. Wait impatiently to get back to the Jewel.

Why was there no Monday edition of the paper on microfiche? If it existed at all, she was sure the library would have had it somewhere. After all, Reg's article was about the Everett massacre. That had to have historic value. You'd think it would have been preserved.

She kept plowing through books about Pacific Northwest history and the IWW and Seattle theaters. Fearfully, she searched for references to a soldier named R. Powell who had died in World War I.

But she found nothing.

When Whaley listened to war news on the radio, she left the room. She didn't ask him if he'd taken the army's test, passed the physical. She only asked him to wait until Friday before he submitted his enlistment forms, until she had a chance to look for the photos at the theater. And she knew he wouldn't have agreed at all, except that he was worried about her and probably thought it would make her feel better.

Friday finally came. When the last bell rang, she slammed her locker shut and rushed home, wanting to leave immediately for the Jewel. But she got held up by Zack, who needed help with a science project. Then Dad wanted her to run a late bill to the post office. . . . To her frustration, it was nearly five when she finally got to the bus stop.

At Third and Pine she jumped off the bus and raced around the corner to the Jewel. She bounded up the back steps, found the key, unlocked the door, and dashed along the hall to Meg Turner's office.

With single-minded determination, she flung open the wooden cabinets. They were thick with dust and speckled with black mold. She stuck her head inside, swept her hands along the wood.

Nothing.

She'd hoped there would be a desk, like in Emma Mae's office. But someone must have gotten rid of it. The only piece of furniture was a rocking chair. Card tables were folded in the corner. Empty cardboard boxes were piled up beside them. Moldering scripts and ancient bills lay in messy piles on the bookshelves. Addie flipped through all of them, but no newspaper clippings or photographs fell out.

She opened a closet and found a mangy fur coat hanging on one of the knobs on the wall. But that was all, aside from rusty hangers. She even stepped inside to check the pockets of the coat and stubbed her toe against a loose floorboard in the process.

"Ow!" Annoyed, she sat down on the floor, pulled off her thin shoe, and rubbed her toe. Then she noticed that the loose floorboard stuck up about a quarter of an inch from the others. The one next to it did, too.

Wait a second. With a rush of excitement, she shifted onto her knees and started prying the board up. It lifted fairly easily. Nothing was underneath it, but—was the next one loose as well? A splinter ran into her finger as she jammed her fingertips under it. She didn't know why she suddenly felt like she was onto something, but she did. Despite herself, she was murmuring, "Oh, please, please, please . . ."

But there was nothing under the second board, either.

Just cobwebs and two spiders frantically spinning.

This was getting ridiculous! Who would store photos under a floorboard? What was she thinking? She stormed out of the office, banging the door as she went. "Damn it!" She kicked her foot against the cold radiator, making her toe throb even more. Then she sank down onto the floor and drew her knees to her chest.

She'd failed in every conceivable way. Like the poor struggling angel, unable to save even one soldier, she couldn't manage to find even a scrap of an old newspaper to save the Jewel.

She put her head down on her knees, closed her eyes, and

the dream was with her again—bombs and guns and gas, and the soldiers running straight into the machine-gun fire.

A chill breeze, wafting in from a crack in the doorway, touched her neck with icy fingers.

She lifted her head and opened her eyes. "Reg?"

Of course not! She shivered, and suddenly her teeth were chattering. How stupid. As if he were a ghost. How could he be?

But there was a small, cold fragment of her heart where she knew that a ghost was exactly what he was.

Hesitantly, she reached into her handbag and pulled out the mirror.

It was the only thing to do. But she was afraid. Afraid to step into a stream of time whose current she couldn't slow, couldn't divert or redirect. Or could she? It all sounded so simple—stop Reg from dying. Stop Whaley from going to war. But life was messy. A million impulses led in different directions. A million decisions, mistakes, and just plain accidents guided where it all ended up. And she knew already where Reg's life ended. How could she know what it would take to change that?

She ran her finger over the forms of the three Fates. *Fates?* Did they have to be Fates? Couldn't they be Graces? Wasn't that possible?

Why had this thing come into her hands?

She thought of her dream, of all the misery she'd seen. And she was trying to push it away, to hold off the terrible meaninglessness she'd felt in all that suffering. In Reg's name chiseled in stone. Was life just like that? Did terrible things just happen for no reason?

Of course they did. She'd known that since her mother died.

But there had to be another side to it, didn't there? What she'd seen in the dream was real. The cruelty and the horror were beyond reason. And yet, the world was bigger than that. In the long run, in the bigger picture, everything *had* to have meaning. It had to. Even in putting on a play, every word, every gesture has to carry meaning, even if the audience can't at first see what it is. If she ever, ever became a director, she would hold to that like iron. Why should the world be any different?

But what if there's no director, and everything is hurtling madly through the universe in absolute chaos?

Addie shook her head. Slowly, she turned the mirror over and gazed at herself in the glass, feeling a conscious power at work.

And it wasn't fate or angels. She was sure of that. The power was in her.

The power that takes people on a stage and turns them into a mirror of the world. The power that holds up a glass to every person in the audience. That's what I've got. That's why I have Meg Turner's mirror. I'm meant to use it.

No. Not yet. Suddenly she leaped up, her heart thumping. Dropping the mirror into her bag, she darted down the hall to Emma Mae's office. She tore through the boxes and found a dress, boots, and a scarf like those she'd seen Meg wearing.

She glanced at her vintage bag, which seemed timeless-looking enough to blend in. And after she changed, she ran back out into the hall and snatched up the mirror again.

Then she stared into the glass, straining her eyes, willing herself back.

For the longest time, there was nothing. Just cold and dark, and dust. But she held on. She didn't break her gaze. No matter what, she wasn't going to let there be nothing but all this ruin.

She stared until her eyesight blurred. Until her head spun.

And gradually, the light around her became brighter, the colors richer. The air warmed, and she could suddenly tell that the back door was open.

A quiver ran up her spine. The breeze that wafted in was sweeter smelling than the dank odor of the alleyway she'd walked through to get here. The hallway was bright with lights from the sconces.

And from the front of the theater, she could hear coughs and the shuffling of feet, and violins and violas. An oboe playing scales. The very air seemed to snap with energy. Opening night!

The door slammed shut. She dropped the mirror into her purse and turned around.

Reg was standing there, staring at her.

Adrenaline surged through her.

"Where have you been?" He looked startled. "You're like a ghost, Addie!"

In a second, she had crossed the space between them and grabbed his elbows. "No, I'm not. I'm not a ghost."

"I swear that no one was there a second ago, and then suddenly, Addie McNeal, out of her mysterious wanderings in the ether—"

"I *was* here a second ago." It seemed a stupid conversation when the important thing was that he was here, living and breathing.

She pulled him closer, throwing her arms around his neck, blinking back the tears that were suddenly hot behind her eyelids.

"What's this for?" He tilted her face up. "You'd think I'd returned from the Antarctic with Shackleton."

Then he slipped his arms around her waist, half lifted her off the ground, and kissed her softly on the lips. Addie hooked her arm tighter around his neck, held him so close the buttons on his jacket pressed into her body, and time, their enemy, slunk away like a scolded cur. All the misery and tension uncurled inside her, and all she could feel was the warmth of his body against hers. When Reg let her go, she just shook her head, smiled, and pulled him back to kiss him again. She stumbled as he released her a second time, and they stared at each other, rattled and uncomfortable and intrigued.

"I guess you're not a ghost."

Addie found her footing and laughed up into his face, and the laugh felt like a bird flying into the treetops, sailing away from time and death and up into the sun. "You knew I wasn't. Try another excuse."

Reg spread his hands wide and gave a feckless shrug. "Do you want me to apologize?"

Addie shook her head, her lips twitching with giddy laughter.

"What's that then?" He let Macbeth creep into his voice. "What are you laughing about, darkling creature of the shadows?"

"Nothing. You don't have to apologize. Just do it again." He did.

"It comes with the territory, if that's any excuse." He was speaking into her hair, and his breath was warm on her ear. "Departing soldiers always get kisses."

Addie sprang out of his arms so fast she would have hit the wall if he hadn't grabbed her. She'd been so overjoyed that she hadn't noticed he was wearing an army uniform— an olive-drab jacket with square shoulders and a big belt, a stiff hat with a visor, and wide trouser legs stuffed into black boots.

"Holy crap!"

"Well, I don't know what *that* means. But I don't think it's pious."

Addie clamped her free hand over her mouth. "You can't . . . you shouldn't . . ."

"Oh, don't be a goose, Addie. I'm only going for train-ing. I'll be back before we ship out."

"Ship out? When?"

"How do I know? Whenever they think we're ready to go to France. The train leaves for the Presidio tonight."

"But"—she knew it was weak, but it was all she could think of—"isn't it opening night?"

The door to the women's dressing room swung open, and teasing and hoots of laughter wafted out.

"I'll have to miss the performance." He pulled her back toward him. "You're not going to the show, are you? Not the night I'm leaving." For a moment his expression was uncertain and Addie thought, *He's not sure of me.* She felt a thrill of exultation, and at the same time, a terrible ache. She put out her hand and touched his fingers. "Even if I were Lady Macbeth, I'd skip the performance tonight."

"Strong words."

Addie thought of the angel in her dream and said, "Stronger than bombs."

They stood for a moment, just looking at each other. He ran his fingers down her spine, and she shivered.

Reg was the one who broke the spell. "Are you game for an adventure before waving me tearfully off?"

"What sort of adventure?" *Things are already under way,* she realized. *The current is swift. I have to see if there's anything I can grab on to—a branch over the water, an oar someone cast overboard—to try and slow it down.*

"I've got to get Gustaf Peterson across town. Want to come with me?"

"Oh, I'll do whatever you're doing," she said quickly. "Just don't go, Reg."

"What? To the *Daily Call* office? Why not?"

"No. Don't go to the station. To the war."

"Addie. It isn't as though I have a choice. You can't just not show up."

"But"—she hesitated—"I know what will happen."

"Oh, come on, Addie!" There was a faint edge of harshness in his voice. "What? One of your magic-mirror tricks again?"

Someone opened a door and a brighter light shone into the hall. Addie self-consciously stepped away from Reg. He straightened his jacket.

Emma Mae came out of her office wearing a long blue dress, its bodice resplendent with azure beads. There was a boa of pale blue feathers around her neck, and crystal earrings dangled to her shoulders. Dazzled, Addie thought, *She looks perfect.* Exactly how she should look on opening night. *When I'm a director . . .* She paused. Where had that certainty come from? But she was certain. *When I'm a director, I'll always dress for opening night.*

Mrs. Powell pulled a round watch from her pocket. "It's a ten-thirty train, isn't it, darling? Thank goodness! We should be past curtain by then. I can meet you at the station café. Do you think it'll be overrun with doughboys?" She looked calm, but a brittleness in her voice betrayed her.

"Oh, I'd imagine so."

Emma Mae touched Addie's shoulder. "I'm glad you made it for opening night. But where have you been all week?"

Addie colored. "I've . . . My father needed me at the bookstore. I'm sorry. I don't mean to be unreliable!"

She could see from Emma Mae's expression that unreliable was exactly what she was. "Well, I'm just letting you know: Meg Turner is gunning for you. She started work on *Peer Gynt*, but no one could find you. Don't you have a telephone?"

The answer had to be no. She shook her head.

"Well, I'd advise you to get one! It's no use being a Luddite. Not if you want Meg to keep you on for *Peer Gynt*. And, speaking of that"—Emma Mae fixed a sharp eye on Reg—"*what* have you been doing to poor Andrew Lindstrom?"

"Nothing, Mother." Reg placed his hand on his heart. "I give you my word."

Emma Mae snorted. "Then how come he thinks you're about to steal the lead from him? He came to my office all but accusing me of nepotism and contract breaking because you told him Meg wanted you to take over Peer when you're home on leave."

"So I teased him a bit. Why not? It's not my fault if he's too stupid to realize I can't just take his part away from him. Anyway, he's been up my nose for months." Reg gave his mother an angelic look. "Don't I get to enjoy myself a little bit before bravely facing the Huns' dastardly assaults?"

"Don't joke about it." Emma Mae's eyes darted around, and Addie thought she must be looking for wood to knock on. "Besides, at the moment, I think Andrew is likely to kill you before you even set foot on French soil."

"Kill me and rumple his costume? Nonsense!" A semblance of repentance crept into Reg's voice. "I'm sure it will be a terrific opening, Ma. I wish I were going to see it."

Emma Mae dropped her voice. "You'll be taking our friend where he needs to go?"

"That's right."

The noise of the orchestra swelled and fell away again. Emma Mae turned toward the sound. "I'd better check that everything's in order—"

The buzzer from the alleyway door made all three of them jump.

"Oh, no," Emma Mae groaned. "I forgot about that wretched APL man! Oh, Reg, why didn't you and Peterson leave already? It's been bad enough with him ghosting around pretending to be our janitor ever since Andrew stumbled onto him. . . ."

"Don't worry, Ma." The buzzer went again. Reg frowned. "Wait a second. You don't mean a four-minute man, do you?"

"What's a four-minute man?" Addie asked.

"You know," Reg said. "Four minutes before the curtain. The pitch for war bonds and patriotism and snitch on your neighbors if they don't support the war? From Mr. Creel's Committee on Public Information? The city's crawling with them."

Mrs. Powell nodded. "This one is with the American Protective League."

"That's what APL stands for? You must be joking. They're thugs. Why did you ask him here?"

"Oh, for goodness' sake! You don't ask them, Reg! They tell you." She frowned. "Just, please, be careful not to be seen when you leave. God knows what will happen then."

"Isn't he staying for the show? If you can hustle him out to the audience, it shouldn't be a problem."

"I'll try. But you'll have to move quickly, too." Emma Mae went and opened the door. A thickset man in a white suit waddled in. He lifted his straw hat, revealing a slick of greased black hair. "Mrs. Powell? Mr. Humphries from the APL. You ready for us?"

Addie glanced behind Mr. Humphries to see if "us" meant there were more APL men lurking in the alley. But apparently it only meant that Mr. Humphries thought of himself as plural.

Addie would not have been able to tell Emma Mae's smile was fake if she hadn't known. "We've been expecting you, Mr. Humphries. What good work you and the committee are doing!"

"You're doing good work yourself, raising money for our boys."

"My son is leaving for training tonight, so we thought it would be a nice gesture."

Mr. Humphries's voice had an oily texture. "Very patriotic, ma'am. Is this your son?" The four-minute man held out his hand, and Reg shook it firmly. "I'd go myself," Humphries added, "if it weren't for these damned flatfeet."

Addie heard a clatter in the hall and looked up to see Andrew Lindstrom. He was flushed and nervous. "I heard we were having a visitor from the American Protective League," he said. "Are you him?"

Mr. Humphries glowed and held out his hand again.

"Why aren't you in costume?" Mrs. Powell said sharply.

"You're looking for people undermining the war effort, aren't you?" Andrew went on, speaking only to Humphries. He was more than flushed, Addie thought. It was like there was a rash on his cheeks.

"Sure," Humphries said. "That's our job."

"Andrew." Emma Mae's voice was whittled thin. "You'd better get ready. It's you and Harrison in the very first scene, in case you've forgotten."

"The witches are first. And this is important." Andrew drew a folded paper out of his coat pocket and hesitated just a second before holding it out to the four-minute man.

Addie stifled a gasp. Then, without a second thought, she snatched the paper out of Andrew's hand.

Mr. Humphries twisted his thick neck around to look at her in surprise. She slapped a pleased look onto her face. "Andrew! You darling!"

She shook open the newspaper and took a cursory look at the close-printed type. As she'd suspected, it was the original copy of the *Daily*, the copy Andrew had snatched from Peterson. "I *thought* you might have the write-up of the previews. Aren't you just wonderful for getting them for me? Meg *said* they'd be useful."

"I didn't bring it here for *you*." Andrew turned to Mr. Humphries. "There's an article in here. Propaganda." He tried to take the paper back from Addie, but she turned casually away, pretending to skim the page.

"What kind of propaganda?" Mr. Humphries asked.

"For the war, of course." Addie looked up and said lightly, "Isn't that what you do?"

Andrew glared at her. "What do you think you're—"

"Thanks so much!" Addie folded the paper, shoved it into her bag, and, wondering if she was going too far, gave Andrew a peck on the cheek. Then she turned to Emma Mae. "Meg will be delighted, won't she? Shall I run this over to her now?"

Humphries was looking from Andrew to Addie, a frown furrowing his froglike lips.

"No. Not now." Reg grabbed Addie's elbow and propelled her toward the back door. "We'll be late for that send-off the fellows are giving me." He turned to Humphries. "One last evening with my girl. I'd love to stay and chat, but . . . you understand."

The four-minute man smiled indulgently. "No need to explain."

"So if you'll excuse us?" They were almost at the door now. Reg grabbed a military greatcoat from the coat stand.

Emma Mae followed them. "All right, then. I'll see you at around tenish, is that right? And I'm to bring the duffel?"

"Thanks, Ma."

Reg pushed open the door and stood aside to let Addie go through first. Hardly daring to breathe, she stepped out into the alley, and the door closed behind them.

SOLIDARITY FOREVER

Reg grabbed Addie's hand and they ran. She had to sprint to keep up with him, and for a few seconds it didn't even occur to her to wonder where they were running to.

But before they could reach the end of the alley, a cart rattled around the corner and they leaped out of its way. The horse shied, the driver flinched, and bottles of milk clinked together in the back. They had to flatten themselves against the back wall of the Jewel between trash cans and a water pump to let it go past while the driver shook his fist and berated them.

"Sorry!" Reg called.

Addie put her hand on his sleeve. "We can't just leave Frida's dad back there. What if Andrew has figured it out and tells the four-minute man about him?"

Reg slapped a hand to his forehead. "You're right. I

thought we could come back later and get him, but . . . just wait here. I'll go."

"I don't think you should." Addie glanced nervously at the door of the theater. "Andrew's trying to get you in trouble. Who knows what he said once we left. I'll get Mr. Peterson."

The cart had stopped and the driver was putting milk bottles down at the loading dock. Addie darted out from behind the trash cans, but Reg grabbed her arm and pulled her back. "No chance. I'm not sending you in there to catch hell for me. Besides, I've got a better idea." His face brightened. "In fact, I've got a *brilliant* idea."

"You have a lot of those. Hiding Peterson. Interviewing the Wobblies. Joining the circus, probably. Why don't you let me take care of this?" For the second time, she tried to go. But he got hold of her shoulders and swung her around, gently but firmly.

"I'll be fine. Besides, you're underestimating my mother. By now she's got Andrew tied to the chair in his dressing room while Meg swings his contract back and forth over a flame. Don't worry."

Addie wriggled to free herself, but Reg didn't let her go. "It's partly your own fault," she said. "You shouldn't have teased him so much."

"Well, he shouldn't be such an ass! How was I to know he'd send a fellow to jail rather than lose a part in a play? Or imagine he'd lose a part, the idiot. No. I'll bet he gave up on his scheme after you snatched away the evidence. He doesn't want Mother to dismiss him, after all." He watched the driver get back into his seat, chirrup to the horse, and rattle away. Then he turned back to Addie. "And, by the way . . ." He drew her closer, leaning his forehead against hers for a moment. "That was pretty marvelous, the way you got my newspaper away from him."

Then he was running back down the alley and up the loading dock. Addie, a bit wobbly in the knees, watched him take out his key and turn it in the lock. What if Humphries was still standing just inside?

She held her breath as Reg cracked the door and peered in. But then he turned back to the alley and jerked his thumb in the air. Resignedly, Addie stuck up her thumb in response.

Pretty marvelous, she thought. She pulled the copy of the *Daily* out of her handbag, and there was Reg's article about Peterson's friends, right on the front page. She read it, moved and impressed. Reg told the men's story so well. And yet, had anyone read it? If the fact that it was missing from the microfiche files at the library was anything to go on, it seemed unlikely anyone had. Ever.

The sound of a heavy door closing brought her quickly to attention. She stuffed the paper back into her bag and looked up to see two men walking toward her: a soldier and a workman. *Oh, good. No problems, then.* She came out from behind the trash cans to greet them.

But the soldier wasn't Reg.

He was a middle-aged man with cellar-pale skin and a hunted look in his watery blue eyes.

"Oh, my God," she muttered. So this was Reg's brilliant idea.

She gazed at Gustaf Peterson in astonishment. In the uniform, he looked like a real soldier. Like that officer's braid on the cuff actually meant something. She wondered briefly how Reg was going into the army as an officer. But it didn't matter. What mattered was that the greatcoat sat on Gustaf's shoulders with an assurance it hadn't on Reg. The hat concealed Peterson's sandy hair, and she noticed that he was clean-shaven. It was a perfect disguise.

While Reg . . . Addie was caught between a shiver and a laugh. It was weird how modern he looked wearing Peterson's rough overalls and a flannel shirt, a flat cap on his head. He could have been one of the guys repairing the earthquake damage at her school.

"You *are* clever," she said when they were close enough to talk.

"Hello, Miss Addie." Peterson sounded positively chipper.

Addie smiled. "I'm glad to see you, Mr. Peterson."

"If anyone asks," Reg told her, shifting Peterson's knapsack on his shoulder, "he's Mother's brother, Rob—Robinson Hamlin. Good thing Uncle Rob moved to Montana ten years ago. No one's likely to question it. Unless we run into really old friends of the family." He pulled the brim of the cap lower over his forehead. "In other words, let's get moving."

As they were turning out of the alley onto the street, Addie glanced over her shoulder. The back door of the Jewel was inching open. She poked Reg's arm and pointed as a man emerged onto the loading dock.

Reg propelled her quickly around the corner. "Probably just the custodian," he said, glancing at Peterson. "The one Mother's been giving so much time off so you can do his job."

Peterson didn't respond. He was looking around, blinking in the fading light, as if every detail of the outside world was new and full of wonder.

The sidewalk in front of the Jewel thronged with men in dress coats and women in velvet jackets and wide-brimmed hats, all streaming toward the theater entrance. Tobacco smoke and perfume infused the air. Above their heads, the theater's electric marquee gleamed: RED CROSS BENEFIT: STANDING ROOM AVAILABLE. It was so crowded that they had to walk in the street, skirting around ranks of parked taxis. At the intersection, Addie glanced down the hill to the Sound. The sunset was streaking out orange and smoky above the distant shores of Bainbridge Island.

For a moment she felt as if she was the luckiest person in the universe.

But then she caught sight of a police officer scanning the bustling crowd of theatergoers, and her heart thudded in her chest. She caught up to Reg and whispered, "Wherever we're going, get us there fast," and they quickened their pace.

It was a relief when they turned onto a side street and Addie saw the Tin Lizzie parked and waiting, its right tires up on the curb. She darted toward its back door, but Peterson stopped her.

"Sit up front, miss. I'll hunker down in the rear out of sight."

Addie got out of his way and let him slide into the back seat. Then she opened the door to the passenger side of the front seat, stepped onto the running board, and climbed in. Reg cranked the car to life, ran around the other side, and jumped behind the wheel.

"There was a policeman," Addie said as they pulled away from the curb. "Did you see?"

Reg nodded and turned onto the main road, swerving around pony carts and trolleys and other motorcars.

Once they were away from the theater's glittering lights and the downtown shops, the city was much darker than Addie had ever seen it.

Occasional street lamps pierced the gathering dusk. As they drove, Reg would be illuminated by their faint glow for a brief moment, only to fade again into the darkness. It felt uncanny. Addie reached out to touch the heavy flannel of his sleeve, as if to assure herself he was really there. He closed his hand around hers and just as quickly let go. But beneath the spark of his touch, Addie felt a wrench in her heart and saw the cold marble and the list of names on the cenotaph, and had to fight down a rising tide of despair.

The car took a sharp turn and pulled over into an alley. Reg engaged the parking brake, turned, and grinned at her. She tried to remember that this was their adventure, and she should be elated at their success. She tried to smile at him. "Nothing to it," he said. "We're here."

"Here? You mean—the *Daily Call* office?"

Reg nodded.

"That's good." She shoved her fear far down inside and climbed out of the car.

As they left the alley and came out onto the street, Peterson stopped short. In the window of a hotel barber shop on the corner was the Wanted poster with his picture on it. Peterson ripped it down and tore it in half. He carried it with him as he turned and ran up the steps of a brownstone with Reg and Addie close behind. At first tentatively, and then more loudly, he knocked on the door.

The door creaked open and a woman's husky voice came from the shadows. "We've been waiting for you, comrades." In the faint glow of the street lamp Addie saw a tall woman with a worried expression on her heavy but pleasant-looking face. She seemed strangely familiar, with her brown hair pulled loosely into a bun, her homely plaid dress, and the thick wire spectacles that made Addie think of John Lennon.

"Who's this?" she asked Gustaf. "Your daughter?" A faint French accent tinged her words.

"Nah, Louise. This is Miss Addie McNeal. And you know the boy." He handed her the ripped poster. "And I got some junk for you to dispose of."

"Hello again," Reg said. He turned to Addie. "This is Mrs. Olivereau. She's the secretary of the Seattle IWW."

Mrs. Olivereau hooked her free arm through Gustaf's and pulled him into the dark hallway. "Quickly, then, all of you. No use standing out on the stoop, waiting for *les poulets*—the police."

They followed her through the hall to a door and up a

stairway. At the top they stopped at another door. Light glowed through its frosted-glass pane, and a rumble of voices could be heard within. Addie watched Mrs. Olivereau turn the knob and racked her brain to remember where she'd seen her before.

Then, suddenly, she knew. It was at the demonstration where Whaley had gotten arrested. Louise Olivereau was the lady she'd seen giving the speech from the soapbox.

Dazed, Addie followed the others into a large loft room. The smells of ink and paste were overwhelming. A fire was burning in the fireplace, and the heat mixed with heavy cigar smoke made her head swim. Along the back wall stood a big iron machine Addie recognized from its brother at the university: a printing press. Editions of the *Daily Call* were strewn everywhere. Posters lined the walls, and her eyes were drawn—again!—to the screeching black cat in front of a full moon, its fur all on end, like the cat on the flyers Mrs. Turner had made. The words above the image read NO WAR FOR WALL STREET.

Four men were playing cards around a table. Three of them were rough-looking men in ink-stained aprons. The fourth wore a rather wrinkled brown suit. He was big in the shoulders and sat with his legs outstretched, taking up as much room as possible. He looked genial, but also powerful, with a close-clipped brown beard and a cigar balanced behind his ear. Something about him made Addie think of a large brown bear. As they entered, he laid down a straight flush. The other men groused and laughed.

The winner chuckled and rose from his chair. He

slapped Mr. Peterson on the back and said, "Well, well. The fugitive goes free. Glad to see you, Gustaf." Then he held out his hand to Addie, who shook it. "Sam Sadler," he said, and Addie introduced herself.

He turned to Reg, smiling broadly. "Thanks for helping out our comrade. If there's anything we can do for you someday, just ask."

"Peterson's mopped our theater for free this last week and given us his daughter at starvation wages," Reg said. "You probably ought to chew me out instead of thanking me."

"Darn good wages," Peterson said. "Who in hell cares about mopping?"

"Don't disillusion Mr. Sadler, Gustaf," Reg told him. "I don't want him to think we in the ruling class are as altruistic as all that."

Sadler laughed, and Addie saw a flash of gold in his mouth. "Don't worry that I've got any illusions about your class, Mr. Powell. At the moment, I see you as an exception."

"You in, Sam?" one of the printers asked him.

Sadler nodded. He sat back down again, picked up the new hand of cards that had been dealt him, and said to Reg, "Glad we could help you out with that paper of yours. When can we expect to see the article?"

"Never," Reg said, with a trace of bitterness. "The provost had all the copies destroyed."

Finally, Addie thought, she would find out. "Didn't you print the edition again, with the article hidden away on the second page?" she asked.

"Sure we did. But when Tom and I got back to campus,

we found a padlock on the office door. So we couldn't print it on our press."

"What?" Addie nearly laughed in disbelief. "You mean that old provost sneaked over and locked you out? How ridiculous."

Sadler looked up at her over his cards. "We've had our windows smashed and our press broken and our friends shot by sheriff's deputies. Your friend got more high-class treatment than that, at least."

"I'll try to feel grateful," Reg said dryly. "At any rate, since I'd just been over here talking with Mr. Sadler about Gustaf, I thought of the printing press these fellows had. So we asked, and they very kindly printed the entire edition for us."

Addie wrinkled her brow. "So there are copies somewhere?"

"Tom and I managed to drop the papers off at the news-stands in the middle of the night. But when we got to campus the next morning, all the editions were gone."

"Professor Hanson had them destroyed? I just—I can't believe it. Are you sure it was him?"

"Who else? He told me himself, when he called me in for 'a rather tedious' meeting in his office, the purpose of which turned out to be expelling me from college. So it seems Tom was right about that." He shrugged in a way that Addie thought was supposed to be insouciant but didn't quite succeed. "It doesn't matter, anyway. I told him I'd joined the army, and he said if the Hun didn't do me in, he'd like the honor himself." He hesitated. "I haven't told Mother yet. You—um . . ."

"Of course I won't tell her!" Addie said, a bit indignantly. And then, realizing what this meant, she added, "Reg, I wanted a copy of that edition—for the pictures, remember? They can't be all gone!"

"Oh, that's right. I'm sorry. Tom has the original. I can write and remind him. . . ."

She thought quickly. "He can just leave it for me in Meg's office at the Jewel," she said. It seemed the safest way. Then she smiled and added, "I loved what you wrote. Make sure I get the whole paper, with the article in it, too."

"Really?" He looked pleased. "Well, if I'm going to have a readership of one, I'm glad it's you. Though you'd better hide it away, even if Meg's just interested in the pictures. I don't know if I like the idea of my mother getting into trouble over my radical connections."

Sam Sadler was watching this exchange with obvious enjoyment even while sorting his cards and bidding. "Too bad about the article. But remember, friend, you can write for the *Call* anytime. We'll even whip up a pseudonym for you, if you don't want to shock your people." He turned to Peterson. "Not to pry, but what's the getup in aid of, Gustaf? You aren't planning a jaunt to the peninsula in those togs, are you?"

"Nah. Reg here loaned it to me. He's enlisted—"

"What a pity!" Mrs. Olivereau exclaimed. "I wish I'd had a chance to dissuade you, Mr. Powell."

Reg ignored this. "It's to put interested parties off the scent," he explained.

Sadler raised his brows. "Anyone interested beyond our usual friends?"

"I don't think so. But there was an actor trying to impress an APL man at the theater tonight. He actually stumbled into Gustaf a few days ago."

"The American Protective League? *Mon Dieu!*" Mrs. Olivereau gave Peterson a worried look. "And someone saw you at the theater?" She cast another worried look at Sam Sadler. "We'd better hope no one finds out we're helping him. It could give the city attorney an excuse for a prosecution. That's all they need."

"Don't worry. Teddy Nickles is picking me up soon." Peterson turned to Sadler. "You heard from him yet?" He pointed at the knapsack Reg had dumped on the floor beside him. "I'm ready when he is."

"He called from the peninsula. The rains have the road in a muck, but he'll make it. He always does." Sam Sadler put the cigar in his mouth and lit it. The tip glowed orange.

"Where are you going?" Addie asked Peterson.

"Camp Disappointment. Sounds homey, don't it? A timber camp out on the peninsula. Frida will come out, too, when the coppers ease up a bit." He turned to Reg. "I'd be in a heap more trouble if it weren't for you and your ma. You let her know."

Addie's ears pricked up. For a moment she thought she heard a moaning sound outside the building, like the beginnings of a windstorm. But then it died away.

"I will," Reg said. He shook Peterson's hand formally. "Good luck to you. Now, the sooner we get our duds switched, the better."

The moaning swelled again. Addie went over to the window, trying to see what was happening, but it looked out only on the side of the next building. The sound was becoming louder and more piercing. She stood stock-still, concentrating. Everyone else was still talking. She held up her hand. "Hey! Does anyone else hear that?"

Mrs. Olivereau came and stood beside her, putting her hand on her shoulder. She turned to the men at the card table, who were still calling out bets. "Shhh! Stop chattering, you ox heads!"

As the room quieted, the sound swelled.

"Fire engine?" Peterson asked uneasily.

Mrs. Olivereau rushed across the room and grabbed him by one arm and Reg by the other. She pushed them toward the door. "Siren. Fire or police, you can't stay to find out. Go!" They stared at her. "*Vite!*"

"But I'm supposed to meet Teddy here. How's he gonna find me?" Peterson objected.

"Think of another meeting place. We'll send him to you."

"Where?" The siren was blaring now.

"The Jewel?" Mrs. Olivereau suggested.

"You're joking," Peterson said harshly.

"What about the lumberyards on Skid Row?" Reg suggested.

"*No!*"

Addie was about to jump out of her skin. She couldn't bear it if, after all they'd been through, Peterson was arrested. "Send him to my—I mean, to Mrs. Turner's house," she blurted out, thinking of the safest place she knew. "Up in Wallingford."

"That's not a good idea," Reg said quickly.

Lights were swooping through the chinks in the boarded-up windows. "They're here! We don't have time to argue. Give me the address." Mrs. Olivereau snatched up paper and a pencil and handed them to Addie. She scribbled down the house number and street and rushed out into the hall with the others, following Sam Sadler down the stairs and toward the back of the building.

The siren's shrieking cut off abruptly. Car doors slammed and people ran up the front steps. Sadler wrenched open the back door, and before they knew it they were in the alley. They stumbled down the steps and ran to the flivver.

They could hear Louise Olivereau arguing loudly with someone around the front of the building. Reg cranked the engine. Addie looked around frantically, hoping the police wouldn't suddenly burst into view. She couldn't imagine how they were going to get away.

And even if they did, she realized, Meg wouldn't be home, would she? Not on opening night. Still, did it matter? As long as they got out of here.

The engine caught, making an unholy racket, and Reg jumped in. He knocked a switch with his finger, and the headlights pierced the darkness.

"Turn those *off!*" Peterson hissed.

"I can't. I'll crash into garbage cans."

"Then leave them on," Addie said. "Just go!"

But as Reg sped down the alley and around the corner,

a man came up the side street toward them. He shouted something she couldn't hear and ran back down the block toward the *Daily Call* office.

"Reg! That was a policeman!"

"I know!"

He shoved his foot down on the accelerator, and the car picked up speed.

For a block or two they were on their own. But then the back of Addie's neck prickled, as if someone had just sat down behind her. She stuck her head out the window and twisted around to see.

Another car was right behind them. A police car? There were no flashing blue and red lights, and if it had a siren, it was off. All these cars looked the same. All the flivvers with their rickety headlights and black paint jobs, like a fleet of hearses.

"Left! Turn left!" she shouted. "I think they're following us."

Reg jerked the motorcar into the left lane and they skidded around the corner.

"They're turning too!" Peterson yelled.

"Oh, no." Addie slumped down in her seat. "Reg! I don't think you should head to Meg's house after all. You'd be taking them right to the guy who's picking up Mr. Peterson."

"What should I do?"

"I don't know!" She thought for a second. "Slow down, for one thing. Drive normally. Then they won't necessarily think—"

"Go to the station." Peterson leaned forward. He put his

arm across the leather seat, and Addie saw the gleam of the brass button on his cuff catch the light of a streetlamp. "King Street. Where you'll catch the train. You want a big crowd. That's our best chance to lose them."

"What if we don't?" But Reg was backtracking already.

"If they catch us, we'll have to bluff it out," Peterson replied. "We've still got a chance."

"Do you think so?"

"Sure," Addie said. "Mr. Peterson has a uniform on. He'll fit right in." Addie's throat felt dry. "He can be your uncle. Isn't that what you said before? It's just acting, Reg. We can do that."

"Then you'd better be ready to pitch in, Madam Director," Reg said grimly.

Addie nodded, looked back at the headlights coming closer, and tried to sound confident. "Of course I will. We're a good troupe. We'll manage."

OVER THERE

King Street Station looked like the site of a city evacuation. A chaos of cars and horse-drawn carts jammed the side streets, disgorging whole families, including grandparents with canes and mothers with screaming babies.

All the way there, Addie kept her eye on the police car, which was still doggedly following the flivver. But luck finally smiled on them as they reached the far end of Jackson Street, so close to the water that the smell of fish invaded their nostrils. An arthritic-looking horse pulling a peddler's cart lumbered into the intersection behind them, nearly clipping their rear wheel, and cut them off from their pursuers. The horn on the police car blared as the two vehicles nearly collided.

"They're stuck!"

Reg glanced over his shoulder and drove halfway up

onto the sidewalk to park. "Jump out then, and keep watch." He pulled off the flat cap and tossed it to Peterson. "We'll switch clothes in the motorcar."

When Addie leaped out, she saw that the peddler's horse had balked and refused to go farther. She wished she could have patted its sad, soft muzzle and told it to ignore the old peddler who was barking, "Git on, you brute! Pull!"

But a second later a heavy police officer appeared.

"Move that bag of bones!" he yelled.

"What do you think I'm trying to do?" the peddler shot back. He slapped a stick against the beast's flank.

The police officer made a disgusted face and shouted something to his partner in the blocked car. Then he turned and began to plow through the crowd of people streaming toward the station. Horrified, Addie pounded the side of the flivver. "You don't have time to change. Get out now!"

She darted into the street, thinking the cop was sure to see her if she stayed on the sidewalk. Reg was already out of the car, settling the strap of the overalls and Gustaf's knapsack on his shoulder. "Damn it, Addie—"

"He's heading this way. Come on, Mr. Peterson."

Addie snatched the workman's cap from where Reg had left it on the seat and jammed it back on his head. Peterson pulled himself out of the back, setting the uniform to rights. A muscle at the corner of his eye was twitching.

They hurried along the row of parked cars toward the station, swerving around opening doors.

Then, just as they were almost at the entrance, Peterson

called, "Wait a second!" He grabbed Reg by the shoulder and reached into the top pocket of his overalls, pulling out a small red booklet with the letters *IWW* engraved over an image of a globe and the name *Gustaf Peterson* printed below. "If anything happens, it'd be best not to have this on you."

Addie plucked it out of his hand. "You'd better not either," she said, stuffing the union card into her bag.

"Good thinking."

They cut through the taxi stand in front of the station as drivers pulled in and out without looking to see if anyone was there—car, cab, pedestrian, or dog—and they had no choice but to merge into the throngs of people on the sidewalk. Addie glanced over her shoulder, and her heart sank as she caught sight of the police officer still bulling his way through.

"I think he sees us."

"What should we do?" Peterson asked.

"Just act like we have a perfect right to be here," Reg answered.

We do, Addie thought with a pang. *This is where Reg is supposed to be tonight, to catch the train for the army camp.*

"Pretend we're seeing you off," she said. "Remember, if he catches up with us, you're . . . Reg's uncle. What did you say his name was?"

"Rob Hamlin."

"That's it. So until we get rid of that cop, you have to be the soldier going off for training."

"All right. Once we shake him off, we'll switch." Peterson

dodged around a lamppost in his path, its light diffusing in the mist around it.

"Just don't speak too much," Addie told him. "And try to sound more American. Flatten your vowels and—I don't know, mutter a bit so he can't tell you've got an accent."

"Flatten—?"

"Like . . . *cat*—make the *a* come through your nose. *Ae*."

"There's no time for elocution lessons." Reg glanced up at the clock on the station's red-brick tower. "We're cutting it close enough."

"But we need to work out what we'll say. Who are you if anyone asks?"

"Dunno," Reg answered impatiently. "Janitor doesn't make sense anymore. Driver? Hired man?"

"Okay."

Their breath hung in veils in the cool night air. Addie shivered, and Reg slipped his arm around her. Briefly, she huddled into the warmth of his body, then, at the same moment, they drew apart, remembering that he was supposed to be a hired man. *And I'm supposed to be . . . who?* Addie wondered.

"Does he have a daughter? Your uncle Rob?"

"Sophie. But she's five."

"Now she's seventeen," Addie said, and kept talking before Reg could object. "I know it's crazy, but I'm not leaving you, and I need a story, too. I'm Sophie." She turned to Peterson. "All right?"

"I heard ya."

Addie walked closer to Peterson—he was supposed to be her dad, after all.

The hands on the huge station clock pointed like daggers to five past ten. "Reg!" Addie exclaimed. "We'd better find your mother, so she doesn't give us away by mistake. Where'd she say she'd meet you?"

"The café. Follow me."

He pushed the bronze door handles, smudgy with the prints of innumerable fingers. The air from inside rushed out, thick and sweaty from the crowd. Addie almost tripped over a little girl in a funny square hat who was jumping up and down in frenzied excitement. The girl's mother caught her hand firmly, sending an apologetic smile to Addie. A man in uniform crouched down, and the little girl ran into his arms.

As they squeezed through the press of bodies, Addie looked back again, hoping the police officer was having as much trouble as they were.

But no. People were stepping aside to let him pass.

The station felt bigger than it was in her own time. Crates of apples were piled up by a kiosk, where a man was doing a brisk business in fruit and newspapers and candy. People sat waiting on smooth wooden benches and in deep leather chairs. The ceiling was much higher, elaborately decorated with carved leaves and flowers, and frosted globes of light hung from it. Tides of perfume assaulted her senses and muddled with the smell of corned beef, fried onions, and the gunpowdery scent of cigars. The aroma of the food grew stronger as Reg led them across the vast waiting room toward the café.

The place was packed. A shining brass railing divided it from the main station, and people sat at a long counter behind the railing. Beyond that, Addie could see crowded tables covered in crisp white cloths. A small military band—a trumpet, a clarinet, a tuba, and a trombone—had set up by the entrance and was blaring out Sousa marches. Soldiers and their friends were lifting glasses and yelling toasts only to be drowned out by the music. Asian women in starched white uniforms moved through the crowds, holding trays aloft. Here and there, she could see lovers holding hands at the tables, their cups of coffee untouched at their elbows.

Emma Mae was sitting at the counter looking out into the station. Beneath the gauze veil that hung from her hat brim, her gaze swept the room.

Her eyes snagged on Peterson first and widened in astonishment. Then she touched her throat, half rising from her seat, as her gaze lit on Reg.

He shook his head warningly as they shoved their way closer through the crowd of revelers. "Don't react," he told her quickly. "And don't tell anyone I'm here or that you're expecting me. There's a policeman following us." He rammed his hand into his pocket, took out a silver money clip, and slid it into Emma Mae's hand. "Hold this for me until Peterson and I can change our gear."

"Should I put it in your duffel?" She pointed to the floor.

"No. Keep it for now."

Emma Mae sank back onto the barstool, her face nearly as white as the marble bust Addie had seen on the piano at the Jewel. Her eyes traveled from her son to Peterson. "I was afraid of this. Andrew talked Mr. Humphries into telephoning the police."

"We figured."

"They'll close the Jewel. He said they could if they find we've been hiding anything—or anyone."

"Let's go." Peterson tugged Reg's arm.

Addie turned quickly and saw the policeman's helmet bobbing above the crowd, only a few yards away. "You can't. He's right behind us. You *have* to bluff it."

Emma Mae looked wearily at Gustaf Peterson. "Who should I say you are? You can't be Reg."

"He's Uncle Rob," Reg said. "Do your best, Ma. We need to get rid of the copper."

Quickly, Emma Mae's features relaxed into a warm and loving expression; her eyes shifted away from her son and gazed at Peterson. She extended her arm over the narrow counter, tenderly folding Gustaf's rough workman's hand in hers. "Rob! I'd nearly given up hope of seeing you!" She gave a tinkling laugh, let go of his hand and dropped the money clip into her handbag.

The waitress, red-faced and harassed, swooped in with a bottle of pale sparkling liquid and two glasses.

"Celery soda. Isn't it ridiculous? So barbaric not to have champagne. Three more glasses, please," Emma Mae ordered.

"Not for the workman." Reg stepped back, slightly apart from the rest.

"Two, that is. One for my brother and one for my—"

"Niece," Addie filled in.

"Sophie." Emma Mae gathered Addie into a quick embrace. "My, you've grown," she said dryly. "Raise a toast with me, both of you. I feel maudlin, but I want our parting to be a happy one."

Reg sprang forward suddenly, and Addie heard him whisper to Peterson. "Give me my enlistment papers. Just in case—they're in the pocket."

Peterson shoved his hands into the deep pockets of the greatcoat.

"No, not that one," Reg said impatiently, but then sank down on one knee and started fumbling with the laces on his boot.

The policeman was right beside him, a big hefty man in late middle age, struggling to catch his breath. He doffed his hat to Mrs. Powell. His blue jacket strained across an assertive belly. "Nice family group," he remarked. He bowed from the neck and pulled a badge from his breast pocket.

Emma Mae looked innocently puzzled, and Addie did her best to follow suit.

"Detective Larson," the man said. "I'm guessing you're Mrs. Powell, who owns the Jewel?"

"I am." Emma Mae tilted her head. "Can I help you, Officer?"

The cop's eyes traveled slowly from Peterson to Addie and finally came to rest on Reg, who had stood up again, eyes still fixed on his feet. But when Detective Larson turned back to Emma, Addie saw Reg glance impatiently at the clock on the wall. Only fifteen minutes now before the train boarded.

"Just a few questions, ma'am," the detective said. "I realize this isn't the best time."

"Of course. I'll do my best to answer."

Larson pointed at Peterson. "Is this man your son?"

Emma Mae laughed her silvery laugh, and Gustaf, taking her lead, managed a faint chuckle. "My son? How old do you think I am, Officer?" The detective smiled thinly, not joining in. "This is my brother. I have two sons. One is a solicitor in Olympia. The other is still at college."

A shadow crossed Reg's face.

"Rob Hamlin." Peterson shook Larson's hand and Addie tensed. He *had* managed to flatten out his Swedish accent, but he still didn't sound native-born. The officer frowned. Peterson, though, went on, gesturing at Addie. "And my daughter, Sophie."

Addie half whispered, "Pleased to meet you," and tried to look bashful.

Larson turned back to Peterson. "I'm sorry to disturb you, Mr. Hamlin, especially at a time like this." He pulled a scrap of paper out of his pocket and said to Emma Mae, "But it says here it's your son who's supposed to be reporting for duty. That fellow who called from the theater told us."

"*What* fellow?"

The detective glanced back at the paper again. "Humphries? He's from the APL, so we got to listen to him. Called us up, told us your son was on his way across town with an escaped prisoner."

"*What?* What nonsense! How would my son come by an escaped prisoner?"

"You tell me. We don't have any reason to doubt Mr. Humphries."

Emma Mae hesitated, as if debating whether to speak. "I hate to cast aspersions, Officer, but as I was leaving, one of the ushers told me Mr. Humphries had brought a flask to the theater and was putting away shots of moonshine like a stevedore. Normally we'd evict anyone who did that, but . . . The point is, if you let a man in that state send you on a wild goose chase . . ." She shook her head disapprovingly. "It doesn't seem right, especially when we're saying goodbye!"

The waitress returned with several long-stemmed glasses clattering in the crook of her arm. "Use what you need. I don't have time for special orders." She lowered the glasses onto the bar and scurried away.

"But I'm not so sure it was a wild goose chase," the detective said. "Your brother and your niece and . . ." He eyeballed Reg. "Who are you, exactly?"

Reg looked sullen. "Mack."

"Mack who?"

Don't say Beth! Addie thought furiously. *It isn't funny!*

"Duffy."

Addie rolled her eyes, wondering if Reg ever lost the urge to make jokes. "I drive for the Powells," he added.

"That correct, Mrs. Powell?"

Emma Mae nodded.

Larson looked annoyed. "Humphries told us your name was Peterson and you were on the lam. Though by my count, you got a good few years before you'd match the man they described. Got a union card?"

Reg shook his head.

Without preliminary, Detective Larson stepped over to Reg and began searching him. Addie's stomach knotted. *Peterson better not have any other Wobbly stuff stashed away in his pockets,* she thought. Anger flashed in Reg's eyes and Addie could tell it was all he could do not to knee Larson in the groin. But then he picked up his character, and his face settled into an expression of resentful deference.

"You're not planning on searching *all* of us, are you?" Emma Mae gathered her velvet jacket about her disdainfully. Addie shifted her bag nervously on her shoulder, thinking of what was inside it.

Larson let go of Reg. "No, ma'am. But your family's got some explaining to do. Even if this fella ain't Gustaf Peterson and everything else that Humphries said was wrong, I still got to ask why these three just came from the *Daily Call* office. That's an IWW paper. On the booze or no—and that's a serious charge, Mrs. Powell—your four-minute man got that right." The detective pulled a small notebook out of his pocket. "The report from Bryant said Peterson's daughter works for you. And there was some kerfluffle over a pistol when he went to the theater to question her. No one's claimed it yet, by the way. Given all that, I think it's fair to ask what your family was doing visiting Sam Sadler and his crew this evening."

Emma Mae turned her gaze on Reg and Peterson. Addie could see a flash of fear, but then it was gone and her expression was composed. "The IWW? What *were* you doing with that crew?"

Reg opened his mouth, and then bit his lip, remembering he was just the hired man. Peterson was keeping quiet.

Someone has to answer, Addie thought. "It was my idea."

The detective swiveled his head and examined her again with his tiny snail eyes. "Yours?"

Addie nodded, thinking, *Oh, great. Why? Why was it my idea? Why would Reg's cousin Sophie from Montana suddenly get the idea to visit the Industrial Workers of the World?*

But then she had it. It was nutty, but it was the only thing she could think of. Sophie was going to save Reg, of course. Wasn't that what girls *did?* Wasn't it in their genes or something, saving boys from themselves?

Grimly, Addie opened her purse and burrowed inside. She pulled out the folded newspaper she had taken from Andrew Lindstrom and handed it to the detective. Reg's eyes were burning into her back—she didn't have to turn around; she could feel them—but she couldn't help it if he was mad at her.

She looked pleadingly at Emma Mae. "I'm sorry, Aunt Emma! I *know* how furious you were with Reg for writing about those Wobblies in the prison."

"Writing about—" Quickly, Emma Mae amended, "That's right. That did bother me."

Addie turned to the detective. "One of the actors was trying to get my cousin Reg in trouble by showing this to Mr. Humphries. I was afraid he could go to jail for it. The dean wouldn't let him print it at the *Daily.* So someone gave him the crazy idea that he could get the IWW to print it." She let her voice crack. "Dad and I wanted to make sure Reg didn't get into any more trouble. You know how he is, Aunt Emma!"

"Oh, I know *exactly* how he is." Emma Mae's voice was brittle.

"So we had Duffy drive us over to tell Mr. Sadler not to accept any business from Reg; that if he did, Charlie would bring a lawsuit." Addie squeezed out a tear. "Please say you're not mad at us."

Emma Mae took Addie's hand and held it to her cheek. "I *am* a little put out with you, Sophie, for giving me such a scare. Detective, I'm so sorry to have wasted your time. And I'm sorry my relatives have made it so easy for you to think we're crazed revolutionists. We really aren't."

Larson shrugged and stuck the newspaper in his jacket pocket. "That does clear up a few things. And I can check your story with Sadler. And with the provost. Who was that?"

"I—" Addie hesitated. "It was Professor Hanson. The point is the paper never got sold. So there's no harm done."

Larson looked keenly at Emma Mae. "Where's your son now? Too busy writing subversive literature to say goodbye to his uncle?"

No one had thought of this. For a moment, Addie's mind went blank. She glanced at Reg. His face was ashen.

Peterson stuck his jaw out. "I told him to get lost. *That's* where he is."

Emma Mae gasped.

Addie held her breath. *Don't say any more, Mr. Peterson. Don't let him hear your accent.*

But Peterson put his rough workingman's hand on

Emma Mae's shoulder. To Addie's relief, he flattened his vowels. "Sorry, Emma. I was mad! Playing the fool while you're working your fingers to the bone. It's more than I could stomach! You've spoiled him all your life, you know that."

To Addie's shock, Emma Mae actually burst into tears. "You're right. I have!"

Addie thought this might be the most truthful thing anyone had said all night.

"All right," the detective cut in. "Enough family drama. Mrs. Powell, you just keep that boy of yours out of trouble. Tell him we're keeping an eye on him."

Emma Mae swallowed and said, "All right, Detective. I'll talk to him. I'm sure he'll listen to me."

Addie glanced from Peterson to Reg, and then up at the clock above the ticket booths on the far wall, hoping that Detective Larson was done with them now.

But Larson pulled off his helmet and draped a leg over a free stool. "I hope so, ma'am. And, to show I've got no personal feelings in the matter, I'll pledge a toast in honor of your brother's service."

He just wants to stick around to see if they're telling the truth, Addie thought in dismay. But she managed to smile vapidly.

Emma Mae kept her composure. "We'd be honored, Detective."

With a steady hand, she poured out four glasses of the soda and passed one to everyone except Reg. She held hers up and said, "Robinson Hamlin! May he honor his country and return safely home." Addie could only touch the glass to her lips. She was afraid she would gag if she tried to drink.

The military band's music roared to a crescendo. Someone started singing "Over There," and other voices joined in. Close by, a bell tolled, and a man with a bullhorn came through the station, shouting, "Ten-thirty to San Francisco, arriving track one. . . . Ten-thirty, arriving track one!"

All around them, people began streaming onto the platform. Women threw their arms around men in uniform. Older men slapped their backs. Children tugged on their legs.

Reg and Peterson stared at each other, and Addie could see shock on their faces. Emma Mae saw it too, and, with great presence of mind, declared, "All right, Rob. This is it. Let's get you on that train."

Detective Larson was watching keenly, and she saw his eyes dart quickly from Emma Mae to Gustaf. He still suspected them. Well, why not? The lines on Peterson's face and the shadows beneath his eyes betrayed deep anxiety. For a moment, he looked old, as he sat, frozen, hands dangling at his sides. She knew he was thinking, *This can't be happening.* You could read it on his face.

But then he seemed to gather his wits, and he rose from his seat.

"No, wait!" Reg cried. Addie looked at him in alarm. What was he doing? He'd dropped the deferential attitude. Everyone else had turned to him. "I—"

Before he could say another word, Addie lurched into the table as though she'd tripped over something and sent the glasses smashing to the floor. "Ow!" she cried, grabbing her knee. It wasn't subtle. But it worked.

The people next to them scrambled away, knocking their own table to one side. Emma Mae swept the skirt of her beautiful gown aside, but it was drenched. Peterson and Larson leaped back out of the sea of broken glass.

"Don't be so clumsy, Sophie!" Emma Mae scolded, picking her way carefully through the shards. Larson offered her his hand. Reg glared at Addie.

"Get out!" The waitress ran up, waving a broom at them as if shooing cats. She shoved Gustaf to one side. "What have you done? Someone will get cut!"

"But, wait—" Reg insisted, trying to get Larson's attention over the hullabaloo. "I need to tell you something."

But Emma Mae managed to give the impression he was speaking to her. "Oh, thank you, Mack!" She put her hand on Gustaf's arm. "Rob, Mack's trying to tell you you almost forgot your duffel." And she grabbed the strap of the bag, lifting it out of the mess of soda and broken glass with a strength that Addie would never have suspected.

For a moment, Peterson stood frozen, a look of disbelief on his face. Then he nodded and took the big bag from her. "Thanks, Emma." Addie saw his chest rise and fall, as if he had just accepted something. He reached into the inner pocket of his jacket and pulled out a folded sheaf of papers, glanced at them, and then carefully slid them back into the pocket. With great dignity, he offered Emma Mae his arm.

Then he met her eyes and a rueful smile slowly rose to his lips, and Addie knew it wasn't acting. The smile was full of warmth and gratitude, and Emma Mae's face lit up in response.

Detective Larson fell in beside them as they made their way out of the café.

Emma Mae looked over her shoulder and said to Reg, in a clipped, authoritative way, "Take Miss Sophie back to the Jewel. It's too crowded for her here. I know she wants to go to the cast party." She gave Addie a kiss on the cheek. "I'll see you there later, darling."

Reg's eyes were blazing, but he just nodded.

Addie flung herself at Peterson, hugging him like a daughter. She felt too stunned to do anything else. "Goodbye, Dad."

Peterson hugged her back and whispered, "Tell Frida."

Addie nodded. And then she watched Emma Mae and Peterson as they made their way out of the café and into the open expanse of the waiting room, Detective Larson following them all the way.

"We'd better go," Addie said. But neither she nor Reg moved. They just gazed through the open doors to the dark, teeming platform as Gustaf Peterson finally made his escape.

HOME

The moon had reached its zenith and was caught, like a saint's halo, on the tip of the great red cedar in her front yard as they walked up the street toward her house.

Addie froze, staring at the place she had lived for so long, but Reg kept walking. It was so quiet she could hear his boots crunching loose pebbles along the rough stone path that passed for a sidewalk.

The drapes were drawn in the bay windows, oddly bare without *Victrola Books* etched on them in gold leaf. There was a porch in front now, and a light glowed behind the deep russet of the curtains. Addie looked up to the second floor, where their family room with the big oak table should have been, then at the third-floor window of Zack's bedroom. Her eyes traveled along the sloping roof where Whaley's attic room, with his music posters and unwashed socks, would someday be, and she felt an odd pang of homesickness.

But when she looked back down the hill at the new houses, some only half built, and at the grid of trolley tracks cut into the asphalt, as if they would always be there, she knew she was in a world that was deeper than the world she had known, as an archaeologist's excavation deepens a familiar landscape. And yet, it was the same world.

Swallowing hard, she caught up to Reg, and the two of them stood silent in a pool of moonlight, looking up and down the street for any sign of Teddy Nickles's truck. Then he turned away, squinting at the house number affixed to the door.

"Reg?"

He'd hardly spoken to her since they'd left the station. Addie shivered. It felt as if something between them had snapped. She looked up into the sky, at the cold, thin disc of the moon hanging like a prop in a play.

"Why won't you talk to me?" She reached out and put a hand on his shoulder. "Come on. . . ." She could feel his muscles knotted under the flannel work shirt.

He turned around and said angrily, "You *know* I didn't want Peterson going in my place."

"But . . ." Addie hesitated, surprised at his vehemence. "You were going to tell the detective who you were. I couldn't let you do that."

"Smashing all that glass to shut me up." His face was all sharp angles.

"I *had* to, Reg. He'd be in jail right now if you'd said anything. And you, too! At the very least, they'd kick you out of the army."

"But—"

"But what? Oh, Reg, *think!* You wouldn't have made anything better."

He shook his head hopelessly. "You don't understand! I said I would go and fight. It's a promise. It's *honor,* Addie. And to have someone else—to dodge out of it! I'm not a coward."

"A *coward?* You? Are you crazy?"

He kept on as if he hadn't heard. "I offered to go. No one made me."

She took a step back and studied him. He looked shabby in Gustaf's hard-worn clothes, and there were dark smudges under his eyes. "What do you mean?" she said slowly. "I thought you were drafted."

"No one's been drafted yet," he said impatiently. "And I'm too young, anyway. I volunteered for a second lieutenant's commission. And now Peterson gets to have the great adventure in my place." He shook his head in disbelief. "Well, I guess at least we can be happy for him."

Happy? She thought of the photographs she'd been looking at with Whaley: the soldiers in their gas masks, the blinded men stumbling their way to the casualty stations or coughing their lungs out after a gas attack. The men with limbs blown off, faces caved in. The war had been grinding along its murderous way for three years, and yet Reg talked about it as a great adventure.

She drew in a shaky sigh, hating herself for knowing so much and not being able to tell him. "I don't understand you. How can it be something to be happy about?"

But he looked like he thought she was the one who was

crazy. "It's a chance to really do something. Really change the world for the better. How many people have a chance to do that?" *Make the world safe for democracy,* she heard in Whaley's voice. Isn't that what they said back in the day?

"You do! That article you wrote. How is that not making the world a better place?"

"No one read it." There was a spark of irritation in his voice. "If you were a fellow, you'd understand. Nothing gets solved if you aren't willing to fight for it."

"Oh, no. I understand, all right. I understand how important fighting is to you boys."

Something in her tone made him really look at her. His voice lost its edge. "Come on, Addie. I told you I'd join up, didn't I? Why are you upset?"

"I . . ." The coo of a mourning dove cut through the mist.

All of a sudden, it was as if she could see everything clearly, as if Reg had just come into focus for her, this intense, brilliant, spoiled, wisecracking, sincere guy wearing someone else's oversize clothing, so full of life and energy, so *alive.*

She sucked in her breath as it hit her.

"I'm not upset," she said slowly. "I'm not upset at all." There was a jangling chorus in her head, a joyful burst of words: *He's not going to die. He's not.*

"Oh, my God!" Her face broke into a radiant smile. "This is great."

"What is?" Reg looked at her in utter confusion. "You really are mad. You know that, Addie?"

"I'm not mad!"

Then, as quickly as it had come, Addie's happiness drained away.

"But what about Mr. Peterson? Isn't he in danger now?"

"In *danger*? Don't be silly. He's safer than he's ever been. Who's going to look for him in the army?"

"But they'll find out he's not you when he gets to the Presidio." It was the only part of the foreboding she felt that he would understand. The least of it.

"I doubt it. He's got my enlistment papers."

Addie frowned, remembering the papers she'd stolen from Whaley's desk drawer. "True. But they'll still know he isn't you."

"Why? All it says is name, address, eye color, how tall you are—we both have blue eyes, he's about my height—and your birthday."

"Well?"

"If Peterson isn't smart enough to change the date, then he deserves whatever's coming!" Reg exclaimed. "Now you're just insulting his intelligence."

"What about the photo?" Addie pressed.

"What photo? There isn't any photograph on the form."

A sound of wheels crunching slowly over small rocks startled them. They turned sharply, and the headlights of a car heading west along the street blinded them.

"It's too bright here." Reg drew her under the sheltering branches of the red cedar. "You should just be relieved he got away. That's the end of the story. He's gone. And I guess I'm still here."

His voice was so miserable, her heart went out to him. She *did* understand how he felt about joining the army. Somehow he was able to communicate that to her, in a way Whaley never had. But Reg wasn't running from anything, like Whaley was. He had everything to look forward to. Or, at least, he had before all this.

"Reg, I'm sorry. I'm really sorry!"

"What on earth for? It's not your fault. It's mine. I set this crazy chain of events in motion, and now . . ." He gave a strange, bitter laugh. "I don't have a notion in hell what I'm supposed to do now."

The wind turned the branches aside, and the moon illuminated his face like a spotlight. In its glow, Addie suddenly saw a look of surprise chase the bitterness from his face. "You know what, though?" There was a note of wonder in his voice. "I don't think I regret it."

"Don't regret what?"

"Taking the consequences. For hiding Peterson, for writing that article. It's like one side of me was cut off from the other, and now . . ." He brought his hands together, fingers entwined. "I'll have to put them both together." He paused. "So maybe you forced me to do that." Then suddenly his eyes were clear and focused. "I think I'm grateful."

Upstairs in the house, a light flared and was extinguished.

"There's a change coming, Addie." He sounded as if he were weighing each word in order to understand it himself. "A change in my life." His voice wavered. "I didn't expect it, and I'm trying to feel—"

The door of the house opened, and lamplight spread onto the porch. Then a girl stepped out and peered into the front yard.

Frida.

She was the last person Addie had expected to see. And suddenly she was the last person she wanted to see. How was she going to feel about all this?

The girl caught sight of them and looked startled. Then she beckoned with her hand.

Silently, Addie and Reg crossed the yard, stepped up onto the porch, and went into the house, straight into a big, open living room.

"Where's Papa?" Frida demanded. "Why are you here and not him?"

Addie couldn't say a word. *Your dad's gone.* And now he might end up in the fighting. The thought tore at her. Behind Frida, Meg Turner was getting up from a rocking chair. For once, she was wearing no makeup, and instead of the fancy clothes she had probably worn for opening night, she was wearing a big, loose sweater and a plain skirt.

"Your father's safe," Reg said, hanging Gustaf's shabby jacket on the coat rack by the door. "The police didn't get him."

"Then why are you wearing his overalls?" Frida's voice was pinched. "You don't wear a man's clothes if he's able to wear them himself. That's for funerals, and going across the ocean!"

"We switched." Reg glanced at Addie for help, but she still felt the weight of her fears and couldn't speak. He went on. "It's a disguise. I didn't *take* them from him. He's on the train for San Francisco. He's got my clothes."

"Your uniform? What . . . why's he in your uniform?" Then she seemed to piece it together. "In the army? My *dad?*" The words evaporated as she spoke them.

"It was either that or jail."

Addie pushed past Reg and put her arms around the girl as if she were as young as Zack. "He's all right," she said, thinking she would really deserve it if Frida hauled off and punched her. "He sent his love. He . . . he wanted you to join him if he got to the peninsula, but it didn't turn out that way."

"He'll figure out another way," Meg Turner interjected in a gentle tone Addie had never heard from her. "And Reg is right. The army is much better than jail."

Over Frida's head, Addie met Meg's eyes. The look of comradeship, of approval, that she saw there seemed totally undeserved. But it helped.

Collecting herself, she grasped Frida's ice-cold hands and led her over to the rocker. The girl let herself be eased into the seat and sat rocking for a moment, pale and frightened-looking.

"I've got a pot of tea in the kitchen," Meg said. "You all look like you could use it."

Addie watched Meg turn and head toward the back of the house. She had to resist a sweep of vertigo as the director swished through a curtain of multicolored beads dividing the room. One day this would be her dad's bookstore. But now there wasn't a scrap of familiarity in the whole place, from the bright turquoise walls to the low coffee table scattered with letters and magazines. Though she did see the door of the closet where she'd found Meg's crates so long ago—so far in the future.

The only other thing she recognized was the gramophone, its great brass amplifier, shiny and new, sweeping out with familiar flair. Dad's Victrola.

Reg went over to it and started pulling big shellac records out of an upright case. Despite herself, Addie smiled. It was exactly what Whaley would do in a stressful situation.

She turned back to Frida. "How did you know to wait for your dad here?"

The color was coming back into the girl's face. "Mr. Sadler telephoned and said there was a mix-up and they'd bring Dad here to catch his ride." She frowned. "He said it was your idea. What made you think this was a good place?"

"Why wouldn't it be?" ·

"Because I've been staying here since I started working at the Jewel. The police know that for good and certain. Didn't you?"

Surprised, Addie shook her head. "Why here?"

"Mrs. Turner offered when Mrs. Powell gave me the job. Our landlord turned me out when Dad was arrested," Frida said.

Meg Turner came back with a teapot and cups on a tray. She put it down, poured some, dumped a teaspoon of sugar into it, and handed it to Frida. The girl held the steaming cup between her hands.

"Meg?" Reg called, holding a record aloft. "May I?"

"Just don't wake Stan." Meg picked up a shawl from the rocking chair where she'd been sitting and threw it around her shoulders. "Secret of a good marriage, I'll tell you right now, girls. I work late, he works early."

"Sounds miserable," Reg said. Addie was relieved to pick up a hint of humor in his voice. "You don't have a romantic bone in your body, Meg."

"I can't afford to," Meg said shortly.

"How I'd hate to be you," Reg teased. He placed the needle carefully on the spinning record and stole a look at Addie. The thin, faraway sound of an orchestra filled the room. Addie smiled to herself, picked up the pot, poured out another steaming cup, and silently handed it to Reg. She'd heard this music before. Melodic. Clear. A cascade of piano notes, slow and deliberate as a stroll down a boulevard on a warm autumn afternoon.

Reg took the cup from her and met her eyes.

"It's Erik Satie," he said at last. "Meg used it in *Twelfth Night*." His expression shifted, becoming oddly shy, as if they'd just met. "Sounds like it, doesn't it?"

Addie nodded, and, not really caring if the others saw, reached up and ran her hand along his neck and across his shoulders. "It sounds like you."

A slow smile answered hers.

Meg Turner looked up from where she sat stirring

sugar into her tea, gazing first at Reg and then at Addie. She raised an eyebrow. "Act One. 'If music be the food of love, play on. . . .'"

A firm rap sounded on the back door, and she went to answer it. A moment later, Sam Sadler burst into the room, with Meg following.

He took in all of them and shook his head in annoyance. "Where's Gustaf?"

"What are you doing here, Sam?" Reg asked. "I thought Teddy Nickles was coming."

"Can't get a logging truck up these little neighborhood streets. He's waiting at the mill on Yesler. Hurry up and get Peterson, will you?"

"You're not taking Gustaf." Reg put his cup down on the table with a clunk. "You're taking me."

"*What?*" Addie cried.

"What!" Sadler roared in counterpoint. "Holy hell, why would I go to all this trouble to transport *you* out of town? Peterson's who I want. Where is he?"

"Past Tacoma by now, I should think. On a train bound for San Francisco."

Sadler shoved a chair out of the way and crossed the room to Reg. "Are you totally out of your mind?"

Reg looked like he found this incredibly funny. "No, I don't think so—"

"*Yes,*" Addie interjected.

Sadler just went on. "Who's going to meet him there? What name's he gone under? I'm gonna go out on a limb here and bet you don't know a single soul in the Frisco IWW. So what in the name of President Wilson's shriveled behind were you thinking?"

Meg Turner, barely repressing a smile, held out a cup. "Tea, Mr. Sadler?"

Sadler puffed out his cheeks as though detonating a controlled explosion and looked from Reg to Addie. "I want you two to explain this to me. And it better be fast and it better be good."

He settled himself on the arm of the sofa, listening intently to their overlapping explanations, moving only to accept the cup of tea and down it in one gulp. Frida drew closer, silently hanging on every word. But when they got to the part about Gustaf boarding the train, Sadler interrupted. "What about the name on the enlistment papers? It isn't your uncle's name. It's yours."

"But that's all the better," Reg countered. "I'm who they're expecting. It's only that detective who thinks he's my uncle Rob. Peterson will know that."

"Hmmph." Sadler looked unconvinced. "As long as that cop was really as sold on your performance as you think." He shook his head. "The best thing would be to get Gustaf off that train, get you on it, and send him on his way. Why in hell didn't you think this through?"

"We did!" Addie exploded. "We can't help it if everything went wrong."

"We were just lucky that Addie was so quick-thinking," Reg cut in, "and my mother and Gustaf caught on so fast. Believe me, if you could get me on that train, I'd be over the moon. But since you can't, you ought to at least help me get out of town, because if I'm swanning around in Seattle when I'm supposed to be at the Presidio, that's going to be a big problem for Peterson. If anyone wants to poke into it. I just think it's better if nothing makes the police suspicious."

"Thank you," Frida murmured. Meg gave the girl a quick smile.

Sadler furrowed his brow and thought a minute. Finally, he said, "I think you're right, friend. You shouldn't stick around here. And I reckon Teddy would take you out to Camp Disappointment. Though, if you wanted to disappear, you could do it in more style than sinking into ten inches of muck out in the rainforest."

"There isn't much else on offer."

Addie watched Reg with concern and amazement. All of a sudden he seemed so sure of himself.

"Just so you're warned," Sadler said, "it's not a pastoral scene out there. The Wobs are organizing in the timberlands, and there's plenty of fight-back from big lumber."

Reg's eyes lit up. "I wouldn't go if I wasn't willing. Besides, it won't be for long. I'll get back into the infantry somehow."

"No, don't," Addie said.

But he ignored her. "And right now, I'd like to get moving. The longer I'm around, the more dangerous it is for Gustaf." He turned to Meg. "You'll tell Mother, won't you?"

Meg nodded. "Of course. I'll telephone your house."

"She's not there. She'll be at the apartment at the Jewel

tonight because of the cast party. I know you don't like those shindigs, Meg, but can you drop in and tell her what happened?" Meg nodded. "Tell her I'll . . ." He hesitated, a troubled look crossing his face. "Tell her I'll try to get word to her."

Addie stared at Reg. He was leaving. Really leaving. Now.

The current was flowing too swiftly. She couldn't stop it—didn't even know if she should. Or if she had already changed its direction.

Then Meg Turner was leading them to the back of the house. "Stick your money in your boot," Sadler told Reg. "And don't take much. Bunkhouse is two bits a month, grub included. If the cops catch you with a wad of cash, they won't buy you're a real timber beast."

Reg laughed. "Don't worry. I haven't got a cent!" The idea seemed to exhilarate him.

Meg reached into the pocket of a coat hanging on the coat rack on the back wall, pulled out a few bills, and stuffed them into Reg's hand.

"Thanks, Meg. I owe you. Hey! D'you have paper and a pencil you can spare?"

The director slid open a coffee-table drawer and handed Reg a small notebook. "You're not going to get in more trouble, are you? Writing subversive literature?"

Reg looked from her to Addie and grinned. "Oh, probably."

Addie met his eyes. "That's good. I think you should give a lot of people a lot more trouble." Despite herself, she returned his grin. She was always telling Whaley to stay out of trouble. But for some reason, what distressed her in Whaley seemed to delight her in Reg.

Sadler opened the back door and stepped out with Frida beside him. Addie heard her ask him if there was any way to get a message to her father but didn't hear his reply. Meg followed them, but Reg and Addie lingered behind in the kitchen.

"Give people all the trouble you can for the rest of your life, if that's what you want to do, Reg," she added. "Just don't go over into the fighting looking for it. Promise me."

"Addie. How can I—" But she didn't let him finish, just pulled him to her and kissed him, hanging on with all the strength she had. She smoothed her palm up and down his back through the heavy workman's flannel, memorizing the feel of him, letting the warmth of his hands sink into her like permanent marks on her skin. In another moment he would be gone.

Then, reluctantly, she pulled away. "Reg, will you give me something?"

He swept his hand over his heart. "Anything." Color flamed into his face. "No jest."

She paused. It was hard to think of it, at this moment. "I need the photos. The ones Tom took of the Jewel that you printed on the front page of the paper with your article. Like I said when we were at the *Daily Call* office."

He nodded, looking slightly puzzled. "You don't think I forgot, do you?"

From the alley behind the house, Sadler tapped his horn impatiently.

Reg pulled her to him once more and kissed her so hard she felt her head spin. For a moment she forgot everything, all swept out on a deep tide in which the past and the present slipped together, collapsed into a single moment.

And then he'd let her go and was saying something. "I'll telephone Tom and tell him to drop them by the theater. I'm sure there's a phone at the ferry dock. Don't worry." He cracked a smile. "No matter how beery Tom seems, he always comes through."

Relief swept through her. "Oh, Reg, thank you!" She threw her arms around him again. But Reg gently pushed her away and put his hands on either side of her face, as if memorizing every detail. Behind him, the shadows seemed to deepen. The horn honked again, more insistently.

"You'll be at the theater, won't you, Addie? When I come back?"

Addie returned his steady gaze and said carefully, "I'll be at the Jewel, Reg. It's my future. Of course I'll be there." That much was true. But she could hardly get the next words out, knowing that they might be a lie. "I'll be there when you come back."

"Promise?"

More than anything she wanted to say yes and to mean it. She *did* mean it! But the words thumped in her head: *Be honest. Tell him. You can't promise anything.*

She promised.

And when he let her go and picked up her hand and kissed her palm, she looked away, ashamed that she had lied to him now, of all times. Except it would have broken her heart if she couldn't let him think that just for once, he could count on her.

He turned and walked out the door, the cuffs of Peterson's work shirt dangling around his wrists.

Addie took a deep breath before she stepped out onto the back landing and went down the steps after him. She crossed the yard to the Douglas fir and joined Meg and Frida. Meg threw her arms around Reg in a quick hug, and Addie heard her say, "Take care of yourself." Frida shook his hand, and he patted her on the shoulder.

"Meg?" Her throat tightened as she watched Reg get into the car. The door closed. Sadler swung the car away from the side of the house and turned it around. "Reg's friend Tom is going to bring a copy of the paper that Reg told you about. With the photos of the Jewel on the front and his article about Gustaf's friends on the second page." She tore her gaze away from the car for a moment, to make sure Meg was listening. "Can he leave them for me in your office? I promised Reg I'd hold on to it. It's—it's important."

Meg put her arm around Addie's shoulders. "Of course he can. What do you think?"

Addie breathed out and turned back to the alley. "Thanks, Meg. You'd better hide it somewhere until I can pick it up. I'm afraid of the APL guy or the police coming back soon." It was hard, hard to give specific directions as she strained and failed to see Reg in the passenger's seat. She forced herself to continue. "You could hide it under that loose floorboard, he said. In the closet in your office."

"Loose floorboard?" Meg asked. "I never noticed there

was one." She squeezed Addie to her side for a moment. "But I'll see if I can find it."

"Thanks." Addie's voice drifted off as she watched Sadler's car drive away up the alley. It climbed until its bulk dwindled in the distance and became a small black flame disappearing over the summit of the hill. A dancing, flickering flame of darkness. And as it crested the hill, the flame just went out.

POPPIES

"Hey, you! Get up!"

Addie groaned and dragged a pillow over her head, but Whaley kept pounding on her door. "I told Mrs. Powell we'd get there before the preservation society people arrive." He cracked the door and stuck his head in. "You alive in there?"

"Uhn."

"You've been sleeping forever, McNeal! What's wrong with you? It's morning." When Addie didn't reply, he just said, "We're leaving in ten minutes." And he shut the door again.

Addie rolled out of bed, limbs heavy, thoughts slow and reluctant.

That's the end of the story. He's gone.

And I guess I'm still here.

The antique skirt she'd worn yesterday lay in the corner of the room, fine and crumpled as a castoff snakeskin.

Carefully, she picked it up, folded it, and started to get dressed. For a second, she forgot what she was doing and just stared out the window to where the Douglas fir stood shrouded in morning mist, looking ghostly and sad. She felt *empty*. She pressed her fingers between her ribs, trying to locate the ache inside her that she was afraid would never go away. It was a part of her now, like her hair and her teeth.

Her gamble hadn't paid off. She had to face it.

There was nothing to show the preservation committee.

After Sadler and Reg left last night, she'd returned to the Jewel with Meg, where the opening night cast party was in full swing and Emma Mae was anxiously waiting for them. She'd asked Meg if she could use the telephone in her office to call her father. But the minute she was alone, she pulled out the mirror. She'd wished that she could somehow manage to shift only a few days forward in time when Tom would have dropped off the article and the picture. There was no way she could have stayed in 1917 waiting for him to bring them by. She'd had no home to go to, and it was nearly midnight, but if perhaps she could have bent time to suit her purpose . . . She'd fixed her mind on it, hoping, believing that it was the power in her that made it possible to travel through time in the first place.

But it hadn't worked.

Instead, she'd found herself back in her own time, in the dusty wreck of what used to be Meg's office.

Why had she even attempted such a foolish thing? In a panic, she'd rushed to the closet to look under the loose floorboard. If she was lucky, maybe Meg would have just left the newspaper there.

But she'd found nothing. Only the torn spider webs.

Well, she'd known it was a long shot. Still, she'd kept searching. Maybe the boards hadn't been loose in Meg's day. In that case, surely Meg would have found somewhere else to hide the newspaper?

She'd searched the whole office, squinting into the dark recesses of the closet, looking for hidden cabinets, pressing against the wood in the back, trying to slide or trigger something. But there were no secret panels. She'd worn herself out tramping around the dark, dank theater looking in every nook and cranny of every room where Meg might have hidden something. But all for naught.

Too many years had passed. Either Meg had never hidden the paper at all or Tom had never brought it to her or someone else had taken it. Who knows? Maybe the police had even confiscated it.

She'd had to face it: There was no copy of the newspaper. No pictures.

She had even, in desperation, picked up the mirror and tried to plunge back into Reg and Meg's world, but that, too, was in vain. And that scared her more than anything. It was as if she'd tried a key that normally worked in a lock and could not budge it.

A horrible feeling had engulfed her—the feeling that something had ended.

What if she could never go back? Had she left without a farewell to anyone or a word of encouragement to Frida?

What if her goodbye to Reg was final? Did that mean there was no hope of ever seeing him again?

It was when she'd put the mirror back in her purse that she'd found Gustaf's union card.

She'd slipped it back into her bag and headed home. And she'd gone straight to sleep, even though it was barely seven in the evening. No wonder Whaley thought something was wrong with her. Because the passage of time in the past didn't register in her own time, her internal clock was confused. She was like a traveler with jet lag.

Groggily, she pulled on a black top, jeans, and a short corduroy jacket. Who cared what she looked like today? She picked up her purse and slung it over her shoulder as she headed downstairs.

In the hallway on the second floor, she glanced at the familiar family photographs on the walls: Zack mugging with green finger paint smeared all over his face, herself twirling in Titania's fairy dress from *A Midsummer Night's Dream*, Dad crossing the finish line of the Seattle–Portland bike race. She was back in her own world. Perhaps for good. Boots and shoes were still bursting out of the tiny closet in the hallway. The smell of frying onions seeped from under the kitchen door, and the clatter of pans told her Whaley was cooking.

Despite this, her home felt nearly as strange to her as Meg Turner's had the night before. It had always been *her* house, her safe haven, but now . . . now it was Meg's house, too. The house where Frida had taken refuge. The house

Reg had disappeared from. The house where Meg had left crates full of costumes and even the treasured mirror that they somehow shared. It would always be haunted. Just as the Jewel would always be full of presences from the past . . . as long as it survived, that was.

She took a deep breath. She had to think. Even if the paper wasn't in Meg's office, couldn't the actual photos still be somewhere? Old photos were on heavy card stock. They might have survived better than newsprint. It wasn't much, but it was the only thread of hope she had. If only she could go back. Now. Right this minute. Find Meg . . .

But the mirror might not do her bidding anymore. She almost couldn't bear to try and be so disappointed.

"Addie! Are you ready?"

There was no *time*. It was already so late, and they couldn't disappoint Mrs. Powell. *Maybe*, she thought without much conviction, *maybe it will go well with the preservation people anyway.* Maybe they'd agree to landmark status even without the pictures. It seemed unlikely. But you never knew.

She pushed open the kitchen door and stared in surprise. Whaley had actually shaved and possibly even dragged a comb through his bristly rust-colored hair. And he was wearing a plain white shirt, not one of his tacky bowling shirts or ripped flannels.

"You look nice."

Whaley grunted. "Don't sound so shocked." He dumped the eggs he'd been frying into a pita and twisted a section of the newspaper around it. "Just thought I'd make an effort. Here." He shoved the sandwich into Addie's hand, made another for himself, grabbed the newspaper off the counter, and stuffed it under his arm. "Let's go."

Zack appeared in the doorway, yawning and stretching. "Sing Addie that song you wrote last night, Whaley."

"You wrote a new song?"

"Shut up, Zack," Whaley said, pushing past him into the hall.

"Sing it to her. She'll *love* it." Zack grinned.

Addie gave him a one-armed hug. "Stop teasing Whaley, you monkey."

"Zacky, get moving!" Dad rumbled from downstairs. "Skagit County, here we come!" He emerged from the far end of the bookstore as Whaley and Addie reached the back door. Quickly, he put a hand on Addie's forehead. "You feeling all right, sweetheart? You look pale."

"I'm *fine*, Dad."

He frowned. "Well, eat up that sandwich. You didn't stay awake long enough to have dinner last night. And tell Becky Powell good luck."

Addie nodded, bundled a raincoat into her arms, wrapped a scarf around her neck, and a few minutes later, she and Whaley headed out onto the damp, foggy streets. Whaley read the news out loud, sidestepping lampposts and fire hydrants without looking up.

There was intense fighting, he read, between U.S. forces and militias in the narrow streets of some city whose name neither of them could pronounce. A holy city, with a shrine, up high in the mountains.

"'There has been no electricity at the hospital for the past week since a bomb destroyed its generator. People are afraid to go to work or send their children to school.'" Addie peered over Whaley's shoulder and saw a blurry photo of a woman cowering near a blown-out shop window. Underneath ran the caption *A local woman examines the damage to her family's business.* She remembered the jagged shards of glass in front of Victrola Books when the earthquake hit, and how upset she'd been. But she was lucky. Really lucky.

The song the military band had been playing in King Street Station, "Over There," came into her head. Everyone had seemed so revved up. So excited. All the kissing of soldiers and blaring of trumpets. But wars were always over there. Always far away.

Except for the names of the dead, Addie thought unhappily. Those stayed here forever.

Then the questions came back, the questions she'd been asking herself over and over: *Did Reg come back to Seattle and join the infantry? Did he go to France after all? Did he fight? Did he die?*

She glanced at Whaley and felt a rush of warmth toward him. She felt herself forgive his stupid fights and the blindness with which he sometimes walked through life. Hadn't she learned how blind she could be herself? How little she understood?

"Hey," she interrupted softly.

"Wha?" He lowered the paper. "Sort of depressing news. Maybe you don't want to hear it."

"Mmm. But thanks for the egg pita."

"Grows on you, doesn't it?"

"Grows something," Addie agreed. "Sing me your song, Whaley."

He hesitated. "All right. But promise me you won't get mad."

"Why would I get mad?"

"Just promise."

"Fine, I promise. What's it called?"

" 'Jailhouse Blues.' "

"Oooh, *that's* original."

"See? You've got a bad attitude already. I don't know if I trust you."

"Shut up and sing."

"It's impossible to shut up *and* sing."

"*Whaley!*"

He stuffed the paper in his jacket pocket and dumped the pita wrapping into an overflowing garbage can on a corner. Addie smiled. Of course. He needed both hands free to play air guitar. Without looking to see if anyone else would hear, he began singing.

> *I went to the jailhouse, baby, just to ease my mind. . . .*
> *Went to the jailhouse, baby, to get sentenced my time.*
> *Judge said, Hey, Whaley,*
> *you done committed a crime.*

He shook his head intently over the blues chords on his air guitar. "Bah-bah, bah-bah, bah . . ."

"Uh, Whaley, has this got anything to do with—"

"Shh."

He threw his head back, and his bony Adam's apple bobbed.

> *Got in the courthouse, baby, Judge sitting up high.*
> *Got in the courthouse, baby, she's just sitting up high.*
> *She said, Explain yourself, Whaley.*
> *I said, Judge, I'm just fixing to die.*

"So you went—"

"Any more interruptions from you, McNeal," Whaley said sternly, "and I'm getting the bailiff to throw you out."

Addie rolled her eyes.

> *I said, I was just looking after my gal, Addie.*
> *Judge said that's no excuse.*
> *I said, I was taking care of Addie;*
> *She said that's no excuse.*
> *I said, you sending me to jail, Judge?*
> *She said, Whaley,*
> *what would be the doggone use?*

"Whaley." Addie folded her arms and planted her feet firmly. "What happened?"

"Don't just stand there. Haul it, girl. I'll sing you the

rest of the song." He grabbed her elbow and propelled her up the steep incline of the sidewalk, singing loudly all the while.

> Got the devil in my soul and I'm full of bad news.
> Devil in my soul, mama, and full of bad news.
> Four hundred bucks and community service . . .
> I got them mean ol' jailhouse blues.

"Hey!" Addie flung out an arm to slow him down, but he just plowed on. "You don't know that, do you?"

"Sure I do." He stepped into the street against the light and she flew after him, yanking him back as a bus barreled by. "Had my day in court. Got my sentence."

"Had your day in court *when?*"

"Yesterday."

"Why didn't you tell me?" Addie exploded.

"Got to stand on my own sometimes. Didn't even have a lawyer."

Addie smacked her hand to her forehead. "But the court *gives* you a lawyer if you can't afford one." She looked at Whaley and saw that she was wasting her breath. "Okay. So no lawyer. And now you've got a big fine to pay. Four hundred dollars! On top of what you owe Mrs. Powell, right?" She stopped, remembering what Whaley had told Enrique about enlisting with a conviction on his record. "The fine . . ." she said carefully, though she knew the answer perfectly well. "Does that mean you're guilty or innocent?"

Whaley looked at her as if she were a nitwit. "Duh! Guilty. They don't fine you if you're innocent."

She tried to squelch the grin that threatened to spread from ear to ear. "Um, Whaley, doesn't that mean you can't enlist in the army?"

He shrugged. "Nah. It's just a misdemeanor. You can apply for a waiver. The guys at the enlistment center told me."

"What about the money you owe?"

"My army pay will wipe out those debts pretty quick, if they let me in."

Addie set her mouth in a determined line. "But didn't you say you'd work it off for Mrs. Powell by fixing up the theater? Didn't you promise?"

"Sure. But I don't expect her to pull a rabbit out of a hat and save the Jewel. Do you? I'm just going today for moral support. Mrs. Powell's got my back; I've got hers. That's all."

The pall that had hung over her when she woke up descended once more. They were almost at the cross street that led up to the south entrance of Volunteer Park. She felt a pang. Would Reg's name still be on the memorial? Or, if he hadn't rejoined the army, if he hadn't fought and died, would his name be gone? Last night, she'd been convinced this was the case. But somehow, all of a sudden, she didn't know.

She glanced at her watch. Only a quarter to eight. They had time. "Whaley! Go on without me. I need to check something."

He gave her a bewildered look. "You're kidding. We've got a meeting to get to."

"I know! I'll catch up to you."

She crossed the street and headed up the hill, twisting

past mansions hidden among vast, ancient trees. But as the water tower came into view, her feet dragged.

No, she thought. *Whaley's right. I can't look now. We're in a hurry. We've got to get to the Jewel.*

But she knew that wasn't the reason for her reluctance. She took two more steps toward the park entrance. Her hands were shaking and she had to force herself to continue.

The fog showed no sign of lifting. If anything, it was heavier than before. Even the tulips were dimmed, as if wrapped in gauze. Addie stopped halfway across the lawn, under the dark branches of a hemlock, remembering the last time she had been here, alone at night, when she had found Reg's name on the list of the dead.

All she wanted was to head back down to Tenth, to catch up with Whaley. Not to have to face this. *There's no point anyway*, she told herself stubbornly. Reg *had* been saved. She'd seen him leaving the city in Sam Sadler's car. Of course his name wouldn't be there.

For a second her spirits lifted. That would mean that she had changed things. That she'd somehow diverted that rushing stream.

Unless, of course, he'd come back from the peninsula and joined up anyway.

And what about Mr. Peterson? She'd had the thought before, that even though it was Reg's name on the cenotaph, it might not have been Reg who'd died. But it seemed too unlikely that Peterson would have stayed in the army and gone to fight under Reg's name. It was too risky. He would have gotten himself out somehow.

No, she told herself. She didn't need to look at the cenotaph.

But as she started back out of the park, a voice in her head echoed, clear as a bell, *Coward!*

All right. She'd look.

She settled her bag on her shoulder, rubbed her chilly arms, and turned back a second time. *The name will be gone. Just be brave enough to look. Then you'll know.*

She stepped through the opening in the hedge, dumped her stuff onto the grass, and threw down the raincoat. All her gear spilled out of the bag, and the coat landed on the ground, but she didn't bother to collect it. She forced herself to walk around to the front of the memorial.

"Addie!" Whaley's voice startled her, cutting through the silence. "Yo! We've got to go!" She turned and saw him standing over by the water tower, beckoning. When she didn't move, he set out toward her.

She stepped around the base of the fountain, crouched down, and scanned the list of names. There. She was looking. She couldn't make herself go directly to the *P*s, but she was looking.

Barnard, Ben-Zackarias, Bolton, Bulasan . . .

Someone else's boyfriends.

Chen . . . De La Cruz . . .

Someone else's dad and brother. She knew how awful it was to think that way, but she couldn't help it.

Jacobsen . . . Jones . . . Lawrence . . . Lindquist . . .

Powell.

The air she drew into her lungs was thin all of a sudden. So thin, it cut. She was high up on a mountain, cold as the snowfields and glaciers on Rainier.

She reached out and traced the letters with the tip of her finger.

Reg Powell? Or Gustaf Peterson?

One of them had died.

She could still feel his hands touching her, still hear his voice.

Her gut said it was Reg, though her mind knew it could be either of them. And it was worse, a thousand times worse than when she had seen Reg's name the first time. Because this time she felt responsible.

Whaley's voice broke in on her. "Holy—!"

She spun around and saw him standing there, eyes wide with shock, the whites showing clear around the blue of the irises. He was holding her mirror, gazing into it one moment, and the next, turning to look over his shoulder.

His hand opened and the mirror slid out, striking the corner of the bench.

Addie dove for it.

Too late. It had already fallen to the ground.

With half a sob, she snatched it up. A thin fracture ran through the center of the glass.

She buried her head in her hands. Tears started in her eyes. Now she'd never return to Reg's time. This couldn't be happening.

She tried to tell herself that it didn't matter. The mirror might still have the power to open the door to that other world.

But she had just seen Reg's name.

Despair washed over her.

"What's *with* that thing?" Whaley demanded.

In anguish, Addie looked up at him. She could barely even register what he'd asked.

But the frightened look on his face shook her out of herself. She'd never seen Whaley frightened before.

"Did you—" Her voice dried up. She swallowed and forced herself to go on. "Did you see something? In the mirror?"

"A girl. She was standing right behind me." Whaley glanced over his shoulder again, as if to catch a second glimpse, then looked back at Addie. "But when I turned around, she was gone."

Addie tried to still the thoughts tumbling through her head. "Is that all?"

Whaley nodded.

"Thank goodness." At least it wasn't some awful portent of doom like Reg had seen. No American flag on a coffin. *Oh, God . . .*

"Just a girl?" She tried to sound normal.

"Yeah."

"Maybe you imagined it." Oh, how she'd hate someone to say that to her!

"I didn't imagine it." The familiar challenging look was back in his eyes, and suddenly he was sizing her up. "You know that. Otherwise you wouldn't have asked me what I saw. And you told me about that statue disappearing. Remember? So don't try to placate me."

"All right!" Addie raised her hands as if in surrender. "I know. I got it. *Sorry.*"

"You've more than got it. Look, Addie, I haven't been so wrapped up in Whaley P. Price these last weeks that I haven't noticed how weird you've been. And it's this mirror." He looked around at the monument, the ghostly trees. "And this place. When are you going to tell me what's going on?"

"I don't know." Maybe it didn't matter anymore. Maybe she could just tell him, because it was probably all over. But it was too painful. She couldn't. Not yet.

Whaley studied her for a moment and then a note of concern crept into his voice. "It's changed you."

"For sure." Her voice cracked. She glanced back at the cenotaph, and the tears spilled down her cheeks. Then she turned her head away.

"Okay," Whaley said. "Now I'm spooked. But whatever, we need to get going. Right? Ghosts or no ghosts." He held out his hand. She took it and he pulled her to her feet.

"Right," she said quietly, wiping her face. "Thanks, Whaley."

As they walked slowly out of the garden, still floating and unearthly in the morning fog, she asked, "What did she look like? Your girl in the mirror?"

"About your age." He considered. "Or—no. Maybe a few years younger. Freckled. Reddish blond hair."

They turned the corner, quickening their pace.

"She was putting a bunch of flowers on the memorial. Poppies." He paused. "Definitely poppies."

Addie licked her lips, which had gone very dry.

"It was weird. She reminded me of someone. No one I know. But still familiar somehow." He stopped. "And there was one other thing."

"What?" Addie had to work to keep her voice steady.

"She was crying."

They went on a bit in silence. At the bottom of the hill, Addie saw the Jewel looming. She hugged herself against the clammy mist. Then she said, "Whaley?"

"What?"

"What does the P. stand for?"

"I luh?"

"The P. Whaley P. Price. What's your middle name?"

He gave her an irritated look. "What does it matter? This isn't about my enlistment form, is it?"

"No. What does P. stand for?"

He rolled his eyes. "Peterson. So? Hurry up. We're going to be late."

CURTAIN

Addie stared at Whaley's strong guitarist's fingers, roughened by carpentry work, and remembered Gustaf's cut and crosshatched hands. Guilt cut through her like a knife. Was it Peterson, then, who had died?

And Frida . . . she could see her standing in the backyard under the Douglas fir last night, waving as Sadler's car disappeared from the alley. She heard her say to Reg, *Where's Papa? Why are you here and not him?*

"Addie? Come on. Don't you want to get to the theater?" Whaley's eyes were resting on her, and all of a sudden, she could see Gustaf and Frida in him, as strong and clear as the sunbeam that had just cut through the fog.

"I know what you're thinking," he said as they descended the winding street back to Tenth Avenue. "That there's no reason for us to rush to get there when those folks are just going to turn Mrs. Powell down anyway. But—"

"No," Addie said slowly. "That's not what I'm thinking."

There were threads she couldn't even begin to connect, but here, she felt, was a chance at some sort of reparation. She tried to keep hold of what she actually knew. One of them had died. And though she now felt it was Peterson, she didn't actually know. But whether it was him or Reg, she did know one thing for sure. The only way to make reparation for death was through life.

She was determined to save the Jewel. She had to. Whaley could make his own decisions from there.

They reached Tenth and turned toward downtown.

Frida and Meg *would* have hidden that newspaper. She was sure of it now. They would have held on to it forever, because of that death. But they hadn't hidden it at the Jewel. Nor in an archive. Nor had anyone turned it into digital signals and loaded it onto the Internet. But it had to be somewhere else. Somewhere she hadn't thought of yet.

She pulled herself up very straight, grabbed Whaley's hand, and squeezed it fiercely. "Wait a second." A conviction had entered her.

"Wait for what?"

"There's one more chance." She looked toward downtown, to where the theater waited, but saw only the rolling rise of the street ahead of her. In the foggy distance, two headlights were approaching, with a row of lights high above them. A bus, heading north.

Abruptly, she reached into her purse and fished out Gustaf's union card. She held it out to Whaley. "This is for you."

He took it and looked at it curiously. "IWW?" He held it closer and a startled expression swept over his face. "Gustaf Peterson? Are you kidding? He's my great-great grandad. Where did you find this?"

There was no way to explain it. "At the Jewel," Addie said.

"But why would it be—"

"Whaley. I—" If she didn't cross the street this instant, she'd miss the bus. "I have to run!" She darted away from him, flying across the middle of the road.

"Wait, Addie! You have to explain this!"

"I can't now! But I'll get to the theater soon! Tell Mrs. Powell—" The bus pulled up, blocking him from view. She jumped on, paid her fare, and grabbed a seat, watching as Whaley got smaller in the distance, still studying the IWW card she'd given him. The card that had belonged to his great-great-grandfather. That belonged to Whaley now. Her heart thumped as she sank into her seat and headed back home.

Almaz was standing outside the bookstore, scribbling a note on a scrap of paper. Her sports duffel was on her shoulder, and she was wearing her team sweatshirt, shorts, and shin guards. She glanced up. "I was going to stick a note in your mailbox to say come to the game at Hale." She gave Addie a severe look. "I've scored four goals in two weeks and you haven't even been there to cheer."

"I know." Addie swung an arm around Almaz's shoulder for a second and then let go. "I'm sorry. I'll come to the next one." She pulled out her key and opened the door. "Can you help me for a few minutes? If you've got time before the game?"

"Help you with what?"

"I have to find something."

"Why are you in such a hurry?" But Almaz stepped inside behind her.

"Because I have to find it before a nine o'clock meeting at the Jewel." Addie shoved aside a pile of bills on Dad's big desk and sat down on it. She glanced at the Victrola on the shelf by the window. Dad had left one of his 78s sitting on the turntable. In her ear the shimmering notes of the piano piece Reg had played for her sounded faintly. Dad had put the Ethiopian posters back on the wall—the bright-colored saints carrying their swords and shields—and underneath, Addie imagined, she could see the turquoise walls of Meg's living room.

"What do you have to find?"

"Those pictures I was looking for. Listen." Addie's gaze drifted around the bookshop. She could see the room as it had been last night, could feel the others who had been there, still sharply, unbearably, present. "Do you remember how Mrs. Turner told us that her aunt used to own this house? And she was the director at the Jewel?"

"Sure." Almaz dropped her duffel by the cash register.

"Meg Turner was her name. She was an amazing woman. She . . ." Addie looked straight at Almaz and felt relieved that, finally, she could reveal something to her. She dug into her handbag and pulled out the silver mirror. "This mirror belonged to her. Mrs. T. and I found it in those crates."

She held it out to Almaz, who took it, handling it carefully, examining the delicate embossing on the back and then turning it over. "Oh, it's cracked," she said. "That's too bad."

"I know."

Almaz returned the mirror, and Addie ran her forefinger lightly along the crack, as if her touch could somehow fuse the pieces together. "It was a talisman of hers—she never directed a performance without it. And she lived in this house until she—until she died. Do you see?" She stopped. "We've been searching the theater for evidence of the Jewel as it was long ago, but we never thought of looking here. And yet Meg Turner lived here for so many years."

"Ooh, I get it." Almaz's eyes lit up. "You're thinking that she had all the costumes from the Jewel and so maybe—"

"That's right."

Almaz spun around, surveying the shop. "But where?"

"I have no idea. But it's our last chance. And there's at least one thing I know for sure." The certainty rushed up in her so fiercely that she felt dizzy. She held up the mirror. "This is mine now. And when I'm working at the Jewel, *I'm* going to use it in every performance. Meg left it for me." She slipped it back into the purse. "And I *feel*—oh, don't laugh at me!—I feel as if she's left me the pictures of the Jewel, too."

Almaz crinkled her nose. Her big eyes, with the dusky

shadows underneath, examined Addie with concern. "Addie," she said gently. "I don't want to pop your bubble . . ."

"You can't!" Addie cried, and jumped off the desk. "Because we're going to find something." She grabbed Almaz's hand and pulled her along to the drama section. "Help me move this shelf."

"You want to look in that closet again?" Almaz surveyed the close-pressed bindings of the books. "It would be a whole lot easier if we pulled out the books first."

"I moved it alone, with all the books on it!"

"Yeah. You don't know anything about muscle injuries. If you played soccer, you'd think before—"

"Are you going to help me or am I doing this myself?"

Almaz grinned. "You're doing it yourself." Then, at Addie's thundercloud look, she amended, "Just kidding.

"Dark in here," she remarked when they'd moved the shelf and opened the closet behind it.

"I know. Hold on a minute." Addie ran back to Dad's big desk and pulled out the bottom drawer. She removed the flashlight he'd kept there ever since the earthquake and switched it on to make sure it worked.

Then she checked her watch. Eight thirty.

She grabbed her phone to call Whaley but put the phone away before she'd touched the button. Look first. Then call.

Or not.

She went back to the closet just as Almaz emerged, disgustedly wiping a cobweb off one of her braids. "I don't think there's much in there, but I can't see too well."

"Let me." Holding the flashlight in front of her, Addie stepped in.

The scent of cedar struck her once again, but differently, because this time it was the smell of the smooth wooden benches in King Street Station the night that Gustaf Peterson had gotten on that train. The scent of Frida's dress when she'd first met her.

She blinked, sternly forcing herself to stop thinking about the past. She had to examine the place inch by inch. The crates were gone, leaving fresh square marks in the deep dust on the floor. She'd hoped that perhaps she and Mrs. Turner had overlooked an extra one hiding in a corner. But they hadn't.

She shone the beam higher up the wall. There was a steel dowel to hang clothes on, which she didn't remember from before. And up above it, a long shelf, just like they had in their own coat closet and on which they threw all their hats and scarves and gloves.

She couldn't reach the shelf and had to climb up on the little bench built into the wall where she'd sat with Mrs. T. amid piles of vintage clothing. Now she could see clearly. And what she saw was . . .

Nothing.

Again nothing. It was always nothing. She shook her head, trying not to let the disappointment overwhelm her.

She leaned forward as far as she could without losing her footing, held the flashlight high, and ran her hand along the shelf to make sure she hadn't missed anything hidden in the shadows.

"Ow!" She pulled back her hand and looked at the nasty splinter she'd jammed into her finger.

"No luck?" Almaz ducked back inside the closet.

"No," Addie said, and carefully stepped back off the bench.

"What are you standing on?" Almaz frowned. "Not a crate, is it?"

"Just a bench." Addie looked down at it. The wood was blackened with age. The seat was narrow, and it wasn't just a seat, but a base as well. The whole thing projected from the wall about six inches. Actually—it reminded her of the old toy chest built into the window seat in Zack's room upstairs. The toy chest that you could open just by taking off the cushions and lifting the top . . .

She looked up at Almaz and saw her eyes widen at the same moment.

"Y'know—" Addie handed Almaz the flashlight.

She bent down and put her fingertips under the lip of wood. Gently, she lifted it.

"Shine the light in here!"

Almaz pointed the flashlight down, and its powerful beam stabbed into the dark recesses of the bench. Addie saw immense balls of dust. Small bits of scrap wood. She knelt to get a better look.

Then, at the bottom, shoved in a corner, she saw a metal box with a black handle on top.

"What's that?" Almaz cried at the same moment that Addie yelped, "Hold up the seat!"

When Almaz had it propped open, Addie reached down

and lifted out the box. It was pretty light, but she could tell it wasn't empty.

"Bring it out here," Almaz said, and Addie carried it back to Dad's desk. The sun had torn away the fog by now, and the whole front of the store was bright, dust motes shimmering in the air. The light struck the golds and reds of book covers in the unsorted piles on the floor, and they sparkled.

Addie's mouth was dry as she settled herself in the big wooden chair and set the box down carefully. On its front, she saw a silver latch with a keyhole.

"A keyhole, but no key." She frowned and pushed a button next to the lock. But the box wouldn't open.

"Let me." Almaz leaned over Addie and tried to twist the lock with her fingernail, but it really was stuck. "You know, I learned something about locks in physics, of all places."

Addie looked up at the clock on the wall. Quarter to nine.

"No time for physics," she said, and opened a desk drawer and found a box cutter. But it wasn't sturdy enough. She shoved aside more papers and found a letter opener, a stapler, sticky notes—"Aha!" Dad's Swiss Army knife.

She pulled out the knife and extracted a short blade.

"Whoa!" Almaz objected. "Don't you think—"

But Addie had already jammed the blade underneath the lid. She jerked the knife to one side, and levered it up. The top sprang open with a creak.

For a moment she couldn't look. The exhilaration shaking through her almost made her sick.

Trying to control the tremor in her hands, she picked up a paper folded in quarters. It crackled as she touched it. A bit of its brownish edge flaked off, like broken pie crust.

"Careful!" Almaz warned. Addie nodded, trying to keep her touch light enough that no more damage would be done. It was agonizing how slowly she had to move. But when she laid the paper on the desk and gently unfolded it, she gasped with delight.

It was the issue of the *Daily* that had been pulled from the newsstands. On the front, she saw Tom's sweeping shot of the façade of the Jewel. The shot he'd taken when he made Reg stand in the street to ward off traffic.

"Ha!" She looked up at Almaz. Her own joy was reflected in her friend's face. "Look! There's more!" Below, between two scant bars of text, were three other shots. Of the dome, open like a flower, the chandelier hanging from its center. The box seats. The carvings of boats on the Nile. She opened the paper to where the article continued on another page.

And then she caught her breath.

It was a nearly all-encompassing shot of the auditorium, from the entrance to the proscenium arch. She sighed softly as she made out the Pharaoh staring sternly down, awaiting the gifts of his attendants. It took in the stage, and the orchestra pit, all the fabulous paintings of the Egyptian gods on the walls. But none of that was what made her shiver. It was the fuzzy, indistinct image of a girl in a dress and an apron walking up the left aisle, half turning in surprise. Startled by the explosion of the flash.

Frida.

She pressed her hands together in front of her mouth.

"Awesome!" Almaz whooped. "This is what you've been looking for, isn't it?"

Addie nodded. "We have to get this down to the Jewel." She grabbed Almaz's wrist. "I'll call Whaley, but look—it's almost nine. How are we going to get there in time?"

Almaz didn't hesitate. She rushed to the door. "I'll get Dad's car. He'll let me. I'm sure. Just be ready. I'll stop in front of the store and honk."

"Thanks!" Addie stood up and took out her phone. This time she made the call.

"Whaley?"

"Is that you, Addie? Listen, you've got to explain about the union card you gave me—"

"It's simple, Whaley. That card means you belong there. At the Jewel. Your great-great granddad left it for you. It's— it's an heirloom." She felt giddy with happiness. "But, listen, there's something else: I've found pictures of the Jewel. From 1917."

"You *did?*"

"I did. Are the preservation people there yet?"

He sneezed into the phone. "Ugh. Dust. No, not yet."

"Can you tell Mrs. Powell? Tell her Almaz and I are on our way. We're bringing the photos with us."

A rustling in the earpiece told her he had put the phone down or was holding it against his jacket or something. She heard him yell. "Yo, Mrs. T.! Addie found pictures for us! Where's Mrs. Powell?" Then a second later: "Tell her it's good news!"

"Whaley!" Addie called. "Whaley! I'm still here."

His voice zoomed up close to her ear again. "Sorry, Ads. Anything else?"

"It changes everything, Whaley. Do you understand? If this works—"

"You don't have to tell me." He sounded happy. Really happy.

Then he hung up.

Addie felt her whole body sag with relief. She'd found it. All of it.

But then she realized there was more. Looking back down, she noticed a picture at the bottom of the metal box. Gently, she lifted it out and held it up to the light.

It was a photo of the troll king and his court.

A tide of excitement washed through her.

It wasn't the same performance as in the other photograph.

It was the same scene, all right—the scene she'd helped direct on that long-ago afternoon when she'd danced with Reg. But in this photo, the troll king's daughter was center stage. It was hard to tell because of the mask, but she didn't think Hettie was playing the role. The actress, whoever she was, was holding Peer's hand aloft and running her other hand through the air below his arm, as if plucking an instrument. *Strike the Dovrë Harp.* Peer was mugging at the audience like a henpecked husband. Addie examined him more closely. He wore no mask, so she could tell he wasn't Andrew Lindstrom.

Then, in the background of the photo, she made out

the troll king himself. The mask concealing the lower half of his face was the same mask Meg had shown her.

She leaned forward, straining her eyes to bring the upper half of the actor's face into focus. She couldn't have sworn to anything. Not in this ancient photograph. But he had smooth, dark hair. And was it just wishful thinking to imagine that the eyes above the mask were blue? They had that amused, ironic look in them. . . .

There was no way to tell for sure.

But there was something about him. . . . Addie turned over the photo and found, in the same hand that had written *R. before the mob* on the photo up in her room, *Veterans benefit—spring 1919.*

Spring 1919.

The war was over by then.

The little moth of hope fluttered up again, pale and fragile, almost invisible in the bright sunlight.

Had he survived? Her heart leaped. She pressed the picture to her chest in inutterable relief.

But if he had, then what Whaley had seen really was Frida, weeping for her father.

Addie put down the photo. Why did it have to be one or the other? *Why?*

But something tugged at her. Drew her back to look one more time.

She picked up the photograph again and turned it over once more. There was something else written on the back. She squinted at it. Oh, it was too faint to see! She held the picture right up under her nose.

The writing was barely visible, and in a different hand—big looping letters, the ink turned gold with age. It said . . . it said . . .

I wish you had been here.

The initial underneath was a sloping *R*.

For a moment she couldn't move. Her eyes ran back again and again over the flowing curves of the script and she stared until her vision blurred. Then she drew in a ragged breath, turned the photo over, and looked back at the troll king's eyes, love and remorse and sorrow and joy all fighting inside of her, churning up a storm.

From her pocket, she pulled out the mirror and looked at its cracked surface. If only . . . oh, if only it could be the key to turn that lock again.

Slowly, deliberately, she tucked the mirror into her purse and, with even greater care, slipped the photo of *Peer Gynt* in with it. She would try again. Even though she doubted it would work, she had to try one more time. But not now.

And even if she could never return—she swallowed hard, trying not to weigh the sense of her loss if that was true—even so, they were all a part of her now. Nothing could take that away.

Outside, a car horn honked. Addie looked up and waved to Almaz. She put aside the turmoil in her heart and smiled as she thought of Whaley hammering up molding and mending the cracks in the walls, bringing the Jewel back to life. And farther into the future, so far she could hardly envision it, she saw herself on the stage, the mirror in her pocket and her book of notes in her hand, directing her cast.

She stood and picked up the precious box with the copy of the *Daily* inside it. She stepped out of the bookstore and locked the door behind her.

And suddenly she had that taste on her tongue again, just as she had the day she'd sat on the loading dock with Reg in the sunlight. The taste of her real life stretching out in front of her.

AUTHOR'S NOTE

This is a work of fiction. However, readers will notice that I've populated my imaginary world with many real events, people, and places.

Seattle readers will detect and, I hope, forgive, a few instances of poetic license. Most strikingly, there is no theater called the Jewel in downtown Seattle. And although there is a Lincoln High School building, there is no actual high school in it. Finally, though the story about Katharine Cornell's late night/early morning performance of Christmas 1933 is true, it took place at the Metropolitan Theatre, which is sadly no more. You can find Cornell's actual account of this—rather than the account I attribute to her—in her autobiography, *I Wanted to Be an Actress*.

The Industrial Workers of the World, also known as the Wobblies or the IWW, were a progressive labor union and political movement most active in the early twentieth century. Unlike most other unions of the time, they believed in "one big union" and organized workers regardless of race, ethnicity, gender, immigration status, or skill. They believed in the power of ordinary people to improve their lives through solidarity, education, and collective action. Many Wobblies actively opposed World War I.

The Everett massacre really did occur in November of 1916; it was a violent reaction by the Snohomish County Sheriff's Department to the IWW's free speech campaign in Everett, Washington. Seventy-four IWW men were jailed.

Though Gustaf Peterson is a fictional character, Tom Tracy was indeed the first of the Wobblies to go on trial, and Felix Baran and Abraham Rabinowitz (among others) were killed by sheriff's deputies. Tracy was acquitted on May 5, 1917, and all the others soon thereafter.

Though they never organized the escape of a fugitive, Sam Sadler and Louise Olivereau were also real people. In 1917, Olivereau was arrested under the Espionage Act. Her crime was sending circulars through the mail encouraging

November 1916 funeral of Felix Baran, IWW member killed in the Everett massacre. (University of Washington Libraries, Special Collections, Social Issues Files Dc/i. neg. #11504.)

young men to become conscientious objectors rather than fight in World War I. During her trial, she demanded, "Will those in power never learn that ideas can never be imprisoned?" She was sentenced to ten years in jail and served twenty-eight months before being paroled. Sam Sadler served two years in the McNeil Island penitentiary in connection with publishing pamphlets opposing the military draft. During and immediately after World War I, hundreds of IWW members were arrested and incarcerated.

Although the IWW still exists today, by the early 1920s, the backbone of the movement had been broken by government crackdowns and vigilante violence. But as Louise Olivereau said, their ideas could not be imprisoned, and their rabble-rousing spirit lives on.

ACKNOWLEDGMENTS

Creating the world of the Jewel required digging into the past. I appreciate all those who helped in this endeavor.

I am grateful to Paula Becker for sharing her deep knowledge of local history; to Michelle Sadlier and Paul Robertshaw for enriching my understanding of early twentieth-century theaters; and to Gregory Hagge, the acting curator of the Fort Lewis Military Museum, for answering questions about all things military in World War I–era Seattle. I am also thankful to Debora Pontillo and her students for welcoming me into their drama classes, to Matt DePies for sharing his military experience, and to all the wonderful librarians at the University of Washington, Bothell.

Thanks also go to Chris Eboch for generously reviewing the entire manuscript, and to Molly Blaisdell, Conrad Wesselheoft, Susan Greenway, Cathy Benson, and Megan Bilder for their close reading. Do Peterson; Wendy Asplin; Natalie Pret; Lisa Citron; Laurie Blackburn; Carol, Robert, Eric, and Peter Spiegler; Mike Panitz; Debbie Bermet; Panos Hatziandreas; and many others kindly answered a variety of odd and often unexplained questions. And, as always, nothing would have been accomplished without the love and support of Richard, Levi, and Joseph.